LITERATURE AND LANGUAGE DIVISION
THE CHICAGO PUBLIC LIBRARY
400 SOUTH STATE STREET
CHICAGO, ILLINOIS 60805

HUDS

HWLCFN

Chicago Public Library

W9-AUG-252

In a temple of trees : a novel

LITERATURE AND LANGUAGE DIVISION
THE CHICAGO PUBLIC LIBRARY
400 SOUTH STATE STREET
CHICAGO, ILLINOIS 60805

FEB   2004

IN A
TEMPLE
OF TREES

a novel by suzanne hudson

MacAdam/Cage
155 Sansome Street, Suite 550
San Francisco, CA 94104
www.macadamcage.com
Copyright © 2003 by Suzanne Hudson
ALL RIGHTS RESERVED

Library of Congress Cataloging-in-Publication Data

Hudson, Suzanne, 1953—
    In a temple of trees / by Suzanne Hudson.
      p. cm.
    ISBN 1-931561-41-9 (alk. paper)
    1. Boys—Fiction. 2. Murder—Fiction. 3. City and town life—
Fiction. 4. Southern States—Fiction. I. Title.
    PS3608.U547I5 2003
    813'.6—dc21

                                                      2003012922

Manufactured in the United States of America
10 9 8 7 6 5 4 3 2 1

Book design by Dorothy Carico Smith.

Publisher's Note: This is a work of fiction. Names, characters,
places, and incidents either are the product of the author's
imagination or are used fictitiously. Any resemblance to actual
events, locales, or persons, living or dead, is entirely coincidental.

LITERATURE AND LANGUAGE DIVISION
THE CHICAGO PUBLIC LIBRARY
400 SOUTH STATE STREET
CHICAGO, ILLINOIS 60605

IN A
TEMPLE
OF TREES

a novel by suzanne hudson

MacAdam/Cage

LANGUAGE DIVISION
PUBLIC LIBRARY
STREET
ILLINOIS 60605

For
Ira B. Colvin
"Ben"

Let the trees God made
Be fed on valley and Hill...
...As the heavens yield their dew

...And with the dew
let harvest and song descend,
goodness and life,
sustenance and help. Amen.

—New Union Prayer Book

Firelight played shadows across the tin roof of the skinning shed where Cecil Durgin lay. He pulled the flannel innards of his sleeping bag up around his neck, against another rush of November's meager chill. Normally much colder at this time of year, the weather was off-kilter, like this night that wrapped him in the seductive sounds of nature and of man. A hundred yards away and up a rise, the lights and music from Big John McCormick's hunting camp spilled into dense thickets, bare oak limbs etched like skeletal grillwork against the stars, overlaid here and there by faint brushes of pine needles. The darkness carried sounds, lulls, louder sounds, down the holler to him, seducing his intrigue, breaking his resistance—crisp sounds of slurred laughter and raucous shouts riding the wind, curling about his aborted slumber.

He was still trying to decide whether or not to slip up to the camp house and spy on the white men. Something was up, no doubt about it, and curiosity had kept him tossing for an hour while apprehension kept him bedded down. The atmosphere back at the big house had been battered and coated with a thick crust of anticipation, the men agitated and laughing too loud, passing sly winks at one another and at the woman. *One woman.* Otis said to be extra cautious if there were only one woman to the five men he listed for Cecil one evening, all boozy and loose-lipped with sloe gin. Those five men were at the camp this weekend. They were having some sure enough party all right, and he wondered what that one woman thought of it all.

Cecil had spent the days prior to the weekend, as he had so many times before, at Camp DoeRun, a cavernous log home book-ended by great stone fireplaces with expansive hearths and balconied by toasty sleeping lofts. He cleaned and made preparations on Tuesday afternoon for the men who arrived on Thursday to post themselves alongside clearings deep in the woods, fix the sights of their expensive shotguns on the elegant bucks roaming McCormick's private forest, and drink the nights into oblivion—swaddled in poker and lies and blended whiskey. Cecil cleaned up behind them in the mornings, after cooking early breakfasts of cheese grits and venison steaks, then again, in the dusky evenings, after dense suppers of barbecued ribs, corn on the cob, roasted potatoes, tomato gravy, and tender quail breasts plundered from the huge deep freeze in the kitchen. He helped with the kill they brought in on pickup beds at sunset, letting the blood, skinning, and gutting, listening with the appropriate degree of attention to swaggering tales of the hunt, laughing at the coarse jokes bandied about, keeping true to his place. He always watched this ritual of manhood unfold with the reverence of a congregation member in a hallowed church of aged bark and chanting leaves, aching for a ritual of his own, a heart full of God, guts and glory, something he was set on getting, no matter what the odds against him. The reality of being a colored orphan in the West Central woods of Alabama spun a fabric of deference and fear about him, along with a hidden determination he learned to wear like the Emperor's new clothes, and some measure of peace came with his secret intentions. At the age of twelve, he was a camp veteran, old beyond his years; he had been coming along on the hunts since he was eight, tending fires and learning to cook from Otis Joyce, at fifty his aging predecessor.

"Give 'em a wide way to go, boy," Otis would slather through his sparsely-toothed gums, eyes fierce and yellowed with whiskey and years. "'Specially when the bourbon's riding high. 'Specially more when they's womens up in here. Put out the food and give a wide way to go, 'cause a white man ain't no kind of predictable. And a boozed-up white man with pussy on the brain is flat dangerous."

So Cecil quietly honed his skills, slipping warily into the role prepared for him by Otis, Big John McCormick, and Mr. and Mrs. Price—Mr. Austin and Miss Sophie to him—the childless white couple who let him live in their heated garage in town, fed him, and gave him small chores—yard work and light duty at Mr. Austin's radio station on the outskirts of town—to earn his keep.

Sheriff Huckaby stood Cecil on the Prices' front porch one July afternoon in 1949, when he was little more than three years old. Cecil's mother had just run off, just up and left, for all he knew, and the sheriff came and got him on the heels of her departure.

"I'm going to get right to the point," Sheriff Huck said. "This little fellow needs a home, and I hear tell y'all can't have no young uns, can't adopt on account of Miss Sophie's a Jew, so I brung you the next best thing. I know it ain't the same, him being a nigger and all, but he might be some help over the years. What do you say?" and he spat off to the side. "Y'all want him?"

Cecil was confused, disoriented, terrified of being sent to the state hospital in Tuscaloosa, where Sheriff Huck told him colored orphans often ended up. There he would be beaten and starved and driven crazy by all the loonies, if they did not kill him and feed him to the squirrels first, the white man said, while his child's mind pictured a rubble of acorns and switching fuzzy tails as the animals gnawed on his toes.

Mr. Austin did not utter a word, but Miss Sophie was thrilled. She had him bathed and fed just that fast, and, after a whisper-hissed discussion with Mr. Austin, tucked into a little water-heater closet of a bedroom off the kitchen. Toys and books were purchased. The Prices' maid, Gladys, tended to him when she was there, so he had two surrogate mothers while he screamed inside for his own mother, the real one who did not care enough to stay with him. Four years later, when Miss Sophie's husband insisted she had grown too attached to Cecil, that folks in Three Breezes thought it improper for a Negro boy to grow up behind the walls of their home, she cried, argued, slammed drawers and doors while Cecil lay on his little bed, listening for the roar of the gas water heater starting up. Gladys attempted to warn him of the coming change. "They is a limit, that's all, boy," she told him. "Even for rich folks, they is a limit to what all the rest of the folks will stand for. And I reckon Miss Sophie can't have you without giving no thought to what folks will stand for."

Two days later, Miss Sophie put her hands on his shoulders and told him to be big about it, about being banished to the car house. Nothing would change between them, she said. It would just have to be more private, private even from her husband. Austin did not understand the love of a mother, she said. Austin's mother had withheld her kisses and kind words. Besides, if they did not keep up appearances, then Cecil might be taken away. "See it as a game," she said. "It's a game in which the two of us will humor the town, humor Mr. Austin, and keep on being a family to one another, all right? It will just be more private, that's all."

Cecil was afraid of the car house, did not want to be alone without the soothing sound of the water heater going on and off, without the nearness of the only mother he knew. But Miss Sophie helped him make the best of it. She fixed up the garage with his pictures and toys and a nice bed and bureau; she had a toilet, sink and shower put in just for him. The water heater was even placed so that he could hear it through the night, and she always checked on him in the evenings when Mr. Austin napped in his big chair or long after her husband went to bed. And she continued to give him abundant affection in private, subtle touches in public, seemed to care when he cried for his mothers, let him attend the Mt. Holy Baptist Church with Gladys, taught him prayers in Hebrew, and toted him to the doctor and the dentist and, when he turned six, to the colored school on Pitch Hill.

His relocation to the garage was the second jolt of rejection that cut him at his center, but over time Cecil grew comfortable with the solitude of his young life. He wondered less and less about his first mother, more and more about the workings of a world he studied from the edges of its respective societies. At school there was laughter and horseplay with the boys whom he rarely saw otherwise, and he envied the place they occupied on Pitch Hill, with their little shotgun shacks, their dirt yards, their families, and their community. He spent the afternoons with Miss Sophie and Gladys in the big kitchen, garnering their approval for his excellent schoolwork, reading aloud for them while they cooed at his intellectual feats. Then he attacked his chores before spending the evening hours in the garage visiting with Tarzan, the brothers Hardy, King Arthur, and the rest of the characters in the books Miss Sophie bought him. When he turned eight, Mr. Big John offered to put him on camp duty, and Cecil went at it with notions of daring adventures fighting wild animals and saving the day, just like his fictional friends.

The reality of it was bland, but it put him in the company of people he watched with the detached eye of a little Buddha, serious in his work, determined in his secret ambitions. He learned when to be the butt of a joke about Negroes and when to laugh at other jokes about hunting, fishing, or fucking. He learned how to nod his head convincingly at drunken longings for more prestige, more political pull, or more pussy. Most important, he learned to keep his mouth shut about everything, but particularly about the whores who were passed about on vagrant weekends, knowing, as Otis took great pains to remind him, "You don't know nothing about where they peckers done been and so you get to keep your'n. Best keep your'n cause you be needing it one day." In the West Alabama woods of 1958, Cecil knew enough stories, at twelve, including his own, to know that life could be taken on any whim or mangled on a dare, that his own silence, indeed, meant life.

This knowledge kept him all the more frustrated with the losing battle he now fought with his burgeoning curiosity. There had been plenty of women at the camp on plenty of debauched weekends, most times at least two or three loud-laughing, man-hugging women who danced close and French-inhaled cigarettes against wet red lips; this was the first time he had been around when there was only one, and Cecil knew that only one woman was required for The Game. Unfortunately, that was about all he knew. With all the other details, all the tutelage Otis had given him over the past four years, the old man kept his own tense silence about The Game.

"Some things ain't fit to speak to a child," Otis told him when he was ten. "But you know it coming when they be having one woman between these five mens: Mr. Big John, Mr. Cash, Mr. Huck, Mr. Roscoe, and Mr. Lee. The same ones every time, unless they let some-

body else in. They will do that every once in a while,
like when they let Mr. Lee in, but him that comes in
stays in." And he explained how Mr. Lee, who was a distant relative of Big John's, was allowed in because of
blood and business connections, not to mention that
McCormick had a strong hankering for a son.

"They is some men, like Mr. Big John, that sets
every bit of they manhood on a male child, done come
out of they own blood, don't you know," Otis said. "Mr.
Big John one of them kind of men. That's how he come
to be called 'Big John,' 'cause he say one day they damn
sure going to be a 'Little John' to follow him all over the
creation."

"But what about Mr. Lee coming in?"

"Like a son, boy. Like a son. You watch them. Mr.
Lee and Mr. Cash be young. You watch them, boy. They
be smiling and laughing on the outside, but they be
fighting all the time, on the inside, just to be like a son
to Mr. Big John, take the place of his son what died." He
hacked up a slug of phlegm. "Shoot. Just want to be a
son to Mr. Big John's money, is all. Uh huh. You let
them get they fist on that money and that money going
to be done spunt."

"But what do they do in The Game?" Cecil was
intrigued, impatient with Otis for getting off the subject.

"Don't matter. You just keep clear of it cause you be
done tore your britches if you don't."

"Why is it only one lady?"

Otis chuckled. "'Cause two ladies going to talk. And
talk spreads for miles and miles, don't you know."

"Do they hurt the lady?" Cecil asked.

"You ain't allowed to ax me nothing no more about it!" Spittle flew from Otis's gums and sprinkled across Cecil's cheek. "But, naw, honey. Don't nobody get kilt or nothing. And that prosecute walk away with upwards of five hundred dollars. A hundred dollars a man. Uh-huh."

Cecil's eyes widened at the figure. He knew about screwing and some of the other things men could do with women—a world of learning came along with the white men's dirty jokes—but what could a woman do that was worth that much money? Enough money for a car or a real diamond ring? But Otis would speak no more of it.

"Just keep away," he said. "If you want your doot in a piece, that is."

Cecil lumbered out of the sleeping bag and stood by the fire keeping the shed tolerable warm, especially on a barely cold night like this. The signature call-letter tune of the radio station came sing-songing down the hill: "Double-you elll-s," pause, "Chiii ca-go," followed by the smooth tones of the deejay and the first beats of "Tequila" by The Champs. The men's laughter masqueraded through the trees—disembodied, like the voice of God, but clearly intoxicated. Garbled shouts bubbled through the maze of bark and brush, but he could occasionally make out actual words:

"Play The Game!"

"Poker face!"

"Go, Hard Cat!"

"Spin her again, Boscoe!" Then there would be a racket of clattering furniture or breaking glass.

"Come on with it, baby!" And the laughter would rise in volume and menacing intensity.

Cecil knew the men well. He knew that Sheriff Jackson "Huck" Huckaby would pass out early, laying his six-foot, six-inch frame wherever he happened to be when the booze claimed victory, sometimes pissing his pants in an alcoholic coma. Lee Davis, the somber young president of the Farmers' Bank, would be the last to leave at the weekend's close, waiting for the place to clear out before he took himself a thirty-minute dump with a *Field & Stream* magazine. Big John McCormick would push the party as far into the night as he could, his graying good looks, his vivid green eyes, and his way with a tale showcased by the wealth and power he had acquired. Cashman "Cash" Cloy, McCormick's overseer-caretaker-guide would join in spurring the men on. The quintessential outdoorsman, Cash once even had a radio show on a Birmingham station, telling folks how to catch fish or shoot dove, turkey, and deer. He could track a deer blindfolded, smell bream beds a mile away, and hit just about anything he shot at. He grappled for catfish in the Sipsey River, the Black Warrior, and the Tombigbee, catching them with his bare hands, never minding the razor fins, and he usually won for the biggest snake at the Cole County Rattlesnake Roundup. He had good looks and charm, like Mr. Big John, but he had no fear, which inspired fear in Cecil.

IN A TEMPLE OF TREES

Finally, there was Big John's weasely little attorney, Roscoe Bartley, also known as "Boscoe" when he was being goaded or ridiculed, pock-faced, bespectacled, and rotund. It was Roscoe, who, along with Sheriff Huck, was most often the butt of a joke—if no bottom feeders or hangers-on were around. Cecil liked him least of all. He skulked, connived, blind-sided, and wore a perpetual sneer hinting at a wholesale lack of conscience. He managed Big John's finances with a cocky sensibility that bought power in the community, yet women did not find him appealing, an aberration in itself, as those who climbed socially would as a rule bed down with anyone who had money or power, no matter how hard they were to look at. Bartley's ugliness was beneath the skin, and Cecil did not begin to trust him. What could "Boscoe" Bartley do with a woman that was worth paying so much money?

Finally, Cecil could not stand the thought of not knowing what those five particular men might be doing with that one particular woman—a woman with movie star looks on the cheap, who had already succeeded in beguiling him with her whimsy. He pulled on his field jacket, zipped up with determination, and began walking up the narrow road that wound through the piney woods, refusing to remember any of Otis's admonishments.

Her name was Charity Collins, this one particular woman, and Sheriff Huck had gone to fetch her mid-afternoon, deposited her at the door, then headed to the northeast quarter section to rejoin his friends.

"Hey," she said, while Cecil lifted one of the deer

tenderloin strips from the bowl of seasoned vinegar in which they had marinated since yesterday. "You look like you know what you're doing."

"I reckon," Cecil said. The large brick grill shot flames up through the wire mesh, sending drizzles of hissing juices to flaming coals. He tried not to look at her too long, but she stood out for pretty, moved with the scented promise of something men would fight to have.

"I seen you around," she said. "You work for that guy who owns the radio station." She couldn't have been over twenty-five or so, close enough in age to intrigue him, and she was stacked like few women he had ever seen. She wore blue jeans, black cowboy boots, and a pink sweater pulled taut across large breasts Cecil forced his eyes to avoid. Her black hair was a cap of fixed waves framing intense blue eyes and soft, pink lips. She smelled of perfume and Ivory soap, and Cecil felt his crotch tingling. She introduced herself. "Charity. Charity Collins. Almost Chastity, but I guess my mama thought twice about that. It's a good thing, too," she giggled. "Ain't it just so pretty here?"

"Yes'm."

"Can you believe how big the house is? And to them it's just a little old hunting cabin!"

"Yes'm." Cecil laid another strip on the grill, the sizzle rising up and around him, a reflection of the electricity popping in the pit of his stomach.

"I can't believe they asked me out here. I ain't never been here before. Some of my friends from the box factory has, though." She leaned in and lowered her voice.

"They choose from the box factory, what I hear. That place is full of good looking women."

Cecil did not make eye contact with her, could not without giving himself away, bathed as he was in her perfumed whisper. He managed an appropriate comment, his standard, "Yes'm."

She nudged him with her elbow, forcing him to glance up. "It's gone on for years, what I hear." Her eyes drew him in to her mood, an aura of giddy excitement, the sweet voice of a confidante. It was too late. He was in love. She leaned in even closer and her breath brushed his face like sun-warmed dandelion down. "There's this lady—older, you know. Sonora. She's been at the mill a while. Anyway, she said she come out here a few times back ten years ago and she wasn't even near the first. What do you think about that?"

He was startled by the question, by his opinion solicited, but his voice would not answer. He was so drawn in, so aware of the physical response she elicited, a breathless, gut-punched feeling that would only let him gape like a stupid boy while he shifted against the barbecue pit to hide the lap of his jeans.

He was afraid she would laugh, but she only squinted her eyes, seemed to be studying his silence, then, in a voice slathered in some kind of husky understanding, said, "Oh, I see." She grinned. "You ain't giving up no secrets." And she winked, letting an eyetooth tug at her lower lip, sending him into a pit of lust flashing images across his brain, images he fought back to keep himself from burning the deer strips laid out on the grill before him.

Her mood moved like mercury. She threw her arms out, then brought them down to hug her own shoulders, all the while doing a slow pirouette. "Damn," she said. "I'm telling you, I feel like some kind of a lady around all this money!"

"Yes'm." Cecil continued to busy himself with the meaty strips. He envied her arms, the arms hugging her shoulders. She was sure enough pretty, sure enough enticing. She put him in mind of a country-girl version of Elizabeth Taylor. He wondered why a girl that pretty would let men pay her to do things with them. She could probably get a rich man if she tried. All a real pretty girl, one that stood out for pretty, had to do to get a well-off man, he had noticed, was to get knocked up.

"That meat looks right fit," she nodded at the grill. "My daddy always said can't nobody cook like a negra."

Cecil's neck tingled like it did whenever he heard white folks use the word "negra," or the aristocratic "nigrah," or "nigger," "coon," "pickaninny," any of the scores of monikers, whether subtly stinging, as Charity's was, or slicingly overt, like the day Sheriff Huck offered him to the Prices. Whatever the context, the words took shape and reminded him, as if he could ever forget, that boundaries were thick and threatening, that silence very often meant life.

"You know," she leaned toward him again and this time he let his eyes cut for a second to the pink sweater. "It's supposed to be a big secret, me being here. Huck said I couldn't even tell my best friend, Janelle, or I wouldn't get paid." She pulled a pack of Lucky Strikes from her purse, slid out a cigarette and lit it. "Of course," she went on, "I shouldn't even be telling you, but, hell, you're here too, so it ain't like you don't know, right?"

"Yes'm," he said. In spite of the breasts and the perfume and the warm whispers, he did not like what he was hearing. The secrecy. The fact of her demanded silence, which made his silence all the more crucial. The one woman. The five men. The brutal fear in Otis's eyes rushed at him. He did not want to know. And he was desperate to know. Five hundred dollars was a lot of money.

She offered him a smile, white teeth framed in pink lipstick. "But you seem okay. You'll keep quiet about all I told you, right?"

"Yes'm," he said, as if he could say anything else. Hell, he would do anything she wanted as long as he could enjoy the sound of her, watch the way her eyes changed expression, the way she moved. He didn't know quite what to make of her. The women who were usually brought to the camp, the women who did not have the legitimacy of being wives or girlfriends, rarely spoke to him. They were easy to regard as whores, sluts and harlots, the words Gladys used for any women who committed adultery. But Charity possessed an open warmth that pulled him with gravitational strength into her orbit. "Yes'm," Cecil said again.

"Goddamn, boy." She giggled. "You ain't one for words."

"No'm," he said, and smiled.

"Hot damn! A new word!"

They both laughed then, and he thought she was more than all right for a whore. He knew Gladys would not approve, and Miss Sophie probably did not even know such women existed, but he was taken with her. He let the sweet seduction of her conversation billow around him like the smoke from the barbecue pit. He learned about her family in Arkansas, how they lived in rot-gut hillbilly poverty, how her uncle came to live with them when she was thirteen and raped her when she was fourteen, how she had come to Alabama with a shoe salesman who went door to door, just so she could get away.

"He made me feel like Cinderella," she said. "He carried me out of the Ozarks like Prince Charming, only without the white horse. Made all kinds of promises, like how we was going to get married and go to Florida to live. Down there in Key West on his boat. You ever been on a big boat? A sure enough yacht?"

"No'm. Just a little old john boat."

"Well, me neither. 'Cause come to find out there ain't no boat. There was a wife, though, in Meridian, Mississippi. I made me up a saying: that fool prince wasn't nothing but a footman. Get it? A foot man?"

Cecil smiled again.

"Yeah, he just wanted to put me up in a sugar shack and have me on the side. Told me all those lies just to get in my drawers. What do you think about that?" She searched his eyes. She seemed to be genuine in her desire for his opinion.

Cecil wanted to ask her how her shoe man was any

different from the men at the camp this weekend, but he knew better. "Sure enough ain't right," he said.

"No shit," she said. "I got me a bunch of shoes, though. Nice ones." She stared off into the woods for a moment, then sighed. "Yeah, it's going to be a long-ass time before I have to buy myself a pair of shoes."

The voices were loud as Cecil crept up to the camp house. They would be at the round oak table near the kitchen, he knew, when he heard the distinct shuffle of a deck of cards; the oak table was where he had watched many a poker game held on stormy afternoons when the deer weren't moving. The clink of plastic chips drifted through the screen door and the slightly open kitchen window. Cecil crouched in the shadows of a holly bush next to the house, the image inside slatted by Venetian blinds.

They seemed intent on a hand of poker at the moment, a shirtless group of hairy masculinity, Charity nowhere to be seen. The radio behind the bar looped the rock and roll piano of Jerry Lee Lewis through the camp house, all the way from Chicago. Bets were placed, raised, A couple of new hands were dealt to murmured talk and plastic chips clacking. Cecil, puzzled, thought to go back to the skinning shed. Maybe she had gone to bed. Maybe he had it all wrong. Maybe—

"Goddamn! Baby!" Cash Cloy suddenly leaned his head back and moaned deeply, body tense. Cecil dipped further into the shadows, pushed there by instinct.

"All right!" Roscoe hollered while the other men laughed drunken bellows and shouts.

"Bring on a load!"

"'Great Balls of Fire' is right, son."

"Bluffed a whole nut, by God!"

"Shit, Cash," Big John laughed. "You had me going. That was one of the best all-time poker faces ever. Made it through five hands, by damn. She-it, you're good."

But Cash was breathless, laying his head on the table. "Uhhh," he grunted.

"Swaller it down and come on out, Baby." Sheriff Huck pushed his chair back and it became apparent to Cecil what was happening as her dark hair appeared from under the table.

"Poker face!" Big John shouted. "Cash is still the all-time champ!"

"No shit," Roscoe said. "He poked her face good. Right? Poker face? Poke *her* face? You see?"

"I got to rest up, cool off the balls," Cash said. "Don't like to use it all up too fast. That way, when I fuck 'em, they stay fucked."

"I want a rematch!" Roscoe pulled Charity up from the floor. She was naked and the abrupt revelation of her flesh to Cecil put him into a confused, lust-filled shock that only let him take in other details bit by bit. She was wearing a blindfold improvised from a red bandana. Cecil flinched when Roscoe squeezed her left breast, then leaned over to nibble at it as she stood.

"Goddamn, you got the tits I mean," the man said.

Charity pushed the bandana down around her neck, wobbled a slight stagger, disoriented, then she giggled, shimmied her shoulders, and pushed her bare breasts into Roscoe's chest.

"Yeeeow!" he shouted.

"I need me a drink," she said, "to wash it down." Her face was wet, pink lipstick smeared, the sprayed hair-do ratty and matted in damp places. Cecil felt swimmy-headed and disgusted, but was compelled to watch her body as she went over to the bar. The brown nipples, framed in white linen flesh that must have been hidden from the sun by a swimsuit, rode the motion of her breasts, a shimmering slow motion, standing out against the chill as she walked. He felt himself get up that quick, and, mesmerized, his hand automatically went to his crotch. She was more than pretty. She was beautiful. He had seen naked white ladies in the magazines Mr. Austin kept hidden in boxes in the garage attic. Once, he had seen a live naked colored lady when he and Tony Mack Franklin went spying one humid night, but she was old, and her breasts and ass had a worn sag to them, the hairs on the mound between her legs thinning. Still, she was live. And naked. He and Tony Mack whacked off behind the Zion Baptist Church, vying to see who could shoot off first. Tony Mack won.

But Charity looked like the pictures in the white girlie magazines, smooth, creamy, made for a man to have a place to put his pecker. When she turned back to the table, Cecil could see the tight-wound sparkles of black curls spilling around the *v* where her thighs met, kissing the very topmost, innermost, fleshy part of those thighs, and he was afraid he would mess himself on the spot. Did he dare do it deliberately? What if they caught him? What if she saw?

"You be wanting that bone of yours someday, boy," he heard Otis whisper through his brain. "Don't be stupid when it come to your wishbone. You be finding a big old juicy jellyroll to dob it in one day and you be wanting that bone then. Wishing for that old wishbone. You miss it if it don't be there."

The men were laughing again, slapping Charity on the ass, pinching at her nipples, pushing a glass of whiskey to her lips. Cecil could tell she enjoyed the attention; her body squirmed, and she ran her palms lightly over her stomach, her breasts, as though in a state of wanting. The boy pressed his palm more firmly to the crotch of his jeans, knowing he was crossing a very distinct line, so taken in by a charge of desire that he did not really care, transfixed by her skin's curves and damp recesses.

"Another game of poker face?" Lee said. "Spin her, Roscoe, and put her back under the table.

Roscoe pulled up the bandana and began turning Charity, as though preparing a child for a game of Blind Man's Bluff, but Big John shouted, "Boscoe, you damn pussy, you don't want to play poker face again. Hell, you couldn't keep a straight face when she was honking your sawed-off little root! Didn't even throw no cards before we called you."

They all laughed, including Charity, who took a giggling fit, the blindfold falling down around her neck again. "I don't think I was on him but a few seconds before y'all called his hand," she gasped. "Shortest blow I ever give."

"Shortest in more ways than one!" Cash yelled, which put Charity in a doubled-over laughing frenzy.

Roscoe glared at the woman. "Y'all are full of bull," he said.

"Anyway," Cash said, "It don't matter how many times we play. Ain't nobody going to beat my record. You're looking at the Hard Cat Man."

Roscoe's face reddened. "Shut the hell up," he said, yanking the bandana hanging around Charity's neck.

"Hey!" she said.

"Relax, baby," Roscoe said. "I'm just trying to help." He untied the bandana.

"You got to be a better sport, Boscoe," Big John said. "Tell you what. I think it's time for Phase Two of The Game. Enough of this penny-ante poker face shit. I think it's time for Big Bets. And cash only, boys."

The men pulled wallets out of abandoned khakis and brown canvas pants, emptying pockets. "I'm placing the first bet," Huck said, lighting a fat cigar, his lips patting it like a bream smacking stifling air. "This one's for Roscoe."

"All right!" Roscoe said.

Charity giggled. "Y'all are something else. Should I be nervous?"

"Naw, honey," Huck said, sweeping the cards and

chips off the table, sending them slapping, dinging and spinning across the floor. "Here. Just you lay right here. I'll bet Roscoe a C-note he can't fuck her for three minutes without getting a nut."

"Shit, Huck." Roscoe said. "My wife would damn sure like it if I could come that fast. Frigid bitch can't get it over with fast enough."

"Oh, I think you can. I think you will. Give her one of them footballs." Huck jerked his head toward Lee, who hung back a little, near the great room.

The banker went from sight and returned. "Open up, girl," he said. He pushed something small into her mouth and ran his hand down her neck, only glancing her chest. Charity squinted at him, then smirked and shook her head. She washed the pill down with amber liquid. She was all obedience.

Cecil gazed at the live naked lady, hypnotized, only peripherally aware of the men's conversation drifting through the window, fascinated by the breasts spilling flesh as she lay back, drawing her knees up, soles flat on the table. He imagined he was at an angle that allowed him to see the deep place between her thighs, felt his breath coming faster. But when he saw what Roscoe was doing, reality came back at him in a huge gulp, along with Otis's warnings and the fear keeping him always in check.

"Wait! Don't put it in yet," Big John said, looking at his watch for a short silence. "Okay," he held up his arm. "Okay, go!"

Roscoe spat in his hand, stroked it down his penis, and began.

Cecil could not see her face, only her body being shoved back and forth on the table, and Roscoe's sneer fading with each motion, eyes closed.

"One minute," Big John said in a while.

"Come on, Roscoe," Huck shouted. "Slam it! That ain't no kind of fucking!" Then he motioned from behind Roscoe, motioned for Charity to speak.

"Faster, Roscoe, honey," she said, raising her legs and throwing them around the man's back. "Please, faster. It feels so good." Roscoe's chubby face pinched up as he picked up the rhythm. Cecil imagined his haunches knotted, flabby butt cheeks drawn in, the hairy back straining.

"One minute thirty seconds," Big John said.

Roscoe slowed, blowing air from puckered lips, face reddening more with each tense thrust.

"Uh-uh, boy, keep on stabbin'!" Lee yelled, an edge of unvarnished desperation in his breath, voice gravelly and unfamiliar. He had been pretty quiet up until now. The look on his face was more restrained than the others' unselfconscious stares, a jarring presence, and Cecil did not know what to make of it.

"Minute forty-five."

Huck motioned to Charity again, pointing at his mouth, mouthing words at her: *Say something.*

Charity moaned, wiggling her legs up higher on Roscoe's back, then pushing her right ankle back around to his chest and up on his shoulder. She panted up at Roscoe. "Goddamn you're good," and her voice dropped to the half whisper that had stunned Cecil earlier. He could not make out what it was but knew she was saying something electric, judging by the effect her words had on the man who pushed between her thighs. Roscoe blew and moaned, slowed and sped up. Cash nodded at Charity. She brought her other heel up on Roscoe's shoulder and half-screamed, half-squealed before stringing out more inaudible words at him through gritted teeth.

"Shit!" Roscoe exploded, while Huck and the other men doubled over in hysterical laughter.

"Where's your control, boy?" Big John said. "I've told you a thousand times to just think about your mama or Jesus or something."

Roscoe blew and sputtered something incoherent.

"You just don't get enough pussy, Boscoe," Huck said.

"Interference!" Roscoe breathed, trying to get his wind. "That's goddamned interference! I'd have made it if she hadn't said anything!" He stepped back from where she lay.

Charity sat up on the edge of the table. "I was just doing what—"

"Shut up!" Roscoe shoved her hard so that she hit the table and rolled over the side, knocking into a chair as she caught herself. "That was damn interference and everybody knows it."

Cecil jerked forward, thinking to help her up, a reflex fed by the manners Miss Sophie had instilled, but Mr. Big John was already taking her arm. "Goddamnit, Boscoe, don't bruise the fruit," he said.

Roscoe pulled up his boxers and sulked over to the bar.

Charity stumbled again as Mr. Big John led her out of view. "I'm fixing to show Boscoe how to exert some self-control. You feeling that pill yet, Baby?" Cecil heard him ask, and she giggled a response.

Mr. Lee drifted over to the bar and took a place beside Roscoe, both their gazes fixed on the adjoining room. The pops and squeals of the great stone fireplaces stabbed into a silence soon filled with the throaty sounds of a woman's pleasure. Cecil felt his arousal reach a new level, overtaking the disgust, and he wished he could see what Mr. Big John was doing with her. He thought about moving to another window that would afford him a view of it but was afraid to risk any noise. Best to stay put.

Cash took a long pull of bourbon straight from the bottle and handed it off to Huck. "Fixing to get good, boys," he said. "Fixing to get real goddamn good."

Cecil let his body sink into a squat, then down to the dirt, arms encircling his knees, the top of his head against the rough wood of the house. Points of holly leaves pricked at his neck and cheek but he did not care. He was cradled by dark and damp earth, unable to walk away from the white men's secrets until they were all played out. He put his concentration on his ears, wishing for the eyes of God, and listened.

The boy knew there would be a much bigger mess than usual in the morning, a mess of bottles, butts, and filth, and men mean with hangovers. He knew the woman would be worn out and probably harder now, maybe not as eager to be brought into the circle of wealth as she had been the previous day. He dreaded getting up, not letting on, revisiting the mundane with his altered perspective. He had certainly, not in a million years, expected to find her lying in the road, wrapped in a bed sheet, not thirty yards from where he had finally slept.

He had waited them out, blending into the blackness, unafraid because he was too paralyzed by revulsion to give himself away. The sounds of The Game curled around him like a cemetery fog, the kind carrying souls who never rested. The echoes bubbled a feverish morality tale with the night until the men began to grow quiet, passing out, one by one; until only one was left there with her, staggering her out the kitchen door to the barbecue pit about twenty yards from where he hid. Cecil smelled them as they brushed by, stale smoke and whiskey wrapped in an unfamiliar musk of sweat and warm breaths. He watched another phase of The Game begin, a coarse, cruel one, as she struggled and taunted, protested through palm-smothered lips. He was terrified he would go to her in spite of his fear, so, when he saw an opportunity, Cecil eased around the corner of the house, taking the back trail to the skinning shed. There he cocooned himself in the sleeping bag, wishing he did not know what he now knew. He hated himself for ignoring Otis. He wished he could take her off and hold her more gently than the white men had. The lush longing he felt for her was mixed with a brittle disgust, though, and he felt guilty when he finally took hold of the hardness that would not let him sleep, unloading into a dirty sock so as not to soil his sleeping bag.

He got only a piece of rest, and the last nugget of night shattered into sunlight too soon. He did not want to face them, but he knew there was no choice but to go through motions, make not to know, start cooking at the usual time, overlooking anything out of the ordinary. But he could not overlook the woman, lying face down, tangled there in the dirty bed sheet draped over her shoulder, twisted about her body like an old woman's corset.

He dropped to his knee. "Miss Charity?" he whispered, rolling her onto her back, the sheet unwinding, rolling her again, unwinding, falling away to reveal splinters scattered over her torso, front and back; a line of red-rimmed, ash-hued circles dotted down her shoulder and over her breast; her left hip and knee ribboned with raw, rough scrapes where they had been skinned. What had to be impressions of tooth marks framed in bruised skin worked their way around the top of her left leg toward her rear, where one definite, large bite mark rested. Matted on her thigh were what looked like some kind of animal's hairs, and a deep, sickened retch tried to rise up in him. He looked at her face. The pink lipstick was long gone, replaced by blood smeared away from a black-crusted cut on her lower lip. She had vomited there in the dirt, and the stench of it clung where it had dried on her left cheek, sticking strands of her hair together in a knotted web against that side of her face.

"Miss Charity?" he repeated, shaking her, not sure what he was seeing. Otis said nobody got killed in The Game, but was she dead? He shook her again, relieved when he heard a weak moan.

"Cec–?" Her right eye came open a crack, the left lashes stuck together, crust-dried together. He leaned down.

"You all right, Miss Charity?"

"Cecil?" she mumbled. "Harcutt."

"What?"

"Harcutt–he wanted."

"I'm going to get help." Her words made no sense, he knew no one named Harcutt, and he was feeling more scared by the second.

"Nuuh!" Fear looked back at him through the one open eye, and her nails clamped onto his forearm, tearing at brown skin. She clutched at him with a surprising surge of strength.

"I got to get help!" He wrenched free, slinging blood as he ran for the camp house, quick with fear, fast with urgency. Panic. It was with him for the first time in his life, mind-jumping, playing out what would become of him if they knew he had seen The Game. He wanted to help her. She was bad off, dying maybe. He had to get Mr. Big John. That was what he would do had he known nothing, and that was what he aimed to do now. A Passover prayer thumped through his head, over and over, with the rhythm of his running. *Baruch ata adonai elohainu melech ha-olam borai pri adamah.* A knot of terror tucked deep in his gut told him he needed to be sick, but he ran on. And when he was tempted to stop he was urged on by a gathering wind rushing through leaves, swelling its sound into a venomous hiss in the temple of trees.

Big John McCormick's ear lay against her chest, the expression on his face unlike any Cecil had ever seen him wear. Was it fear? It flickered across the man's eyes, then, as if it were a window shade being let up fast, flashed away into a cold, determined stare. "Goddamn, Cecil, she's dead," Mr. Big John said. He pressed his fingers against her neck. "Dead as a post."

Cecil stared at her, the stuck-together eye, the scratches ribboning down her torso, welts of red skirted by blue bruises. He had never seen a dead person outside of a coffin. He glanced up at the trees, searching for the essence of her. Did her spirit go up to God already? Or was it hovering there in the trees, playful and watching? Was that a breeze or was it her soul fluttering up to Heaven? Was she even going to Heaven? After all, she was a whore. She committed adultery.

Miss Sophie said there was no Heaven, that folks were to live their lives in the here and now, live to please God and not look for a reward in an afterlife for doing right, but the preacher at Gladys's church said different. And Mr. Big John was saying something different still.

"...a heap of goddamn trouble."

"Sir?"

"I said, you have fucked up something bad, boy. Real bad. You got yourself a world of trouble here." He paused to let it sink in, green eyes like spring water bouncing reflections of algae along mossy banks. Cecil backed away, the dawning of reality rising fast.

"I ain't going to ask you what you were thinking," Mr. Big John said. "I ain't going to ask about them scratches on your arm, but you best keep them covered till they disappear."

Cecil fingered the raw skin her nails had raked into angry red rows.

"I ain't going to ask anything," Mr. Big John went on, "because, truth be told, I don't want to know."

"But—"

"Shut up, now. Just shut up." The white man's voice was acid-toned, a mean sound unfamiliar to Cecil. Yet he knew the sound was layered with implications and demanded to be obeyed.

Just last summer Charlie Quiddons, a deacon at Gladys's church, had been accused of raping a white lady. Close-mouthed, Lord-loving, meek little Charlie Quiddons, whose thin, five-foot frame could not even threaten a child, supposedly held a big-boned, one hundred-sixty-pound white lady down, bruised her round the neck, and screwed her on a Sunday afternoon in July. Charlie went missing for ten days before his burned up body was found on a creek bank near Tippin's Eddy, at the foot of a burned-up cross.

Cecil shut up.

Mr. Big John stood. "Go clean up the house. Lee will take you home at the usual time, and you ain't got to do but one thing: keep your goddamn mouth shut.

You understand?"

Cecil nodded.

"We're going to keep you out of trouble, but this is not to ever be talked of. Not ever. You got that?"

"Yes, sir."

"Go on, then. Go fix breakfast."

"Yes, sir."

As he walked up to the big house, Cecil could hear Mr. Big John pacing back and forth, dirt, rocks, and leaves crunching under his fine leather boots, a steady rush of mumbled curses sputtering angrily into November's impotent chill. He let his heart take in the chant of the pine limbs, hoping to find her, but the trusting spirit of Charity Collins was nowhere he could make out, and he knew, with the most hollow, sinking feeling of his young life, that she had taken a piece of his own soul with her.

On any given Sunday morning Cecil Durgin would take an hour-long drive through the game preserve, across Round Swirl Creek, and down the rutted logging roads crisscrossing McCormick's spread. The drive would be slow, contemplative, even soothing at times, walled behind sentinels of bark and foliage. Sometimes he would stop and watch the woods, all whitewashed in silent brightness, little slices of light splitting and splintering the maze of still-life, searching for her. If it was raining like a son of a bitch or graveyard cold or suffocating with heat, Cecil would likely be in the woods if it was also a Sunday morning. This was the only place where he knew, deep down, he was meant to be.

On this Sunday he was visiting, one more time, with the familiar guilt which came, and with more and more predictability, whenever he disappointed his wife. He was wondering, one more time, if he should just be done with marriage, let Earline find herself a man who could keep off of other women. Maybe he should teach himself Spanish, cloak himself with a whole new set of words, and go away to Mexico, let himself be absorbed by yet another culture, shed his present life like a snake slipping its skin. After all, the children were grown and gone, to bigger towns where time had moved a little closer to the next century. Three Breezes, Alabama, was, in more than a few ways, stuck in the past, stuck like Cecil's own conscience, full of untapped intentions and unspoken truths.

The pickup bounced over red clay washouts, jarring Cecil with the reality of his reliance upon Earline, his dependence upon her strength and her ability to wait him out, a wait going on for two decades now. She had given more than any man deserved, and if he was a real man he would leave her—or make it right. Petite and dimpled at the cheeks and elbows, Earline was a tender mix of innocence retained from youth with a deep, even wise understanding of him. When they made love she held him cautiously, her warm brown skin like minted bronze against his. Yet when she looked up at him with almond-shaped eyes the color of buttered molasses, those eyes would sometimes take him with a startling passion; and that sudden glance blurred, for him, the deliberate lines he had set up in order to survive. It was in these moments that her eyes expressed what her body had been denied, what he sensed she wanted, though it was never discussed.

He caught his own eyes in the rearview mirror, eyes in their mid-forties. Goddamn, he was a grown man, way grown enough to use his brain when it came to his urge to rescue emotionally stranded, romantically ship-wrecked females. But in the same moment, he knew it would go on and on as long as the woods remained mute, as long as he held on to what Earline considered to be dubious reasons for keeping his own silence.

Ironic, he thought, that a person with such a silent soul would have made a living with his voice, as a radio disc jockey with a Christian preacher for one alter ego and a verbally outrageous, money-tossing talent agent for another. Maybe it was the comfort of just having a voice, any voice, to fill in the quiet gaps he was forced to guard. Whatever the reasons, he was by now a fixture in Three Breezes, a prominent businessman who moonlighted as a cook for the McCormicks and others, just to keep a finger on their pulse. Just to know they were fully aware of his presence, a presence he knew, even if they did not, alternated between shadow and form.

The shadows were everywhere, it sometimes seemed to him. The unusual circumstances of his growing-up years, cloistered in the garage of his phantom parents, threw reaches of dimness into every other aspect of his dealings with folks in the vague, white world. He did not have the luxury of complete exclusion, as did other Negroes, instead walking a marginal tightrope along the borders of the Prices' lives. He addressed them as "Miss Sophie" and "Mr. Austin." He followed the required codes of society while he deciphered the hieroglyphics lying just beneath the surface. He learned to read Miss Sophie's every expression, to know when he was to remain on the periphery of a social encounter with pale interlopers or when he was to retreat to the confinement of the building which once housed Mr. Austin's black Studebaker. He also knew when he could immerse himself in the fantasy of family living in the Prices' home, most nights taking meals with them, developing an awkward bond with the man who did not want to be a father to him but tried to become a fraction of one, out of love for and loyalty to his wife.

The forays into social life on Pitch Hill, too, were shrouded in brown and gray fogs. Even though he had friends and a place laid out for him in the black community by Otis and Gladys, he could still hear the uncertainty in the voices of the outcast, feel the subtext of suspicion in their expressions. In spite of this, he was included, was invited to the birthday parties of the other children, and became popular as he grew older, popular as an athlete at the colored school, popular with the girls who glanced up at him, coy and with easy give in their open stances, popular with the boys who kidded him with genuine affection and called him "whitey" and "Mr. Clean" because of his upbringing.

Every once in a while he slept over with his friends, went into their homes, breathed in the familial atmospheres and puzzled over the way each little shack full of humans had a distinct scent hidden beneath the dinnertime smells of pot liquor and larded grits cakes. Most often he stayed with Tony Mack Franklin, whose mother made a point of giving Cecil a place of honor at the table, hugged him, and called him her adopted son. But in spite of the veneer of unconditional acceptance there was always a hazy feel of all that was unspoken between them, the questions unanswered, his alien heart. And the disfigured darkness inevitably crept in, at least within his spirit, and he had to look elsewhere for form.

He thought he had found a certain kind of form in

tortured her, making murderers of them all. He was not motivated by the soulless cravings fueling the white men, he told himself, continuing to justify his entanglements. And, indeed, the encounters did give him a rush of peace and a heady charge of passion, brief respite from the pain inhabiting him since the age of twelve. It was a little like the thrill of bringing Jesus to others, offering up radio show salvation. It had an addictive quality to it, he knew. And he knew he would always go back to it, to the chance of making it up to her, hoping in vain for resolution.

He parked his truck and let the motor idle while he squinted into the trees. Sometimes he caught a glimpse of her, a searing flash of skin and dark hair, and for that isolated instant he would be overcome with the brief peace of another second chance. This time he would put it right. This time he would come out from behind the holly bush piercing his face and neck. He would charge out of the shadows with his Ka-bar knife, the one he carried every day now, in a long leather sheath secured to his belt. He would cut the throats of the men who hurt her, watch their blood puddle across the lawn at DoeRun, and not give a damn if they strung him up or sent him to prison. And he would have at once spared Earline her pain and obliterated his own, having done what his conscience intended before it was cowed and hemmed in by fear.

He pulled back the coverings of tree limbs with his imagination, sifted layers of leaves through his field of vision, tried to conjure her up from the mists mingling with her spirit. He put his full concentration on a bank of vines, hoping to wish her from beneath the tangled, rooted stems and into his arms. He thought he heard a faint, muffled giggle, a sound padded by damp earth and cool, green cover. It had to be her. He watched for a long while, every nerve ending in his body vibrating with determined expectations. He waited as the humming anticipation faded to a whisper and fell silent. It was only then he could complete his ritual of solitary searching, giving up his latest attempt to will her out, to coax her back to life and finally force his relinquished redemption.

Miss Honey Drop Davis could sing gospel with the ache of salvation that is just out of reach and blues with the raw yearning of one who has known the fleshy salvation that is love, therefore reaching more desperately for it. She had a fierce talent. She was the Real Deal, and Cecil Durgin had recognized this, had agented and promoted her, and finally held her hostage under contract.

She also had the looks and presence to send males into dog-pack heat, an exotic sensuality settling about her in an aura of tense readiness, full lips, fuller breasts and hips, knowing eyes set in amber skin, taking sultry for their color. Men jockeyed for position, squirmed with desire, became all boisterous exaggeration with one another, and went overboard to impress her.

"She's got a hot voice and a hot look, gonna melt you down like smelted iron, gonna make them juices run down your chin. Mmmmm–*Miss* Honey Drop Davis–gonna make you sure enough *drip*," went Cecil's promo on the weekly secular broadcasts at WDAB, his inherited radio station. "Come and get just a little drop of that sweet, thick honey. Man, them sticky drops, I mean. Get your tongue around it. That's what I'm talking about. She'll be at the Ready-Go Lounge in Columbus and you can make her yours. Come on, now. Come on with it, Miss Honey Drop." Then he would play a cut from one of her tapes and the airwaves would vibrate with the promise of sexual perfection.

The woman who carried the Cecil-bestowed stage name grew up as Kim Davis in Philadelphia, Mississippi, but moved to Cole County after meeting Cecil three years earlier. At twenty-eight she was nearly two decades his junior, but was intrigued by this kind-hearted man with the worldly edge, muscular and charismatic, who could hold an audience, in his own way, just as well as she could. She was sweet on him, but he was strictly business until finally, just last spring, she had exploited a road trip with him to Birmingham along with a bruised collarbone, courtesy of her most recent boyfriend, and climbed into his bed, fueling her fantasy that he would leave his wife, take her to New York or Chicago or Hollywood, and make her famous.

He ran his fingertips over the dark bruise that spread below her neck like black velvet. He kissed it over and over while his breathing came warmer and faster with each pass. And then he made love to her with the passion of a rollicking Pentecostal church service, finding rhythms and angles which caught her up in a shimmering net of orgasmic flashes, sealing her fate. He gave her the time and touch she never got from other men, men who were so overpowered by her lush sensuality they became automatons, intent only upon fucking themselves to ejaculation, without regard to her cravings. She was drawn back again and again, needing that touch, whining and begging him to take her away.

"Daddy, please," she would moan, biting at his chest, chewing her way down to his thighs, covering him with her mouth. "Don't tell me no."

But he would. "Baby, you got me wrong," he would say. "I love my wife. She knows me. Feeds my spirit." And this would make Miss Honey Drop all the more needy and demanding.

Then came the offer, just last month, to cut a demo in Muscle Shoals, sign with a big time promoter, with an outfit out of Memphis.

"But, Baby, you know I can't release you yet," he said. "You got two more years under contract to me." And she broke a wine glass in anger, thrashed at him with her deep red nails, and let him melt into her with the promise of sex so good she dared not let it pass.

Thus went her cycle of neediness, anger, sex, neediness, anger, sex, until she came to a moment when it all had to give, one way or another. It happened three nights ago, late Thursday night. She was into her last set at the Dew Drop Club, out the highway to Repass, when he came in. This was not unusual; he stopped in on her gigs routinely, sometimes having a drink with her or a furtive sexual rendezvous in the dressing room. What was unusual this night was the woman with him—his wife, Earline. In all the time he had been promoting Honey, he had never brought his wife along, certainly never subjected her to the deferential attention he showered on that churchy, squeaky-clean bride of his. He was making a point; that was obvious. He was reminding her he was nobody's fantasy, least of all hers.

She barely made it through her last three songs, so close to tears her voice held together only by pure force of her will. The audience loved it, though, this raw pool of emotion poured into deep blues. As she stood on stage, lights hot on her skin, a slick sheen of sweat at her neck and chest, listening to the cheers and applause, she knew she wanted more. And she knew she would have more, with or without Cecil.

So it was that Sunday noon found *Miss* Honey Drop Davis heading out to make preparations, gas up the car, drop off the last of her bills. She had choreographed her exit, blocked out every step so she would wrap up her errands by paying a visit to WDAB. She had fermented in hot tears since Thursday, aching for a big, big audience in Memphis, and she was determined to threaten and bulldoze him into trashing the contract no matter what it took. A Smith and Wesson automatic, a prop for her last curtain call, was nestled in her spangled, green-beaded pocketbook, determined as she was to cut herself loose from him once and for all. She checked her make up in the entrance mirror of her Columbus apartment, picked up the keys to the Maxima, and threw open the front door as if she were walking out onto a grand stage, making her big time debut.

Ronnie Pierce shoved a fistful of Toasted Cheese Curls into his mouth, stared at the picture on the soundless television, and tried to think what to do. He didn't want to fuck up and make his brother mad, that was for damn sure. He wondered if he should just go on down to the jailhouse and see would his brother give him the instructions he needed on a daily basis, then decided Claud would probably just cuss him out for coming to where John Law was. On top of that, his big brother would kick his ass later on, kick his ass especially hard if the Law got wind of what Claud called his "commissioned" work, the jobs he did for those rich men over in Three Breezes.

It was the kind of work Ronnie had some understanding of, having been raised by a man who did the same kind of work until he died. But Ronnie never caught on to the degree his brother did. His brother was a natural. That was all there was to it. Claud was one mean motherfucker, had kicked Ronnie's ass on a weekly basis since they were toddlers, and had no patience with what he called Ronnie's "thick-tongued, dumbass questions" or his "shit for brains news flashes."

"This milk's done gone sour," Ronnie might say, pouring curdled clumps down the drain.

"Oooh! It's another news flash from the SFB Network. I think you better call CBS and CNN and let them know you're all over that big-ass story," Claud would say back.

"Looks like a storm making up," Ronnie would observe.

"Live, from SFB news seven, an up-to-the-minute report from retard-at-large Ronnie Pierce," Claud would say. "When water starts falling out the sky be sure and tell me it's raining, okay?"

"You want me to change that flat on the pickup?" Ronnie would ask.

"No, shit for brains. I thought maybe the fucking pickup fairies would come out of the woods and do it," Claud would say. "You know, you ain't going to win no Pulitzer Prize by asking them dumb-ass questions."

Claud didn't like to answer a lot of questions, particularly ones about day-to-day things, like was it going to rain or do you reckon we ought to check them spark plugs on the bass boat or did you know we're out of beer. And if Claud didn't like everyday questions, then he flat sure wouldn't answer too many questions about what he called his "business ventures," like the patch of marijuana he cultivated or the "secret operation" he set up in the padlocked shed near the barn.

Ronnie was forbidden to go anywhere near the shed, but curiosity took him there a few times when Claud was not at home. He peered into the dimness through cracks in the weathered boards, was mystified by the beakers, flasks and empty medicine boxes, the Coleman burners, the plastic gas containers marked, not "G" for gasoline or "K" for kerosene, but "AnAm," for he didn't know what. And then there were times when the smell from the shed crawled across the dirt yard and bit its way up his nostrils, sending a foreign, metallic taste to the back of his throat. Whenever Ronnie complained about the fumes, his big brother would tell him it was the smell of money and not to bitch about it. Occasionally, Ronnie would press his nose into a wad of bills, just to see was Claud telling him the truth. But the money did not smell anything like the chemical odor of Claud's "business venture" shed.

But it was not the business ventures that stirred Claud to his most puffed-up swaggers. It was his commissioned work in which he took the most pride and about which he needed to boast. And, since this work was the most secret of all his secrets, he settled for boasting small fragments in Ronnie's direction. "Got to go do a nut squeeze for the bank boys," he would say, grinning his sadistic grin for his brother. "Damn Bernie McDougal ain't made a payment on his vehicle in four months."

"Got to go scare a Ford out from under a poor old widow woman," Claud would say. "'Dry puff on board.' That's what her bumper sticker ought to say I bet. Reckon I ought to check her out? Reckon I ought to hang a horn in her?"

"Got to go incinerate a tin can, make the insurance man go ka-ching." Claud would say. "Folks ought not to get a doublewide unless they going to cover the note. And now they done messed it up so bad it ain't even worth the repo for the bank. That kind of shiftlessness shocks and appalls me, you know it?"

On three separate occasions folks drove new cars up to the gates of the Pierce property and left them there. Claud cursed each time. "Fucked me out of a nut squeeze," he said. "Must have heard I was making the repo instead of some pussy motherfucker." And Ronnie knew not to ask any questions if he did not want a knuckled fist to his torso. It made his big brother right hard to live with, but Ronnie just figured mean motherfuckers like Claud were bound to be that way.

Ronnie had gathered it took a lot of energy and brains to be as mean as Claud was, always thinking about commissioned work and nut squeezing. It seemed to Ronnie his older brother didn't just act mean; he breathed mean. He carried mean around in his gut, and he carried smart around in his head. Claud was way smarter about life than he was.

His daddy had been that way, too. His daddy and Claud were two peas in a pod. It was a family joke, even. "Me and Daddy's two peas in a pod," Claud would say, "and Ronnie is a pod full of pee." Then he would kick his ass. Again.

Claud punched, kicked, throttled, bullied, bit, spat, and glared his way through their childhood. If he wasn't picking a fight with another boy or bloodying Ronnie's nose, he was victimizing some animal or another. He shoved firecrackers into the butts of squirming, spitting kittens, creating what he called "kittycrackers." He conducted "bullfrog batting practice," knocking the amphibians across the creek with his Louisville Slugger.

He created a game called "drop and roll," in which he doused barn mice with charcoal lighter fluid before setting them on fire, just so they would make a flame that would last long enough to eat down through the skin. "Drop and roll!" Claud would holler at the panicked little fireballs running in crazed pinball paths across the dirt yard. Then, when the scorched animal lay blackened, hairless, and delimbed in the mud, twitching, writhing, and emitting weakened squeals, Claud would poke at it with a sharp stick or with his pocketknife and say, "Damn. If the thing would've just dropped and rolled it'd be just fine." Then he would collapse into laughter.

Ronnie would watch these little torture sessions with a gut-level fascination combined with secret, helpless frustration, but he participated nevertheless, just so his brother would not call him a sissy and beat him up one more time. He would participate so Claud would not tell their daddy what a pussy Ronnie was, because being a pussy earned the harshest beatings of all from Cee-Boy Pierce. He would participate when told to, but every once in a while, when he saw the chance, Ronnie would sneak and rescue one of the targets of his brother's meanness, like that one mouse, Lester, that Claud had kept in a cage in the barn.

Ronnie had been eight, his brother ten, when Claud started doing experiments on Lester, blinding him in one eye with a rusty nail, binding him to a board with freezer tape and holding a Zippo lighter to his back legs while the brown bulb of fur struggled and squealed into the gamey stench of burning mouse flesh. Then, after a few days of watching the creature drag itself around with its two good front legs, Claud made an announcement: he planned to finish Lester off by staking him out on a fire ant hill.

That night Ronnie sneaked out to the barn and rescued Lester. He kept him for a few more days in a deep box in the back of the tool shed before the little rodent died of the injuries he had suffered at the hands of Claud Pierce. Claud hardly missed him and simply moved on to other animals.

Other animals sometimes meant bigger animals, as was the case the time Claud beat a wounded buck to death with a bunch of barbed wire wadded around a creosoted post. Claud had gone into a rage when he could not finish off the deer he had shot because Ronnie had forgotten the box of shells he was supposed to bring along.

"You goddamned retarded, no-nutted fuck head!" Claud yelled, then popped him on the jaw with the familiar, hairy-knuckled right hook.

"Just cut his throat," Ronnie whined from his familiar place on the ground at his brother's feet.

"Cut his throat my ass. I ought to cut your skinny-ass gullet, you stupid motherfucker." And Claud ignored his knife, instead snatching up a post from some ancient, fallen fence, a snarl of rusted barbed wire tangled around one end. Then he commenced to flail at the dying creature. A steady stream of profane indignities were spewed forth at Ronnie as Claud tore through the thick hide of the struggling animal with clustered spikes of metal, fueled by the kind of rage that only the elder Pierce boy could harbor.

Other animals which were potential targets of Claud's wrath, however, did not include his daddy's prized bird dogs, the ones Ronnie and Claud were to take care of, were to feed every day. And they were to hose down the dog pen behind the barn every evening as well. "And don't you never in this world lay a hand on them dogs, you hear me, Claud?" Papa Pierce said. "I want their training left to me and Forrest Sims. You and Ronnie just take turns tending to them." But within a few days, the care of the dogs had turned into a solo effort.

Made me do everything, Ronnie thought, licking orange crumbs from his orange-stained fingers. Why I ought to do anything for him now? He ran his lower lip out at the thought of how the maintaining of the dogs fell entirely on his shoulders, how he hadn't minded at first, but when mounds of dog shit piled up faster than he could hose them away, he began to get frustrated. It was a stinking, nasty job and Claud knew it. Claud wasn't about to help and would beat Ronnie to tangerine pulp if he told their daddy. Ronnie was in his usual no-win situation with his brother.

Hard shit, soft shit, balled-up and blown-out shit, Ronnie felt like all he did was scoot shit out of the pen with a hose pipe. But one day he stumbled upon what he thought to be a clever solution. He had forgotten to feed the dogs for a couple of days and observed a resulting drop in shit production. Ronnie decided that his life would be much easier if the dogs did not eat so much. Thus, he reasoned his way into withholding food from the pedigreed animals. And it worked. The piles of shit grew smaller in number and in individual volume. Ronnie's job was at once manageable. Until his daddy noticed that the animals were beginning to look gaunt and rib-cagey.

"They don't shit so much if they ain't too full. And it ain't so hard to keep the turds scooted away," Ronnie offered when Old Man Pierce questioned his sons about why his bird dogs had dropped off so much.

"Goddamn, boy," Cee-Boy Pierce thundered. "You got every bit of the sense of your stupid slut of a mother, you know that?" And he administered a Cee-Boy beating, claiming that Ronnie was killing the dogs with his idiot self. Then he ordered Claud to take over the whole feeding operation, with Ronnie to serve as a shit scooter only, and the sole shit scooter at that. On top of it all, Ronnie got a second beating from Claud, who was pissed off about having to finally participate in the care of the dogs.

Ain't nothing I done never been right enough for him, Ronnie thought, studying the orange stain on his fingers from the Cheese Curls. I ought to not even bother trying to help him out now. I ought to not even bother with Cecil Durgin.

He crunched on another mouthful of bumpled, finger-sized nuggets, knowing that, in spite of all the resentment he felt and the beatings he had endured, he would help his brother out for one overriding reason.

He would help his brother out because it was a rare

opportunity to show Claud he really could be of help, was, in fact, way smarter than everybody thought he was. He could be a mean motherfucker too, if anybody would ever just give him a chance. Well, now he'd been handed a chance, because his brother was supposed to be somewhere and he wasn't going to make it. Claud had got himself locked up across the state line, wouldn't be out till who knew when, and he'd promised those rich men he would take care of Cecil Durgin *today*.

The man named Lee had been out to the trailer a few days earlier. "We got us a critical election coming up," he said. "I need to see your brother about putting some hurt on Durgin. Neutralizing him."

Ronnie envisioned a Terminator-like character blasting Cecil into fragments with some kind of a ray gun before Claud took the visitor into the trailer to talk it over. Claud didn't allow Ronnie in on any conversations related to his commissioned work. "You're such a shit for brains you'd probably tell it all over the fucking county, get me arrested quick, you stupid motherfucker," he would say.

But this time Claud was much more excited than usual, and he told Ronnie some of what was said. It was like he was a kid again, with a new animal to torture. "I finally get to work on Cecil Durgin, that nigger Daddy used to be on all the time. Daddy always said that nigger needed a new pair of overalls, and now I get to do it."

"Do what?" Ronnie reached for Lee's word, struggling to get on the same ground as his brother. "Neutralize him?"

"You goddamn right. You just let them pussies get in a bind and they call us, just like Daddy said they would. You just let some politician threaten to tax their fucking trees and look at how fast they run around trying to hold on to their money. I'm picking his ass up on Sunday."

Ronnie caught some of Claud's enthusiasm. This was the most information Claud had ever disclosed to him at one time. No matter that he did not understand a whole lot of it, like what overalls had to do with anything, but he didn't dare ask and risk his brother's wrath. "Can I go?" he asked.

"Shut the fuck up. You think I'm going to put the SFB network news cameras on my commission work? You keep your stupid ass cameras away from there."

"Hell, I ain't got no cameras, Claud," Ronnie said, but his brother shoved him aside and went back into the trailer.

Ronnie tipped his head back and emptied the contents of the Cheese Curls bag into his open mouth. He aimed the remote at the silent television and let the reception land on a lady in a leotard. The image tickled some life into his loins. She was on all fours, engaged in a repetition of bringing her knee toward her chest then straightening the same leg out behind her. Ronnie liked the way her butt wiggled with the motion of her leg, the way her lips steady moved with words for him alone, the way she periodically flirted a glance at him along with a wet-lipped smile. It flat made his rat crawl, got his intentions all sidetracked and in a mental tangle.

"Goddamnit," he blurted, throwing the Cheese

Curls bag on the floor, standing, and adjusting the crotch of his jeans. "By God," he said aloud. "I ain't about to beat off. I'm fixing to do this here thing for Claud." And he steady thought of how Claud would look at him in a whole different light, stop thinking of him as a doofus and a retard, stop telling him to shut the fuck up every time he opened his mouth. Claud would see he could be tough and smart like their daddy was. Claud would see, and then he would let him in on his life as a big time, sure enough, known-for-it, bad ass mother fucker.

Wade Connors fumbled under the seat of his patrol car and brought out a copy of *A Brief History of Time*, thinking to read while he waited for Cecil to get there. He was on a physics kick lately; for months he had only read titles related to the paradoxical theories that, surprisingly, gave him a sense of order and calm in the chaos of the universe, and he liked to think on it. Last fall he was on a self-help kick, immersing himself in pop psychology until he had trotted out and examined every dysfunctional emotional demon he could unearth from the repertoire of his own damaged psyche. Before self-help it was Zen everything, from Motorcycle Maintenance to Confucius. Before that it was a Stephen King-Edgar Alan Poe-athon. And before that *To Kill a Mockingbird*, four times in a row. Sometimes he got stuck on a particular writer, sometimes a genre, as with the true crime binge he went on one summer, in between

Victorian erotica and short stories set during the Civil War. This was the way he went at reading—consuming books by random categories, getting down inside an author or a subject until he had answered his questions or had more questions than ever in his quest for the ultimate answer. That, he decided, was becoming pretty futile, but this quantum physics shit was right on the mark, and he felt as close to the answer as he had ever felt in his life.

Too, he was reaching for the book to help him keep from stewing over the upcoming election. The reform which would raise taxes on property would be pushed through the next spring and already the panic was underway, paper mills and the big landowners supplying them determined to stack the legislature with opponents of any change whatsoever. And if they succeeded, and if folks went to voting a straight ticket like the dumb asses they were, well, Wade's job could disintegrate like Scott tissue in a toilet bowl. He needed Cecil's help in a big way.

He was parked in the gravel yard at WDAB, a squat brick building perched on a hill just south of the Three Breezes City Limits sign. It felt more remote than it actually was, surrounded by dense pine and oak shielding it from view of the passing cars on Highway 33. They could see the transmitter, though. That big-ass stick, boasted to be "the biggest stick in the state," sent little old Cole County way the hell out across the airwaves, all over Mississippi and Alabama. It was erected there in the 1930s by a hard-shell Baptist preacher from

Columbus, Mississippi, who had big dreams of becoming a famous radio evangelist. It had to be sold, though, when it eventually came out how the preacher fleeced his flock and romanced a rich old widow woman to get the money to put it there in the first place. Austin Price came in, bought the station, and enhanced the stick in increments. Cole County was just a dark little tucked-away crevice in the South, but for that big old stick. Sheriff Connors thought it ironically fitting that the station had passed from a '30s holy roller to a '40s atheist and then to a '60s Negro preacher who could be considered half Jewish. Maybe it was an example of chaos theory in action.

Wade considered Cecil the man a paradox: black-white, Christian-Jew, whore hopper-family man, master of the spoken word over the radio, and man of few words in person. Most of all, he saw Cecil as outwardly serene but sensed a molten core which was anything but, a perception he couldn't explain. Even Cecil the deejay was a multiple personality, alternating between the Sultan of Salvation, who peddled gospel music and common-sense scripture; and the Moonpie Man, who purred over jazz and blues. Maybe the mix of enigmatic contradictions had something to do with the odd circumstances of Cecil's journey through life. In any case, Wade, several years his junior, had always looked up to him. That in itself was odd, given the times. Odd that his choice of a hero to worship was one who was outside the bounds of his own race. But in Wade's estimation Cecil forever seemed to have it all when it came to cool.

In Cole County Cecil's voice wafted over the air waves of WDAB, "a little dab'll do ya," the station just outside the county seat of Three Breezes. Weekday mornings, which were hired out to a white deejay, were devoted to agricultural news and items of local interest along with country music and easy listening. On weekday afternoons, beginning at 1:00 P.M., folks tuned in to Cecil for a variety of chit-chat, Top 40, R&B, jazz, blues, a little country—a patchwork of sounds, something for everyone, and his show went late into the night—heavier on rock and roll, R&B, and blues—on Fridays and Saturdays. But Wednesday evenings and Sundays—a.m.'s, afternoons and evenings—were set aside for the gospel groups Cecil promoted, along with his common sense preachings, community notes, and spiritual advice for whoever called in.

His rich, velveteen voice, thick with the African-American dialect of Mississippi state-line mud, drew in listeners of all classes and races; many praising God right along with him; others hungry for a slice of rural culture straight out of the early days of radio, jarringly anachronistic in the years building to a new millenium. No mass-produced tapes of hyperactive, egocentric disc jockeys had ever been broadcast over the airwaves of WDAB. Cecil was among the few remaining of a dying breed, the sure enough live, no-rehearsals-allowed, hometown deejay, who still preferred old vinyl to the cassettes he played as well, and who took it as it came.

Yet his was not considered a throwback to the radio shows of the '40s, as he had done his broadcasting since he was a teenager in the early 1960s, creating his own individual stamp on the genre; his longevity only legitimized the flavor of his style. Too, Cecil learned the business well under his tutelage with Austin Price. It was Old Man Price who set up Cecil's initial foray into the business on-air, a biweekly rock session which began when he was only sixteen and soon spilled over into the weekends. The sounds of Little Eva, Chubby Checker, and the Dynatones crackled across the hills of Cole County with a vibrant innocence, gathering in mostly colored fans who were not previously well-acquainted with the station. This boosted Austin Prices' advertising market, which surged as Cecil was discovered by even more area teenagers. Within a few years the show had become a Motown-laden soulfest and Cecil was a solid hit with even the white kids in the county, just getting their first taste of Sam Cook, Martha Reeves, Wilson Pickett, and Otis Redding.

When Wade was in high school, he was aware of scandalized whispers about white girls going out to the station to hang out with Cecil, but Wade thought nothing would be more cool than to kick back with a real disc jockey and listen to good music all evening. The less-than-appealing parts of Cecil's job included, of course, his duties as Old Man Prices' chauffeur and general gopher, but he managed to carry even those duties out with an aura of suave calm Wade envied. Over time, Cecil learned the business inside out, from bookkeeping to advertising, with no formal schooling necessary. By 1982 the station was his, having been willed it by Austin Price.

His religious talks were earnest and homespun, his blues promos earthy and charged with sexual innuendo. He walked the line between salvation and sin with a rare and innate agility, imbuing his work with an informal honesty which allowed him to conduct his life as needed, no rush, no agenda. If a friend dropped by the station he would either step outside and let the air waves go silent or have a willing partner for a boisterous on-air chat. If need be, he would leave to preach a funeral or emcee at a blues club or honky-tonk. Thus, the radio programs he anymore personally conducted were, on occasion, hit and miss; yet folks knew, in spite of the silence, he would always be back. That was the essence of what Wade admired about Cecil. Cecil was solid. He might have a wounded spirit, or a secret wellspring of rage, but the fact that he was so unflinchingly solid demanded a level of trust from others Wade had found to be rare indeed.

Wade had just settled back with his book when Cecil's pickup wheeled into the parking lot, a few minutes late, as usual. And, as was usual when he met with Cecil to talk political favors, Wade had to fight back the feeling that he was intruding, with his petty little world, on a true man of God, albeit a bawdy one. Cecil seemed to have the spiritual strength of an Apostolic Army, but he definitely had the moral flaws of a lost Lamb under siege, and Wade knew he was going to have to try to confront one moral flaw named Kim Davis, along with the politics.

"So it's going to be a mean one, huh?" Cecil asked.

"Meaner than any I've ever been in. Seems the big dicks in Monkey Town been counting noses like crazy. They done all the polling they need to tell them Cole County'll probably be the key to the swing vote when that tax bill comes up."

Cecil shook his head. "So they ordering up one legislator, right?"

"Absolutely."

"Well, that shouldn't be too hard to pay for."

Wade laughed. "No shit. I just don't want the guy they pay for to carry off my votes, you know?"

"I hear you."

Wade cleared his throat.

"What you need? The usual?"

Wade shifted against the fender. It was just like Cecil to get straight to the point. "Well, yeah, the usual, but you need to know they'll be on your ass, too."

"Ain't nothing new."

"Well, it's fixing to be. I hear the big mucks around here are already plotting your character assassination. They don't mean to pay taxes on all the trees this side of Tuscaloosa."

Cecil gave a gentle chuckle. "I'm scared shitless, man."

Wade reached into the open window of his car for the mangled cigar he kept close by for an occasional gnaw, having given up smoking back during the self-help phase. He was never sure how much to say, how much he was supposed to know about Cecil's personal life. "Look," he said. "I ain't saying you should be scared, but you better take this one seriously. Folks get downright crazy-mean when it comes to big money. If you got any secrets, like maybe some sugar off to the side, they bound to find it."

Cecil narrowed his eyes. "Come on, man. Them mucks you talking about. It's just Old Man Davis, Roscoe Bartley and them, right?"

"Basically."

"They won't touch me."

Wade zipped a streak of tobacco-infested spit across the gravel. "Ain't nobody can't be touched. Everybody has something to hide."

"That ain't what I said. Ain't what I meant," Cecil said. "It ain't that they can't touch me. They won't."

"Well, ain't you confident."

"Just a little," Cecil laughed.

Wade was not too surprised by Cecil's lack of concern. Even though folks did get crazy-mean when big money was at stake, Cecil, whose reputation for getting out the black vote was so legendary he was routinely visited by politicians of all stripes right up to the state level and sometimes beyond, kept his own power very low key. And, unlike most citizens of Cole County, black and white, he was not intimidated by McCormicks and Bartleys and others who had been entrenched in absolute power for generations.

"All right, then," Wade said. "Thought you ought to know they mean to dismantle you this time. But, if you ain't worried, at least be on your guard, okay?"

"Yeah."

The sheriff got into the patrol car, turned the engine over, then leaned out the open window. "Oh, and Cecil?"

"Yeah?"

"You'll be singing my praises, won't you?"

"You and Jesus, man. All the time."

"Thanks."

Wade wound the car through the pines and back to the highway, trying to think of another way to avoid the office. His deputy, Ray Jones, was keeping an eye on their only prisoner, one of the no-'count Pierce boys from deep in the woods. Ray, also known as "Booty" in honor of his obsession with women back in the high school days, wanted his boss back in time for him to go to church this morning. They had already agreed to do a Sunday afternoon in the office catching up on paperwork, so Wade had a couple of hours to kill. He thought about stopping in on Tammy Sims, but knew she would be out snake hunting today. If it was not a Sunday he could go hang out at the Co-op for a while, listen to the farmers who brought in gossip to trade for Treflan and fertilizer, empty seed barrels rolling across the beds of dented pickups. Hell, maybe he would just ride around a while and listen to the radio. He turned the radio on to Cecil's deep-voiced Sultan of Salvation.

"Here goes a sound that'll get right down in your spirit and get your limbs to jumping," the Sultan said. "Yes, Lord, make you move. Sling them arms, jostle them legs and play them shoulders. The Lord loves it when you let your shoulders play. So here comes The

Blind Boys of Alabama to get your blood going and
your shoulders to playing."

Wade grinned. He spat a line of cigar juice through
the car window and turned up the volume, sending a
jubilant rhythm out into the oppressive, high-noon heat
of a Sunday in August.

Cecil put on a pot of coffee, letting the music fill the
small radio station, considering what Wade had just told
him. So the good old boys still believed they could
intimidate him, believed that his silence was held out of
fear, even now. They had no inkling how he ached for
the day when he could reveal everything without creating other victims of The Game. He shook his head.
The fact that Lee, Cash, and Roscoe, the surviving trio,
continued to believe they could control all aspects of his
life was a testament to their overblown egos. He had
been sparring with them politically for years, more
aggressively over time, as Cole County crawled toward
the present. After his initial defiance, at the age of seventeen, Cecil let a few years pass while he worked quietly at his subterfuge, building his influence by degree.
The early 1970s were his fruitful years, when he could
finally step into his role as spokesman for those in the
community, particularly those who were young and
black, who had some things to say, things that most of
the white folks did not want to hear. And by that time,
the weight of Cecil's unique position was permanently
set in, and the fact that he could enjoy a measure of

safety, albeit a small one, could work to his advantage. By the time the American Bicentennial rolled around, Cecil Durgin was at the height of an influence that Cole County had never experienced from a nonwhite.

From then on, Cecil could always be counted upon to deliver the vote, he knew, because, aside from being a self-ordained minister active in the church community, he had, via WDAB, the ear of all of Cole County, not to mention a good portion of two states. So he bargained with his enemies for the good of the general population, delivered winning ballots in exchange for more jobs at the mill or for a swimming pool at the Pitch Hill Community Center or for new desks at Cole County High School, which had long been abandoned by white students for the racial safety of Cole County Christian Academy. He knew how to play the game, but he also knew, in spite of a youthful sense of invincibility, just how far the game could go. Consequently, in spite of his bravado, Cecil Durgin always kept close a reservoir of caution, just in case.

Cecil reached his left hand inside his shirt collar, then over his right shoulder, fingertips glancing the scarred skin raised into silken folds forming the "Mc" that looped down into another "C." The McCormick brand, the premiere West Alabama symbol of old money, endless stretches of timber-laden hills, prime cattle, and the murky, muddied secrets he carried, had rested upon his shoulder since he was twelve years old, set there by the son of a Klansman—a son with a viper's sense of fun and sport. Cecil did not take great pains to hide the scar, but he never talked about the letters etched in his flesh, rarely touched them in a conscious way, and considered them a presence that tested his faith and willingness to hold in. He sensed that folks were curious about it but knew not to ask, just as they knew not to ask too many other questions about what went on in his personal life or in his hidden thoughts.

He was keenly aware there were two camps, two theories about the inner workings of Cecil Durgin. The first, that he was a womanizing opportunist, was held by most of the white population and a fraction of the black population of Cole County. The second, that he was a spiritually serene Holy man who had a few flaws and committed indiscretions, was held by most of his friends, along with white folks like Wade Connors, and the black community in general. And Cecil knew neither was the truth.

Cecil cued up the next trilogy of songs, leaned back in his swivel chair and took a long swallow of coffee. Damn, he was being introspective today. Usually he left the self-indulgent meditations upon his own psyche out in the woods where they belonged. But thoughts were sticking with him today, sticking to his ribs like a big breakfast, playing havoc with the façade he had constructed over time. The one thing his outward serenity forever failed to assuage, the dark backdrop of guilt that shaded his heart, was very much with him today. Today he knew with more clarity than usual no matter how many he helped, entertained, spiritually advised, or romanced back to safety, it would never be enough. He also knew the white men's political attacks and character assassination plots were nothing more than gnats in a dog's eyes compared to the knowledge of where Charity Collins lay every night.

On the surface, he knew anything he could not change could be accepted and borne while the anger was shoveled into his heart. Miss Sophie Price had taught him that when she had shown him her ability to hold serene in the face of indignities, indignities that were a direct result of his own failings. She even put him in mind of Jesus, gently bearing Cecil's sins on her shoulders, on a vicious night that still tested the dormancy of his emotions. Throughout his adult life, Cecil attempted to transpose some effigy of Christ over the core of beliefs Miss Sophie gave him, and something about the mix came across in a palatable way to his radio audience.

Cecil thought it troubling that white preachers often seized upon the meanness of the Word, the threat of hellfire, the Rapture leaving most everyone to slaughter while those few True Believers rose up through the clouds, up to God's Heaven. But Cecil rarely contemplated hell or a shallow God who would practice such vengeance, preferred instead the kind words of Christ, the turning of the cheek, the steady presence in the face of adversity. These beliefs successfully camouflaged his rage, became the edifice of the Reverend Durgin's spirituality, hidden embers of shame miles beneath his calm countenance. No one would ever have the satisfaction of breaking him down because broken down was where he came from; he knew broken down from the inside, from a place his enemies could not get their minds to comprehend. So most of the time they left him alone. They had, at least, for the past decade or so.

He took a block of calls and prayed for Leota Ponder, Moore Hadley, and Eric Salter. He introduced another trio of songs and thought about getting the Sunday paper he left out in his truck. He liked to talk about news items or the editorials, find ways to relate current events to spiritual life. Instead, he flipped through yesterday's neglected mail. He took another sip of coffee. He turned over another envelope, then another. Then he stopped, his forehead wrinkled, and he held up an envelope addressed in a very familiar hand. He tore into it, knowing it could not be good if she was leaving a note when she could have just called. Not unlike another note she left, at the station, under the center mike at the jockey's desk, over twenty years ago. He still remembered that one, word for word: "I need your help, please, please. This is as bad as it can be. No one can know. I'll be here as soon after dinner as I can get away. Please don't leave. Wait for me. Please. –S." He did as she asked that time, as he would any time, as he knew she would for him.

This new note was similar in its tone. "Must talk to you. Absolutely MUST. Very urgent. As urgent as it can be. Please meet me at the camp tomorrow afternoon. Sunday. I'll be there whenever I can get away. Trust me. –S." And, in spite of the fact that they had not spoken in years, in spite of the scarred letters scripted by hot iron to his shoulder, he knew nothing had changed. The trusted silences and hidden oaths of childhood could still be relied upon. Cecil leaned back in his swivel chair, leaned into the gentle peace of rediscovered loyalty.

Miss Kate McCormick tuned in to Cecil Durgin's program every Sunday, especially after she began to falter in her dutiful attendance at the First Methodist Church. She listened to his program in spite of herself and to spite her late husband, Big John. The driving, clapping rhythms even lifted her spirits a bit, brought a sliver of life to the embittered zombie she had become in her role as a widow, a woman whose confrontation with the mirage of her past put her in a semidaze. But for some perverse reason Cecil could pierce it. She sipped her Long Island iced teas to the cadence of his preaching, news of wakes, funerals, weddings and births in Cole County's black community. Sometimes her daughter, Sugar, would join her, but not today. Shug and her husband, Rob, had driven to Starkville to look at yet another horse, so Miss Kate watched the robins, sparrows and one lone bluebird at the feeder outside her bedroom window, while she sipped the cold, mint-sprigged drink, embracing the layer of numbness that would come in time.

"Yes, brothers and sisters, we know you will want to visit Mizres Arness Johnston. She's took down with the cancer, Lord, and we had a most prayerful time just yesterday. Prayerful time, Lord. You know you can pray it all away in Jesus' name. So let this tune carry you to prayer. Here's 'Bearing Me up in Jesus' Arms' by the East Church Trinity Choir."

Miss Kate tapped her once-upon-a-time burgundy manicured nails, now chipped and ragged, on the marble table top with the thump of the bass. She looked out over her family's 350-acre farm from her second story bedroom window, and beyond, to the rippling hills of timber buffering Camp DoeRun, just a little slice of her late husband's timber land blanketing the western part of the state. Big John McCormick increased his own inheritance twenty-fold before he died; built her this lush Victorian farm house; gave her diamond trinkets– "sparklies," he called them; and made love to her enough to produce a son, stillborn, and six years later their only living child, Sugar Lee. He lied, cheated, whored around, and confounded her with his driven need to put his deceptions right square in her face then proceed to accumulate more land, more money, and more lavish gifts for a wife he rarely touched once she became a mother.

When he died from an out-of-the-blue heart attack a little over two years ago, she withdrew into the green satin cocoon of her bedroom, the bedroom she occupied throughout their marriage, separate from his. She spent afternoons and evenings with Long Island iced teas and vodka tonics. She recoiled from the puzzling maze of figures her attorney, Roscoe Bartley, attempted to explain. Big John had handled all of that; her brain shut down when confronted with numbers.

She listened to Cecil preach and play music on Wednesdays and Sundays, in spite of herself, tempted, at times, to call in to his program for advice on those evenings when the alcohol did not do its job and stop her recognition, scene by scene, of years wasted. Once upon a time, she would have fought her way out from under the hopelessness to take the spotlight from her larger-than-life husband. Once upon a time, there were parties and laughter and trips to Atlanta and New York with her best friend, Sophie Price. Once upon a time, she met an old boyfriend in Chicago and spent a weekend more passionate than ten years of making love to her husband all rolled into one. And Sophie covered for her.

But when Sophie's betrayal dawned on her consciousness, and Sugar Lee left home and would not even visit, there was only her husband and herself and the act of going through the motions, smiling and chatting at barbecues, making shallow small talk with Sophie and the other faces in her life, Cecil's looming large among them. Aside from those parties, she and John spent most evenings in front of a flickering television, awash in alcohol and lies. Her husband's death served to put it more sharply in focus, the slipping of her self into a surrender of regret and addiction.

Her husband's death also served to bring Shug home. Finally, after twenty years of traveling with John to visit their child, her daughter came back with her husband, her own bastardized version of Big John, in tow. Shug's husband Rob had all of Big John's cold business sense with none of his charm, and Kate did not trust him, never liked him. How her daughter, who was throughout childhood the leader of the pack, who called all the shots during her teenaged years, could have married such an oppressive, overbearing braggart was beyond her. But Kate could tolerate Rob as long as she had Shug home again. And her child was, after all, home. Shug came home, briefly, to attend her father's funeral; then, just seven months ago, came home to stay, to give her husband over to help run the timber business. Kate's daughter was home, but the distance between the two of them was a Xerox of the distance she knew with Big John McCormick.

She thought of Cecil, the oddly comforting, heavily dialected voice of the radio preacher, the spiritual center of Cole County, who cooked for Big John at the hunting camp or at the barbecues they threw at the farm twice a year, until two years ago. She watched him grow up, grow from solemn child to lanky boy to the kind of man she admired in spite of herself and in spite of the degree to which she hated his existence. Cecil had always been a presence in the ritual and routine of small town wealth; Big John insisted. Cecil was meshed into her pores from the beginning, gradually taking the fight out of her, of late becoming a voice of aberrant hope, in spite of herself. It was through Cecil that Miss Kate was feeling something like optimism about making a reconnection with Sophie Price, her only real friend over the years. Even though she had resisted Sophie's attempt at rapprochement, her isolation had been pierced and she wanted to forgive. It was the secret need to be forgiven, though, which had her caught stock-still in the head-lights, and she knew their reconciliation would only happen if they could look their mutual betrayals in the eyes.

As the song wound down, Miss Kate leaned back in her crushed velvet chaise lounge, waiting for the deep, steady voice to speak reassurances to her. She lit a Virginia Slim menthol. But the last strains of the music melded into a raspy rhythm, electric, repetitive, filling the silence that was her life.

"My god, Cecil," she muttered. "Where have you gotten off to?"

The radio answered with the same sound, spiraling on and on, serenading the birds at the feeder, the farm-land planted in rolling undulations of low soybeans and high corn, and the hills of pine and hardwood beyond, grim and guarded.

Miss Kate gazed at the tree line on the farthest, darkest ridge.

"Cecil?" she whispered.

"That's some fucked-up shit," Wade Connors' deputy, Booty, said, hanging up the phone.

Sheriff Connors looked up from his dog-eared paperback. "The hell you say. What's up, B?"

"This here." Booty flipped on the radio to WDAB, the squenching, thudding staccato droning across the office, up the stairwell, and echoing into the cells on the second floor.

"Hey! Turn that crap off!" Claud Pierce, the only prisoner, in for being drunk and disorderly at four a.m., yelled down.

Booty eased down the volume. "That was Miss Sophie Price on the phone, out to Tammy's nursing home," he said. "Going on and on about something's wrong at the radio station. Afraid about Cecil. She was wild with worry."

"Shit," Wade grunted.

"Yeah, I told her wasn't nothing new for Cecil to get sidetracked," Booty went on, "but she said since that station used to be hers and her husband's before they give it to Cecil, that she ought to have a say."

"Shit," Wade grunted again.

"I can still hear that shit!" Pierce yelled, louder. "It's fucking with my hangover!"

"We going out there?"

"Naw," Wade said. "Let ol' Cecil take him a dump in peace."

Earline Durgin merely rolled her eyes when the jubilation of the East Church Choir ended in the rhythmic grate coming in steady time from the radio in the church kitchen. In the early afternoon she was washing up after Mount Holy Baptist Church's once-a-month Sunday dinner on the ground. The smell of fried catfish, onion hush puppies, and ham-fatted greens padded the conversation between Earline, Martha

Hughes, and Selethia Poe, stalwarts all, never failing to step in to the Christian Duty they relished.

"Lord, girl," Selethia said. "Old Cecil getting old and forgetful. Old Timer's Disease, I'll bet." Her fleshy arms worked a dishtowel around the outside of a cast-iron Dutch oven.

Earline shook her head, faltering in her determination to keep her thoughts about Cecil to herself. "He's an old timer, all right. An old timer eat up with making time."

"Naw!" Selethia said. "You don't think he's up in the radio station with that whore, do you?"

"That ain't the sound of no lovemaking," Martha said.

"Shut your mouth," Earline snapped. "I'm the only love he's making. There's a difference between making love and dipping that stick of his in some skanky whore like Miss Honey Pot or Miss Honey Pie or whatever she calls herself."

"Miss Honey *Drop*," Martha said in her solemn voice. "But her real name is Kim. Kim Davis. Guess her real name ain't good enough for a club singer."

Earline hated having these conversations, devoting valuable time to the discussion of Cecil's most recent in a fragmented series of girlfriends. It was the only drawback to their relationship, these girls he took up with every great once in a while—needy, lost girls or headstrong, self-destructive women he was compelled to take care of. The first couple of times she had found him out, early in their marriage, she had yelled, cried, threatened to throw him to the curb; knowing she would not go back on her promise to him, a promise she made with the knowledge of a level of intimacy few women were lucky enough to experience. It was a promise made in the abstract and overwhelming in its reality. The first time she had the gravity of her promise put before her, she stared at him in stunned, breathless shock, exhaling one weak word. "Why?"

"You know why," he said, as if it were a predetermined aspect of his nature. Then, in a faltering cadence and a gentle tone, letting her feel a piece of his anguish, he said, "Earline, it ain't likely to change just because you wish it would." So she gradually grew more quiet about it, relying on wishes as abstract as her promise.

"Well, her stage name's good enough for a whore," Selethia said. "What I hear, she giving that stuff out of both britches legs."

Martha shook her head. "That's just what some wish was true. What I hear is she don't do nobody much. Them boys just want to make like she is so they think they got a chance."

"Don't matter," Earline said. "That man of mine might need to dip that stick every once in a while, but he's always going to come home to me. He knows it. I know it. Jesus knows it." She struggled not to let her real feelings show. The mantle of strength she wore throughout her marriage kept them together, she knew, and, with patience, the obstacles—those women Cecil took on to rescue—would be cleared. They had to be. She had gambled everything on it.

"Well, it ain't right for a Man of God to be doing

such as that," Martha intoned, bringing her spine to the ramrod straight bearing she assumed at her most self-righteous moments.

"You ever knew a Man of God that didn't?" Earline countered. "A Man of God full of passion's going to do it every time. But, naw, he ain't going to do it at the station. He knows I'd be like to catch him." She forced a counterfeit chuckle. "Then I'd have to hurt him." But she knew she would never do that, either. He had already been hurt enough.

"Praise Jesus," Selethia giggled.

The three women swished steel wool against pots and pans, or rattled stainless steel utensils into open drawers, or scrape-tapped leftovers into Tupperware bowls, setting a jangling cacophony against the steady fuzz and thump of Cecil's abandoned radio program. Earline thought of the tenderness with which he treated her, the subtle touches she wished would flare into something out of his control. They took care of one another, kept confidences, gave close to unconditionally. She was fortunate in so many ways, frustrated her friends saw her as being too easy with Cecil or, worse, weak. But Cecil was a product of a rare and insightful life. He was the essence of her blood-rushing pulse, and even at her lowest moments, when she did consider leaving him, she knew she was lying to her own heart.

Earline shook her head again. She studied the soapy water, islands of suds disintegrating into tepid liquid. "What I'm going to do with that man?" she asked no one in particular.

A Confederate flag tattoo was emblazoned across Claud Prices' left forearm, "Never Forget," in Old English script beneath it. He lay on his cot at the Cole County Jail, arms crossed over his chest, staring at the ceiling. A couple of knuckles were split and his left eye was swollen, all from the fight he had picked with—who was it? Jimmy Johns? Or was it Jimmy's brother Leroy? Well, no matter. It had landed him in the Cole County jail and that was the point. He fucked up and drank too much brown. Brown whiskey always made him crazy, and now it was interfering with the plans he had made for today.

He wondered where his own brother, Ronnie, was right about now, whether he was like to show up here at the jailhouse, blabbing his stupid mouth about how his big brother had commissioned work to do. He silently cursed himself for saying too much to his baby brother, who wasn't no rocket scientist, didn't always know what to do with the little bits of information living in his otherwise empty head. All Ronnie seemed to know how to do was lay around the trailer, look at the TV, ask stupid questions, and beat off like a man who had just been told his pecker was scheduled for amputation. If it wasn't for blood ties, Claud thought, I would have put him out a long damn time ago.

He wished his daddy was alive. But Charles "Chuckie" Pierce, also know as "Cee-Boy" or "CowBoy," had died back in 1984 of cirrhosis, although some said he died of just plain meanness, and Claud knew he had died from anger marinated in untaken revenge. He was a cop for the Repass Police Department, across the Mississippi line, ten miles from Three Breezes, an old-school cop who knew what went on in the darkest corners of Turner County, Mississippi, and in neighboring Cole County, Alabama, late of a night.

He taught his boys to shoot his pistol when they were old enough to support the weight of it in their little hands; showed them where the stills were that he had supposedly busted up, then gave them each a twenty dollar bill for their silence; and cursed their mother, who ran off with a Yankee on a motorcycle when Claud was only seven. He taught them to fight, and fight to win, no matter how dirty or how low they had to go. He took them to Klan rallies and stock car races, porno movies, strip clubs, and prostitutes who showed them any appetite had a quick fix as long as you had the cash. If his daddy was here, he would know how to deal with Cecil Durgin, would love every minute of it, too, since Cecil Durgin was his favorite nigger to hate.

"Listen at him," Chuckie Pierce said when the sound of Cecil's voice first rode the airwaves into their home. "Listen at that blowed-up son of a bitch talking that nigger shit. Playing that Detroit nigger music. That motherfucker has needed a new pair of overalls ever since he was a kid. Somebody ought to give the bastard a new pair." And over the years, as Cecil's political influence grew and Chuckie's waned, Old Man Pierce would go on drunken rants ending only when he finally passed out. "Big Ass Pete," he would slur. "Thinks he runs the vote. Walking round over there in Three Breezes in them Big Ass Pete suits, driving him a big car. Thinks he's the big boar coon that walks just before the dawn, don't he? Got hisself a fucking radio station, now. Got it off a white man. Sending them goddamn motherfucking nigger radio messages way the fuck over here into Mississippi. Done fucked me up."

"Go after him daddy," Claud would say.

"I goddamned sure ought to."

Cee-Boy talked to anyone who would listen about how he would get that Durgin nigger into a new pair of overalls no matter what it took. And that was the kind of talk which finally brought Jackson Huckaby to their trailer one evening for a very private talk about Cecil Durgin.

"Ain't you boys got a date or something?" Sheriff Huck asked.

Cee-Boy pressed a twenty dollar bill into Claud's palm. "They got one now," he said. "Go on, boy. Take your brother after some pussy. Don't come back till you get a bate of it."

The next morning, Claud's daddy's face was swollen to hell and back, but he was cussing Cecil with even more ragged rage. "You see how it is, don't you, boy? You see where the lines lay, don't you? You see who runs the motherfucking show. A nigger loving son of a bitch who sits in the hip pocket of a fucking multi-millionaire."

"You going after him, Daddy?"

"Shit, can't nobody do that, not while he's connected up with the big boys, motherfucking McCormick and them. Goddamn motherfuckers. Well, they going to be sorry one of these days, when they nuts is right before being took by that piece of shit nigger. Ain't nothing like some rich sons of bitches to get things good and fucked up. Goddamn pussies."

Old Man Pierce would sputter and bake in his vitriol, his two sons simmering in its juices while they watched their father grow weaker and weaker from the poison of it all. "You mark my words. They going to regret they didn't get rid of that woods tic of a nigger long years ago, back when I put my first hurting on his black ass. And when they get backed up in that corner, you know what their chicken shit asses is going to do? They going to call on us. The goddamn little snot-nosed pussies is going to call on us to do what they ain't man enough to do, just like always."

It worked on the old man something fierce. The bile of bitterness chewed on him from the inside, gnawing through every particle of his spirit, and he was dead long before his liver shut down, saturated in gin and moonshine whiskey.

"You just watch, Daddy," Claud whispered to the ceiling, just as he heard the unmistakable sound of dead air on the radio, curling up from the sheriff's office downstairs. That dead air could only mean one thing. Claud sighed deeply. If the sound was any indication, then Cecil wasn't even at the station today, probably off with that whore of his.

"Hey! Turn that crap off!" he yelled through the bars, then settled back to squint his determined eyes at the ceiling and formulate another plan for dealing with Cecil Durgin.

The white Mercedes bumped over the tired old highway running from Columbus, Mississippi, to Three Breezes, Alabama, an NRA bumper sticker nodding with the rear fender. The car was coated with the dirt road dust Shug's husband, Rob, hated, the windshield dotted with dried insect corpses. He would spend hours waxing the finish and polishing chrome, only to have it recoated with Alabama dirt inside of a day. It was an ongoing, futile war with an environment he tolerated only for the status and influence it gave him. Rob was still fuming, so Shug kept still until it occurred to her to turn the radio on to Cecil Durgin's Sunday afternoon program.

"If I'd known he was going to be a goddamn Jew about it I wouldn't have bothered," Rob said. "Asking a goddamn fortune for that piece of shit nag."

"I know, baby." She eased up the volume. It had been humiliating, the whole scene back at the Blackburns' spread in Starkville, Rob spitting insults and showing out. She was at the end of her tolerance with Rob's tantrums, but she was not sure what to do next. Cecil's Sunday program, she knew, would set Rob on a path of ridicule she hated, yet she preferred it to his seething temper.

"And the visitation going to be this Thursday evening at four P.M. and on into the night at Potter's Funeral Parlor. So cook up a red velvet cake or a butter pound cake or a triple chocolate cake and come on out to Causey Logan's funeral. His widow is the most delicate and refined Miss Toomie Logan, and you know how Miss Toomie loves the sweetses."

Rob chuckled. "Delicate and refined? Miss Toomie who works at the Stop and Go? That woman weighs three hundred pounds, at least."

"Speaking of sweet, you know the sweet love of the Lord is a powerful thing, and it gives unto us the power of prayer, like I was saying to Mizres Johnston just yesterday. Yes, brothers and sisters, we know you'll want to visit Mizres Arness Johnston. She's took down with the cancer, Lord, and we had a prayerful time yesterday. Prayerful time, Lord. You know you can pray it all away in Jesus' name. So here's 'Bearing Me up in Jesus' Arms' by the East Church Trinity Choir."

"That nigger has to be the biggest bullshitter on the planet," Rob said. "It would be damn near comical if not for the power that fool has."

Shug's neck tingled, but she deflected the faint urge to defend Cecil to her husband. She was beyond tired of Rob's slurs and self described "holy mission to queer the vote" of the black residents of Cole County. It had to be done, her husband said, because the election was the most critical in years. Big timber stood to be taxed like never before if the liberals and other miscreants got their way. Immersed as he was in his new role, that of southern timber baron, Rob had been having hushed talks with her father's old friends, conversations upon which she eavesdropped, vague and threatening conversations heightening her senses and stirring old passions. After years of putting the whole of her energy into not seeing her husband as he really was, Shug was tired. She was tired of his theories about the tainting of the economy at the hands of the Jews, the decline of the white race, Christianity imperiled, and she ached to speak up, confront his paranoia.

It was only since her return to Three Breezes, seven months ago, that something wanted to let loose. There was some piece of her heart she had forgotten to silence, some whittled-away voices lying in wait at her daddy's farm, now whispering their way back into her. She was beginning to recognize the voices, both the voices of her two closest friends from her life in Three Breezes. She knew that recognition made it only a matter of time before she would speak up, destroy all the soiled security she had assembled with Rob. It cut right through the shame and frightened her, because, so practiced was the suppression of her own voice, she still could not quite uncover what was left of her old self, the one who would have never been intimidated by twisted ideas or even unpredictable rages.

She glanced at Rob, his knuckles tense on the steering wheel; he gripped it with the nervous energy keeping him in a white-hot state of anxiety. He was a pacer, an eye shifter, a glancer-over-the-shoulderer, a collector of guns and conspiracy theories, of racial epithets and Aryan literature. Shug had come to walk a deft line crystallized by his fears, his domination, and her own discombobulation. But her head was clearing, and what she was coming to see was daunting but, just maybe, doable.

Ironically, Rob had come to her rescue in the beginning, saving her from the fallout of her wild years. She met him when she was a freshman at UCLA, the school she chose simply because it was as far away from home as she could possibly get without falling into the Pacific Ocean. Robert Overton was a senior majoring in accounting, opinionated, intelligent, quirky in an endearing way, different from the boys to whom she was accustomed. He was from Augusta, Georgia, so there was an immediate connection between the two southerners adrift in a sea of hippie-fied West Coast Yankees. Most significantly, he was a born again Christian, a "Jesus Freak," an active member in Campus Crusades for Christ, and his salvation shielded her from the neon places within her soul, signs flashing with cold beer and hot sex.

Her vulnerability lay in the fact that she was in emotional tatters, private and overpowering. At the pit of it all was the secret of an older man to whom, at seventeen, she handed her heart with blithe naivete telling her they would live happily ever after. He was a handsome, charismatic, married man, who went down on her at her father's hunting camp; carried on an intense, pleasure-ridden affair with her for four months; and who, in the end, was more loyal to her father than to her. When she had realized she was pregnant, she was convinced Cash Cloy would come through for her, take care of her. He would put his arms around her, say how sorry he was, and offer to marry her, just as soon as he could get a divorce. He never loved DeeDee anyway, he would say. His boys were getting to be teenagers and they would adjust. He would kiss her fear away and put everything right. He would stand up to her father and tell Big John McCormick exactly how things were going to be.

They met at DoeRun on a Tuesday afternoon, as they had every Tuesday afternoon for four months. He gave her a kiss like a sucker punch to the mouth, sandpapered his face into her neck and squeezed her ass hard. He told her she had it all, made him crazy, and they lay on the sofa squirming against each other with the heat of lovers who were accustomed to fevered rushes of passion instead of laid back brushes of affection.

It was then she whispered in his ear what she had been suspecting and was now certain of, and the effect was like that of a gas burner going out with a deep pop. He stood without betraying a single emotion. He did not drop to his knees and proclaim love and loyalty. He simply wrote down an address and phone number in Birmingham, pulled out his wallet, leafed through some bills, and handed her four hundred dollars. "This should more than cover it," he said.

"You won't go with me?"

"There's a million reasons not to."

"But I want you to."

"No, Shug."

"But I'm scared."

"Hell, girls do it all the time."

"Can you meet me when I get back?"

"Sugar Lee, I think this is all played out." And he left her there on the sofa at DoeRun, Villager dress wrinkled and damp, numbed by the shock of unfamiliar rejection, and, for the first time in her life, being hit right square between the eyes with a definite "no."

She had a clear recollection of scribbling a note to Cecil, just in case he wasn't there, and carrying it to the station, determined not to cry, fighting the urge to ram her MG into a tree trunk. Then she went home with a manufactured story for her parents, a story about a last minute weekend visit to Birmingham-Southern, saying she wanted to see what the sororities were like there, and yes, this was a spur of the moment thing, but they wanted her to go to a college nearby, and maybe she would really like it there, and yes, she would come home often if she decided on Birmingham.

It was Cecil who commiserated with her, then demanded that she buck up, phoned in a replacement for himself at the station, made all the arrangements, told her what to expect, and drove her to Birmingham. For the first time in their years of deep friendship she heard him cuss and threaten a white man, calling Cash Cloy a conniving, murdering coward motherfucker who deserved to have every hurt he had ever done come back around to him, and then some.

It was Cecil who waited for her the next morning at the doctor's office, where she was sedated and spreadlimbed, icy stirrups sending chills up her open thighs. The steely clink and rattle of instruments, the slurping suction pulling tissue from her hostaged womb, the pasty-faced nurse who leaned down to tell her she was doing fine, just fine, the hollow ache of her raw insides oozing blood were pieces of the detailed story she shared only with Cecil. He let her cry into his lap. He sat with her in a motel room, brought her ginger ale and Ritz Crackers, and reassured her she had done the right thing, she was not evil.

"Was it a soul, Cecil? Did I kill a soul?"

"No."

"How can you be sure?"

"I just can."

"How?"

"Shug, I seen a soul go out of somebody on account of me. I seen walking around folks ain't got a soul, like Cash Cloy. I know you. You don't need to worry."

She nestled against him on a funky bedspread at the Holiday Inn and finally slept.

Five months later, after a self-destructive frenzy of one-nighters and chemical highs, Rob got the abridged version of her experience: "I had sex with several guys over a couple of months and ended up pregnant. I had an abortion."

He told her the acceptance of the Lord Jesus Christ as her personal savior would wash her sins clean. She could feel as peaceful as he did if she would just give her heart to Christ. So she went through the motions and, finding no peace, attempted to receive it parasitically, through her husband. She gave her heart to Rob, in the beginning, expecting the peace of Jesus to come at any moment, living inside the anticipation of it while the rest of herself shut down, over time.

They married as soon as he graduated, and he insisted it was pointless for her to finish college since he expected she would stay home and raise their children. They settled in Seattle, where he had connections to a lucrative career, while she immersed herself in clubs and volunteer work, taking on a persona as hostess who was the envy of the other wives in their social circle. She watched her husband become more angry and judgmental as the years went by, the born-again spirit and oddball intelligence, initially attractive, becoming rigid and accusing, akin to some kind of craziness. And because she could not go home, she let the role swallow her: wife-committee person-fund raiser-volunteer-organizer-party giver-too busy to think-big smile-don't let on. Whenever a doubt nudged her, a questioning of her self, she simply threw better parties, got written up in the society pages more often.

The only thing she knew not to do was have the children he kept her corralled at home to raise, and she knew it on a deep-in-the-gut level, by instinct. So she did not have children, deliberately, choosing instead to swallow the birth control pills she kept hidden in the toe of a pair of cowboy boots she never wore once she left home. Rob credited her barrenness to the will of God, so she simply existed within the boundaries of her own deception.

But now she was coming to grips with the irony of looking to Rob Overton for peace, the beatific countenance of his college days having shriveled over the years into the scowl-lined face of a man who had come to despise her, his life and lack of progeny, and the Lord, and did not even know it. At the marrow of it was Rob's disapproval, seeded years ago by the brief confession of the abortion, growing large into the present, their marriage having basted in his quiet self-righteousness until it was now coated with a thick glaze of overcooked resentment.

She thought again of Tammy and Cecil, bewildered by her failure to make contact with either of them before now. She thought of Cecil out at DoeRun when they were young, how she trailed after him, impressed as she was with the grown-up responsibilities he had. And she got to know the not-so-grown-up side of Cecil, the playfulness of cold splashes of creek water, pinecone skirmishes and dirt clod wars, forts nestled in the brush. There were games of hide and seek, Animal Rummy, and Monopoly. They rode Tarzan and Lucifer, her daddy's quarter horses, all over the woods, creating hidden trails while the grown-ups sipped cocktails at dusk. There were private dramas revealed, promises made and kept from everyone else. There was kinship.

By the time she was old enough that her mother deemed her rides through the woods with Cecil inappropriate, it was too late. The closeness between them was a given and they exercised it as an ongoing. If she couldn't spend time with him around her parents at the camp house, well, she knew where to find him. She would wander down to the barn to help him brush the horses, or she might ride Tarzan over to DoeRun if Cecil was there, help him set out for cooking or fish with him at Round Swirl.

When high school rolled around, she and Tammy, a cold six pack of Busch, and a tin of Charles Chips would join him at least three nights a week out at WDAB. If full-length albums of nonstop Wilson Pickett, Sam and Dave, or Aretha Franklin were going out over the air waves, that meant the girls were there, to talk and joke and get the expert advice of one four years their senior. There was a hint of flirtation between Cecil and Tammy, but with Shug and him it was a protective camaraderie, an us-against-the-world feeling she found nowhere else. It had been only natural that she sought out his help when she turned up pregnant by her father's business associate and impostor of a son.

Something jarring grabbed her thoughts, an odd, insistent sound. "Bearing Me up" was playing on the radio just seconds before, but now came a thumping beat framed in a static-laced hum through the car's speakers.

"Damn fool does this all the time," Rob said. "Loses his train of thought, gets distracted. Runs around the countryside sticking his nose in where it's not his place, especially at election time."

Again the apprehensive tingle rinsed down the back

of her neck. Her husband and the other men, her father's old allies, were up to something. She had listened from around corners and near cracked-open doors as Rob asked question after question about the McCormick Trust, the mountain of millions her father had accumulated, invested, multiplied. She caught the uncomfortable, squirming tones of Roscoe Bartley and Lee Davis when they offered up answers. Cash had the good sense to stay away from her, but she was certain he was in on whatever it was. She had gathered Rob was to meet all three of them out at DoeRun at nine o'clock this very evening, and she had a plan of her own, finally. But it was the mention of Cecil's name by the men, hooked up with threatening words, that really caught her attention, making her realize she had to see him. Cecil was a part of her, was, at the very least, an inextricable part of her past, of the high school days when her little blue MG owned the back roads across the state line to the Mississippi juke joints, slow dances with redneck cowboys who pressed their crotches into her thigh and left wet kisses on her neck. Cecil had been there to listen to the goofy problems of two boy-crazy teenagers whenever she and Tammy needed him. And he had been there for her when she had the wind and the will knocked out of her with her lover's rejection. Now she could be there for him.

She wondered if Cecil found her note at the station. If so, he surely would have read it by now. She already mentioned to Rob that she planned to go riding later in the afternoon. Lullabye needed the exercise, she told him. She needed the honesty, she told herself.

"It's no wonder we can't get anybody decent elected," Rob was saying. "There is a bunch of damn black folks in Cole County."

"That is a fact," she said, in her most passive voice.

"It's a fact that's fixing to change, at least on the ballot count."

"Oh?"

"Yeah, Mr. Radio Man's going to shut up on this next one."

The sound of the absence of Cecil Durgin was pounding at her false calm. She could not let on, not let on, not let on, she thought along with the rhythm scraping across the airwaves. Finally she reached over and, with forced nonchalance, changed the radio station, determined not to betray her fear or the secret of her allegiance to Cecil Durgin.

Cecil's initial concern and easy slide into his old affection for Shug did not last long. It fast became something like agitated curiosity folded into a suspicious foreboding, then outright worry for what might be going on with her. Still, he went through the patter of his usual newsy monologue, mentioned Miss Toomie Logan's funeral and her love of sweets, and a prayer over Mrs. Arness Johnston's skin cancer segued right into a song. "You know you can pray it all away in Jesus' name," he said into the mike. "So here's 'Bearing Me up in Jesus' Arms' by the East Church Trinity Choir."

He switched off the mike and opened Shug's note again. He was so engrossed in the words he did not hear Kim drive up, did not hear a sound until her heels clicked an angry staccato across the terrazzo floor. When he looked up to meet her expression of full throttle fury, he felt a familiar wash of disgust take him. It was a predictable feeling arriving, as it always did, when reality crystallized before him. The heady charge so vital to the early-on life of his vagabond romances, coming with the knowledge of putting something right and offering a safe haven, inevitably faded into an old reality, as it now had with Kim. The reality was he was no hero; he was, in fact, a double-faced cheat, a marital fraud looking for another helping of guilt. And the drama he hated, the scenes to come in the final act, would be tired, full of stale lines bound to dwindle to a denouement of poorly edited tears. It was definitely over, just as he knew it would be, and he owed it to Earline to move Miss Honey Drop on out of his life, go back to trying to do the right thing as opposed to that which he craved. Still, business was business, and he intended to hold her to the contract as long as possible. He was also determined not to discuss it, or anything else, just now.

"What do you mean you got to go meet somebody? You ain't got the afternoon program going good yet. Who you got to meet?" Whatever her intentions were in coming to the station, they were now chased away by knee-jerk suspicion and territorial jealousy.

"A friend." Cecil knew he would have to keep his

answers brief and light if he were going to avoid one of Miss Honey Drop's rages, which usually involved creative cursing, the hurling of objects through the air, and enough tears to launch a schooner.

"What's her name? Do I need to mess her up?"

"Relax. There's nothing to worry about. It's an old friend. I got to go out to the hunting camp."

"What camp? You got yourself a honeycomb hideout? And what friend? You know you ain't fooling me, Cecil. And you know I don't take no double-timing shit off of nobody, even if your stupid-ass wife will."

In an instant he came to the verge of lighting into her about Earline, but he knew it would not accomplish anything other than to hold him up. Instead, he poured her a cup of coffee and set it on the desk.

She was mumbling a string of insults aimed at Earline's appearance at the club a few nights before. "Low-ass motherfucker, bringing your church-hymn-singing, print-dress-wearing, no-hipped woman up in my place of business. I swear to God I'm going to mess somebody up."

"Look," Cecil said with firm finality. "I'm going to do this because it's important. And you don't have to like it. But I promise we'll talk business later on this week." He picked up his keys.

"I ain't believing this shit. You think I don't know what's the deal? Who the fuck is she?" Honey opened her handbag, withdrew the Smith and Wesson, and nodded it at the ceiling. "I'm fixing to flat-straight fuck somebody up."

Cecil shook his head, walked over to where she stood, and took her purse. "Baby, you're way too high strung to be carrying this damn thing around." He opened her purse again and took the gun from her. "When you going to get rid of this thing?"

She sank into a chair and began to sob. "You fixing to go meet up with somebody new. I know it." All of her bold intentions were gone, obliterated by the neediness that swelled within her ample bosom, and the tears poured forth.

She expected Cecil to play his rehearsed role, comfort her, tell her she was going places way bigger than Cole County, and she would be the one to leave him, not the other way around. But he was through with that speech. Today he simply put the gun back in her purse and laid it on his desk. He let her have a short but healthy sob session, then handed her a paper towel to mop up the floodwaters and said, "We ain't going to do this right now. We just ain't. We're going to talk about it in a few days. I got to go."

She hiccupped, blew her nose into the paper towel, and reached her hand out to him.

"Look here," he said, stepping back

"What?" she sniffled, dazed by his lack of reaction to her tears, his lack of interest in her affection. "Don't you even give a shit?"

Cecil stepped forward, took her hands and pulled her to her feet. Then he touched her cheek, shaking his head again, marveling at the hugeness of her talent and the smallness of her regard for herself. "I got to take care of this. Right now." He led her around behind the jockey's desk. "Here's your coffee. When this song quits, you just hit this button and another tape will start, okay?"

"Shit."

"Okay?" She plopped into the chair, lips set in a sull. "Reckon I'm fixing to help him out, now," she mumbled. "Play some Jesus music for his low-ass self."

"I'm gone." Cecil walked toward the door.

"Wait a minute," she said.

"What?"

"How do you know I wouldn't shoot your sorry ass with that old gun?" she said. "How do you know I still won't?"

Cecil chuckled. "If somebody was supposed to kill me it would have happened a long time ago. I reckon the Lord don't mean for me to go that way."

"Maybe," she said.

"Besides," Cecil laughed, "you're probably a lousy shot, Baby. Hell, a high-strung woman like you is bound to be." And he walked out to his truck, leaving his latest version of Charity Collins sitting at WDAB, his departure accompanied by the sound of a coffee mug shattering against the closed door of the station.

Tammy Sims heard it, through the headset connected to the portable radio hanging on the handlebar of her four-wheeler. She was out hunting rattlesnakes and cottonmouths, had been for most of the afternoon, skirting the creek banks and hills near her trailer, riding to the soulful beat of the best music there was, when she cut the motor to study the tendrils of a Resurrection fern. She took off the headphones, letting them hang loose around her neck. As the scraping thump of a broadcast silence thudded into her flesh and into the scorching heat of the languid summer afternoon, she did not think it odd that Cecil Durgin failed to break in at the close of a rocking gospel melody. After all, he was prone to distractions, so she had paid it little mind at first. Cecil was known to leave the jockey's desk—go to town for a sandwich, get sidetracked by some community ill, such as a hospital or jail visit. He would be back to cue up the next gospel song in an hour or two at the most, if not in the next few moments.

But he did not come back, not in a few moments, not in an hour; and, for some reason, the sound wore into her, into the history she shared with Cecil and the truest friend of her girlhood, Shug McCormick. Consequently, she let the pulsating scritch and thump stay with her the rest of the afternoon, becoming another piece of the overlay of sounds woven into her woods.

The metallic, squenching thumps coming from the cast-off headset blended into a more familiar sound, just as a rustle near an outcropping of sandstone caught the laser's red dot from her pistol. "Bastard," she whispered to the sizzling, rattling sound of a fair-sized diamond-back, a four-footer, maybe. The Ruger's explosion bounced and echoed from hill to hill to creek bottom and back, the snake ricocheting from the rock, twitching against mulching leaves and moist dirt.

Tammy's croaker sack held two other carcasses, a much lighter kill than she had routinely taken three summers ago. By August of that year she had tallied the corpses of eighty-seven poisonous snakes, many of their skins now lining the walls of the living room in her doublewide. She worked at thinning the population so that she could safely bring the nine residents of her old folks' home—The Wildwood Assisted Living Facility—down to the wooded creek bank for picnics and nature excursions. She could feel a little easier about it. But she had not overcome her fear of snakes, not by a stretch. Snakes and the dark sent her into a little girl's nightmare of amber dimness soaked in the sour-sweet scent of whiskey on her stepfather's breath, no matter how many rattlers and moccasins she slaughtered.

She unplugged the headphones and used a sturdy red oak stick to coax the dead reptile into the sack while the radio etched its empty rhythm across the holler. It was amazing how it had been thumping away all afternoon, no change in volume or tempo. The snake's head flopped from side to side, fangs stabbing at the still August air. The heaviness of the ropes of dead flesh in her sack made her give a shudder, punctuated by the radio's droning cadence. The woods seemed to take a breath and, in that gasp, Tammy stared at the tiny radio. She had an eerie feeling, out of nowhere, out of the fuzzy bump of the battery-powered box; she began to sense a desperate quality to the once benign sound—an insistence, an invisible promise of a crescendo that could only be malevolent. In one rushing motion she turned the knob to the "off" position.

She glanced up at the sky. Night was coming on, sunlight dimming fast, so she loaded up her kill and the plant cuttings she sealed in two Ziplock bags—one holding the moist, lacy leaves and fronds she would press into her log of indigenous flora, the other holding the dried cannabis sativa she would enjoy later this evening.

She fired up the Yamaha engine. She couldn't let the sunset overtake her. Night shade in the snakey woods was blacker than a moonless night. And, while she could certainly kill snakes with a practiced aim, she could never shoot the dark.

Miss Sophie

Miss Sophie Price strained to hear the sound of Tammy's four-wheeler coming back from the woods. Instead, the dinnertime rattle of plates and utensils drifted out to the long porch stretching across the face of the Wildwood Assisted Living Facility. Mayree, the cook, had prepared a summer vegetable dinner of squash and onions, fried okra, pole beans, and mashed potatoes doused with dark brown gravy made from left-over roast drippings. The other residents laughed and conversed in voices squelched by age, enjoying another home-grown meal. But she was too worried to eat, too afraid for Cecil.

"You better tell that boy of yours to keep quiet," Roscoe Bartley had said just last week, when he visited her to go over her will.

She did not ask why, only threw a look of defiance and said, "Or what?"

He chuckled. "Come on, Sophie. Folks have been killed for less."

She kept to her confusion, refusing to give him the satisfaction of any kind of reaction to his gray-area, vague sounding threat. But she was afraid for Cecil.

She was afraid for him forever. Afraid when she first

heard the rumors about the baby born to Otis Joyce's niece Renee over on Pitch Hill. It was routine sport, back then, for white men to make occasional forays into the colored section of town, leaving a scattering of light-skinned toddlers with eyes of honeyed amber or pastelled with rinsed-out blue, or watercolor-washed in green, like Cecil's. Such babies were not uncommon, but this baby was something else, something akin to royalty, if the hushed rumors were true. This child's existence could bring out festering greed, resentments cured like meat over several generations, or just plain meanness.

She was afraid when Sheriff Huck brought him to her, Cecil all of three years old and tired out from crying. She was aware that it had all been arranged in advance. Austin would not speak much of the details, only conceded that money had changed hands, via Huck, that Renee Joyce, the mother, had been "intimi-dated," then paid to migrate north to Chicago where a good job awaited, and that the result was the purchase of one healthy Negro child to be reared in the orbit of his father. The Prices were chosen because of Austin's bank note on WDAB, which was immediately paid in full; Sophie's childlessness, remedied at once by a son of a darker hue; and their odd status as folks of an appro-priate class who were also outsiders when you got right down to it. The citizens of Three Breezes did not quite know what to make of the couple's aberrant religious practices, Austin's agnosticism and Sophie's Judaism, both of which were the equivalent of atheism to rural Alabamians, who were further confused by the fact that the couple was likable, had no scars, X-ray eyes, or devil horns. Consequently, those in the Prices' social circle were polite, but there was always a judgment suspended on the periphery of every interaction, an edge of mistrust Sophie had known all her life.

She grew up in a South Alabama timber town, her father, plagued as everyone was by the Depression, managing Goodman-Evergreen, one of her grandfather's ribbon mills. Evergreen was a universe away from the exotic places and scintillating personalities she watched at the Ritz Picture Show in town, pretending to be the lady in the elegant gown, on the arm of a seductive rogue. In the reality of Evergreen, she was a member of the town's only Jewish family, surrounded by Methodists and Baptists who, even in the financial shambles of their grainy-gray, washed-out lives, wore the smug certainty of the Heaven-bound. She was allowed to attend Sunday school with her friends, but they were only rarely allowed to go with her family to synagogue in Pensacola or Mobile. They felt sorry for her, they told her, because she would never go to Heaven, unless, of course, she accepted Jesus Christ into her pagan heart. Her teachers were kind to her, but they, too, patronized and babbled at times about the Lord, saying daily prayers in Jesus' name, flinging stinging little darts at her heart and spirit. But Austin Price was intrigued by a girl outside the norm, and she with him.

Just out of high school, she was working in her father's office at the mill for only two months when

Austin bounded in, a dye salesman based in Columbus, Georgia, sixteen years older and different from anyone she had ever met in her life. With deep dimples puckering in even more as he drew on a cigar, he wore pale blue seersucker that set off the cornflower blue of his eyes. He bought her a sundae at Mitchell's Soda Fountain and bubbled with dreams. Like Sophie, he wanted to be around folks with broad ideas, cities full of art and music. In fact, he felt he was destined for the music business, but could not quite figure how. She latched on to him and married him against her father's will, without the two-year degree from Gulf Park College she had planned on getting, without her family's blessing, garnering a Goodman shunning worthy of an Amish community. But it was worth it. She was swept up in a love born of passion and counted on Austin to take her places where she would be seen as an intellectual, where the free thought swirled about in rich currents of cosmopolitan conversations.

Instead, he heard of a radio station he could get for a fraction of its worth, and Sophie found herself in an even more culturally barren outpost—Cole County, a place nothing more than thick woods and hills intersected by rivers, small farms patchworked into the landscape. Three Breezes consisted of a courthouse square surrounded by a post office, hardware store, grocery store, jail, drug store, café, the requisite Methodist and Baptist churches, and the Co-op, which seemed to be the hub of activity in town. McCormick Lumber Company was behind the square, its creosote plant and box factory hugging the railroad tracks near a small depot.

The only bright spot in the wasteland that was Three Breezes, aside from Austin, was Kate McCormick, effervescent, outrageous, full of spunk and polish. She was a flashy beauty adept at storytelling, an art lover who made annual trips to galleries in New York and Paris. And she was thrilled, she said, that Cole County now had something as exotic as a real live Jew. She devoured Sophie's traditions, observing Chanukah and Yom Kippur along with her, accompanying her to Temple Beth-El in Birmingham with an enthusiasm her childhood friends in Evergreen could never muster. She prodded Sophie to teach her, then latched on to some favorite Yiddish expressions that evolved into a Southernized "catty code" to be used at parties, where the two women could remark on flat hairstyles, obnoxious husbands, thunder thighs, and bad outfits as the situation demanded. They became fast friends in spite of the uneasy alliance between their husbands. Big John bought ad time from Austin; the two men needed each other enough to maintain a polite aloofness, but had little in common. Austin did not like to hunt. Big John had little patience with Austin's lack of conformity. But their wives melded a confidence that took them deep into one another's lives, into the secrets they kept from the rest of the world.

Each had the essence of what the other wanted. Sophie had the kind of rich love from a faithful man Kate was denied; Kate had the ability to bear children. Her deceased son, John Jr., was evidence of that. But

Sophie had not been able to conceive, sank into depression when she felt the prickly cramps announcing her next period, cursed the brick-red stains taunting her failure at becoming a mother. Throughout the war years she and Austin tried, but she only ended up crying with Kate. She was ashamed of her selfishness, of mourning the pre-fetal entity leaving her body in the form of menstrual fluid each month, ashamed, when she thought of what was going on in Europe, to be petty enough to want more than the good life she had. She berated herself for envying Kate, whose husband cheated on her, visited whores in Birmingham and Mobile, and, finally, produced a bastard son right under her nose.

Sophie was afraid for Cecil when she first laid eyes on him, a fear mixed with the instinctive need to care for a motherless child, she a childless mother. She was afraid of what the underpinnings of this shadowy contract might mean for him. She already suspected what it meant for her. It meant more criticism from a community she discovered would not even allow her to adopt a white child into her "mixed" marriage to Austin. Still, her resentment of the judgment harbored against her made her even more determined to have her own family, via Cecil, whatever the cost in gossip and disapproval. But this determination also threatened to take the one friend she did not want to lose.

Kate said nothing of the child, apparently knew nothing, but time would take care of that. Most secrets had a way of oozing out like pus from a festering sore, and when she did find out, Sophie dreaded what was to come of their friendship then. Yet even this seemed to pale in comparison with the child gazing up at her, abandonment and terror in his child's eyes. The child was worth the sacrifice. As it was, Kate gave birth the following year to Sugar Lee, named for the pet name Kate had been called by her own mother and Lee Davis, one of John's surrogate sons. As it was, the friendship between Kate and Sophie thrived for fifteen years until the reality of Cecil's lineage sifted through Kate's denial. Whether she heard it from a well-meaning acquaintance, from her own husband, or whether she simply figured out what was staring her in the face, Sophie never knew. But the slow chill curling about the times they were together was palpable, and those times grew less and less frequent.

Miss Sophie squinted into the gathering dusk. She sat in one of the rockers on the porch of the Wildwood Home, rocking a slow, deliberate creak into the wood floor. Maybe she had known something bad was coming, had a premonition that it would all catch up with Cecil. After all, she had finally decided to confront Kate about his presence in their respective worlds, to resuscitate their friendship, to revisit old haunts.

The rush of water from the dishwasher in the Wildwood Home told Sophie dinner was over. She watched the woods for Tammy and contemplated the mother-son relationship, if it could be so categorized, she had with Cecil. When he was a child she had wanted to take him away, had, in fact, begged Austin to move them all to a big city or even to another country, someplace where no one would care that they did not come in matching hues. Then she would be able to behave like a real mother and give him what Three Breezes did not allow, full participation in her family.

"But he's not your son, Sophie," Austin said. "And even if I agreed that it would be a practical solution, do you really think I would go back on my word? Even if I could feel about him the way you do, do you really think Big John would sit still while we traipsed across the globe, hiding out in Peru or somewhere? Look, I made a promise to keep him here until he was grown. I gave my word. And he'll be all right, better than all right. You'll see."

And, up to a point, Cecil was all right. Austin took him on as a project rather than a son, while she provided as much emotional nourishment as she could, within the boundaries they were pushing outward by degree. And Sophie's private pride in the young man she was rearing helped her through the years. She appreciated the sense of fairness that came with Austin's passing of his business to Cecil, the respect Cecil garnered from that passage, and the justice lying in the fact that John McCormick, whose political cronies now feared Cecil's power, had made it possible, when the debt had been paid off, for Cecil to own the station free and clear. Yet she did not know Cecil the way other mothers knew their children, could never know beyond a basic affection, the social barrier between them as deep as the secret life they shared. Still, she could keep her silent pride, love him, and fear for him.

Her fear was consummated by that one Sunday and the close of that one weekend in November over thirty years ago, when Cecil came home from Big John's hunting camp, went to the garage, and cried with an intense, agonizing tenor of grief, much as he had cried for his mother when he was three. Her fear turned to horror when she coaxed fragments of his story from him, then to blind anger as she realized he was being set up and she could do nothing to put it right. She could not even tell Austin. The circle of danger would only extend and wrap around him like the tentacles of glimmering ribbon that used to curl and brush primary colors and pastels around her as she ran through her grandfather's mill. Absolute silence was the only option. If there were ever a sliver of a hint of betrayal, Cecil would surely pay with his life, kin or no.

She held on to him, there in the garage, for a very long time, until dusk began to take the afternoon. Finally she pushed him upright, clutched his shoulders, and gave him the full strength of her gaze.

"Let these be your last tears over it, Cecil," she said. "Let these be your very last thoughts of it, because there is nothing that will ever be done to change one speck of it. Any more thoughts of it will put you at the end of a rope and you know it."

She left him then, left him to his loss and the degrading realization of the even lower esteem in which the white men held him. She left him there, joining his first mother as someone he could not depend upon to save him.

Eleven days later the men came, white-hooded and silent, materializing out of the pines, buffeted by sage-brush, drifting across the gravel lot at WDAB like swamp phantoms. Austin was in Birmingham on business. The men must have known this. She and Cecil were at the station that evening taking care of some cleaning and bookkeeping. The men must have been watching, waiting for the right moment.

When Cecil saw them his eyes begged her to let him run. Instead, she took his hand. "It's all right," she said. "It's impossible that they know anything about what happened. It's plain they've only been sent to scare you. And I'm here. They would get you alone if they were more than a warning."

There were three men and two children, smaller even than Cecil. The jarring presence of the children, wearing angel-wing white, of their innocence perverted, filled her with a rage she could hardly contain. But she resolved to appear calm.

All were silent as they approached the door, all except one, the largest one, whom the other adults addressed as "Cee-Boy," who carried a pistol and waved her and Cecil outside with it. "Ain't that sweet?" Cee-Boy said. "The little nigger boy and his white mama."

"She ain't white. She's a Jew," another man, holding a long piece of iron, said.

"I ain't never seen no Jew, Daddy," the smaller of the two children said, his voice girlish and angel-wing clear.

"Hey. Little nigger boy," Cee-Boy said.

"Is it a real Jew?" the child said again.

Miss Sophie squeezed Cecil's hand, silently urging him to speak.

"Answer me, little nigger boy," the man repeated.

The two children giggled, echoes spilling out to the sage.

Miss Sophie squeezed harder.

"Sir?" Cecil exhaled.

"You think you got you a white mama?"

"No, sir."

"Let go of her hand then, little nigger boy."

Again the children giggled. Sophie was struck by their dimpled little hands, their crisp, chirping voices.

She gave Cecil's hand another squeeze before releasing it. One of the men grabbed him by the left shoulder, pushing him into the other man, who snapped a pair of handcuffs to his wrists.

"You behave now, little nigger orphan boy," Cee-Boy said, while one of the men ripped Cecil's shirt front open so that it draped from his shoulders and hung low down his back.

Someone muttered, "Down on your knees," and Cecil was shoved to the gravel, pointy gray rocks biting into his dungarees. She knew he must be full of terror and she wanted to reassure him, but kept her silence for him. She could not risk agitating the men.

She smelled gasoline at the same moment she heard a deep whoosh come from the metal drum where Austin and Cecil burned trash. The two children stood near the barrel, hot red flames illuminating the diminutive replicas of the men who swore slurs at Cecil.

"The goddamn little piece of shit thinks he's white," one of the men said as the one called Cee-Boy took Miss Sophie by the arm, jerking her over to stand before Cecil.

"Look here, little piece of shit nigger," he said, standing behind her, laying his hands on her shoulders. "Do you think you come from this? Look here." He slid his palms to her breasts, squeezing hard. "Is this where you suckled when you come into the world?"

She felt removed from herself, knowing this angry, evil man was touching her, but unable to have that knowledge sink in enough to react. She stared into the flames stabbing up at the ceiling of stars, shutting off her fear, latching down her shame and her fury.

The other men were laughing. Cecil dropped his eyes, which brought a knee into his back, knocking him windless. "Pay attention!"

"Yeah, do that," said Cee-Boy, stroking the clothed flesh of Sophie's chest with a throaty chuckle, then sliding his palms down to her stomach. "Did you grow down here in this white woman's belly? Huh?" His hands kneaded her abdomen, crawling down over her hip bones. She knew the hands were there, rubbing lewd motions down between her legs. She could feel the man leaning in behind her, pressing against her, but she was a fire nymph, walled within the curling flames, seeing the world through the yellow-orange cast of heat. "Answer me, little nigger boy."

"No, sir, I didn't."

She thought she heard a small break in Cecil's voice.

"Aw," Cee-Boy said. "Is it gonna cwy? Is it gonna cwy for its mama? Bless it's itty-bitty nigger heart." And the laughter of the men swelled up around her.

Let him be strong, God, she prayed, while Cee-Boy worked her dress up, up to where the tops of her nylons rested on rubber knobs overlaid by stainless steel clips, where, kneeling behind her, he plundered touches over the flesh of her thighs, up between her legs. She crawled deeper into the vivid flames. Cecil must have looked away again, because she heard him get another knee to the back, another reprimand. "You listen and look here every second, you goddamn piece of shit," said one of the men near Cecil.

"Hey," Cee-Boy said, jerking the elastic of her panties aside. "Little nigger bastard boy. Did you come out of this womb, out of this pussy here?"

"No, sir." Cecil's voice was hushed.

The other men laughed louder and whistled, their deep-voiced amusement eerily laced with the high, bell-clear giggles of the two children.

"You sure? Reach your hand up here and take a feel. See is it familiar. Come on."

More deep laughter blistered the night, its surreal echoes taking the trees.

"I can't." Cecil's voice was barely a whisper.

"Goddamnit, I said feel of it!"

She felt herself being pushed forward and several hands shoving Cecil's hand into her thighs. She thought she heard the boy make a choking sound. It was then that she let the fire have her, curling into the bowels of it as if it were some glowing embryonic membrane silencing the world. The jump of light, crisp and sharp and daggered by flames against the night sky, took her gaze from deep within the belly of heat. It was like being on the other side of reality, inside the skin of another soul, a place where she wanted to stay forever.

Something pulled her out, though. A sound. A loud yell. A scream. No, a horrific howl so full of agony she wanted to be deaf, ached for deafness to take her ears. They could degrade her with their filthy hands, shame her with their foul talk, and she could hold together, she knew. She could refuse to give them the satisfaction of her tears or her vitriol. But she could not bear to hear Cecil's pain, needed to stop them, had to stop them, could not, was held about the waist, still, by the big Klansman, and the words crawled up into her chest, taking form as they rose from deep within her abdomen, up, up to the back of her throat, releasing themselves into the dense chill on winter's cusp. They burst free of her mouth full of truth and lies and self-loathing.

"My baby!"

The men laughed even louder. The two of them were holding Cecil to the gravel, the taller of the two children putting a glowing iron brand to the back of his shoulder, withdrawing it, sending Cecil's scream shattering into shallow breaths and moans until he lay quiet in the rocks. His right shoulder lifted and receded with his breathing, the "McC" taking shape in her consciousness and in the raw searing of his flesh.

"Is that okay, Daddy?" the child asked Cee-Boy while one of the men removed the handcuffs latching Cecil's wrists together.

"How come Claud gets to do that and not me?" the other child whined.

"'Cause I ain't a shit for brains, like you," the first child responded.

"Claud gets to do everything," the second child whined again.

"Shut up!" Cee-Boy hollered before turning back to her. "You want your baby?" he taunted."Hey, boys, the nasty whore Jew-lady wants the little nigger boy."

More laughter.

"Y'all deserve each other," the big man went on, "but personally I think the little nigger boy is getting the shit end of that deal. Jews is no better than field rats but they claim they done been chose by God. At least niggers knows their place." He waved his arm and the other men began to move toward the woods. "That god-damn mark on your back's going to remind you every day who you belong to, boy, so don't forget. And don't forget to keep your big fat nigger lips closed."

The flames were coming down a notch just when the men's white forms dissolved into the brambles and sage, as if they were being absorbed into the winds blowing all around the county, invisible, but always present. The unfamiliar smell of burned flesh crawled across the parking lot. He was breathing easier now, and she moved toward him. He had been damaged by heat and flame, the same fierce slice of hell so comforting to her just moments ago. That the fire could have two opposing forces within it was mysterious to her, a jarring impression she would contemplate over years of retribution. But at that moment she had to tend to the boy.

The sound of Tammy's four-wheeler came like the faint buzz of shade-shadowed mosquitoes. Miss Sophie stood, straining to hear, as if hearing could will it to move faster. Hurry, she thought, having convinced herself, prepared herself. She trusted Tammy Sims, trusted her heart and her tenacity. Tammy Sims would know what to do.

Tammy was the soul of the Wildwood Home, "The Wild, Wild Woods," she called it. Her charming combination of bawdy humor, righteous obstinance, and innate kindness was the essence of her, something Miss Sophie noticed when Tammy was only a child and a regular playmate of Kate's daughter, Shug. The two little girls grew through jacks, hula-hoops and dress-up, then into teenaged running buddies. They were an odd pairing, the pampered princess and the neglected pauper, but the chemistry worked, though Sophie was aware of Tammy's irritation with Shug lately.

"The damn bitch has been here going on a year and ain't even so much as called me," Tammy fumed just yesterday.

"Phone line runs both ways," Sophie said.

"She gets married when she's supposed to graduate

college, which wasn't even an option for me back then. Didn't invite nobody to the wedding. She won't come home to see her mama and daddy. She calls me and writes me for a few years, then nothing. What kind of friend is that?"

"A troubled one?" Sophie said.

"Maybe she's too goddamn good to come to the trailer, got some rich boy husband."

"You're acting like a frog bouncing across a lily pond of conclusions," Sophie said. "There's a real easy way to get to the bottom of it." And as she said it she knew she was speaking of her own falling out with Kate as well.

Sophie could still picture Shug and Tammy, filling Kate's big house with the electricity of youth. They were both wild, boy crazy, brimming with sex appeal, although Tammy's attractiveness was outside the margins of standard issue good looks. Her muted, soft-edged beauty was obviously not inherited from the Simses, the plain-faced, sharp-featured, clannishly isolated bunch Tammy's mother, Sonora, had married into three years after Tammy's birth, finally giving her fatherless child the legitimacy of a man's surname. The buttermilk-hoe-cake upbringing giving the Simses a pallid cast contrasted with Tammy's ephemeral bronze freckling of a healthy blonde sheen, a polish at once natural yet aberrant when juxtaposed with the rest of the family, folks not her blood kin. Sophie heard that Forrest Sims, Tammy's stepfather, was part farmer, part outlaw before he died, doing neither with any consistency. He ran with bootleggers and cock fighters at night and laid around the house during the day while his wife Sonora worked at the box factory to keep them in groceries. He shot himself in the head—accidentally, his side of the family said; on purpose, his wife maintained. Whichever it was, his violent end did get Miss Sophie her current home, as he had plenty of land, land that found its way into Tammy's possession and became The Wildwood Home.

It was Shug who posssessed the green-eyed, thick red-haired beauty that got noticed. She was the more outgoing of the two, the McCormick cockiness saturating her genes. At first glance she seemed to always run the show, but Tammy's force of will would rear its head if an underdog needed her defense. It was as if Tammy were content to go along with her friend in order to keep the peace, but would always remain willing to take charge of Shug's recklessness if there were a higher principle involved.

Shug went away to college right after high school, while Tammy went straight into a bad marriage that dragged on for a dozen brawling years. "When I got together the strength to throw that man out," she told Miss Sophie one evening, "I knew I could arrange my life just like I wanted it, and I wanted never to have to account to anybody about what I do. So there won't be another husband. Ever. I love the woods and I love old people, and that's plenty to love without a man in the way." So she sold off a little of the farmland and a good bit of the timber her stepdaddy left her and put up her old folks' home, where Sophie, alone in life, gnarled with arthritis and brittle-boned, landed in 1987.

Miss Sophie offered her big house in town to Cecil and Earline, but it still sat vacant because Cecil was not yet ready to move in, not easy with the idea. Earline confided that, on one level, Cecil did not want to appear to show off; but on a deeper one he was loathe to leave the little ranch-style structure at the edge of Pitch Hill, where he and Earline raised their family, where he knew something of a home, a hint of belonging. Earline, though, had all kinds of plans for Miss Sophie's abandoned two-story, plans she shared on those late afternoons when she and Cecil visited his mother at the Wildwood Home.

There were nine residents, seven women and two men, plus two live-in aides, an itinerant R.N., a cook, and a cleaning lady. There was a miniature chapel, and local preachers who took turns presiding over Sunday afternoon services. Sometimes Cecil conducted the services. Rabbi Meyer even made the trip from Birmingham every four or five months or so. Tammy was constantly in and out, planning outings, cookouts down by the creek, flitting back and forth from her trailer a hundred yards back behind the building like an errant butterfly.

The facility itself was homey, secluded, and tranquil. Miss Sophie knew she was fortunate to be in such a place when so many were cold, clinical, and cruel. It never occurred to her to leave Cole County, not after so many years, not when Austin was buried at the Dry Creek Cemetery, where her own plot beside him waited to be filled. No, this was an ideal place to die, next to nature, surrounded by kindness.

"You should have seen the devils I killed today, Miss Sophie." Tammy dismounted the three-wheeler and pitched her croaker sack up to the porch. "Blew their little snakey brains out."

At forty-one Tammy retained the soul of her beauty. Her honest, natural looks would have been cheapened by makeup, and she scoffed at women who visited hairdressers and tanning beds. "Been there, done that," she would say. "Spent my teenage years playing dress-up glamour queen. Hell, Shug and I had all the girls in our class as handmaidens. And we damn sure cultivated that musky power we queens have over men. Caught myself a handsome dog of a man who got me so addicted to his love I overlooked the little things—you know, like his lack of an IQ, the time he knocked up my own aunt, how he stayed gone for days at a time, how he drank his way through my money. And I've seen enough shit to know that history can repeat itself. So, sure, I'll go glamify my big fat ass, hit the Stop and Come Inn, and rustle me up another beer-belching, coke-sniffing, whore-humping fool who likes to whup me round the head before we make love. Oh, yeah, I'll run right out and do that." And the old folks would laugh at her crusty candor, share their own war stories with the big-hearted girl who had messed up as badly as the next person. Miss Sophie at once wondered why she had not thought to trust Tammy long before now.

The younger woman glanced mischief at Miss Sophie. "You want to take an up-close and personal look at some slaughtered devils? I believe Mephistopheles himself is up inside my body bag."

Miss Sophie shuddered. "You know those things give me the willies. And I'm already beside myself." Her voice broke and she sank back into the rocker.

"Damn, what's wrong? Has Miss Ida been in your things again? You know, I believe that pillar of the Baptist Church was a kleptomaniac in a former life. You want me to kick her butt?"

The old woman laid her face in her palms.

"What in the world?" Tammy knelt before her, pulling at her wrists.

"It's Cecil."

"God, I knew it. I felt it. When I heard the radio this afternoon a rabbit ran right straight over my tomb."

"I called the Sheriff's Office," Miss Sophie said, "but they laughed it off. Like everybody else, probably."

"Laughed? Why the hell would they laugh if Cecil is dead? My hand to God, that Wade Connors is a—"

"No. I didn't mean to say he was dead."

Tammy exhaled. "Thank God. Damn, you had me going. I thought maybe Cecil keeled over from a heart attack in the middle of Gospel Glorifications. So, I'm confused. What is the problem? An accident?"

"No. I don't know. Maybe. All I know is he's gone and I have to find him." Her arthritic hands trembled as she pushed wisps of gray from her cheeks.

"Calm down, Miss Sophie. I'll get you some sherry and we'll—"

"No. Stand up."

"You've gotten all worked up over nothing. I bet old Cecil's off on a call. Or maybe with that sweet thing I hear he's been–"

"Stand up. Now. Then stand me up."

It was as firm a command as Tammy had ever heard her utter. She helped her out of the chair with a palm to the old woman's sharp, shaky elbow.

As Miss Sophie stood, there rose within her more of the certainty she felt at the thought of confiding in Tammy, and her eyes met and gathered in the strength of an ally, something she never had before, not in this fight. "I have been such a coward," she said. "And over the years I've just tried to will it away. I've wanted to forget it but that is impossible. Maybe if I say it to you, then I can say it to Kate."

"Miss Sophie? You're only confusing me more."

The old woman locked her fingers onto Tammy's arm and pointed out across the lawn to the edge of a thicket being fast swallowed by evening shade. "Just let's you and me walk out to that bench yonder and let me tell you these things. No one else can hear. You see, I have these things in me and I need to tell you. I need to tell you just as much as I can get out. I can't have all of this die with me."

It was approaching midafternoon when Cecil Durgin pulled onto the grassy lawn at DoeRun, a lawn sprawling paisley: curved patches of rye grass swirled emerald patterns in dark jade, then became the green-black velvet of damp-moss at the edge of the surrounding woods. It was a place as familiar as any home he ever had. He wasn't sure when Shug would be there. "As soon as I can get away," the note said.

It had been a long time, and he had often wondered about her, worried over her deliberate avoidance of Cole County. It wasn't like her to stay down, to play the coward, no matter how badly Cash Cloy busted up her spunk. She maintained some contact, at first, but the letters dwindled to once a year Christmas cards, then nothing but the occasional newsy tidbit from Miss Kate.

"How's Shug doing these days?" Cecil would ask at a barbecue while he prepared the meat or at a cocktail party as he tended bar.

"She's just fabulous," Miss Kate would gush. "Got a plaque from the mayor just last month for another fundraising event. Stays busy."

But it sounded hollow to Cecil, not like the Shug with the carefree spirit, to be nothing but busy. Once, about five or six years back, she called him, late at night. She sounded drunk. "I miss you so much," was all she said. "I miss y'all so goddamn much." And the line went dead, leaving him frustrated, needing to know she was all right.

He eased his pickup around behind the house at DoeRun, down the old logging road shielded by a stand of trees, just in case someone was to drive up, however unlikely, then took a seat in a rocker beneath a ceiling fan on the side porch. He smoked a cigarette. Then another. He read his Sunday newspaper, front to back. Then he reread a few articles. He finally got up and carried the newspaper around to the back of the house. He kept the editorial page, which contained a couple of pieces about the land tax referendum, and tossed the rest in a trash barrel near the barbecue pit. He was certain he would have a good bit to say on the subject of land taxes on his radio program during the coming weeks. Might as well start collecting information and opinions. He stared at the place beneath the kitchen window where he had long ago spied on the five men and Charity Collins, the years between then and now no deterrent to his sense of responsibility and longing for another try. He napped for a long while in the big rope hammock strung and shaded between two cedar trees. He never once thought about leaving.

By close to 6:00 P.M. he'd had enough of being lazy in the summer heat. He walked back around to the front of the camp house, deciding to go ahead and fire up the air conditioner. No telling how long she would be. He had his own key, had since he was a boy, trusted as he was without merit. He could have been all cooled off by now, but he did not like the oppressive feel of the big house, the history of his interaction with it, or the remorse and grief tangled in the lives of others he had known here. He swung back the heavy oak door and flipped on the lights.

The camp house had changed little over the years. The faint smell of musty wool, cedar-chipped smoke, and sticky sap met him as he entered. Stripped pine columns bearing split-tree roof beams beyond the sleeping lofts gave it the feel of a rugged cathedral or a Medieval mead hall, deep spaces steeped in tales of Canterbury travelers passing through. Travelers like Cecil, who stood before one of the massive stone fireplaces, looking up at a herd of buck heads charging through the rocks. Each wood plaque bearing its trophy also bore an engraved gold square carrying a tiny history:

18 POINT-NONTYPICAL
180 BOONE & CROCKETT
CASH CLOY
BUCK WALLER STAND
NOVEMBER 25, 1988

12 POINT
JOHN MCCORMICK
ROUND SWIRL CREEK BANK
DECEMBER 18, 1953

There were eight racks on this wall alone, more on the opposite end of the great room, and others scattered about the cathedral. Most were from the particular five men who were regulars over the years, but there were also a few from others who joined the hunts from time to time. Roscoe, Huck, and Cash even had sons represented, sons who played football, scored with women, fucked the whores their daddies bought for them, and killed animals to do their fathers proud. Sons who had surely devised and were now carrying on their own version of The Game. Cecil reached up to stroke the cement-hard neck of one of the peaceable creatures sprouting antlers in a magnificent web above him. His index finger glanced across the gold square.

12 POINT
LEE DAVIS
CHEWED LIP CLEARING
NOVEMBER 29, 1963

Cecil laid his folded newspaper on the coffee table. Old Lee. It had taken him years to get his first, and, as far as Cecil knew, only deer. Lee just plain wasn't cut out for it. He was a lousy shot, skittish in the woods, and often wore a pained expression as he watched Cecil skin the kill. Yet he came to the camp at every opportunity, invested hundreds and hundreds of dollars in the best gear, pored over the magazines. It suddenly dawned on Cecil that Lee had been studying during those long A.M. visits to the john, sure enough digesting and making room for his developing *Field & Stream* mindset. But Lee, who in his youth was a semi-peer of Cash Cloy, would never live up to his promise. Cash would maintain his romantic edge, but Lee would slip into subservience to the masculine mystique he could not capture. He studied and emulated the men, trailing Cash, his winning competitor for Big John's favor, like a Blue Tic hound; but, after bringing in this deer, the group dynamic took on a different flavor. Cecil witnessed the transformation first hand, and it, in turn, transformed his perception of the men. In 1963, Cecil learned the men were colder than killers, they would turn on one another for sport, and they certainly never deserved what little respect he held for them prior to that time.

It was a pivotal year for Cecil, all the way around. His nerves tingled with the electric current of new possibilities riding the air in winding breezes around the South. He could feel it inching its way toward Cole County, spent most of the year in a state of edgy anticipation. In 1963 Cecil was seventeen, an expert by then at his camp duties, able to anticipate and react without being told most of the time. In spite of the broadcast of some of his opinions about Governor Wallace back in the summer, Cecil grew almost as popular as Otis as a hand out on the hunts. And after the events of the summer, the harsh comeuppance he was given, the humiliation of being used like a dog to fetch for the white men, he decided to be more active in his observation of the men. He decided to be much more productive in his use of time spent with them, to watch them with an eye toward the eventual upper hand. Indeed, he made it his mission to intellectually ingest them, to know them from the inside out, keeping secret his contempt, holding close the jaded sensibility they inspired in him.

There was, however, an arena in which Cecil had always been willing to give the men the positive regard they were due, and that was the arena of the deep woods when they were out on a hunt. It was in the wilderness where the rules were the most strictly followed, with no enforcement necessary. It was a given, a matter of honor and manhood; there was a right way and a wrong way to proceed through the bloody rituals of the forest. In fact, the code of the hunt seemed to Cecil to be the glue holding together what few high principles the white men shared. Their conduct in the field was the only thing he ever saw them undertake with a sense of unblemished fairness and sporting purpose. And he would have never come to any other conclusion had he not seen a different scenario unfold. He would have been as amazed and impressed as the next person by Lee's out-of-nowhere trophy had he not been in the field with him that day, had not seen yet another game unfold in which Lee himself was stalked and laid bare by his best friends.

There must have been twenty-plus hunters there that weekend, several from other parts of the state, royalty in Alabama lumber mills, men creosoted with money and bravado. Some brought registered hunting dogs and their own "boys," Cecil's counterparts, albeit older, who would bed down with him and Otis in the skinning shed, where they would pass a bottle of sloe gin, trade tales, and share a few secrets, harmless ones, about the white folks.

In the predawn darkness of a Saturday they climbed into a covey of pickups with their shotguns, hangovers, and Thermos jugs of hot coffee, to be driven out to clearings along the West Ridge of McCormick's forest. Big John liked to get right to it, forgoing the milling conversations over mugs of coffee, routine along Alabama's back roads early of a morning during deer season. The conversations would come later, in the early evening, behind the afternoon hunt.

In two of the truck beds, Otis and Cleon, who always introduced himself as "Mr. Leroy's niggah from down to Monroeville," carried the dogs. There were seven tracking dogs this time, four in one group, three in the other. The two men were to set them out just after dawn, after the hunters were situated at their designated posts. Cutter, Jack, and Old Mabel, Big John's prize Blue Tics all, danced clacking toenails in the back of the truck Otis drove. With them was a Walker bitch named Cora Mae, new to the hunt, a rare beauty brought up to the camp by Mr. Leroy Lanaux, lord of his own manor in South Alabama. The dogs sniffed and paced, sometimes nipping and growling at one another. Cora Mae had just come off a heat, so the excitement of the dogs, keenly fixed on their need to run down a deer, often escalated to scuffles over Cora Mae before Otis would holler them apart from the driver's side window. Cleon hauled Sheriff Huck's two Red Bones, Joe and Juliet, along with Mr. Leroy's second dog, a Blue Tic named

Viceroy.

Cecil found himself in the bed of the truck Lee Davis was driving, along with Cash and Roscoe, the two white men perched on ragged orange crates. Headlights skidded and bounced through the dense cathedral of pines as the vehicle rumbled along the rutted dirt road. The men were as quiet as the hour, 4:30 A.M., for most of the drive, breaths trailing frosty in the frigid air. Roscoe pulled his hat down at the furred earflaps. "Gonna be a fucking cold one, ain't it, Cecil," he said, finally.

"Yes, sir. Sure is."

Cash jerked his head toward the cab of the truck. "Gonna be colder for him. That somebitch sitting inside with the heater full blast. At least we're getting used to it."

The three of them chuckled. "Hey, Cash," Roscoe said. "Lee tells me he's going to get him one this weekend. Says today's the day."

"Shit. He couldn't hit a bull in the ass with a bass fiddle."

This got a bigger laugh from the group, Cecil included. He was allowed to laugh, when it had to do with something like Lee's lack of shooting ability, but never to his face.

"He'd shit hisself if he did hit one," Roscoe said.

"That's a mighty big if." Cash turned to Cecil. "What you think, boy?"

Cecil grinned on cue, delivering the joke he had been invited to deliver. The invitation was crucial, as an unsolicited joke was taboo. "I think he be butt-blasting that shit clear cross the county, that what didn't puddle up in his boots."

The men hooted and let the jostle of the wheels lull their humor while Cash took on his squinty-eyed, thoughtful look, the dangerous one. He reached down and plundered through a brown canvas bag, coming up with a box of triple-ought buckshot, Lee's preferred size. "You boys interested in seeing Lee shit hisself?"

"Are you fixing to—? Naw, man, you ain't," Roscoe said.

Cecil was brought up short. Cash used double-ought, as did most of the other men, but here he was, pilfering some of Lee's triple-ought. Did he mean to shoot a deer for Lee? Break a rigid code of the deep woods and cheat on a kill? If the men were this cutthroat with one another, how murderous could they be where he was concerned?

"Come on, man," Roscoe said. "That ain't right. Besides, Lee wouldn't lay claim to one that wasn't his."

"Yeah? Well, I got fifty bucks says he would."

A slow smile took Roscoe's face, then, "No, man. It ain't right. Lee's had it rough this year, what with Bev leaving him and all, running round with Johnny Gossman."

Boscoe. Cecil inwardly rolled his eyes at the false display of conscience and concern. Over the years Cecil noted the pecking order of the men shifting, Roscoe coming up a notch with every kill, Cash always on top, Lee in decline, becoming more the butt of the joke than Roscoe or Huck ever were. And it was all a function of his inability to bring in a buck, the critical rite of passage he had never undergone. Consequently, Lee garnered degrading nicknames hidden inside humor—the obvious "Dead Eye Davis," "Old Three Shot," "Arnold Oakley, Annie's little brother," and this weekend's fresh one, "Lee Harvey Davis," a dark reference to the President's assassination only a week ago, all because of his failure to finally kill one, just one, deer. Cecil also watched Lee's pudgy shrew of a wife, brown-haired, big-eyed Bev, at camp parties, how she flinched when her husband rubbed slow-dancing into her, how she warmed to other men. She never belonged to Lee. Like his unbagged buck, she was another hurdle he could not clear, another passage he could not make. And Cecil's encyclopedic knowledge of the men grew in increments.

"You goddamn right he's had it rough," Cash said. "Don't he deserve a little happiness? Don't I deserve fifty bucks of your money?"

"He ain't going to lay claim to it if he ain't shot it."

"Well goddamn, Boscoe, if you're right you get some spare change. If I'm right we got one on Lee and he don't even know it."

The other man let the smile take his face again.

It was still dark when they arrived at the trail where Roscoe and Cash were to get out of the truck and hike to two separate clearings, Roscoe to Dog Leg Creek and Cash to Over the Bluff. Cash would have the land just up from where Lee and Cecil were to take a place at Chewed Lip, at the south end of a scattering of small open fields, each of them separated by a hundred yards or so of trees spilling into the frosty-moist clearings where the deer would come to feed.

Otis and Cleon were to set the dogs out near the highway running north and south through the northeast quarter section of McCormick's land. The wind was right, and Cash had tracked the movement of the deer with a sharpened expertise. If all went well, the dogs would run the deer into the scattering of men, camouflage-meshed into the browns and olive greens of the November forest.

Cecil came along often, toting gear, looking after the extra ammo, a spare shotgun or bow, rib-nudging a silent heads-up when bone-colored tines materialized through overlaid limbs, the animal crystallizing through the fog and weeds to take a spray of shot, preferably in the neck or chest. He followed Lee down a trail dusted with frozen dew, black dirt smells shrouded in the rush of creek water sounds a quarter mile westward. It was a beautiful world, the deep woods. Cecil respected it with the deference one would show a church sanctuary, letting the purity of it enter his pores and bring its peace all up inside him, in short segments of fine moments, forgetting the perversions of life he had seen played out before him in this Eden of his.

They arrived at Chewed Lip Clearing, so named because it was where Yancey McCormick, John's pale, wormy cousin, had, in a fit of buck fever, bitten clear through his lower lip and pissed himself before he missed a fourteen point back in '52. Big John got it instead, like he got everything else in life that his cousin, along with John the last of the McCormicks, could not manage. Cecil reached under his jacket and into his vest to check for extra triple-ought, the k-bar knife Otis had given him when he was ten, and the plug of Day's Work he would pull from. He had found it helpful to have something to chew on, give himself a place to direct his energy. They had to be still and silent for what seemed like eternities at a time, a branch snap or faraway rustle of leaves cueing an intensification of the senses, a searching of the trees for another signal, maybe just barely perceptible. This morning would be no different. He hunkered down on the wet grass and waited, letting the woods take him to his own private clearing.

Cecil dozed as the cusp of morning wore long in segments of muted light. First it was the deep copper glow reflected from a horizon-hidden sun finally pushing its way shadowy through tree trunks as three doe ambled into the clearing, their feeding interspersed with stock-still alerts to sounds only they could hear. When the day's birth of yellow-white rays filtered through chilled fog, the big buck came, the eight point rack carried like a crown on a blueblood prince. Lee's grip tightened on the shotgun, which had been fixed through a shooting slit, at the ready, since the three doe had walked up, for almost a half hour. He breathed trembling breaths into the stock as he made to pick his mark on the animal, to lay it out with a shot to the chest. But the twitch in the man's jaw told Cecil what he already knew.

"Buck fever get Mr. Lee's butt every goddamn

time," went Otis's voice through Cecil's brain as he watched the barrel of the shotgun rise and fall in the shooting slit. It gave a slight lift in the man's hand with each throb of the pulse in his neck, a throb that must be booming through the white man's ears with the resonance of a tympani, waves of vibrations sending repercussions to the stock as it rested in his damp palm. A lift of the stock, then down, lift, down. A whisper of a bounce, but enough to send thirty-ought shot fired wild.

The buck strolled through the planted vetch, padding its hooves into melting frost, owning the clearing. Sweat glinted in slick drops on Lee's upper lip, defying the frigid morning air. His eyes closed hard, then opened. Finally, his shoulders rose slowly, with the deepest breath possible, aimed at steadying the barrel. But it was an audible breath. Too audible. The buck alerted and bolted in one quick second, just as Lee bore down on the trigger, sending a spray of shot into a wild privet hedge and tangled tree limbs.

"Fuck!" came through gritted teeth. "Fuck, fuck, fuck!" He turned his deep brown eyes to Cecil, spitting expletives in a gravelly whisper. The look was frightening, and for a second the boy thought the gun might be turned on him, just so Lee could have the satisfaction of finally shooting a living creature.

But something broke the look in two. The gruff echoes of the dogs barking, trailing, faraway sounds lacing the woods to the east and north, some barely a whisper, but others coming louder in increments.

"They out. Up around Buck Waller," Cecil said, low.

"Trailing easy."

The sounds were varied in pitch but similar in cadence, punctuated by silences, fifteen, twenty, thirty seconds each. Cecil could make out Cutter's deep bass, which told him Big John's hounds and the Walker were closer than Cleon's group of dogs.

Cecil stood to join Mr. Lee. "What you think?" Lee asked.

"Won't be long to strike. Not with the wind out the west."

In a few short minutes the rhythm of barks branched apart and Cecil studied the chorus working closer their way, sending ripples of other sounds out across the forest, as if unseen life were awakened and on the move.

"Cutter leading one other. Ain't Old Mabel, though," Cecil said, when, of a sudden, the woods were filled with an explosion of howls, a cacophonous symphony of one long, rolling moan of the dogs in unison as they struck.

"They jumped him," Cecil said. "Done lit him up."

The volume intensified in minutes, went down a few decibels for a short while, then picked back up.

"They're pushing him, ain't they? Reckon they're going to push him on out?" Lee put a soft, pale, banker's hand to his face and rubbed at more nervous sweat.

"Hell, they ain't pushing him," Cecil said, biting back his irritation with Lee's anxiety, deciding to have a bit of secret fun. "It's all they can do to keep up. Must be a good 'un."

From far to the north came a sprinkling of gunshots. Lee flinched.

"Got bucks scattering like quail. Cleon's group," Cecil said, subtly pushing at the white man's fear.

"You think this one'll make it all the way down to us?" Lee's panicked expression told Cecil the white man did not want it to happen, did not want to be put on the spot yet again, wanted instead for Cash or Roscoe to intercept the animal.

"He ain't fucking around. And he's headed for home straight out." Cecil jerked his head toward the game refuge backing up to the creek on the western border of McCormick's land.

"Where they at now?"

Cecil listened, sorting out the pitches and volumes of the dogs' moans and bays. "Steady moving southwest. Not long before the hill in front of DogLeg. And it ain't none of Old Mabel or Jack. It's that Walker done took the lead like I knew she would. Ain't got much of a nose, but she sure can run. Damn, he must have jumped up right in front them, the way they complaining."

Lee rubbed his palm across the slick wood stock of the gun, lips moving in silence, as though he were praying or invoking some spirit of Luck.

"Be ready," Cecil said, steady shoving at Lee's tattered nerves. "He's either going over the hill or coming through the cut. If he comes through the cut he belongs to you or Mr. Cash. Be ready 'cause you going to have to shoot fast."

Lee checked the safety, lips still moving, but quiet.

"By the way he's covering ground he's toting a rack. And Gyp right on him, I mean, breathing up his butt," Cecil said.

Echoes of woody brush breaking and the occasional loud pop of a tree limb worked their way to the two of them. Lee ran the back of his hand over his face, trickles of sweat swimming down to his neck. His breathing picked up with the volume of the dogs' barks, with the anticipation of meeting his trophy.

"Never seen one move this fast. Ain't nothing but a race. Wait—" Cecil strained forward, then, "That's it. He's coming through the cut. Be ready."

Lee looked as if he might pass out, and Cecil could not help enjoying it. Mr. Lee might just shit himself after all. The boy almost snickered, but kept himself in check.

Suddenly came an explosion north of them, from Cash's clearing. They turned toward the original sound which now echoed from hill to hill, couched in other sounds, coming louder, sounds of breaking limbs, sharp, clear cracks echoing behind the ripples of gunfire.

"Missed him. Going to pitch him this way, though. He's heading cross the creek to home."

Lee raised the shotgun, tense, and as ready as he could be, panting. Cecil thought he could even make out an occasional whimper. The thump of hooves grew louder, as did smaller sounds, leaves and ground twigs pounded into dirt, the blow of breath that could only be from a wounded animal, the dogs booming like big guns just behind it.

The buck burst into the clearing, snorting and stumbling toward the opposite end, terror-eyed and spackled along its backside with blood. It tossed its antlers from side to side, snorting louder, filling the woods with the surrendering sound of rank death, while Cutter and Cora Mae surrounded and harassed it. Hot breaths rode the air on white vapors, a stagger taking its gait until it wove crazily toward waiting trees, sinking side-angled kneeward. Cecil felt what he always felt as he watched one of these kills, a dense disgust and mellow sadness destined to stay with him for days, a matter-of-fact mourning of the loss of a piece of Paradise.

He was watching the dying animal so intently the explosion from Lee's shotgun gave him a violent start. Shot sprayed the ground near the buck, dotting its hind limbs with pellets as it fell full over, legs kicking, making to get up, but only kicking at sun-dappled air, breaths slowing and spacing.

The wild, musky smell of game and death met Cecil's nostrils as they walked over to where the buck lay in a tumble of blood and matted grass, eyes fixed in a stare reflecting pine-needled clouds. The boy pictured a spirit rising, playing among the treetops, curling its essence into the spirit of Charity Collins. He could see her face in the shadows and woods shade. She smiled at him from the pine-needled boughs, piercing his heart one more time, and he fought to keep himself focused on his tasks. He pinched off a corner of the tobacco plug and handed it to Lee, then got a rope around the Walker, the blooded bitch sniffing at the kill before dropping panting to the ground, exhausted. He didn't see Cutter, dreaded chasing him down if that crazy hound had gone after another deer.

"Goddamn," the white man said, dribbling brown juice down his chin as he worked the chaw. "I finally did it." He grasped the right side of the rack, lifted the deer's head, and let it drop limp to the bed of grass. "I finally fucking did it," he said again.

It was then Cecil caught sight of the mound of fur in the vetch, fur bloodied and shimmering red against brown and white. Cutter lay dead in a thickening of the high, green grass, cleanly hit in the side of the head with a thirty-ought slug.

That evening, when the men gathered at the skinning shed with their whiskey, carcasses, and braggadocio, Cecil watched another game unfold, a cat and mouse game played outside of the mouse's beknownst. He watched and knew the frigid regard in which the white men held one another.

Big John had been characteristically gracious, graciously silent, about Cutter. These things happened, he said, his lack of words showcasing the anger and disdain lying behind them. That Lee had shot Big John's prize Blue Tic was the icing on the cake for Cash, Roscoe, and others of the men who never missed an opportunity to play on another man's weakness, taking cruel jokes as their own armor. Still, much was made of Lee's first kill, however tainted, and Cash had him recount his adventure over and again, first to Big John, who merely tolerated it, then on down the line. He gave the occasional

back slap and amazed "No shit, man!" to Lee's manufactured account of how Cash must have sprayed the
buck's legs, sending it spooked and running hard into
his own clearing, how he tried to get a fix on its neck as
it passed, but ended up flat out and low. So he fired into
the flank, a sloppy shot, he knew, and it would be messy
cleaning if the gut was blown.

"Ain't that the fucking truth," Cash said, winking at
Roscoe. "Me, I make a special point of getting them in
the front end. Makes for neater meat. Guess I had a off
day today. But, hey. Lee got his ass a buck! Done made
the kill club! Even killed hisself a pedigreed canine. Way
to go, man."

Lee had fallen apart, panicked, when he realized he
had shot the dog. He had paced, cursed, cried, plotted,
and retched. Cecil merely went about his own business,
sickened anew by the white man's ineptitude. He tied
Cora Mae to a tree and slit the buck's throat with the k-
bar, his own private ritual, as he liked to leave the
warmth of the blood at the spot where any given animal
fell. It was a Cecil Durgin stamp on the hunt, just as
Otis's proclivity for cutting a silver-dollar-sized piece of
the hide was an Otis Joyce stamp. It was ritual. It was
almost a religion. Cecil watched the rendering from the
carcass puddle and spread, creating a bloody bog in the
matted vetch, a crimson swamp soaking into the dark
soil beneath it. Shortly Otis arrived to get the dogs, and
by then Lee was resigned to what he had done. These
things happen, Big John said, but everybody knew these
things rarely did.

Four carcasses were already hanging, heads down, from beamed hooks beside the shed, while Cecil prepared Lee's twelve point. The men stood in small knots, eating the fried chicken and corn on the cob Otis had prepared, or passing bottles of Scotch and bourbon while they swagger-laughed their stories at one another. Lee and Cecil stood before his buck.

"Goddamn," Cash said. "Ain't you going to dress your own deer?"

"Cecil helped me get it. He can help me skin it. I'll do the rest," Lee said in what seemed to be memorized lines.

Cecil pressed the blade into the fur and flesh of a hind leg, careful not to slice through the sinewy tendon at each knee joint. The back legs were spread, then tied to a metal bar. Finally, the animal was hoisted to the gutting beam. Enmeshed in the ritual, he nodded an acknowledgment to Charity, the woods sprite who hung back amidst the tree trunks, always residing in his peripheral vision. He took a breath and continued.

Cecil sliced through testicles and rendered the animal dickless, tossing the useless flesh, so much like hers, into a gutbucket that was set beneath the wild game corpse. Then, with a surgeon's precision, he ran the blade up the inside of either leg to the previous cut on each side, around each knee, then down to the front legs, again circling the knee joints. The skin came down with ease, peeling back until the gray form of the animal was revealed.

He cut hard through the breastbone, then held the

IN A TEMPLE OF TREES

knife out for Lee to take over, at once aware of Lee's face taking on the bone-ash hue of the antlers at his feet. He don't want to do it, Cecil thought, with a twinge of satisfaction. He ain't going to make it.

"You want me to take the head off, Mr. Lee?" He savored the man's fear, tasted it as if it were a delicacy for his soul to devour in secret.

"Yeah. I'll take it from there. Where's the goddamn whiskey?"

"Here you go. Let's drink to old Cutter. He got his reward for running a buck to Lee Harvey Davis." Cash handed him a bottle of Dewar's and Lee threw his head back, swallowing the light amber courage.

Cecil pulled the knife through neck muscle, dragging in places, but careful not to meander off course, to make the taxidermist's job more difficult. This was the trophy, the evidence of victory, the centerpiece of the bragging rights. He set the head at the base of a nearby longleaf, hide caped out, while Cash ran his hands up inside the carcass. "Well, come on, buddy. Get your blood. You earned it." And he slapped his bloody hands to Lee's cheeks and forehead, hard, too hard, punishing hard. Spirit killing hard.

Lee's face was pale behind the animal's blood rubbed across his skin in a primitive smear, and he held his knife a shade tentatively. His upper lip had erupted in the familiar glaze of sweat in spite of the night's chill. At the same time Cecil was repelled by Cash and Boscoe's victimization of their friend, he was also glad to see Lee getting a fraction of what he deserved, and

Cecil's tongue wrapped around a secret taste of revenge.

"Yeah, boy," Cash was saying. "Going to be nasty up in there. Looks like you busted up some innards for sure. I'm telling you, you blow a gut and it almost ain't worth fucking with." He grinned at Cecil and Roscoe snickered.

At once the degree of Cash's viciousness dawned on Cecil. Goddamn. He had set everything up. Slick as the scales on a mountain stream Rainbow Trout, Cash had reiterated his superiority. Cash the sure shot. The Great White Hunter of all hunters. Of course, it made perfect sense. Cash had placed a shot in the precise spot where Lee would have his senses and lack of temperament for the kill tested to their outermost limits. Cecil himself had thrown up a couple of times, when a busted stomach sent out the most foul, slushy-green shit smell he ever imagined, and Lee had never even gutted a deer. Cash, using smart timing and the finesse of his expert shooting ability, had chanced a bet that the dogs would run the deer up on Lee's stand, and they had. He had bet that Lee would claim it, and he had. Now Lee was about to pay a price for both of their deceptions, and for old Cutter to boot.

The white man ran his knife through dull, pewter-gray skin, organs and entrails slooshing down and forward, a sucking, sloshing mass of greens and clay-grays. Wincing at the precursor-smell rising with body steam, Lee plunged hands and knife toward the heart, letting it fall splashing into the gutbucket below. Cecil was cognizant of the subtle gags Lee was choking back while

Cash and Roscoe laughed and nudged at one another.

"Oooowee! That is some stinking-ass shit," Roscoe said.

"You need yourself a barf bucket?" Cash said. "Or a *bark* bucket? Get it?" And he howled like a dog.

"Shut the fuck up," Lee said, taking the knife around to where Cecil indicated, severing the membrane of the liver, sliding it quick-slug-like into the bucket. It was then the full power of the gut stench hit them. Men backed away, moving their stories apart from the smell. Cash roared. Lee had his hand against the stomach and intestines, having held them in place as Cecil instructed, then let them slide out and cascade into the receptacle.

"Yep," Cash said. "Busted the gut. See there?" He pointed at Lee's bloodied hands. A green-yellow slime of half digested grass and acorns punctuated the pungent shit stink that steamed from the emptied carcass and covered Lee's own flesh. Cash reached down into the bucket, into the torn entrails that leaked yesterday's meal, and, with a flourish, came up with some of the intestinal ooze on his fingers. "Here you go, buddy," he said, in a cold, retaliatory tone, smearing a mustache of stench beneath Lee's nostrils.

It was too much. Lee heaved and retched onto the carcass, coughing vomit into the gutbucket while Roscoe, Cash, and the others cat-called and whistled at him as if he were a girl. Lee made to collect himself, wiped off his face, and took a seat on a bench under the shed, head down, weak, mumbling curses. Cash walked over with cold nonchalance and offered him a smoke, which sent Lee into a wave of dry heaves. Any other victim might have aroused sympathy in Cecil; instead, he savored the man's shame. He also made a vow to himself to remember this. Should he ever begin to convince himself they would never hurt him or those he cared about, he would remember how ruthless they could be with one another.

"You know what you done, don't you?" Cash asked Lee. "Done gone and puked on the meat. Going to have to hose it down good, I mean."

"Yeah, yeah, I know," Lee said, pale flesh peeking through deer blood and humiliation.

"But what the hell," Cash said. "Congratulations, buddy." His voice was iced with irony. "You finally got one. Oh, yeah. Make that two, counting old Cutter, may he rest in peace. Congratu-goddamn-lations."

Cecil walked over to the round oak table, where, on a legendary night that very same weekend, he had watched Big John McCormick lose a thirty-two hundred dollar hand of poker to a timber baron from Brewton, Alabama, without batting an eye. The old man was a class act under pressure, a malevolent adversary when the real chips were down. He had to give him that, but he was loath to give him much more. McCormick was infected with the malady he observed in most of the wealthy men, however jovial or charming, who haunted the camp, a hard, detached demeanor born of always having the upper hand, a cold certainty with which others' lives were maneuvered. Certainly Big John had manuevered Cecil's life.

Cecil's awareness of his supposed connection to Big John McCormick had come in prickly little waves of vague realization. It was very much like when a limb had been asleep and was beginning to regain feeling, painfully, with the whispered comments swirling about his assigned periphery to the white world, and all-out ribbing from his own friends on Pitch Hill.

"Hey, Cecil," his best friend, Tony Mack Franklin, would say. "I been wanting me one of them slick GTO's. Reckon you could get your daddy to buy me one?"

"Hey, whitey," someone might joke. "Can you loan me a grand or two?"

He laughed it off or shrugged his shoulders at it because he did not want it to be true. He did not want his father to be a man whom he did not respect. That there was much more than a fraction of Caucasian blood trickling through him was undeniable, and he had tried to come to terms with it, but he could not, on a spiritual level, tolerate the thought of McCormick blood tainting his own, shooting white-water rapids through his veins.

The fact that McCormick's genetic stamp would make him half brother to Shug was the only palatable aspect of that situation. She had grown up around him, four years younger and forever at his heels. She shadowed him at the camp, questioned him, pestered him, yet there was a good-natured slant to it. He always liked her, watched her, watched out for her. She and her friend Tammy grew from giggly-loud children into voluptuous young women in a heartbeat, high school boys sniffing them out at the hunting camp parties. Cecil knew they crossed over to the opposite creek bank to make out with the boys, or went down behind the skinning shed where a brand new barbecue pit, never used, had been set on a slab just after Charity Collins' disappearance.

When Charity's abandoned car was found at Tippin's Eddy, there was a cursory investigation that ended abruptly. Austin Price editorialized on his radio station, questioning why there were no leads being pursued, but stopped giving it air time after receiving midnight phone calls threatening anonymous retaliation on him and Miss Sophie. A couple of Charity's relatives from Arkansas showed up to demand answers, but went away in a mysterious rush. Sheriff Huck implied the same relatives might somehow be involved in the case of the missing woman. By the following spring, Charity Collins was not even a memory in Cole County. And true to their word, neither the men nor Cecil ever spoke of her again, not to one another, anyway.

Charity Collins visited Cecil, though, came to him throughout his teenaged years in sweet wet dreams when she would kiss his face and chest and take him in her mouth until he baptized her face with his orgasm. But always the dreams turned into nightmares in which faceless white men hung her by her ankles and gutted her like a deer, batting her heart back and forth in a game of volleyball, playing jump rope with her intestines, pushing horse-hair tails into her ears and nostrils. He would wake up in damp sheets of salty sweat and sticky ejaculate, shaking and tearful.

It was a strange thing, but Shug sometimes put him in mind of Charity Collins when he least expected it. Even though the two girls occupied opposite ends of the social spectrum, even though sexual attraction for Shug was jarringly absent, there was a facet of frivolity in the both of them, a sense of fun that inevitably led the two young women into dangerous situations. Cecil never failed to notice when Shug, a freshman in high school all at once stunning, was led by any of half a dozen senior football players to the skinning shed, boys so fermented in sudsy beer and rampant hormones their dicks became heat-seeking missiles. He noticed when older men danced with Shug, Tammy and the other girls, charming them with their lack of horniness, their libidos laid back, tucked away until just the right moment. Cecil was aware of her relationship with Cash Cloy even before she was, back when the white man's eyes first brushed across the tight jeans cupping the firm butt of a cheerleader not yet conscious of the power she wielded.

When Cecil's ears caught the sound of a horse's hooves way up the dirt road, he stepped out onto the back porch. She would no doubt be on Lullabye, a blooded Appaloosa her father purchased for her only weeks before he died, hoping to lure her home, Cecil heard. The cantering thump came as a louder cadence now, and he could see her flashing through the trees, her once gold-red hair muted by age and woods shade.

The horse galloped into the yard and Shug lifted her arm to wave at him. Seeing her at that moment made him realize how much he had missed her, one of the few who were deep-rooted in his heart.

At once he thought about Otis, with his strong hands, kind spirit, and demanding demeanor. Otis walked the line between master and slave with the agility and honor to which Cecil aspired, but knew he never reached. The agility he had, the guileless ability to naturally turn any situation to his favor using his empathy, love of principle, and the perceptiveness he honed in his study of the men. Honor, however, was impossibly out of reach, buried under a barbecue pit in the woods. Honor was, for him, bound up in his masquerade as a man of the cloth, a man who let himself be seen by others as righteous since he could never see himself in that light. Otis was dying of cancer, he heard a while back, and he imagined it would be an honorable death Otis was dying, promising himself to get by to see him.

Up until he was thirty years old, Cecil visited Otis often, usually stopping by early in the evening with a bottle of sloe gin. Other evenings they would nibble on a six pack of airplane shots, tipping the miniatures to their lips while they smoked Alpine cigarettes, later Salems. They would debate where the best fishing holes were, commiserate good-naturedly about their wives, and wonder what the weather was going to do.

"Reckon it's going to clabber up and come a squirt?" Otis would say.

"Might. Corn sure does need it," Cecil would reply. They stayed in the safe zone with one another, even though Cecil was drowning in questions on the inside, rumors he was desperate for Otis to either verify or put down.

For some reason, 1976 was his year to go demanding answers, perhaps because he had turned thirty and figured, enough of this bullshit; or perhaps it was the whole bicentennial thing that made him reevaluate his life in the context of history and the incompatible, rumored mixture of African and Scotch-Irish in his blood. It was an all-around angry year. He was furious about the rumors defining him, bits and pieces of whispers he had to cull from, careful not say too much, protect this one, not offend that one. It festered in him like a sore from a tropical fever, until he found himself sitting opposite Otis on the slanted front porch of his little shotgun house on Pitch Hill.

Otis stabbed a thick index finger into the air, the way he only did when he was serious about his anger. "They is some things you flat out ain't allowed to ax."

"I'm asking anyway," said Cecil

"You always axed too many questions 'bout deep down business. Done it since you was a boy." He shook his head, yellowed eyes marbled with busted blood vessels.

"What is it to you? Why won't you tell me about my mama?"

Otis had simply set his jaw and shook his head.

"What the hell are you scared of? It ain't like I'm

going to say anything to anybody. But even if I did, couldn't nobody do nothing to you."

"Boy, if you believe that, you'd buy human shit from a turd seller."

"Old man, you're still living in the 1940s. Things are different now."

"And if you believe that," Otis spat in his toothless way, "you got a turd for a brain. And you done forgot yourself to boot."

"I ain't forgot nothing. I wish to hell I could forget what little I do know. Forget it and put the truth in its place."

"Done forgot yourself, I said. Done turned off into a businessman. Slick. Got a smooth voice, nice car. They's talk you be getting that station someday and won't you be some kind of smooth then." Otis laughed his aging cackle. "You be a regular pillow of the community. Maybe even the white community."

"What you getting at?"

"I'm getting at this: It don't matter none where you come from, and so there ain't no need to know about it. It don't matter who done who to get you. You black. All black. Boy, you think they going to let you up in they country club, let your children in the Three Breezes Academy done been set up for the little white children? You better remember where you come from."

"Goddamnit!" Cecil exploded. "How you going to tell me to remember where I come from when you won't tell me where I come from? How is it that you hold all the cards when it comes to me? Is it maybe because we're kin? That it?" His voice dropped. "Please, Otis. Tell me something. I won't say anything to anyone else. Not even Earline," he lied. "I won't go looking for nobody. I won't go chasing down my mama."

Otis was quiet for a moment, then, "Too many questions makes a mess. But go on, ax."

Cecil did not hesitate for any portion of a second. "They say your niece is my mother, making you my kin."

"Renee. Sweet as the day is long. Pretty girl. Bright skinned, like you. Lucy and me brung her up. She come to us when our own was most growed up."

"Where is she?"

"Chicago."

"Do you hear from her?"

"Some."

"Does she ask about me?"

Otis looked at the floor, rubbed his palms over his thighs, then looked full at Cecil. "I'm going to tell you this much," he said. "Then you got to leave it rest. You hear?"

"Yes, sir."

"I got some things. Letters and whatnot. They wrote out to you, from Renee. I already told Miss Sophie about them, and I told her when she say it's all right I'm going to give them to you. Miss Sophie, she all right. She the onliest one, though."

"But—"

"Hear me, now. When she say it's all right. Not no time sooner."

"So the two of you talk."

"Right regular," Otis said. "But that's something I ain't going to speak of no more with you."

The feeling that Miss Sophie and Otis were co-conspirators in the deceptions surrounding him gathered in Cecil as a storm of betrayal, but the fury he felt was overwhelmed by more curiosity. "Tell me why, Otis. Why did my mama run off and leave me?" Cecil studied every subtle reaction that passed across Otis's face, which at once clouded over.

"Just sorriness. Some folks is sorry like that."

"Is this the same girl who was sweet as the day is long?"

"I ain't saying no more to you about it. Not now."

"But someday? The letters?"

"Someday."

"Who is my daddy?"

"No more."

"John McCormick?"

Otis ran an ancient palm across his face. "Why you got to make me say what's best left alone?"

"All I want is what's mine to know. I know what they say. All I want to know is if it's the truth. It's my truth. It belongs to me."

"Yeah," Otis surrendered. Then he spat hard over the porch rail and repeated the name with more venom than Cecil ever saw him issue. "John McCormick."

There it was. And it left him unphased. But it had been a given, after all, something he had always felt. The real answer Cecil needed was about the circumstances of his own conception, whether he had sprung from something decent, or at least partially decent. "And how did he come to be with your neice?"

"Boy, you need to stop this."

"What happened? What are you afraid of?"

"Stop it right now. You got to remember I ain't no businessman, no big time radio disc jockey. Sure as hell ain't no future owner of WDAB, no big fish in this little old pond. You want to sit there and tell me I ain't got nothing to be afraid of? Then you come on and live up in this little shack and see how you get done. You'll see. You'll see you ain't nothing but a shotgun shack piece of shit nigger not worth they time."

Over time, Cecil's anger at Miss Sophie for the secret of the letters was tempered some by their very existence. The fact that his mother had bothered to write them was proof that she cared, at least. But he stopped visiting Otis so often after that conversation, and he now felt pained at the notion he might have only been visiting Otis out of a simple need to know the facts, not a genuine affection for a mentor who had been confirmed as a great-uncle. Maybe he was staying away to wait for the someday when Otis would feel free to talk without fear. Or maybe he was beginning to understand Otis had to protect his own by keeping secrets, even though they might help someone else.

Shug and Cecil sat at the round oak table as if not day the first had gone by. Initially, they laughed and remarked on how odd it was to be face to face again after living adult lives apart from one another. Then they owned up to what a shame it was they had slipped into their own respective worlds, and what screwed-up little worlds they were.

They sipped cold beer and crunched pretzels, like so many times before, when Shug would tell him about the most current true love, the latest must-have-him guy. But now she was a woman, a grown woman who was maybe, just maybe, ready for the truth or some part of the truth. And she was a woman who was throwing around words like "neutralize" and "exterminate" and telling him he was in some kind of awful jeopardy. Maybe they meant to have him killed, she insisted. But it did not make sense and Cecil said so.

"You just ain't used to this stuff, that's all. See, Shug, these small town politico types like to talk a game, play tricks, send bag men to the black churches. Skull-duggery. Agent, counteragent. They're like little kids playing 007. And they even use a lingo. Makes them feel like Big Ikes."

"But, Cecil. 'Neutralize'?" Her green eyes reflected a mirror-image of his.

"Hell, yeah. Look. This ain't the Mafia. They just mean a character assassination is all. Probably some personal dirt. And I admit there's plenty of it out there, but maybe nobody'll care."

"I don't know," she said. "You don't understand how—raw Rob is. And he feels threatened. More threat-ened than I've seen him in a long time. And he's para-noid as it is. What is so important about winning this election, do you think?"

Cecil stretched by drawing his shoulders in big circles, then rolling his head as he tried to relax. He had not realized just how worn down he was until he found himself back at the place where it had all begun. "It's pretty obvious," he said. "It's what Wade Connors mentioned to me just this morning."

"What's that?"

"Just about that push to restructure the tax code. You know, land taxes, to get big business—timber and whatnot, that is—to pay up."

"Sure, that's it. Rob's been going on and on about land taxes. I guess I shouldn't tune him out so often, but politics is so boring," she said. "No offense."

"None taken. Anyway, they want me to shut my mouth on air about it. They know how my folks will vote."

"So, yeah. Of course. It makes sense that they'd have to have a personal stake in it, right?"

"Yeah. That would have the most direct effect on you and yours. It ain't like they're in it to save humanity or anything."

"The McCormick Trust. That's the other part of what I need to tell you. See, I finally realize it's time I look into how that's being run these days."

"It's a big chunk of change," Cecil said. "The kind folks don't want to let go of, you know?"

"And it might affect you and yours, too, Cecil." She raised her eyebrows and nodded.

He looked squinty-eyed back at her, unsure if the

reference was intended.

"Hell, I know you heard the rumors, just like I did. Maybe it's true," she said.

"No maybe to it," he said. "I got it from Otis years ago."

"My god!" She slammed her palms down on the table. "Why didn't you tell me? How could you keep that from me? Does my mama know?"

"Shug, you know that wasn't for me to do unless you asked. You never was one to want to hear shit on your daddy. But it was bound to be true, if we go by the way things have played out with me and you. It makes sense."

Shug smiled. "Oh, I've heard more shit on Daddy than you know. I'm getting immune to it, I think. But this isn't shit, not about you. This is good stuff. And I don't have a bit of trouble believing it, even without Otis. I think I've always known, really. Still, I guess even with what I do know, there's a lot I don't know about my daddy, huh?"

"Everybody's got stuff hid up in them," he said. "Human nature."

"So do you think my mama knows?"

"Now how am I going to know a thing like that?"

She shrugged. "I just think you probably know more than most people about all kinds of things."

"Well here's something you should know: I ain't after none of your mama's money."

"What if you're entitled?"

"Don't want to be."

"Let's do this," she said. "Let's just agree that, down the line, fair is fair. Okay?"

"You say so."

"You know I mean it, too."

He did.

"But, like I said, I have to find out what's going on with the trust," Shug said. "So I want you to do something for me, tonight."

"What–"

"They're coming here, all of them, plus Rob. They're coming at nine. I heard him talking to Lee about it. Something about letting Rob 'in on it,' whatever that means."

"I think I got a idea what it means."

"Well, so do I, and I was thinking about hiding up in the loft and getting the real story."

"Hell no, you ain't."

"Well I won't if you'll agree to do it instead. That's the favor I wanted to ask. See, I don't know how I would get back to the house before Rob did. I never go out at night. He would catch on to something."

Cecil shook his head, knowing already he would agree, knowing moreover how crazy it was. "Damn, Shug."

"I know. It's us being little kids again, spying and sneaking around. But this involves you, too, you know. I'm still not convinced what they mean to do or not do to you."

"That ain't what I'm thinking, Shug. I ain't worried about that. They won't touch me. I'm thinking I been here before."

"What do you mean?"

"Nothing. Look. Sure, I'll see what I can find out."

"Will you stay the night here, too? Let me see what I can get out of Rob tonight. You know, when we're close. That's when his guard is way down. Then I'll meet you back here in the morning and we'll compare notes."

"You look downright disgusted."

"Prostituting myself to Rob is pretty disgusting, finally. But humor me. Please?"

"I don't know about staying here all night, Shug. I got a lot—"

"I'm doing all of this because I know them, too well. There's a side to them, all of them, that's capable of anything. You know?"

Cecil sighed and nodded.

"You'll stay the night. I'll call Earline so she won't worry, then you stay until I come back in the morning. Okay?"

"All right," he said, although he wasn't sure why. It wasn't because he gave any credence to Shug's imagination-running-wild concerns about his own endangerment. It certainly wasn't out of any kind of fear of the white men. In fact, he was intrigued by the idea of getting one over on them, busting her sorry husband. Maybe it was partly that he did not want to listen to Miss Honey Drop's bitching or look into Earline's wounded eyes and see the pain he was putting her through. Maybe it was just plain time to be here, in the place where he was so uncomfortable and agitated, where he was truly alone with the harpies and sirens cluttering his brain. Probably, for some strange, gut-wrenching reason, he needed to be here, inside this cavern of the past. It was not a pleasant place to be, that was for damn sure, but something deep in his belly told him it might be time to get himself through this post-poned rite of passage, if he could. Probably the exhaus-tion he felt was a gathering of his own worn out con-science.

Shug took a shaky breath and pulled the muted red ponytail from her neck, wiped at summer sweat, then mirrored his feelings back at him. "I am so sure enough exhausted. Tired."

"Of what?"

"Of being disappeared. Of being scared. Of being like my mother. She says things, you know. When she's been drinking, which is pretty much all the time."

"Like what?"

"Like how she hated Daddy. And it kills me. It does."

"I'm sorry, Shug."

"The other night she was talking, babbling on and on about Cash. I swear, I think she might have had an affair with him."

"Damn," Cecil said.

"I mean, she said a lot. About Lee, too. And you." She took a deep breath. "Did you ever? You and my mama? Did you?"

"Goddamn, Shug, that's crazy as hell."

"Sometimes I think Mama's crazy as hell—crazier than she used to get when she was drunk. She has this fixation on you, listens to you all the time on the radio."

"Sounds to me like she either enjoys my program or she knows what I am to you. But Lee and Cash, well, who knows?"

She sent him a hesitant glance, then, "You remember why I left."

"Sure. Sure I do."

"That's when I disappeared from myself, when I hurt so bad and took up with Rob. And you know what, Cecil? Rob is not a nice person. At all. Actually, he's a very mean person. He's capable as hell of putting someone on you. Mama thinks he's already stealing from the trust. That's really what got me paying attention to Rob's phone conversations, and it looks like she's right about what Rob wants."

"Money'll do it, all right," Cecil said. "Man, you really can pick them."

"Can't I, though? I guess he thinks he's got a hand on my inheritance."

"So how do you feel about that?"

She smiled. "It's funny. I almost feel relieved. That's the word, only it just now came to me. I've been out of love with him forever. Just too at home in my own little rut to do anything to change."

"How in the hell did you get so drug down by that man?"

"Oh, I did it to myself. And he was different back then. So close to God. So spiritual. It was like he had all the answers, like I could keep myself safe if I latched onto somebody with the answers. You know?"

"Seems like we both been trying to get our salvation from somebody else."

"I'm a damn idiot," Shug sighed. "And about a minute from ending up like Mama. Mad at a whole life because I got so stuck on image, looking like I had it all together. Is that crazy?"

"No crazier than the next person. At least no crazier than me."

They were quiet for a moment and Cecil was glad she was not questioning him about his own demons. She still understood his silent signals.

"Do you ever see Tammy?" she asked.

"Sure. Whenever I go see Miss Sophie. You ought to ride out there with me next week."

"I would, only—I just don't know if I can face her. I've missed you and her so damn much. But I've lived out the kind of life she would hate. Hell, I hate it."

"Come on, Shug. It's Tammy. She ain't never give a shit about window dressing."

Shug laughed. "That's the truth. You know, when we hit junior high and everybody started noticing how goddamn rich my family was, Tammy was the only girl in my class that didn't act like a big fat suck-up."

"So what you worried about now?"

"I don't know. I always wanted her to think of me as tough and all together, you know? Even though she did see how upset I'd get over Mama and Daddy, I wanted to be as tough as she was."

"Look, Shug. Tammy ain't all that tough. She's like the rest of us, deep down. Just playing her part."

"Maybe."

"No. Definitely."

"You know what, Cecil? I think I was sick with pride. One second I had too much and the next I didn't have one bit. I just knew I would have him either way. I was so sure Cash and I would be together, that I could have any man just because–" She stopped.

"You were just real, real young, Shug. Okay?"

"I don't want Tammy to see how shallow I am."

"*Was.*"

"I mean, how pathetic is it to be prepared to accept a man who's only after money or influence or something bigger than you are? Can you ever see Tammy doing that?"

"That's enough, Shug." Cecil leaned back in his chair. "You don't get to be pitiful for more than ten minutes and your time's up."

Shug laughed and held her beer bottle up in a toast. "Here's to the pathetic life I've been acting out."

"What about it? That life? What about Rob?"

"What about it is I think I'm just before finished with him."

"Can you go through with that?"

She chewed on her lower lip for a second. "I guess I'm fixing to find out," she said. "What about you? Are you doing right by Earline?"

"No. Sometimes I think she'd be better off without me."

"Don't be ridiculous. Just give up your girlfriends."

"I got to give up my ghosts first."

"I don't get it."

"Never mind," he said. "Just some shit I need to think about. That's what I'll tend to this evening." Even as he said it he was shot through the gut with fear. And even as Shug's horse galloped her away from DoeRun, he began to feel the ghosts circling.

The early band at the White Horse Club sucked, so Claud Pierce sat at a long bench behind the pool tables in the back room, watching Shirley Ellis lean her little tits across an expanse of green felt as she took shot after shot. He drank a Budweiser, then another, then a third, seething at his no-brained brother. When they were teenagers, Claud invented a phrase, "terminal infantile literalism" to describe the way Ronnie processed life's random pattern of information. Yet he still couldn't believe the scene he had come upon on the way home from the Cole County Jail—his dumb ass baby brother Ronnie masturbating in the middle of a dirt road while Cecil Durgin's nigger girlfriend sat in the truck reading goddamn *Field & Stream*. Of all the stupid things Ronnie had done in his entire stupid, terminally literal life, he had finally outdone his stupid self. So Claud had cold-cocked him and then ordered Ronnie to carry the woman on to the trailer, where Claud threw a couple of codeine tablets down her throat and locked her in one of the bedrooms. He had Ronnie nail a sheet of ply-wood over the window and after an hour of ranting and railing at Ronnie's stupidity, Claud slammed out of the house and headed for the White Horse. He had to sort it all out, decide what to do with her.

Beyond the bizarre autoerotic incident, which in and of itself would have been harmless, Ronnie had pretty much ensured that they would have big trouble with the law. It was a fucking felony. He had brought the bitch over the state line against her will, and she didn't seem to be the type that would let that go. Besides, she had some connections, folks who would look into it unless it was handled right. No way around it, somebody was very likely going to get charged with kidnapping, he figured, and he had to come up with a plan to make sure it would be Ronnie and Ronnie alone. Either that or get her all the way gone, as in dead, an option that he was not ready to eliminate just yet.

At the same time, he was turning the Cecil Durgin situation over and over in his head, rage spilling into rage until he could almost taste blood. It thudded through his ears with the furious rhythm of his heartbeat, echoing his daddy's words. Goddamn the son of a bitch, acting like the King of Cole County over at that jive ass station of his. And another vein of anger joined what already stemmed together in his gut, the hatred he carried for Cash Cloy and all the other pretty boy rich fuckers who ran things counter to how they should be run. His daddy had been right. They should have fucked that nigger up a whole lot better years ago, maybe even put him out of their misery for good.

Shirley leaned over to pop the cue ball with the long stick she worked between index and third finger, a mane of bottle-blonde curls dipping at the Harley-

Davidson wings pulled tight across two firm little mounds of breasts that only yielded a hint of cleavage. She glanced up at him and winked.

Claud made no response at first, simply took another swallow of Budweiser while Shirley pumped the stick six, eight, ten times. "Don't fuck your stick too long," he said finally. "You might make it come."

She responded by raising her left hand and giving him the finger. Then she grinned. "Maybe I will make it come, you think?"

He smirked and took another long swallow of beer, ignoring her question while he put Cecil back in the focus of his thoughts. Yeah, his daddy had been right about everything, but especially right about Cecil Durgin. That puny little firebrand he had laid on Cecil's shoulder had only kept him quiet for about four or five years.

It was the summer of 1963 when Cecil turned Cole County upside down, for a minute, anyway, but something had been coming for years. The Civil Rights folks set Cee-Boy Pierce ablaze with a renewed purpose, to defeat them no matter what; and he carried his two boys to Klan gatherings, to rally after rally all over the South. They went to meetings of the White Citizens' Council. They rode along with night caravans into pockets of rural black populations, firing shotguns out of car windows and leaving scattered, malevolent gris-gris of threats and flames.

It was The Little Rock Nine that set his daddy off, early on. Then Martin Luther King came along. Then, when Governor Barnett failed to keep James Meredith out of Ole Miss, Claud's daddy made a declaration: "This goddamn shit is personal now. They goddamn sure done made it personal, bringing it up in this goddamn state. Fuckers." He was more short-fused than ever during those years, and Claud and Ronnie were on the receiving end of more blind rages and hard-edged beatings than ever. Claud knew full well that it was building up to something, had to be taken somewhere, and it seemed natural for it to come upon Cecil.

In the summer of 1963 Governor Wallace stood in the schoolhouse door at the University of Alabama in Tuscaloosa, "right up the goddamn road," Claud's daddy said as they watched the TV news images. "That ain't much more than a hundred miles up the goddamn road. They already made it personal, but they damn sure in my goddamn yard now." Even the successful takedown of Medgar Evers did little to lift his daddy's spirits, and Claud knew that something had to give.

Cecil was seventeen then, had a radio show on the air a couple of nights a week. "Nigger music," Cee-Boy would spit, but it wasn't music the town was talking about a few days after the Tuscaloosa integration and the Evers killing. Instead, it was an editorial commentary, the first editorial Cecil, a skinny, snot-nosed boy, had ever delivered on air, and it would be the last he delivered until over a decade passed.

"Get in the truck, boys," Cee-Boy said the moment he got the phone call about what Cecil said, how he ridiculed George Wallace and came full out for "every single Negro citizen, every single Christian citizen, and every other citizen with a conscience" to rise up against segregation and work to use the vote to do it. Cee-Boy Pierce fishtailed his pickup all over the gravel road leading to the highway, then laid rubber as he headed for Sheriff Huckaby's office, a steady stream of curses sloshing around in the cab.

"Fuckers ought to have let me snip his nuts right then, the dickless motherfuckers. Letting a nigger kid go round thinking he's the big boar just because his mama's cunt got stabbed by some big boar white man. Piece of shit nigger."

"You know what you ought to do?" Ronnie offered. "You ought to lay another brand on him. Let me and Claud, like we done that other time. Only I'll do it this time, okay?"

Cee-Boy Pierce let fly his right arm, backhanding Ronnie in the mouth. Then Claud popped him on the back of the head, for emphasis. "Goddamn retardo," he said.

Sheriff Huck, reared back in his wooden swivel chair with his heels resting on his desk, did not appear to be surprised when Cee-Boy and his sons burst into his office. He let Cee-Boy have a good ten-minute rant before he held up his palm. "You're right," he said. "You're preaching to the choir. And we've already done met about it, me and the boys. This is something that's going to be stopped right here right now."

"Well I want a piece of him," Cee-Boy said, spitting into the trash can.

"Like I say, it's a thing to be flat sure put down and it will be. Hell, even Austin Price—"

"Austin Price ought to be busted up right along with him," Cee-Boy said. "Jew-fucking nigger lover."

"Only Austin Price ain't about to be busted up and you know it. Anyway, he's already made some things clear to Cecil."

"Like what?"

"Like he was way out of line. Like he'll be lucky if nobody messes him up. Like how he needs to keep his mouth shut."

"That ain't enough," Cee-Boy said. "I want a piece of him."

"That's another thing you ought to know by now. You ought to know you ain't going to get no piece of him. Not piece the first. But it's going to be taken care of. Me and Cash are going to take care of Cecil. With Big John's blessing."

Claud could feel his daddy's rage. It seeped from his pores and inhabited the space between them like an invisible hound of hell. He knew his daddy had no say in anything with McCormick's stamp on it, not in Cole County. Sure, Cee-Boy was king of Turner County, ran the bootleg operations, the crap games, carried a badge, even busted unions in Birmingham for the Big Mules, took orders from Bobby Shelton and the other players across the Southeast. Cee-Boy Pierce was a big god-damned part of the show-runners, in Turner County, Mississippi. But he wasn't no match for McCormick's millions, for McCormick's land, for his oil wells down in the Florida panhandle, McCormick's nigger son. And it drove him over the rim and into a volcanic fury.

"And what in the hell are y'all going to do? Make him skip recess? Write a hundred sentences? Ain't you got no kind of an idea what—"

"I said we'll handle it," Sheriff Huck said, dropping his feet to the floor for emphasis. "We got something lined up here shortly. Got a dove shoot this weekend. Cecil will get the picture."

"A fucking dove shoot? Hell, it ain't even dove season. You carrying the puffed up little nigger to a dove shoot? Hell, yeah, that ought to show his big boar ass. Why don't you carry him to the picture show and buy him a Chilly Dilly and a cherry coke while you're at it. Shit, don't even put him in the balcony. Let him sit with the white folks."

Sheriff Huck stood, his huge frame demanding respect and deference. "I told you, Chuckie, it's being handled."

"Handled my ass."

"It's being handled," Huck said again, and his tone made it clear and final. "Don't fuck with it. And you tell that to every last one of your hard tails cross the line. You know what's what, and you know how to keep it that way, you hear me?"

Cee-Boy glared a full thirty seconds. "Yeah, I know what's what. I damn sure know that. Problem is, don't nobody over here in Cole seem to get it."

They left then, but Claud knew his daddy would not let it go, could not let it go any more than he could give up breathing. Claud knew his daddy would have to get some kind of temporary satisfaction in the internal war he fought with the powers that were, that were just up the highway, one county over. And he was right. A few nights later Cee-Boy rounded up Stoney Crow, Bugger Red Maxwell, and Forrest Sims, loaded up his sons, and went riding the backroads, looking for an easy mark. It was not difficult to find one.

"Nigger up ahead, on the left," Bugger Red said, and the two Pierce boys watched out the rear window and into the bed of the truck as the targeted man protested and pleaded, then was roughed up and thrown in, his hands cuffed in front of him.

"You look like you could use a new pair of overalls, boy," Cee-Boy said when he reached the creek bank at Coalfire, where the man was laid out on the sand. And Cee-Boy set to popping the man with a bullwhip, beating him so hard the denim tore in bloody slits all up and down his backside. Claud was allowed a turn with the whip, felt his nerves tingle with the crack of the leather, felt the power of having a life in his hands, of deciding on the degree of pain to be inflicted. Ronnie, too, took a turn, but used it like the pussy he was, tentative and weak.

When the man lay with his denim in bloodied tatters, breathing soft moans into the sand, the dark skin of his face patched with light gritty grains that sparkled in the moonlit dark, Cee-Boy went over to the truck and reached in. "Here goes your new overalls," he said, chunking a fresh pair at the man, who did not move.

"Goddamnit, ain't you going to thank me? Done went to all this trouble to give you a new pair and you ain't got nothing to say?"

"Thank you." It was muffled, but it was said.

"What? What did you say? I ain't hearing right."

"Thank you," came the reply, before he added, "sir."

"Let's go, boys," Cee-Boy said. "We done our good deed for the day." But he still was not done with the bitterness. The taste of it lived in him, seemed to be secreted by his salivary glands and soaked into his words. "Goddamn Huck," he said. "Goddamn all of them. They know what they can do with their great long goobers. They can throw them big goddamn dicks over their shoulders and burp them for all the good they do. Motherfucking pussies."

Claud sucked on a fresh bottle of beer. Shirley leaned over the pool table, aiming a tight-jeaned ass right in his direction. Yeah, old Shirley had some pretty good stuff inside those jeans, but he couldn't let go of the thoughts, counterthoughts, and subtexted thoughts in his brain long enough to think about doing her. Not tonight.

Tonight he kept replaying how right his daddy was, all the way around. And his daddy was most of all right about the little club of rich boys who were so used to running the show, who always would run it, as long as their money kept the show in production. In that moment, with a sucking band thudding a sucking rhythm through the White Horse Club, Claud had to smile at the irony of his role in helping them with their own production, acting from time to time as part of their stage crew, when it suited them. And on the heels of that realization, it came to him full force that they would not let his daddy fuck with Cecil Durgin because Cecil Durgin was seen as better than the Pierces on account of Big John McCormick. Cecil Durgin had just a little trickle of high-class blood in him, so he had to be worth more than some trailer-dwelling piece of trash like Cee-Boy Pierce. Yeah, McCormick ran the show all right. Even now, even fucking dead, McCormick ran the show.

At that moment, Claud felt the pure tenor of his father's hatred through and through, understood more clearly than ever what moved the man who was such an indomitable presence in his life, and the thoughts kept gnawing on him. They bit at him, chewed on him, and masticated him into the deeper realization that he didn't really have to pin anything on Ronnie, after all. He didn't have to panic himself into a corner; he could simply take charge. He could go ahead on and fuck Cecil Durgin up, but good, and he didn't care at all what happened after. Hell, he could go ahead and fuck Cecil up to suit his dead daddy, and if things went too far, well, he didn't give a shit. He didn't give a shit because he would take that whole bunch of rich-ass pussies down with him if he had to, and wouldn't prison be sweet then? But he knew, too, that Cash Cloy, Lee Davis, the lot of them would save his ass if they thought it would save their own. And he had some information to bargain with, going back to how his own daddy's operations overlapped with some of Sheriff Huck's, and now, with Sheriff Huck's buddies. Hell, he could take all kinds of revenge for his daddy and stand a pretty good chance of getting away with it.

But first he had to find Durgin. He cursed himself for doping up the nigger chick so fast, but he had been needing to let loose on Ronnie's idiot ass right then, so they had shoved her into a bedroom at the trailer to sleep it off. But he wasn't too worried. She wouldn't be a problem at all. That bitch would put him on Cecil straight out, would do it gladly by the time he got through with her.

Shirley sauntered over, set down her beer, and straddled his lap, grinding against his crotch. "Hey," she said.

Claud took a sip of Budweiser, set down the bottle, and ran his hand up under her tee shirt, mashing his palm into her breast, squeezing hard.

"Mmmm, I been missing you," she said.

"That right?" He squeezed harder. Maybe he would go on and get a little, after all. Shirley knew a few things that put her out front of the pack.

She ground her crotch more firmly into his. "Don't you want to go out to the parking lot for a little while? I got some reefer in my car." She pushed blonde curls back from her face and grinned.

Claud looked at her for a moment, the white hair, the pleading eyes, the chipped front tooth where her ex-boyfriend hit her with a beer bottle. Then he thought about the clean, white teeth of the rich girls back in high school, and the girls who crossed the state line to drink at the Mississippi honkytonks, girls like Big John's daughter, who knew they were perpetually out of the grasp of hands like his own, hands with dirty fingernails, callused with hard work. And everyone he had ever known in his life, everyone who had seen him as trash and scum, every moneyed man who had paid him to run interference outside the law, every state line society woman who had seen him as a pair of hands that would never press against her powdered, perfumed purity, melded into two faces, those of Cecil Durgin and Cecil Durgin's nigger whore of a girlfriend.

"I got to go," he said. "I got some pussy back at the house I need to knock off in the morning. Get on off of me."

With her palms against his chest, she pushed herself up and grabbed her beer. "I don't get you," she said.

Claud gave an ironic laugh. "No, you don't. Not tonight, anyway."

She spun, flipping blonde-dyed curls, and stomped off toward the bar. Claud appreciated the swing of her hips, the switch of her ass, the whole package of her attitude, until she was swallowed up by a crowd wrapped in a haze of cigarette smoke, blue jeans, and bad music.

Tammy Sims studied Wade Connors' face across the porch of her mobile home as she spoke, but could not get a feel for what he thought of her story, the one Miss Sophie passed to her. Tammy's inclination was to go straight out after Cash, Roscoe, and Lee right this very minute, put a dog cussing on them along with some handcuffs. But Wade only nodded, "The hell you say," interjected into her monologue every so often. Bastard. He was hard to figure sometimes, but that was one reason she liked having him around, a regular visitor at her trailer. This was no visit, though. She had called him as soon as she got Miss Sophie situated, saying, "Wade, I need a law enforcement officer out here. Bring your bullet." Then she went about her weekend ritual of snake-skinning, laying the rattles and sheaths out on the tin roof of a shed to dry in the morning sun the next day. Finally she showered away the subtle reptilian smells, the dirt trail dust, and got ready for bed.

Now, still damp from her shower, she sat with Wade on the porch, waiting for him to declare his intention to arrest someone for Charity Collins' murder. Citronella candles danced light across summer scents of rosemary and mint leaves from her herb garden. The screened porch was shrouded in tree limbs moon-glowed by an occasional breeze, blankets of chirping crickets and gulping frogs, and, finally, the sweet-weedy odor of the marijuana she grew out in her woods. If he was going to sit there dumbstruck, she was going to by god smoke a joint. She exhaled a thin cloud across the porch, tossing a glance of defiance along with it. "You ain't going to arrest *me* are you?" She took a sip of iced tea.

Wade laughed and leaned back in the rocking chair where he sat. "From what all you just said, looks like I got me a murder to look into. Me and Andy G. know how to prioritize. So go on and smoke your old nasty dope."

"Intend to, ass-hole." She took another drag just to prove her point, then knocked the fire off the end and set it aside for later.

He had spent plenty of time on her porch in recent months, late afternoons when he sipped on a beer while she told him about the ways of the old folks. Other times he might swing by for a cup of coffee before work or show up for a midday lunch, courtesy of Mayree, the Wildwood cook. It was pretty incredible, he thought, that Tammy Sims had bestowed upon him a drop-by-anytime status no one else had with her. He felt a bit honored by it. Besides, he enjoyed her company. And he had to admit to himself that she was nice to look at, even nicer now, with her light, barely brown hair down, the wet ends brushing freckled shoulders. She was wearing a blue cotton nightgown, a thin little piece of nothing in which she moved about unselfconsciously, outwardly comfortable as she was with him. He could make out the white borders of her panties whenever she stood. He could follow the subtle motion of her breasts as she rode an old metal glider back, forth, back. He could discern the darker push of her nipples beneath the sheer fabric when the light was right, even as she moved. He felt as if something feathery was blowing around in his stomach, and he focused on making conversation.

"How's Miss Sophie?" he asked.

Tammy sighed. "Oh, you know. Nervous wreck. I

had Rita give her a sedative."

Wade chewed on his cigar, staring into the night's metropolis of sounds.

"Well, what about it?" Tammy said.

"What about what?"

"Damn you, Wade Connors, I just told you about a murder. You're the law, ain't you? Ain't you going to get off your do-less ass and go solve it? Oh, wait a minute. I forgot. It's done been solved. All you got to do is pick the sons of bitches up."

"Don't know that that's possible," he said.

"Hell, Wade, it ain't like they're on the run or nothing. They're probably at the country club over in Columbus, having a martini and all you can eat steak and lobster."

"I got to look into some things." He spat tobacco juice into an empty coffee can at his feet.

"Well, shit. That's all I can say. Except for this: ain't it right up on election time? You want my vote or not?"

He grinned. "I ain't worried about your vote. That's one thing I know I got."

"How can you be so laid back about this? I'm so mad I could spit blood."

"You see a body anywhere?"

"What in the name of the Apostles are you talking about?" Tammy demanded.

"Oh, not much," Wade chuckled. "Just the corpse of Charity Collins. You know. Dead. Which is how you generally know somebody's done been murdered."

"No shit."

"No shit don't cover it. A corpse is pretty much one of the requirements, don't you know."

"I'll help you beat it out of them. You know Lee Davis don't want his soft little face messed up. And Cash Cloy's as in love with his own good looks as he ever was."

"It's a good thing I am laid back about it and you ain't in law enforcement. Your temper wouldn't never let you make a decent case." But he was turning Miss Sophie's story around and around in his head. This was big, as big as it got, and he didn't want to fuck it up.

"All right, then," Tammy said. "What about the walking-around, opposite to dead body of Cecil Durgin? Where the hell is he?"

"I've studied about it, asked around."

"And?"

"Well, his wife Earline ain't heard from him, so I ran by the station. Only thing interesting there is his girlfriend's car and a busted up coffee cup."

"So you think he's just shacked up somewhere?"

"Looks to be," he said. "Maybe they like to make up after a good fight."

"Well if that ain't just like you, to think he'd be shacked up with another woman."

"Either that or he's gone whole hog. Took off with her."

"Oh, come on, Wade."

"Hell, it happens. You ought to know that, right?"

Tammy took a piece of ice from her glass, put it in her mouth, and blew it across the porch at him. "'Course

I know, ass-hole. But Cecil Durgin is a far cry from Jerry Wayne Tolbert. The son of a bitch I had the misfortune to marry was born to be a cheat. Cecil might play around a little, but he wouldn't never leave Earline. We used to talk about shit like that."

"Point is, I just don't see any reason to go at the thing without Cecil confirming it first. Let's face it. Miss Sophie's old. She's probably shy a few brain cells."

"You're a goddamn fool if you believe that. She's sharp as she ever was."

"Maybe," Wade said. "I guess we'll see."

"Maybe you're the one that's light. Do you even remember ever hearing about that girl's disappear-ance?"

"Just a few things over the years," Wade said. "I asked Huck about it when I took over, but he said wasn't nothing to it, that she'd run off is all. But I admit, Miss Sophie's tale is interesting, especially the part about old Huck being out there that night. Too bad he's already took his story to the grave. I want to hear it from Cecil, though. Straight out of his mouth."

"Oh, you'll hear it, all right. And if you don't plan on looking into anything, you can bet Miss Sophie and me will be."

"If you want to do my job for me, help yourself. I got some reading to do anyway," Wade said. "Girl, you must have one sad, boring life."

As soon as he heard himself say the words, it hit him. He was describing his own life. He read his way through the days, books interspersed with the small-town duties of an arm of the law, then went home to his catatonic addiction to cable TV before he swallowed a Valium, or two or three, and finally slept. Alone. He only had to have his heart busted up once to know he would not give it away again, so he laughed and joked with scores of acquaintances, then scampered into himself when no one was around. And it was a lonely place. It was unusual for him to be visiting anyone at night, aside from a bar every once in a while. It was even more unusual for anyone, at this hour, to be visiting Tammy Sims in particular. She was more of a loner of an evening than he was. Most times, Booty-Cop took night calls, but her call gave him a lift of anticipation and curiosity. It was a welcome excuse to pay her a visit. And, what with the story she recited, the blue nightgown, and the good company, he considered this visit well worth forgoing a few hours of television.

"Well," Tammy said, "I hope you've got room in your jail down there for, oh, three very prominent citizens. Let's see, that would be one putrid little sissified banker, one fat-ass old lawyer, and one full-of-hisself good old boy."

"Good thing we turned Claud Pierce out today," Wade mused, "or the motel might be getting full."

"Claud?" Tammy leaned forward. "Did you say Claud?"

"What about it?"

"It's just that Miss Sophie mentioned that name as one of the children with those Klan guys who attacked her and Cecil."

"Come on, there's lots of Clauds around the state line," he said, while he silently inventoried and eliminated the ones he could think of.

"Does this one have connections with the old Klan folks?" she asked, feeling her face heat up. Her own stepdaddy had been active back when she was in high school, would have laid her out had he known how much time she and Shug spent alone with Cecil.

"Could be," Wade said, and by his tone she knew it was a yes. "But what I'm really curious about is your interest in Cecil. Aside from Miss Sophie, that is. Got any beer?"

Tammy went into the kitchen, the light through the open door catching her shadowy form beneath the silky fabric, the curve of her waist, the swell of her hips, and he couldn't help wondering what it would be like to brush his palm down her back, all the way from her shoulders to her thighs. Whatever it was that drew him to her was magnified now by an unfamiliar longing, something he never felt with the women he met in clubs, women he never brought home, content as he was with a fast blow job or a quick fuck in the back seat of a car. Tammy had the sharp common sense and the easy humor it took to engage him, draw him into a dimension he did not know with other women.

She brought out a Budweiser and handed it to him. The pop and spew of the aluminum can took her back to the clubs in Columbus and out narrow highways, where she and Shug would pull over to pee, open another can, and go chasing down adventures. When the bars closed, she told Wade, the two of them would land at WDAB to share silly little teenybopper secrets with Cecil and ask for advice. During the girls' senior year, Cecil, then twenty-three, had just gotten engaged to Earline, the preacher's daughter he said had everything he imagined a woman could. "He told us he would give his life for Earline," Tammy said. "He said he would consider that an honor. Shug and I thought that was sweet as hell."

"I'd call it stupid," Wade said. "To be that wrapped up in a woman."

"You would," Tammy said, thinking of her own stupidity when it came to men.

Jerry Wayne Tolbert and Cash Cloy were all she and Shug had to show for their forays into the opposite sex. Both men were overpowering, Jerry Wayne in wild, intimidating strength, and Cash in charisma and raw sex appeal. Both were steeped in danger, Jerry Wayne's brand bound up in unpredictable flashes of not so pure kindness and utter meanness, Cash's hinging on his status as an older, handsome, married man, who also happened to be Big John's Hemingwayesque right hand. Tammy and Jerry Wayne carried on an in-your-face brawl and kiss, while Shug and Cash had an ongoing secret rendezvous at the hunting camp or out in the game refuge. Jerry Wayne had Tammy snake bit with needy addiction, and she was jealous when Shug went away to college, leaving Cash behind. "Cecil was the only one who knew about Shug and Cash, besides me," Tammy said.

"And what did Cecil think about all that?" Wade asked, intrigued. He always suspected Cash of dipping into the boss's daughter.

"Cecil thought it was fucked up, of course, which it was. He said Cash Cloy collected women the same way he collected deer heads, and Jerry Wayne was a coward who could only be cruel to anybody who cared about him."

"Damn that Cash Cloy," Wade said. "Right under Big John McCormick's nose, too. That guy has a set of balls that won't quit."

"So did Shug," Tammy countered. "At least she did before Cash and that goddamn Rob got a hold of her."

"And what happened to old Tammy's balls? I seem to remember a chick who didn't take much shit if she was backed up in a corner. How do you explain your years as Mrs. Tolbert?"

Tammy stared off into the night-blackened woods, the dark hobgoblin of her deepest self. Darkness held the thick, syrupy smell of whiskey riding warm breaths across the slurred dreams of an eight-year-old, when her stepdaddy would stand beside her bed and put her small palm to the thing that lived there beneath the curve of his huge, hairy belly. She would try to shove pictures into the grainy dark, try not to see him, not to feel the mash of her tiny hand into his, but she could not pretend his looming form away or conjure anything that would color the dim shadows of her bedroom, not while she looked into the dark. So she would close her eyes tight, so tight it hurt, sending bursts of light against her closed lids. And all the while, as he moved her palm along the creature he coaxed with his own, she would see nothing but the black-eyed Susans growing along the highway, or yellow buttercups at Easter, or her mother's azalea bushes, hot pink and white. She would bathe herself in floral colors, fending off the dark and the molding of her fingers to the creature taking shape there, his boozy breaths laced with cigarette scents bearing down on her eight-year-old body. She strung the flowers into garlands spiraling out around the little bed until his breaths hit hard and the thing spat venom across the pistins and velvet petals she had laced through the thick layers of the night.

Wade was startled to see an expression of unhappy bewilderment on her face, a serious look she rarely offered anyone, least of all him. They maintained their high school friendship over the years with a steady banter of good-natured insults masking the just out of sight attraction, and there was never any talk of serious concerns. Even when Wade was a deputy, years earlier, and came to arrest Jerry Wayne on assault charges, charges Tammy dropped the very next day, they joked with one another.

"I had to kick his ass, Wade," she said. "He wasn't scrubbing the kitchen floor shiny enough to suit me, so I had to knock him around a little. You understand how it is."

Wade sighed at her apparent stupidity, the pink palm print blistering her cheekbone, the cut kissing her upper lip, and her unwillingness to change it all. "Just you kick his ass a little harder next time," he said. "Or call me and let me kick it around a little bit."

She laughed, slapped his upper arm in mock anger, the way she always did, three times, palm, backhand, palm, and said, "Go catch yourself a real criminal, Barney Fife. And don't forget your bullet."

"So?" Wade asked again. "How do you explain your marriage to that son of a bitch?"

She narrowed her eyes at the moon-bathed woods, and the look of fragile uncertainty had "pretty" written all over it. "It's strange you should ask that," she said, "because ever since Miss Sophie broke down this afternoon and told me all she'd been through, I've been wondering myself. How do so many of us get lost, or mistreated, or all wadded up with folks who are so bad for us they spoil us for the next person?"

Her eyes were liquid reflections of moonlight, another shock to his senses. He had never known her to cry. She was always so hard-nosed, tough. "What. did you come up with?" he asked. "I sort of need to know, too."

She smiled. "I know you do. I know a lot more about you than you think I do. But here it is. There's one answer that's real easy."

"What's that?"

"Just that I wanted to get my stepdaddy to love me and Shug wanted to get back at her daddy. I mean, Cash was like a son to that old man. Hell, Big John was eat up with wanting his own little boy. Remember? He didn't make no secret of it at all."

"I see what you're saying."

"Sure. Shug had to at least be a little jealous, you know? She had to be mad at her daddy, so what better way to get even?"

"And you?"

"Obvious. Marry a man who'll treat you as bad as your stepdaddy, the only daddy you ever knew. You got daddy's love, right?"

"You've thought a lot about this."

"Yeah, but Miss Sophie put another slant on things. I told you I had the easy answer. I didn't say it was right. Bullshit is easy, but it ain't necessarily true. Hell, it usually ain't."

"So what messes us up?" Wade took a long sip of beer.

"One thing. Just one," she said. " Secrets." Tammy's eyes spilled then, sending glowing pokers into Wade's gut. Crying women were things he went out of his way to avoid, and he was relieved when she continued talking. "It's so sad to think of all the secrets we keep in us, how they just eat us up inside. What Miss Sophie went through was too horrible to think about. But we all have those things in us, you know? I have them. You have them." She wiped her face, rubbing tears into freckled cheeks. "But Miss Sophie scraped up the guts to say it all out loud, and now things can maybe be put right. You see my point?"

Wade bit down on his cigar. He was beyond uncomfortable with the whole conversation, but drawn to it at the same time. He rose and walked over to sit beside her on the glider, then nudged her with his elbow, an attempt to take refuge in humor. "Go ahead, then," he laughed. "Tell me one of your secrets."

"I'll tell one of yours, instead," she said.

"All right. But make it a good one."

"Oh, it is," she said. "It's one you think nobody knows."

"Well?" he said.

"It's just this: you are one scared shitless mother-fucker."

"I'll give you that," he said. "But I guess it takes one to know one."

"Yeah," she said. "I guess that's one reason Cecil was always so understanding with Shug and me. I mean, imagine how scared he must have been, only twelve years old and knowing all what he knew."

Wade nodded, thinking back on the times Cecil had been on the edge of his life. He had been there for Wade to envy for his presence in the hunting culture of Cole County and for his freedom and his free-wheeling disc jockey personality, yet now came the revelation that Wade's hero had been cut at his most vulnerable, manipulated into secrecy as a child. Cecil had been used by a gang of men who always did as they pleased, never minded repercussions, and threatened children if necessary.

Some wrinkle in Wade's memory at once smoothed out so that a picture crystallized. It was a mental snap-shot he had long ago tucked into some part of his interior where he kept the thoughts and images he did not really want to have. It unfolded on its own, though, unstoppable, and he described it to Tammy as they sat on the to-and-fro sliding glider.

It was a picture of a group of men standing near a pond alongside a plowed field in the afternoon heat of early summer, waiting for the dove to come in. He was with his daddy, at a shoot on John McCormick's land. It was an oddly rushed gathering, and at the wrong time of year for dove hunting, but Wade's daddy shrugged it off. "Look here, boy. We ain't going to shoot them all. Just a few. Just enough to check your shooting eye. Besides, Cash Cloy wants to work his dogs. Says they're lonesome."

Wade's daddy had instilled in him the code of the hunt, a disdain for poachers who took what they wanted from wherever they wanted; and trespassers who plundered the back sides of posted ponds; and cheaters who slaughtered doe out of season or set out at three or four A.M. on the day of a hunt, to shine and kill a deer, then waited until daylight to drag it out of the woods; and petty liars who claimed birds that weren't theirs; and riffraff who dynamited for fish or dragged seine nets up little sloos. These things mattered. Other laws, laws that applied to life in the hamlet, could be broken. At six, he could wink back at his daddy when they visited Sister Frankie, the colored bootlegger, of a Sunday. At ten Wade could drive the backroads in his daddy's truck. At twelve he could drink a beer at the camp house while he watched the men play poker. And at fifteen he could even fuck the whores the older men brought out to the camp house. "Training wheels," they were called, and Wade had been with more than a few.

But the laws guarding the outdoors were never to be taken lightly, and where there were no laws related to sport, then honor mattered. Wade still felt ashamed of the time, at the age of eight, when he used a treble hook in a clear pond to snatch orange-bellied bream right off their sandy bedding. He snatched seventeen bream off the bottom without offering the first worm before his daddy noticed and lectured him about it. His daddy was principled about such things, and now his daddy was taking him on an off-season hunt.

"But—" Wade began.

"But what?"

His daddy's face wore an intimidating, challenging expression, and all Wade could manage was, "But it's illegal."

"Yes sir, I reckon it is." His daddy looked thoughtful for a moment, then he blew a sigh. "But hell, the game warden's up the Tenn-Tom, checking fishing licenses. And if he should show up, all it'll take is a fifty-dollar bill from Big John to get him gone." Still, the whole event, looking back on it, seemed contrived; his daddy's demeanor out of character; and, looking back on it, Wade felt he could now put it all in its proper context.

Big John, Lee, Roscoe, Cash, Huck—they were all there, along with maybe a dozen other friends of McCormick's, men and their sons. Cecil and Otis were there, too. A couple of dogs, a Lab and a Golden, lounged panting in the shade beneath John McCormick's pickup.

Wade was about twelve years old, so Cecil could have been no older than sixteen or seventeen.

He described for Tammy his being in awe of Cecil's status as one who knew the ins and outs of any hunt, able to predict what its given prey would do, called upon by the men for his perspective, a quiet and capable expert in his own right. As a young boy who wanted to spend all of every day in the woods, Wade thought Cecil had it made. He got to go on all the best shoots, got to fish exclusive ponds, got to take hunting trips to prime land around the southeast with Mr. Big John. That had to be the life.

But on this specific day, Wade sensed a shift in the usual atmosphere of spirited humor, overlaid now by a glinting blade-edge of sharp resentment. There was a tense undercurrent in the men's bearing toward Cecil. And on this day their interactions with Cecil went from kind regard to perverse ribbing tainted with low-down meanness.

It started off with the cap, Wade remembered. Cecil was wearing a brand new-looking cap, nothing fancy, just new and clean, with some kind of fertilizer logo on the front as if it had come from the Co-op. Early on, during a lull, Cash Cloy walked over to Cecil, squinted at the cap, shook his head, and quick-snatched it off Cecil's head. Then the tossed it up in the air and blasted it with bird shot as it met the ground. "You know better than to wear new shit out here," was all Cash said, while the other men chuckled, muttering to one another. Cecil only looked bewildered and attempted a chuckle himself, before dropping his eyes, keeping them down for a while.

Somehow Wade sensed, at the time, it was a direct result of the talk about integration and Civil Rights filtering of late into Cole County. There seemed to be an outward anger building toward black folks in general. A few days earlier, his own daddy was cursing about something Cecil said on the radio, but Wade did not know what. And now, on the heels of Tammy's revelation, Wade wondered aloud if the men had not been going to an inordinate amount of trouble and manipulation to make a point, with four of the men sending a very distinct message: You'd better keep your mouth shut about a lot of things, Cecil, but especially about Charity Collins.

The full force of the men's abuse of Cecil grew with one of Cash's jokes on Roscoe Bartley, his usual target at the time. Cash took Wade's daddy off behind a stand of pines and had him pee into a plastic funnel in the mouth of a Wild Turkey bottle while Wade looked on, intrigued, as always, by the antics of the men.

"Damn if I ain't out of piss," Wade's daddy said, shaking his penis after putting out about an eighth of a bottle of urine. "Go on, boy, and add some."

Wade and then Cash contributed to the creation of the no-proof Wild Turkey piss, Wade feeling grown-up, important enough to be included in some kind of prank, even though he had no idea what the prank was to be.

"I know what will really sweeten it up," Cash said. "Hey, Cecil!" he yelled. "Come over here a minute."

Cecil gave the man a puzzled look when Cash told him to pee in the whiskey bottle. "I got to have this full of piss," Cash said, "so it'll look drinkable, like it hasn't been long opened."

"But—"

"Just piss in it, goddamnit," Cash commanded. "And don't nobody say a word to Boscoe."

Cecil unzipped his canvas trousers and topped off the pee the rest of them had contributed. Then they went back to the shoot.

"Bird, Billy, behind you," someone called.

"Goddamn, they fogging in fast."

"Got the wind pushing them."

"Bird, Huck."

The dove came and went in waves, meeting with bursts of shot from Remington and Winchester pumps.

"Low bird," someone would warn.

"Got one in the bushes. Fetch, Maggie!" And the Golden would race to the brush, returning the downed creature to Otis, who opened a big aluminum ice chest and dropped it into a feed sack fat with the kill. They wouldn't bother about sorting the birds, would probably send the bloodied mounds of gray feathers to Pitch Hill with Otis, who would in turn share them with family and neighbors.

Finally there was a lull in the appearance of any birds, and Cash reached into the bed of his truck, bringing out the whiskey bottle full of piss. "Wild Goddamn Turkey," he said to Roscoe. "We ain't going to be shooting much longer. You want a drink?"

"Hell yeah," Roscoe said, leaning his shotgun, a Belgium Over and Under, against the side of the Ford.

"Best stuff made," Cash said, unscrewing the cap. "Here you go, buddy."

Roscoe took the bottle and threw his head back. Almost immediately, the bottle came back down and Roscoe was sputtering and spitting onto the turned earth while the men and their scattering of sons slapped their legs and sent a chorus of laughter across the field of dirt clods. It was funny, Wade remembered, until it turned against Cecil.

"What in the hell is this shit?" Roscoe said, still spitting.

"Well it ain't shit at all," Cash said, while the men roared. "It's piss."

"What?"

"Yeah, piss. You know, pee. Urine. Like that."

"God Almighty!" Roscoe said, gagging a little, spitting some more "Goddamn your ass."

"Eighty proof piss, contributed by Ben and Wade Connors, myself, and Cecil Durgin," Cash smiled and let this sink in.

Roscoe's eyes grew larger. "Cecil?" he said, spitting. "Nigger piss? What the fuck—"

"Hell, Roscoe," Cash laughed. "It ain't going to kill you. We was just having a little fun. Right boys?" He let his expression go serious. "Right, Cecil?"

But Roscoe had already strode over to where Cecil was standing and slugged him across the face, sending him into the mounds of plowed dirt. "Did you know what he was up to?" he demanded. "Did you, boy?"

Cecil, dazed, squinted up at him. "No, sir."

"You better not be lying to me or I'll beat the shit out of you. Did you know what he was up to?" he demanded again.

"No, sir," Cecil said, then he dropped his head. Wade remembered feeling humiliated for him, sensing a dim anger for something he was not quite understanding.

"Leave him alone, Boscoe," Cash said, laughing. "He didn't know what I was going to do with it."

"Fucking nigger piss," Roscoe said, and he spat one more time, in the dirt right beside where Cecil sat, sending flecks of white spittle across the boy's pants leg. "Somebody give me a cold beer. Jesus."

In just a few minutes the afternoon was slipping into sunset as another wave of birds came in. Crashes of gunfire sent pellets against the sky, birds plummeting zigzagging paths to earth.

"Yeah," someone said.

"Got him," someone else said.

"I believe that one was mine, Billy."

"Good one," came from another.

Wade thought he himself might have even hit one, a rush of conquest searing through his bones. Then he noticed Cecil was still sitting in the dirt and it at once dawned on him. The older boy was seized up with fear, afraid to move without a word from someone—one of the men, or even a boy, like himself. He wasn't sure if he was allowed to make the gesture, but he couldn't ignore what his conscience told him was the right thing to do.

Wade extended his hand down. "Here you go, Cecil."

"Yeah." Cecil took his hand and rose.

"I think I got one," Wade said, trying to talk past the demeaning halo of shame settling upon Cecil's bowed head.

"All right," Cecil said, flat-voiced.

Otis was just about to set the dogs to their task when Huck said, "Don't you reckon them dogs are tired Cash?" And he jerked his head toward Cecil.

"Hell yeah, they're tired," Cash said. "Carry them on back to the house, Otis."

"Kennel up, dogs," Otis shouted, and the pedigreed pair jumped into the back of Mr. Big John's pickup.

"Cecil!" Cash shouted. "Get on out there and start picking up them birds."

Mr. Big John walked over to where Cash stood, and Wade, the only one near enough to hear, caught their words.

"I think you made your point," Mr. Big John said.

"Not just yet," Cash said.

"That's enough."

"It's got to be done," Cash said.

Mr. Big John sighed. "I'm going to the house." And he walked back over to where Otis had the dogs loaded up. "Let's go," he said, climbing into the cab of the truck while Otis stepped up on the rear bumper and threw his leg over to join the dogs. Mr. Big John raced the engine, spinning tires throwing up a burst of dust, and sped off, tossing Otis and the dogs around in the truck bed.

"Go on, Cecil," Cash shouted again. "Go get the goddamn birds. Them dogs was wore out. Good thing we brung you along to take up the slack."

Cecil glanced at Wade, and the green eyes set in brown skin were listless with surrender and crippled pride. Wade tried to give him a glance of reassurance in return, confused by the men who, to Wade's knowledge, had never been overtly unkind to Cecil. He watched as the older boy, the boy whose life he envied and coveted, walked out across the field with a feed sack. Cecil picked up the kill, fallen from an azure September sky now blushing bronze in gradual declensions of shades, with the lowering of the sun. Cecil picked among the dirt clods, walked along the furrowed rows of mounded soil, small clouds of field dust rising from his steps. He moved with a posture of supplication, kneeling and rising, bringing the limp-headed little fluffs of bloodied gray, one after another, up to the feed sack. He walked and stooped, walked and stooped, gathering the small creatures dotted with shot and blood, the blood and a few stray feathers sticking to his hands, while the men, guns broken, barrels to the dirt, stood silhouetted against the sunset, passing bottles of bourbon and fine Scotch whiskey.

"God," Tammy said at the close of Wade's harsh reminiscence. "God."

The two of them were silent for a moment, then Wade said, "I wanted to help him. You know, pick up the birds. But I knew I shouldn't or I'd be breaking the rules. It's the damndest thing. I just sensed that I wasn't supposed to help him, you see?"

"You were only a kid. What else could you do?"

"Yeah," he said, clamping his teeth down on the cigar, rising.

As he stood, Tammy caught his hand and pulled herself up. "You were just a kid. Just like Cecil was when–Jesus, I hope he understands that there was nothing he could do. For that girl."

"How could he understand that? With the way they did him?"

"That's where we come in, don't you think?" And she rose on her toes, took the cigar from its perch, and put her lips against his mouth, just for a couple of soft seconds. "You see how scared you are? Can't even kiss a person back."

He let his hand slide down her arm. It was impossibly soft. "I might could," he said. "I'll give it some thought."

She smiled. "Well, if you're going to do much kissing, you might want to rethink the cigar."

"Don't know about that. I ain't much for change."

"Oh, I don't know. I'm coming to see that change is a good thing." She put her palm to his cheek, running her thumb across his chin, then rose again on her toes. This time he could feel the push of her body against his own when she touched his lower lip with her tongue, a gentle little brush of her tongue, before she returned his tobacco and said good night.

Miss Honey Drop Davis opened her eyes, just a crack, to a black room and the smell of rank perspiration. She wanted to open her eyes all the way, but they would not work for her. She wanted to throw the sheets back from where she lay in an unfamiliar bed, one minute a slow-spinning merry-go-round of a bed, the next minute a sluggish roller coaster of a bed, the next a raft of a bed on rolling waves. She was all consciousness sliding sideways in the darkness, nauseated, ears humming, and she could not for the life of her get her arms and legs to move. Her head was thick, and trying to shuffle the fuzzy thoughts around took every bit of her will and concentration.

Cecil. Where was he? He had been at the station. Had she confronted him about the contract? Her mind began to doze. No, she told herself, you have to stay awake and figure this out. Think.

He couldn't talk now, he told her. He had to go to the hunting camp and meet somebody but he wouldn't say who.

Is it a woman? She demanded.

Nothing to worry about, he said.

Sure, nothing to worry about, she thought, trying to get another fix on where she was. She could hear rock and roll music, booming bass, frantic drumbeat. Everything was mixed around in her head. I'm on some kind of a bad drunk, she thought, feeling her eyelids close, slipping into the unconsciousness that suffocated her like a fat feather pillow. But she was not panicked or clawing against this overpowering angel of sleep. Instead, it was nice. It was deep, relaxing, and now she wanted to be down inside the dark. She wanted to let it take her into its anesthetic blackness and keep her there. She let her eyelids relax, abandoning the struggle, feeling herself fall the short rest of the way into it, not caring, not knowing, and slept.

As the dusky evening bore down on nine o'clock, Cecil made sure the lights were off, the door locked. He decided the air conditioner would seem less suspicious if left running; otherwise, the men might wonder why the house was so cool, wonder who just now turned off the thermostat. He decided Shug's idea about hiding in the sleeping loft made sense. It would be dark up there, the men unlikely to go near the stairs. Still, just to be on the safe side and to give himself a clear view of the living room and bar area, Cecil decided he would watch through the railing from beneath one of the four-poster beds in the loft.

When Cecil heard a car approaching, way up the dirt road, he climbed the stairs to the sleeping loft directly above the kitchen and TV area. He lay on his belly and slid beneath a bed, positioning himself so that he could look through the chenille-fringed hem of the bedspread, through the railing, and down into the open great room. He couldn't help feeling a bit foolish, hiding there like a little kid, but he had a gut feeling Shug was not wrong about the great swindle taking place right under her nose. The sons of bitches. He had watched them over the years, learned their capacity for self-interest. Tonight, once again, he would watch and learn.

He wondered for an anxious second if they might

stay the night, but that would not make sense, not on a Sunday evening when they had to work on Monday. Probably they would have a few drinks while they talked business, then leave. Cecil witnessed a good bit of business talk at DoeRun during its decades of existence. In fact, Big John's desk and safe were still here, angled in the back corner of the room where the walls were lined with framed maps of the McCormick pine forest. Cecil could remember plenty of times when they carried on passionate arguments, the men standing around the desk, studying large papers they unrolled and spread out before them, talking about pulpwood and heart pine and dry holes and natural gas. They made more than a few big decisions about big money at this castle of a cabin in McCormick's big woods.

When Cash Cloy, Lee Davis and Roscoe Bartley came in, laughing, cursing, accusing one another of leaving the air conditioner on, mixing ice-clinking drinks of Scotch, Cecil drew back just a little, there beneath the musty mattresses. The rattle of the ice cubes, the tenor of their voices, the fact that he watched from an unseen place, all blended to give Cecil the feeling of being a boy again, a boy all set to be laid low by the things he would witness. The men had put on several lamps, giving their little stage an eerie, confined glow, while Cecil watched from the shadows over their heads, thirty-two years obliterated by the raw shock of revived emotions blistering his gut, even now, in the lightning strike of a passing moment.

"All I'm trying to tell you is, if Cecil turns up

maimed or dead or something, we're fucked." Cash
Cloy was saying, slouched back on the sofa, resting his
heels on the heavy pine coffee table. Age coated his
good looks with a sprinkling of gray curls and a weathered tan, both of which only served to make him more
striking to the women who still pursued him, hoping to
tap into the McCormick jackpot.

Lee Davis spoke from an oversized leather chair
near the bar, where he sipped Scotch to steady his
nerves. "But nobody specified he should be kidnapped
or," he hesitated, "killed, right?"

"Who would be that fucking stupid?" Cash replied.
"Unless it was you."

A braided rug served as a backdrop to Cecil's point
of view. It roped around in circles of brown, rust, beige,
and olive, resembling a giant target. So he was right.
Shug had been overreacting to the men's intentions
where he was concerned. In a brief burst of relief and
confidence, he smiled to himself, thinking these men
had become nothing more than sad parodies of their
youth, buffoons with sagging testicles and thinning hair.
Then, just as quickly, Shug came to mind and Cecil
thought better of taking the men too lightly, with too
much humor. He was nudged by the insistent, building
sense of deja-vu. And once again, he let himself feel the
emotional reality of how far they had gone in the past.

"Y'all wait a minute," Roscoe said. At sixty-three he
seemed to consider himself the patriarch of the group,
an attempt to fill Big John's role as level-headed referee.
"Let's just back the hell up. Tell us what you said to him,

Lee."

Lee squinted for a moment, too long, as if feigning thought. "All I said was what we talked about."

"I should have gone," Cash said. "Lee don't know how to talk to them boys."

"Shut up a minute," Roscoe said. "Think. What do we know for sure? What are the facts?"

"Booty-Cop said Miss Sophie Price is making a fuss, that Cecil is missing," Cash said.

"And there's no way on earth to connect us to that," Roscoe said. "Only thing we did was get Lee to pay a visit to Pierce, give Pierce a few hundred to carry Cecil out to the woods, tell him to think about backing off, maybe plant a little seed behind that honey hole of his, right?"

Lee fidgeted, took another drink. Cecil hated the fact that Miss Sophie was upset about him, but he appreciated the fact that he was relearning not to underestimate the extent of the men's arrogance. Hell, they actually got some outlaw, some mouth-breathing redneck flunkie, probably, hired up to try to scare him into toeing their line. Unbelievable.

"Right, Lee?" Roscoe challenged. "You had a talk with Claud, didn't you?"

The name sent a chill of unconsummated recognition over Cecil, a piece of the kaleidoscope of his memory, broken loose and lying at the bottom of the tube, but he couldn't think how the name fit. He focused with new purpose on the conversation.

"I talked to Ronnie first," Lee said. "Then I told

Claud all that about Cecil's girlfriends, this latest woman and all. Gave him five hundred."

For a moment Cecil marveled at how much his political dismantling was worth to them, but he could not shake the odd, familiar feeling to the name they tossed around—Claud. It caught in his mind like a synaptic hiccup. There was something to be uncovered in that name.

"Wait a minute," Cash said, rising, taking on his intimidating stance. "Wait a goddamn minute. What did you tell Ronnie?"

Lee ran his hand through the graying beard he had taken to wearing in recent years. "Well, I guess—I guess I told him more of the same."

"What would that be?" Cash demanded, standing over Lee's chair. "What were your words?"

"I don't know. I might've—"

"Exact words," Cash said.

Cecil watched Lee's physical response, the way he shrank back from this person he tried to emulate when they were young. Cecil could almost see them as they were, years ago, playing poker at the round oak table, like they were that one particular night, and a swampy bog sucked him down into the past, the men's voices echoing in the high-ceilinged room, just as they did back then.

"Fuck," Lee stammered. "I wasn't with Ronnie but a minute before his brother ran him off. I might've just said something like we needed to neutralize Cecil Durgin."

"Jesus goddamn Christ! Well, there you go, Roscoe," Cash said. "That's what you get when you send a stupid fuck like Lee to talk to goddamm Claud Pierce. He talks to Ronnie. And Lee don't talk Ronnie's language and it makes for misinterpretation, you know?"

"What kind of misinterpretation?" Lee asked.

"Like you don't know what a dumb ass fool like Ronnie Pierce would do to 'neutralize' somebody. You dumb fuck."

Roscoe held up his hands. "Everybody just relax. Stop jumping to conclusions. Didn't Booty say Cecil probably ran off with his piece of ass? Didn't he? Goddamn, y'all are carrying on like a couple of women. There's nothing to worry about."

"Shit," Cash said. "I hope you're still saying that next week."

"I will be," said Roscoe. "Anyway, Ronnie doesn't get involved in Claud's doings, from what I understand. Look. The thing we got to turn our attention to is how we're fixing to solve the Rob Overton problem."

Nervous perspiration beaded up on Cecil's upper lip, and he swiped it with his index finger. This was too familiar, hiding and watching them, a familiarity taking him back to the dank earth beneath the holly bush, back to the minutia of those degrading moments playing out to his peripheral eyes. But now they were talking about Shug's husband, and his concentration went toward confirming her suspicions.

"So we all agree there's only one thing to do about

it," Roscoe said. "We all know that."

"Oh, I don't know," Cash's tone dripped sarcasm. "Maybe we could have him killed instead, you think? Old Lee Harvey here could pick him off like a sniper, if he didn't shoot himself first. What about it, Lee Harvey?"

"Goddamn, Cash, let it drop," Roscoe said. "Nobody has had anybody killed around here."

"Not lately," came the bitter reply.

"Shut the fuck up, Cash," Roscoe said. "Don't take your ass into territory that's gated and locked up. Don't say or do anything that goddamn stupid."

So they did acknowledge what they had done, at least to themselves. But there was no sense of responsibility or regret. Cecil took on all of that. He watched them move about on the big bull's-eye of a background, watched as Cash drew up his knee and push-kicked the sole of his boot full into the leather chair where Lee sat, still sipping his Scotch. The back legs of the chair left the braided rug and scraped the hardwood in a little skid, sending Lee's drink sloshing ice and liquor to the floor.

"Goddamn, Cash. What'd you do that for?" Lee yelled. "Now I got to make me one from scratch." He went to the bar, then came back and dabbed at the spill with some paper towels.

Cash strode over to the long couch and plopped down on it. "Okay, I'm with the program," he said, switching over to a light tone, his way of messing with Lee. "What's the deal with Rob? He's kind of a runty little bastard. Tight-assed. I never would have figured

Shug to go for him."

"Well, she did," said Roscoe. "And ever since they've been back he's been studying the books, looking into the trust, asking all kinds of questions about how we take bids on the timber, and on and on."

"So exactly how much does he know?" Lee dropped ice cubes into another glass of Scotch.

"He's not stupid. I'm pretty sure he's got it all figured out."

"You think he told Shug? Or her mama?" Lee asked.

Roscoe leaned back in his chair. "I know this is chancy," he said, "but I get the feeling Rob doesn't mind keeping things back from Shug, not with this kind of money involved. He would have said something to her by now and we would have heard about it for sure. I think he'll be quiet if we let him in."

Cecil filed their every word concerning Rob away in his brain. This could make it all very simple for Shug, if what they were saying was true. But Rob would be there shortly, he knew. It would be something else to get it first hand from that sorry husband of hers. He wiped his upper lip again on his knuckle. It was claustrophobic there beneath the bed, with the men's voices rising up and corralling him like a spooked pony.

Cash sat up. "Now that's low. That's low down. Shug don't deserve that kind of shit."

Shug didn't deserve your kind of shit either, Cecil thought. But at the same time he was satisfied Cash could show some sense of justice, however jolting and

ineffectual, where Shug and her husband were concerned. Yeah, Cash could make to care something for
Shug, but Cash wasn't offering to get himself out of
whatever deal the men had going to plunder
McCormick's fortune.

"Well it's the same kind of shit that'll keep the rest
of us in some extra cash for the time being," Roscoe
said. "Matter of fact, I want to talk to Rob about selling
off a few hundred acres of timber from the east end."

"Who's bidding it?" Cash asked. "The usual?"

"The usual plus one," Roscoe said as he walked
toward the door. "And I think the new boy just drove up."

"I don't like it," Lee said. "Life would be a lot easier
if we just had Miss Kate to deal with. All we'd have to
do is keep ordering up cases of Absolut."

Cash cut a look over to where Lee sat, slowly getting
inebriated in his linen suit. It seemed to Cecil the years
gone by only intensified Cash's contempt for Lee, contempt no longer half-heartedly masked by jokes and
treks into the woods of a weekend. Both their marriages
ended in divorce, but the two men could not even forge
a bond from their parallel loss. Lee tried, in his familiar
way, to lock into some aspect of Cash's world, plug into
the kind of machismo he could not scrape together in
himself. And he failed so often he gradually gave up, let
apathy and Scotch have him.

As Roscoe ushered Rob Overton into the great
room, Cecil inventoried his first impression, an initial
estimation of Shug's husband. What he saw right off the
bat was a swaggering rich boy wanna-be who was not

near good enough for her. Based on what she had told him earlier that day, Cecil figured he was a parasite in disguise, a brag-about-it-I'll-pray-for-you-even-though-you-didn't-ask-me-to Christian, a coward who hid behind self-righteousness, a hell of a hypocrite. Bottom line, a loser, like Lee. They belonged in the same category, along with all the Lees and Robs in the world who aspired to be the Big Johns and the Cashes.

There were a few rounds of perfunctory small talk, played out as if on a fairway, with all the sincerity of a ball sneak-tapped to a spot on the green where a birdie was a sure thing. There were smooth chuckles, a couple of jokes of the "did you hear the one" variety, and a round of drinks before Rob was invited to give his perspective over to the group. And Shug was right. Rob knew enough to know the men were somehow making a couple of large side profits from the trust through a couple of questionable corporations.

No argument ensued, no marking of turf, no threats of legal scuffles. Instead, there was loud laughter, laughter Cecil recognized to be insincere even if Rob did not.

"Damn, you're good at what you do, boy," Cash said. "Hey, Roscoe, we need this guy."

"You think so? I ain't so sure," Roscoe said, playing at a touch of "bad cop."

"Hell yeah," Cash said. "The man's got to know as much about hiding money as he knows about finding it."

"That's a good point," Lee said.

"I'm not convinced," Roscoe insisted, and Cecil caught Rob's pained look of confusion. They were not about to let Shug's husband think he could just march up and take the upper hand. "What do you say about it, Rob? What can you bring to our little group."

Shug's husband fidgeted with his belt buckle. "It's like they said. I'm a natural with money. Always was. Made a name with the firm in Seattle."

"Already got two accountants," Roscoe said.

"And Rob here can do the work of three," Cash boasted. "Ain't that right, Rob?"

"Don't mind if I do say so."

"Well..." Roscoe squinted at him.

"Come on, Roscoe," Lee said. "Let him in."

"Oh, all right," Roscoe said. "Come join the team."

"Congratulations, boy." Cash said, handing Rob a fresh drink, taking the empty glass over to the bar. "You ain't got no idea what kind of fine club you're in."

"But you need to know the guidelines," Roscoe said. "And nobody deviates from the rules."

"Like?" Rob asked.

"Like we're honor-bound to the common good, have been for decades," Roscoe said. "It's tradition. If you're with us, then it's from here on out. That never changes. Understand?"

Rob took a sip and nodded. "I think that's the only way it can be," he said. "And I look at it as part of my responsibility to Shug."

Cecil rolled his eyes. This guy was even worse than he thought. Balding and wiry, he wore a look of arrogance along with the uniform: khakis, a starched white button-down with the sleeves rolled up above his wrists, alligator skin belt, and topsiders sans socks. He probably had a closet full of the same damn uniform.

"Well sure it is," Roscoe said.

"I didn't see it that way at first," Rob said. "I had to think on it a lot. I had to pray about it, about how to handle this where my wife is concerned. It could be misunderstood, so I wanted you fellows to hear me out."

"Feel free," Roscoe said.

"Well, as y'all know, I'm a Christian. And I've always been a believer in the man as head of the family. I was brought up that way, and it's the right way."

"Just don't let my wife hear you say that," Roscoe laughed.

Rob maintained a serious face. "I have a responsibility to Shug, to take care of her," he said. "And a part of my taking care of her is to handle her money, make decisions she shouldn't have to worry about. That's why I'm going in with you. So I can better take care of my wife."

His reasoning was certainly well practiced. Shug's husband obviously thought it all out in advance, knew right where he would fit in. Cecil watched as Rob set his glass down on the coffee table, on a folded newspaper, on today's Editorial Page, which rested where Cecil had left it. He had forgotten all about it, felt his body shift forward by millimeters, as if to swoop down like a bird of prey and carry away this evidence of his presence.

Cash spoke up. "Well it sure as hell sounds noble.

Going to look out for Shug. By God, ain't she a lucky girl."

Cash was on to Rob, that much was certain. And, if he took notice of the newspaper on the coffee table, Cash could be on to Cecil, too. He watched the men in relation to the folded paper. If someone picked it up, noticed it was today's, then they would surely wonder how it got here, wonder who brought it here. They would begin listing everyone who had a key, a circle that only extended beyond them to Miss Kate, Shug, Otis, and himself.

Rob reached down and picked up his drink. Cecil could make out the circle of wet on the newsprint. "Beyond that," Rob said, "I want to be sure I don't walk off empty-handed. I mean, just on the off chance that she and I, you know, don't stay together."

Cecil was so focused on the newspaper he did not take in the significance of Rob's words until Cash began interrogating him.

"Whoa, now," Cash said. "What's that all about?"

"It's personal."

"There ain't nothing too personal to put in between this bunch. Part of the deal is you lay it on the table. Anything that affects the group. Put it right here." He slapped his palm on the coffee table. His fingertips hit the newspaper.

Cecil flinched, then forced himself to relax. So what if they did discover him here? What could they do? He would still know what he now knew about Rob. They had already said too much. In the space of a heartbeat, though, Cecil knew they would go as far as they needed to go, do whatever it took, to hold on to their respective pieces of Shug's fortune. "You and yours, too, Cecil," she had said. And even though he had been adamant in his initial refusal to share it with her, wouldn't it be a fine feeling to take it from the swindling, conniving hands now raising glasses of premium liquor to their lips, the hands of the men who had, more than once, set out to break him down.

Rob's voice rose. "You wait a damn minute. I don't feel that I should have to—"

"But you do," Roscoe said. "We all do. The common good, all that. You can't have it both ways. Let's be god-damn clear about that."

Rob's face reddened. He stood, knotty-fisted and quivering. "I'm not used to taking orders, hanging my dirty laundry out. You three are the ones who have been raping the trust. I wonder what my mother-in-law would think about that."

Cash chuckled. He picked up the folded newspaper and rolled it up while a prickling jolt of fear shot down Cecil's spine. "He don't seem to get it, Boscoe." Holding the rolled up paper in his right hand, Cash tapped it in the palm of his left. "Hey Lee, you want to kick his ass or should I?"

"Shut up," Lee said, scratching at his beard. "Ain't nobody beating nobody up."

But Cecil wished somebody would get beat up. Any of them would do. It would be a sort of entertaining kind of revenge. He watched Cash twist the rolled paper between two fists. Keep twisting, he thought, so it's ready for the trash and not ready for getting noticed.

Roscoe stood. "You better know something, Robbie. We've been here a lot of years, go way back with the McCormicks. We're as much family as you are. More. So you feel like getting into a pissing contest with this bunch, you better drink several hundred gallons of water. You want to take any information to Kate McCormick or your wife, then you better consider what they would think of this conversation. You need to always keep that in mind."

Cash rose, tossed the wrinkled tube of a newspaper behind him on the couch, and sauntered over to where Rob stood, on the opposite side of the coffee table. "Want to open up the safe?" he said to Roscoe, who had taken a seat at the bar. Then he turned back to Rob. "You got to see ol' Big John's safe. That safe yonder." He indicated the antique block of iron beyond the fireplace, behind Big John's desk. "Now sit your ass down."

Rob sat, wearing an expression of fresh intimidation, while Roscoe walked over to the safe.

"See, our fearless leader Roscoe, being a right swift attorney, is very thorough. And he likes to play games, some serious, some fun," Cash said. "You like games?"

Cecil felt a swell of nausea wash through his stomach at the mention of the word. In one breath, the month had gone from August to November. It was as if he were twelve years old, spying on the white men. Roscoe set about opening the safe, began turning the dial, little muted clicks whispering across the room and up to the loft.

Rob gave a nervous laugh. "Sure. I like games."

"Good," Cash said. "Then you'll appreciate this."

Roscoe pulled open the door to the safe to reveal piles of papers, videotapes, small cassettes, and reel-to-reels. "We've always documented major events relevant to the group. Good documentation keeps us all in line," he said. "You wouldn't believe all the serious conversations catalogued in this thing. And the not so serious." He fumbled through a stack of videos, then slid one out of its cover and tossed it to Lee. "There are even tapes of me in here. Me bringing in a twelve point. Me and Cash sitting on Lee's head, gassing him. Me in compromising positions, even, but I'm honor bound to keep them all. Hell, some of them reel-to-reels go back over thirty, forty years ago. Back when Big John got that first tape recorder. Some of them probably disintegrated already."

"He'll put the tape of this meeting in there," Cash said. "We'll pull it out from time to time when we want to make a memory."

Roscoe laughed. "Part of your initiation is to put up with Cash Cloy's stupid jokes." He picked up a hand-held recorder from his desk. "And, yeah, I'll be sure to file this away."

"Yeah, boy," Cash said. "See, Rob, you're kind of a serious fucker. So I'll be on you when you least expect it. Sort of whip the sense of humor into shape. And old Lee, there, he'll teach you to shoot."

"I shoot just fine," Rob said, his voice back down to

its resigned volume. "And I don't need any help with my sense of humor."

"What sense of humor?" Cash said. "And what about you and Shug?"

Rob sighed. "All right, damnit. She's just different since we came back here, that's all. Okay? Just a real gradual change into I don't know what. It's just different. That's all."

The sound of a woman moaning cut into the conversation. Lee had apparently put the video in and turned on the TV beneath the loft where Cecil hid. Although he couldn't see the picture, Cecil could make out the flickering glow fanning out across the men on the target. "That's one of the not so serious tapes," Roscoe said. "We get kind of crazy out here sometimes."

"Lisa!" Cash yelled. "I remember her. Lisa with the fine butt. She was a good old gal. But this is some boring stuff. Show him something from Game night."

Cecil studied Rob's face while a fresh tide of nausea flooded his stomach. Rob was mesmerized, eyes reflecting the soft light from the television. Religion or no, pussy gets them every time, he thought. Pussy was the great equalizer.

"Naw," Roscoe said. "That would be too overwhelming for the boy. Save it. And cut the volume. We got to talk."

The woman's moans went silent, but the strobe of the television still played across the room. Lee walked out from under Cecil, went over to Rob, and threw a booze-friendly arm around his shoulders. "Pretty good show ain't it? Wait till you see a live one. It'll be our way of welcoming you in. You like poker?"

"Don't gamble," Rob said.

"Oh, not that kind of poker," Lee said. "We got our own special game we play, maybe once every year or so. It's a game where you get any fantasy you ever tucked away up here." He tapped on Rob's temple.

Cold perspiration and a stab of sick dread took Cecil again. It was still so fresh, especially now, as it replayed in the back of his head like a needle stuck on a forty-five.

"Save it, Lee," Roscoe barked. "We got to talk business."

"Oh, come on, let him know what the boys got to offer in the woman department," Cash said.

"Yeah," Lee squatted and breathed liquor at Rob. "You have secret desires, right, boy? Something you don't dare share with Shug 'cause it might be too far out from her sexual territory? Something that turns you on so much you'd do it all the time if you could. You know what I mean, right?"

Cecil studied the younger man's face, the flicker of intrigue that brushed across his eyes. Of course he knew. This money-grubbing husband of Shug's would be on their next whore like white on rice.

"Y'all are out there on a useless tangent," Roscoe said.

"Fantasy," Lee said again, winking at Rob before he meandered back to the big chair.

"Can we get down to business now?" Roscoe said.

Rob cleared his throat. "So tell me how the bidding process goes." He got up and took a seat across the desk from Roscoe.

"Well, it's pretty straightforward," Roscoe said. "Lee there manages the McCormick Trust, pays all our salaries, supports the family, as you know. Cash acts as broker, being as how he's overseeing the farm and the timber. What he'll do is cruise the sections I have in mind, do a little surveying and marking, then he'll set the minimum bid. You'll give us a good price, right, Cash?"

Cash chuckled. "Fair market value."

Cecil had to believe that whatever he learned tonight would be worth the specters and ghosts oozing out of cracks in the ceiling beams, curling around him like the vapors guarding tombstones. They were coming at him fast, whispering to him that she was waiting for him, had been expecting him, knew he would see to her.

"Naturally I take care of all the legal aspects of the trust," Roscoe went on, "so I'll advertise the sale and gather up some bids. Enough bids, you know."

"What about me?" Rob asked.

Roscoe smiled. "You, Mr. Overton, are to be hired for professional services by GreenTree Lumber, Inc., down in Barbados, who I assure you will be the successful bidder and ultimately the purchaser of the timber we're offering for sale. All you got to do is submit a bill to me, which will be promptly paid, along with any expenses you might incur."

"Expenses?" Rob leaned forward.

"Hell, you know," Roscoe grinned. "Two or three phantom employees would certainly go unnoticed. Aside from that, all you got to do is keep your mouth shut and you won't wake up with an ice pick stuck up in your head. Clear enough?"

"Yeah, real clear," Rob said, as Roscoe began unfolding some tract maps and plats.

Cecil watched Rob watching Roscoe. Rob was loving this, Cecil decided. Yes, by god, this boy was a snake. Old No-Shoulders himself, if his fixation on the Lord were any indication. This was a guy who could use the Holy Bible to justify indiscretions, lies, and downright criminal behavior. Cecil had known folks like him all his life, folks full of spit and fire, fast on the draw when it came to the accusatory finger, slow on laughter. And once there were a couple of rounds of The Game to showcase the musty corners of Rob Overton's secret interior, that would be the nail in his coffin. And that secret interior was bound to have some interesting twists in it. Yeah, this was a guy who could be tapped over the edge of sanity with ease, if need be, and the other men knew it. This guy was a natural for the role they would all eventually scramble to avoid, that of scapegoat, fall guy, too bad so sad. It had not happened yet, but Cecil knew they would be prepared. If the shit ever hit the fan, then an easy-to-crack looney like Rob Overton would come in handy.

The video was still throwing out light, reflections of hunting camp parties, when the business talk wound down. While Roscoe worked at the late Big John

McCormick's desk, planning out ways to steal the late Big John McCormick's money, Rob, Cash, and Lee lounged in the sitting area in front of the TV. The men were silent for a while, until an apparent turn of a camera, an odd angle, perhaps, elicited a response from Rob. "Damn," he said.

Cash Cloy laughed and raised his glass. "I want to drink a toast to Rob. You know, boy, I think this could be the beginning of a beautiful friendship."

Cecil watched the men watching the silent screen, their faces fixed on the screen, each face fixed with the same primal expression he remembered from the one particular night. It was a look of rank intensity laced with cold confidence, a look that would strip away the armor of its prey and quarter its exposed flesh with a slow blade. And beyond the men and their soulless stares, through the kitchen, and out the door, he knew she was waiting for him. Charity Collins, their blundering victim, was out there in the humid dark, expecting him to come and put it all right. Cecil watched the men watching the screen, at the same time promising her a rendezvous, wishing he could make it all fade to black.

She couldn't decide what time of day it was, but it felt like mid-morning. She had to go by body clock, since her fingertips had earlier discovered, upon opening the room's only window, that it was covered with a sheet of plywood, the door closed and locked on the outside. The room eeked a damp odor of sock sweat, the smell suspended in the dark like paper mill smog. There was a lamp, though, and she reached up to switch it on. The honky-tonk rock of Lynnard Skynnard backdropped the clutter everywhere: several rods and reels leaning in a corner, an assortment of pornographic magazines sprawling a montage of tits on the floor next to the bed, two tackle boxes, a chest of drawers spilling jeans and T-shirts, a couple of mounds of what had to be dirty clothes, which explained the smell. Honey Drop Davis sat up, too fast, on the edge of the bed. She put her head down, dizzied by a spinning grogginess making her queasy all over again. Pills. They had given her pills, she remembered. In between all the yelling and cussing, they had agreed that she needed to be unconscious for a while. Two white boys the age of men at least a decade older than she was, one a mook-ass halfwit and the other a cold-eyed vessel for all the demons of Dixie.

She could hear snatches of the argument before she passed out, and she willed some pieces of it to replay through in her head. "Where the hell did you ever get the idea you was supposed to shoot his ass?" and "You ain't got no verbal skills. Hell, you got a terminal case of infantile literalism. Don't you fucking know that words have more than one meaning?" and "This ain't like the good old days, shit for brains, when just any old nigger could be offed."

And what in the hell, she wondered, was she doing here? She couldn't make sense of any of it.

The mean one was still yelling and cussing in spurts, going on twenty-four hours later. She could hear him once in a while, above the rock music thumping through the trailer. Yes, it was a trailer, she remembered, where the scrawny, ponytailed one called Ronnie brought her. A trailer where the other one called Claud made her swallow some pills that knocked her on her ass.

Claud was the one who brought her up short with unfamiliar fear, but it was Ronnie who picked her up in the first place. He slung gravel when he wheeled into the parking lot at WDAB yesterday afternoon, just a while after Cecil left, ran off to some hunting camp to see some slut, probably. She was not about to follow Cecil's instructions and get a new tape started on its way to whatever rural radios were receiving WDAB's transmission that day. He slammed through the door and hollered at her. "Where is he? Where the fuck is Cecil Durgin?"

"Who wants to know?"

It was then that he pulled the nine-millimeter out of the back of his jeans. That fast and for no apparent reason. But he struck her as more nervous than anything else. "You just better cooperate with me 'cause I ain't nobody you'd like to have to deal with, okay? I'm a mean motherfucker, okay? Now where is he?"

She thought of the Smith and Wesson in her own purse, the sequined emerald green bag cradled beneath her right arm. She also knew not to go for it, not now, not with that big barrel of steel pointed in her vicinity by a very skinny, very ugly, very jumpy Saltine. "Look, Sweet," she said. "Calm down. He'll be here any minute I bet."

"You a goddamn lie. I bet you know right exactly where he's at."

"Even if I did, you think I'd put a crazy white man toting a gun onto him?" As soon as it came out of her mouth she wished she could take it back. She heard one of Cecil's sayings in her head: *You done let your alligator mouth overload your mockingbird ass again, Honey-gal.*

"Shit! Why does everything get fucked up when I do it? Huh?" He threw his fist against the wall, sending a framed picture smacking into the floor just as his expression morphed into one of recognition. "Wait a goddamn minute," he said. "I got a gun so fuck you, okay?"

"And I want to know why you come up in here with a gun."

"Can't you just do like you're supposed to? Huh? Shit. Don't nobody do right by me." He grabbed her arm. "Come on."

"What for?"

"You're fixing to go with me."

She wrenched free. "I ain't going nowhere with your crazy ass. You might as well just shoot me now."

"Well–Well, you think I won't? Huh? You think I won't blow your face off? Huh?"

Her mouth took her across the line again, too far. "No, Baby. I think you'd fuck that up, too."

"Goddamnit! You ain't the goddamn boss of this here!" He got another grip on her arm and tightened it as she tried to clamp the same arm down harder on the purse. "I come all the way across the county to round that nigger up and goddamn if he ain't here. Don't nothing go right for me. Nothing. Fuck!" He jerked on her with more wiry force than she imagined he could have, sending the green spangled purse skidding across the floor.

"Who the fuck do you think you are?" she yelled, drawing back her leg to aim it dead into his left shin, eliciting from him a kicked-dog yelp. He did not, however, let go of her arm.

"You can't do that!" he said, lifting his wounded limb, hopping sideways. "You've done hurt my leg, now."

"You can't come up in here waving a gun at me and expect me to kiss your narrow ass. I don't do no kind of ass kissing." And she drew back, kicked him again, harder.

"Ow!" He hop-danced her against the wall, their

feet sending pieces of the broken coffee cup tinkling across the floor. "Fuck! Them is some pointy-assed shoes."

"Leave me the fuck alone!" She squirmed against his hold, but he had too much of his meager weight pressing her into the wall, left forearm against her chest.

"You're going to get your ass still," he said, and the deep, hollow clack of the hammer being thumbed back gave her pause.

Her beaded pocketbook was long gone, she was pinned against the wall by someone who could crush her windpipe if his arm slid any higher, and she was in the dark about who and why and all the etceteras that went along with it. She had to use her head. "You're mashing me," she said.

"Well, you made me do it, acting like a crazy fool."

He was flat sure disgusting, with that mangled pony-tail raked in greasy brown rows back from his forehead, where a raised vein pulsed a blue line across his flesh. He was close enough for her to see a scattering of tiny skin tags along his left eyelid, rubbery little bits of flesh mixed in amongst thin eyelashes. He leaned even closer to her face, and, along with a set of nicotined teeth, she could see that his expression was more fearful than menacing.

"I'm going to catch hell because of this." He pressed the barrel of the pistol under her chin. "You've done fucked it all up and you're coming with me. I ain't about to show back up at the trailer with nothing."

The steel was cold, the blue vein throbbed, and he

was too tense and haphazard for her to chance any resistance. Not now. She was right fond of her face, so she decided to wait until her head was not in danger of being exploded before she acted. She would think of something, she knew. He didn't seem too bright. She nodded yes.

"You ain't going to be a pain in the butt, right?"

She nodded again. She couldn't think what this man might want with Cecil, but, angry as she was when she first arrived at the station, she was now overcome by a need to protect her man, or her ex-man, or whatever Cecil was to her now, with a little curiosity thrown into the mix. What could this boney-assed redneck have to do with Cecil Durgin?

He lowered the gun and pushed her toward the door.

"Hey," she said. "Would you be a Sweet and grab my purse for me? I don't go nowhere without it."

"Aw, to hell with the purse," he said.

"If you say so, baby, but if some laws come up in here, find my car out yonder, my pocketbook on the floor, and no me, well, you know they going to think foul play right off."

He narrowed his eyes in pained contemplation. "Shit," he said. "You stand right there, by the door." He kept the pistol trained on her. "Don't do nothing with your feet. If you kick me when I come back over there I'm going to shoot you for real, okay?" He backed over to the purse, scooped it up, and put it under his own arm. Then he led her out to a dented-up blue pickup patchworked with Bondo, "Get in." He pitched her handbag into the bed of the truck.

"Why'd you do that?"

"'Cause if you're like the women I know you got some of that Mace shit in that bag. I ain't stupid, you know."

"You going to tell me what this is all about?" she asked as they pulled out onto the highway. She studied the serpent tattoo coiled around and around his right forearm, the fingernails acting as vessels for black grit.

"Can't."

"But you would if you could?"

"Yeah." Out of nowhere he decided to pound on the steering wheel, five times, punctuating each hit with a "Fuck!"

Honey had run several scenarios through her head, plans for the upper hand, and the only sensible one was to keep him talking. Her own weapon, after all, was out of reach. Besides, she had only shot the thing a few times, certainly never at a real, live person. She only planned to use it to threaten Cecil into releasing her from their contract, and that had damn sure turned into one big joke. Best to rely on her charm for the time being.

"Claud is going to be pissed," he said. "Peee-oh'd," and he looked as if he might cry.

"Who's Claud?"

"My big brother. Mean motherfucker, too. Way meaner than me."

"You think he might kick your butt?"

"He's done kicked it all my life. Thinks he's the only one knows how to do anything right."

Honey sighed. "Don't I know, Baby. I got a big sister my own self. Marietta. Been telling lies on me since we was on all fours. Kept me up in some trouble when we was growing up. But I'm fixing to bust out. She's going to be sorry as hell."

"What you going to do?"

"Not much. Just make me a name as a singer. Win me a Grammy or two. Ain't nothing going to hold me here."

Ronnie opened a pack of Kools and offered her one.

"No, thank you, Sweet. Bad for my voice. So what's your name?"

"Ronnie."

"I'm Kim. That's my real name. Just Kim. Not even Kimberly. One damn syllable. So I sing under 'Honey Davis.' Except Cecil's done got to billing me as 'Miss Honey Drop.' But who am I kidding? I ain't nothing but a fucking 'Kim.' A one-syllable individual."

"Least it's easy to spell."

"Yeah. But I'm still a one-syllable individual trying to live a twelve-syllable life." She tugged at her skirt. "You like music? What you listen to?"

"Rock. Country. Not no nigger music." The unlit Kool bobbed as he spoke.

She resisted the urge to explain the history of rock. "Sweetie, you got to like a little blues or jazz."

"Jazz? Jazz is pure fag music."

"You ain't right."

"Hell, I seen this jazz singing man on the TV. Had on these shiny shoes like a woman. Hell, he flamed so much you could set his hair on fire and nobody would notice."

"Well you ought to listen to a little more before you make up your mind, Sweet."

"No way. Who the fuck listens to jazz? Can't nobody understand it. Hell, you can't dance to that shit."

"All right. Blues, then." Honey leaned her head back, closed her eyes and sang a few bars of "Got Took by a Thief Called Love" with all the sexual energy of a live club performance. Then she cut her eyes at him. "What you think? I wrote it myself."

"Damn if you don't have a nice voice. It's still nigger music, though."

"Well, Sweet, what else I'm going to sing?"

"No shit. Hey, you know what?" he said, flipping open a metal Zippo, sending lighter-fluid fumes across the cab of the truck, "I sure hope Claud don't make me hurt you. You ain't so bad." He snapped the lighter shut and she caught a flash of a cartoonish Robert E. Lee waving a Confederate flag etched on the stainless steel.

"I don't see why Claud would want you to hurt me," she said.

"'Cause you know too much."

"Wait just a second, Ronnie. Let's think about that a minute. I don't know shit."

"Well," he said, "you know I come hunting Cecil with a gun. If something was to happen to him, you'd put the law on me, wouldn't you? You a damn lie if you say you wouldn't."

"All right, yes. But you could have avoided that whole problem if you'd have just come in the station and asked, real nice, where's Cecil, then come back later if I didn't know. There's something to be said for manners."

"Aw, to hell with manners. Besides, I was nervous," he said. "I was real nervous. I didn't know you was going to be up in there."

"So what you wanting with Cecil?"

"I was trying to help—no, hell no, I ain't telling you nothing."

"I figure I got a right. You've done carried me off. I figure I ought to be let in on it, you know? Fair is fair."

He ignored her, so she tried another approach. "You know, Ronnie, you could always carry me back." She gave him her most luscious smile. She could work this guy, she knew. Easy. She just needed a little time.

"Shit, I would. I really would. But I reckon I better run it by Claud first, now that I've done fucked everything up."

"Come on, Ronnie. I'm just a shit load of trouble. Everybody says so."

"Forget it."

"Hey, I bet you could use some money. I got eight hundred dollars in the bank. Swing by the Farmers' Bank and let me get it for you, okay?"

"Ain't going to happen."

She sank back in the seat. "So where are we going?"

"Mine and Claud's trailer. 'Bout thirty miles."

She had decided that was good. Thirty miles was a nice long piece. You could sure enough jerk a guy around in the time it took to drive that far. "Is it just you and Claud?"

"Yeah. He run off his last girlfriend two months ago. Serena. She was a old bucktoothed thing. Hell, she could eat a apple through a knothole. And mean? Talk about a bitch."

"Y'all didn't get on, huh? You and Serena." Three Breezes was way behind them, Mississippi straight ahead, so Honey settled in to the conversation.

"Hell, no. That bitch was always doing shit just to piss me off."

"Like?"

"Well, like–" He screwed up his face for a few seconds, deep in thought, then blurted, "Like putting the stick butter in the refrigerator. I like the butter to be warm, okay? You know, room temperature. So it's easy to slap on the toast, don't take so long to melt, okay? But hell no, she said it'd go rancid and we'd all die. It wasn't even none of her butter, neither. She liked tub butter. She had her butter soft already. Ain't that a bitch? Didn't even use no stick butter. Which do you like? Tub or stick?"

"Well, hell, Ronnie, anybody with half a brain likes stick better," she said. "But what happened to make your brother run her off?"

"Claud said she was a sye-co-fant."

"A what? A psycho?"

"A sye-co-*fant*. He's all the time using big-ass words.

Claims I ain't got no verbal skills. Calls me some kind of a infant about it. He said a sye-co-fant is one to follow behind waiting for the crumbs to drop. He said Serena was only good for throwing crumbs to. And he was right. She was all the time playing up to him. He don't like women that's all the time kissing his ass. Done told you he's a mean motherfucker."

"What about you?" She turned her body toward him, throwing her arm across the back of the seat, wishing she had dressed a little more provocatively today. A nice view of cleavage would come in handy about now. Well, at least she had her legs to work with, a short skirt. "What kind of woman do you like? A ass kisser or a bitch?"

"I ain't picky like that. I just want one with a warm pussy."

"Come on, Ronnie, cute guy like you can be picky as he wants to be."

"Yeah?"

"Sure, Sweet. You ain't trying to tell me you don't have a lot of luck with women, 'cause I ain't believing that shit. There is some flat out dumb-ass white girls running round here if they don't have nothing to do with you." She slipped off her green patent leather heels and turned all the way sideways, leaning her back against the door, drawing her left knee up, foot on the car seat. Give him part of the view, she thought, smugly satisfied when he looked. He was a total amateur. This would be too easy. "Yeah," she went on, "me, I got men after me like bloodhounds, but I'm jonesing for one that won't leave his wife. Ain't that some shit?"

"I went out with a married woman one time. Her husband threw brick acid all up in my bass boat. That was all she wrote."

"Was it worth it?"

"Hell no. You kidding? Ain't no kind of pussy worth a bass boat."

"I don't know, Sweet. I've had men act all kinds of crazy just to get a half a look at mine. It's right pitiful to have a big old strong man crying and begging for it."

"Ain't done it."

"Oh, yeah, Baby. All the time. Just last week I had a white insurance salesman offer me three hundred dollars just to get a look at my tits. I ain't lying."

"Did you?" His voice had the eager tone she was coaxing.

"Oh, I've done shit like that before. I mean, cash is always nice. But I was going with Cecil when this happened so, no, I didn't. Of course, looks like Cecil and me are over and I ain't long for this part of the world. So, you got three hundred dollars? You got three hundred dollars I'll show you some kick-ass tits." She laughed her hoarse, seductive laugh.

"Can't be that good." He squinted his eyes at her chest.

"Must be, 'cause I get that shit all the damn time. But what about you? Cute guy like you bound to have a woman. You been bullshitting me about that, right?"

"I do all right. Well, sometimes. Not as good as Claud, though. Hell, women get all over him. He gets more ass than a toilet seat. He's got this what you call magnetic type of a personality, which I ain't."

"That ain't so, Baby. That just ain't so. You got a real sweet personality, just the kind decent women like."

"Yeah?"

"Hell yeah, Sweet. And I know what I'm talking about 'cause I know what women want. I'm the love guru. Folks talk to me all the time about their love lives. You ever been in love?"

"Well, just once. Sarah Pugh. Except she said she wouldn't give me none unless I married her. So I did. I went and married her ass, brung her out to the trailer to live with Claud and me. But hell, she didn't appreciate nothing. Sat on her fat ass all the livelong day and looked at the TV. Then she started going out to the clubs of a weekend. Wouldn't clean up or nothing."

"But she gave you plenty, huh?"

"Plenty of nothing after about six weeks of being married. Got to where she didn't never want to."

"That's cold."

"No shit. I was so horny back then that—I had a beard and a mustache back when we was married, and I'd get so horny I'd wake myself up in the dead of the night with my finger in my mouth. Had to shave the shit off where I could get some sleep."

"Ooh, Child, what happened to her?"

"What happened was I throwed her out for fucking Claud."

"No!"

"Yeah. That bitch was a damn lie. She weren't worth

the pussy she was mounted to."

"But weren't you mad at Claud?"

"Naw. She was a whore. She done it with half the county. I guess she had done saved it up for so long she thought she better get all she could, once I broke it in. And she's still giving that stuff away. Done skin't every pole in a hundred square miles."

"No!"

"Yeah, that thing is about as blowed out as a throwed retread on a eighteen-wheeler. Probably be like fucking a dried-up mud hole."

"Well, she was crazy to give up a cute husband with a nice personality—"

"Ain't magnetic, though."

"Magnetic ain't so good."

"Claud says it is. He's got a magnetic personality."

"No. Look here. You ever held a magnet over a bunch of nails?"

"Yeah. So what?"

"So what is this. It picked up a bunch of nails, right?"

"Supposed to."

"Picked up the shiny new ones and some of the old, rusty, bent-up ones, too."

He turned to her with a blank expression. This guy was dumber than she thought.

"What I mean is, you got a magnetic personality, you're going to draw some shitty women your way, right up in amongst the good ones," she said. "But the good ones, the decent ones, will just naturally come to a man like you, and come of their own free will. No magnet necessary."

"I lost that old magnet anyway," he said.

"You got any other family?"

"Well, I got a mama and a sister somewhere."

"Somewhere? You don't know where your own sister is?"

"Naw, it's been since she was a baby. She's all growed up and haired over by now. See, they took off when I was five. Daddy wouldn't let Mama have me and Claud. Said boys belonged with their daddy and she was a whore, besides."

"Your sister?"

"No, my mama."

"Seems like you folks is crawling with whores."

Ronnie laughed. "No shit. It's hard to find a decent woman that ain't butt-ugly and knows how to take care of a man."

"Well, this woman right here knows just how."

"Shit."

"You tell me I ain't right, then. It's like this. A man wants two things. A mama and a whore. The problem is most women want to be their man's friend, don't want to be a mama when he's low and needs to be puffed up. Or else they take care of him like a mama and don't want to be a whore in the bedroom. Every man wants a whore in the bedroom, right?"

"Why would you get a whore if you got a wife?"

"No, Baby, your wife going to do for you anything a whore would do. See?"

"I reckon."

"Look here. If Sarah had give you a good blow whenever you wanted her to she'd have lasted longer as a wife, right?"

"Hell, yeah. But she never done that. She thought it was against Christ. Told me I was eat up with sin." He turned down a narrow dirt road. "Bent Spike Road," the sign said. This trailer of his was going to be isolated. She was feeling more and more pushed into a corner.

"Shit, Baby, anybody gets a blow job from me thinks it's the Second *Coming* of Christ." Miss Honey Drop did not like the idea of going very far down this rutted road. Maybe it was time to turn things around. "You like a good blow job, Baby?" She let her foot slide down and over, pressing it against Ronnie's thigh, then lifted her right foot to the seat to give him the whole view. He looked.

"Who don't?" He squirmed in the driver's seat.

"Nobody that's had one of mine. But I don't give them out to just anybody." She pressed her toes harder into his thigh. The paved road had disappeared. She moved her right knee from side to side, successfully mesmerizing him.

By now his driving was suffering because he was focusing more on her green nylon panties edged in black lace. "What you doing?" His voice had that generic male tone of arousal, telling her she was definitely getting somewhere.

"Oh, I'm just doing what comes natural to me when I meet a good-looking guy I like." She kept the knee moving, opening and closing her thighs.

"Yeah?"

"So, what you think?" Honey slid her foot over to his crotch to gauge her effect. Damn, I'm good, she thought, when her toes found solidity beneath the denim. "You want the best blow job in the Southeast?"

"Hell, yeah," he breathed.

"You better be sure. They say it's so good won't nothing ever feel right again. You sure you want yourself a Second Coming of Christ blow job?"

"Damn right."

"Pull over, then." She sat up to move next to him, marveling at how weak men were, as a rule.

He slammed on the brakes and skidded the truck across gravel, then unzipped his jeans in a rush.

"Slow down, Baby," she said. "Take it easy. Miss Honey Drop's blow jobs got to be savored. Going to make you drip." She rubbed her hand over his penis and glanced down. It looked like a stunted mushroom with a slitted little eye in the middle. Damn, she was a desperate bitch to be bargaining a blow job with this racist, no-dick idiot. She wondered if she would be able to get through it without gagging.

He moaned. "What you waiting for?"

"I told you I don't give these out to just anybody." She steady rubbed his penis, eliciting more moans and sharp breaths. "This makes us a connection. Two people who will treat each other right. You agree?"

"Anything you say. I can't stand this. You got to get started else I'm going to squirt."

"Mmmm. Just so we understand. I want to do it just like you want it, with a little of my trademark technique thrown in. I had a engineer out of Vicksburg tell me I ought to get a patent. How you like it, Sweet?"

"I like it now."

She leaned down and gave it a little nudge with her tongue, then straightened up. "Say please."

"Please. Goddamn, please."

"And you going to turn round and take me back to the station after, right?" She rubbed a little faster.

"Right. Yeah. Damn right. Shit! I mean—what the fuck?"

"Fair is fair, Baby. You get, I get, right?" She drew her hand back.

"What the hell? Why you want to stop? Come on, now. Get at it."

"Well, Baby, I do want to. I really do. But I can't give without getting back, you know?"

"You'll get back. I'll tote you back to town as soon as you take care of this here."

She studied his expression, seeing the look she knew better than any other. The lying look of a one-track man. "You know what, Sweet? I think you ain't about to hold up your end of this deal."

"Fuck!" he beat the steering wheel with his fist. "You been fucking with me the whole fucking time!"

"Ronnie, come on. You don't need to take me out to your place. I ain't no good to y'all."

"Shit! You been fucking the hell with me. Well, you done done it now. You done got my goober hard. You done got it all fucked up." He took his penis between thumb and middle finger, as if to offer proof. "What I'm going to do with this? Huh? What I'm going to do with this now? When my pecker gets done thisaway it don't go down by itself. Ain't no way. What I'm going to do with this?"

Honey sighed. It was clear he was single-minded about getting Claud's stamp of approval on the whole deal. "I don't know, Sweet. Maybe you could stick it up your brother's ass."

Ronnie flailed at the steering wheel, sputtering expletives. "I ought to make you go on and do it," he said. "I got the gun, you know."

"I ain't about to suck your old knobby dick for nothing," she said.

"You a damn lie! The thing ain't knobby!" The blue vein on his forehead welted up across his forehead. He opened the door and stood next to the truck, again indicating his sawed-off midget of a member. "You can't look at my pecker and say it's knobby."

"Sure I can," she said. "It looks like the back end of a turnip root."

"It ain't done it!" He was red-faced, livid, a greasy-haired, ponytailed Rumpelstiltskin, on the verge of stomping his foot and splitting the earth open, with his solid little button of a penis nodding in agreement.

"Believe me, Sweet, I've seen all shapes and sizes, and you a low-built motherfucker. That there is a knob."

"Shut the fuck up!"

"A damn nubby knob."

"Ain't!"

"Is, too. It ain't no more than a nubbin."

"A nubbin?" He took it again between thumb and cussing finger, seemed to be contemplating her critique. "Well, whatever it is, it's damn sure got to be drained."

"Well I sure as hell ain't going to be the one to pull the plug."

"Shut up and hand me that jug of motor oil in the floorboard."

She picked up a plastic bottle of Penzoil. This was a good sign. When he got his head under the hood to put oil in the engine, she could get her purse, her gun, and get the hell out of there. She was formulating the plot in her head, how she would drive right over him if she had to, when it came to her what he was doing. He had oozed some of the oil into his palm and set about masturbating.

"Good God almighty," she said. "I've seen a lot of sick shit in my life, but I ain't never seen nobody beat off with Penzoil."

"Does right tolerable," he panted. "And I like the smell."

"Well, shit, go off in the bushes or something. I don't want to watch you go to flinging that mess at me. Are you crazy?"

"Shut up," he said, blowing and sweating in the summer heat.

"Go on away from me with that shit!"

"Shut up, else I'm going to aim it right at you," he panted.

"I ain't believing this shit," she muttered. "No-dick

redneck motherfucker going to beat off with goddamn thirty-weight. This here is some sick motherfucking shit." She turned the rearview mirror so she could check her makeup, her hair, then picked up a magazine rolled up on the dashboard. A whole magazine about fishing and chasing down deer, but she would be damned if she was going to acknowledge what he was doing. She started flipping pages, summertime cicadas vibrating, punctuated by the slapping sound of Ronnie giving himself a lube job.

It was then she heard the car, back toward the highway, but approaching them. She moved the rearview again, so she could see the road behind them. She could get help. Scream. Jump out of the truck and flag them down. She stared at the masturbating moron opposite her, arm pumping like a piston on an old-timey train engine. He seemed oblivious to the sound of the vehicle just around the curve, and she did not dare turn around and draw his attention to it. His eyes were fixed on her, but they had that glazed-over look she knew so well, that typical male I-done-tuned-everything-out, even-you, 'cause-I'm-just-before-coming look that she hated. Cecil never got that look. He would always stay detached until he had driven her over two or three orgasmic cliffs and be done with it.

Car wheels loud on gravel and a blaring horn broke into Ronnie's sexual reverie. "Goddamnit, it's Claud," he said, wiping his oily palm on his shirt. "Shit! Why didn't you tell me somebody was coming?" He bent over and pulled at his jeans, which had puddled around his ankles.

"Apparently not you," she said. She got hold of the door handle, was just about to jump out when Ronnie referred to his "mean motherfucker" brother, who was slamming out of a dusty, two-tone beige and white Monte Carlo and walking over to Ronnie's parked truck. She watched him through the dirt-filmed rear window, struck by how he moved with a deliberate saunter, saying nothing. He was taller and thicker than his brother, but still railey by general standards. When he reached their vehicle he leaned down to meet her eyes. His own were iceberg-blue, translucent, set in a weathered face, skin scuffed and scarred from what must have been a recent fight. This set of eyes belonged to a man who could not be worked as easily as his brother. These eyes belonged to a man who probably really was a "mean motherfucker." Blond strands of hair wiggle-wormed from beneath an Ole Miss cap, and when he smirked, shaking his head, Honey could feel his disgust pricking her soul. There was something disturbing and threatening in this man. She drew up some spunk, though, and managed a greeting. "How you doing, Sweet?"

"Yeah," he said. "Sweet is right, ain't it? It's damn sure sweet to come up on my shit-for-brains brother in the middle of the goddamn road, tongue hanging like a running coon dog's, beating his meat, with a nigger whore in the truck."

"Imagine what I been going through," she said.

He stared at her, not a whisper of humor on his face.

He shook his head again. "You ain't nothing but a smart-ass." He turned to his brother. "What the hell is that? Penzoil? I hope you got some fucking GoJo in your truck."

Ronnie did not move, oil-stained britches caught around his knees, hands limp at his sides, toadstool of a penis still slicked and poised at the ready.

"That thirty-weight's going to rot your pecker off," Claud said. "What you need is small engine oil."

"Won't do it. I done used it before. Long as you keep it out the pee hole it's all right."

"Goddamnit, you want to put your pecker up, Ronnie?" Claud said.

The younger brother came to life then, tugging his jeans up, mashing his stubby, rigid little companion into them. "She done it," he said. "She went to wallowing on me. Promised me a gummer and then went back on it. You know how I get, Claud. I had to get some relief."

Claud stared at his brother for the better part of a minute, a seething stare that sent Ronnie into more of his babbling explanation.

"Hell, my pecker don't know how to act. You know how I am, Claud. Anything rubs on my pecker it's all she wrote. Hell, it gets hard if I tuck my damn shirt in. You know that. You know it's going to be pinched up in my britches until I get it greased up and relaxed. You know–"

"Shut up, goddamnit! You goddamn shit for brains!" Claud drew back a fist, connected with Ronnie's left cheek, and laid his brother out in the gravel. "I don't want to hear another fucking word about your sorry

excuse for a goober," he said. "I already know you got
to rub on it every time you get still. What I want to
know is why the hell you headed to my fucking trailer
with a nigger bitch I ain't never laid eyes on."

Ronnie struggled to sit up, grunting. "Damn, Claud,
I was trying to help you out." He held his cheek and
pulled himself to his feet by grabbing the side view mirror
on the pickup. "I went after Cecil but he wasn't–"

"Why you want to tell her his name, shit for brains?
You bout as stupid as a sump pump."

"But she knows Cecil. She's his girlfriend."

Claud leaned back down to peer in at her. "Well I'll
be goddamned. Honey Drop Davis. I heard all about
you."

"Heard what?"

"How you want to bust up Cecil Durgin's marriage.
How you fancy yourself some kind of entertainer."

"Who told you all that?"

"None-ya," he said. "Now that I see you though, it's
clear there ain't much to you." He turned back to
Ronnie. "Well, why the fuck is she here?"

"'Cause he weren't there and she was. I'm sorry,
Claud."

"Goddamnit, you still ain't answered my question."

"What question was that?"

Claud leaned down to her again. "Why the fuck you
here?"

"You know, Sweet, I ain't got the first idea. But I
really need to be getting on back now. Lord, taking the
Maxima in for a oil change ain't never going to be the

same."

Claud reached into the truck, left hand cupping her chin, and gripped her face between thumb and fingers, a vise on her cheeks. He leaned in close enough for her to see the pores in the skin around his unfeeling stare. "Don't you say another goddamn motherfucking word."

She could feel the fear then, the tremor of fear that vibrated louder and louder in her ears, the rush of blood and adrenaline, the thumping of her heart. He would hurt her if she gave him an excuse, and she knew she would have to think smart if she was going to outthink this one.

He pushed and released her face, shoving her back into the passenger's side door. Then he turned back to Ronnie. "This conversation ain't going nowhere. We need to get out the road, so go on home. I'm right behind." He sauntered back to his car.

Ronnie tugged at his zipper and climbed back into the truck. He made to adjust his crotch, squirmed, winced. "See? The thing ain't going to be right till it's done shot off. You know, you a damn shit load of trouble."

Honey sighed, slid her feet back into her shoes. "That's what I already tried to tell you, Sweet."

They drove for several more miles down the dirt road. It ultimately ran through a locked gate flanked by two tall poles bearing Confederate flags. That had not been a good sign, but, if not for Claud, Honey would not have felt an ounce of intimidation. She had been around folks all her life who snatched at the perverse past of the Old South as if it were handed down from Moses, folks who grabbed at defiant symbols because their feeble brains could not process history or religion in a way to render them productive. Still, she maintained her façade of nonchalance while Claud railed at his brother, who whined and protested. Finally, Claud shoved some pills into her mouth and had her wash them down with a can of Budweiser.

Now she groped under the bed for her shoes, the sexy green stilettos Cecil loved. She had to collect her things, collect her thoughts, and get herself out of here. None of this made sense. None of it. Goddamn, he jerked off with thirty-weight. She had a sudden, stomach-turning thought, stood, hiked her skirt, and thrust her hand into her green panties, black lace snatched aside. Surely, he didn't. God, no. She let her fingers reconnoiter between her legs. No, it didn't seem so. She brought her fingers to her nostrils and sniffed. No. That was definitely all her. Thank God.

She glanced up. The entire wall behind the bed was draped with a Confederate Flag, and she remembered seeing another one above the sofa when they had brought her inside yesterday. Shit, those damn flags were everywhere. Hadn't they heard about Appomattox?

She sat down on the edge of the bed again, putting her thoughts on fast-forward as she rolled her options through her head. She would promise to let it all go if they would take her back to the station. She would list all the places Cecil might be. She would tell them she would leave town. Today. Hell, she had been wanting to get to Memphis for a while now. She would be businesslike with Claud, lay it all out for him so he knew she was not bullshitting him. She would be forceful with Ronnie if she found herself alone with him again. She figured Ronnie might go along with her if she simply took charge and let him know he was to do what she said. If necessary, if she perceived a threat to her life, she knew she would pick up a gun, her own or one of theirs. She would work her way out of this one, out of this sardine can of a home with the Dixie décor. She knew she would get clear of the whole mess.

Just as she had herself calmed and convinced of her capability, the door pushed open. Claud Pierce stepped inside the room, shirtless, a lit cigarette dangling from his lips, the wide leather belt on his jeans unbuckled. A cluster of keys was hooked to one of his belt loops, and he was barefoot. The head of a snake peered over his left shoulder, fangs bared, drops of ink falling into a patch of curled hairs on the man's chest. He gave her a long look of sneering contempt, blue eyes cutting through her confidence, sending her headlong into a muffled panic, more unfamiliar territory.

She didn't betray her fear to him, though. "I need to talk to you, Claud," she said, in her most assertive tone.

He held up his hand and squinted his eyes, commanding silence. "No, you don't. You don't need to talk to me just yet. What you need to do right now is shut the fuck up and speak when you're spoken to. And I'm speaking now. I'm telling you to think real hard and let me know right now do I need something. Do I need to go get me a weapon for this visit we're fixing to have?"

Instinct told her she was cornered and he would bat her around like a cat playing with a wounded moth, and she couldn't answer for a moment. "I don't understand," she said, finally.

"It's simple. See, you're going to give me all the information I need, and then some," Claud said.

"You wouldn't need a weapon for that. I'll tell you anything you want to know."

He walked over and stood in front of her, over her. He reached down and took her wrist in his hard grip, pressed her hand to the crotch of his jeans, and gave a strange laugh that was mostly a gravelly choking sound. "You're going to give me all that information you put in front of my baby brother, too. That information you got him all fucked up with. That information down between your legs. And you're going to do it nice. So tell me right now do I need a weapon to keep you being nice, or will my motherfucking bare hands do?" He grinned a sneer at her.

She tried to withdraw her hand, but he pushed it with more force into his jeans, clamping his burning grip tighter around her wrist. A sour, sickening dread unfolded inside her as she began to realize what was just before happening. A flurry of choices rushed through her head, flipping like a Rolodex through her thoughts. The instinctive one, to fight like a crazy woman came first, but she knew immediately not to venture into that contest, not with a man so cold and prone to doing who knew what. But it went dead against her nature, to even consider being compliant. She was desperate to fight, to cry, to scream slick curses at him, attempt to match his coarse hatred of her; but another instinct, untapped until this moment, told her that her typical, time-honored defenses would only give him victory. And his victory would come at a very high price for her. Instead, she had to refuse any reaction, keep as cold as he was, and remember everything. She would get out of this situation, eventually, and when she did, he would know the rough side of Miss Honey Drop Davis.

With a strange sense of surrender, she steeled herself, raising her chin, and met his eyes, shutting off the emotions and thoughts that might sabotage her survival. "No," she said. "You don't need no weapon."

Shug walked down the hallway toward her mother's bedroom, thinking to try, just try, to reveal herself, tell her how unhappy she was with Rob, tell her about the new life taking shape in her head, ask her to help her do what needed to be done, urge her to be fair to Cecil, and to Miss Sophie. She said more to Cecil yesterday than she had to anyone else in twenty years of trivial cocktail party chatter. But then, he inspired trust, a gathering of nerve, and honesty, however difficult. He always had. There was never a time when she did not feel like they were kin, and now they could build a united front of siblings against the users and frauds of the world, the tiny little lagging-behind world of Cole County.

It seemed such a big world when she was a teenager, playing the role of benevolent queen in a sea of ladies-in-waiting, girls who latched on and gushed over her looks, the Bobbie Brooks wardrobe, the big house, the sports car. They really did think she had it all. But Tammy knew. Tammy got an up-close and personal look at the interior of the McCormick nuclear family, round for round. She could huddle up with Tammy in her huge attic bedroom, all done up in lilac, violet, light blue and yellow, pansy-patterned wallpaper keeping its little floral faces vigilant, a veneer of cheer against the nightly chaos. Sometimes they would creep down to the third step and she would sob while her best friend sympathized, but only up to a point, until Tammy would tell her, in her common-sense way, it was not a big deal your parents went on nightly drunks, too often culminating in dark curses and slamming doors. It was not an aberration, your mother's desperate bids for affection or lust, or anything encompassing touch; her failed attempts at seduction, the tears and serpent-tongued insults coming with the inevitable rejection. All parents fought, Tammy would say. Hell, her own certainly did. Okay, so your father prefers whores to your mother. Maybe he has some kind of a mama problem. Maybe he can't get it up with a woman who has borne his child. It doesn't mean he doesn't love her. He damn sure loves you. This obsession he has with replacing your dead brother is just some kind of a male something, an ego rush. So what if he visits the cemetery more and more, spends more time with Lee and Cash than he does with you. And then there's the talk about Cecil. No, of course he would never claim Cecil outright. It would wreck his reputation, could even take down his business. And sure, that does make him a man with skewed principles, but not many principled people make it financially. That's just a law of economics. Look at me, dirt poor as my people are, and be grateful you were born rich. While you were having steak dinners growing up, I was eating canned sardines, Spam sandwiches, and Vienna Sausages. While you were on shopping trips at Rich's Department Store in Atlanta, Mama and me were picking over the tables at the Methodist Church's monthly rummage sales. Hell, look at my stepdaddy, Fat Forrest, who slaps me around and bothers me all kinds of ways you don't have to worry about, and be grateful you got a daddy who'll spoil you rotten, even if he won't give you his understanding. Anybody can feel sorry for theirself, but let's us don't.

Shug reached for the doorknob to her mother's bedroom. She had spent so many years reaching, never touching. It was as if they were at the touch-resistant poles of two separate magnets, an invisible cushion of secrets and denial between them. Still, she took a deep breath, got her palm around the glass knob, and entered. Her mother rarely rose before noon on weekdays, thick-brained from the two-thirds of a bottle of vodka she usually consumed in the course of an afternoon and evening; Bloody Marys began at two P.M., Long Island iced teas anytime. Shug sometimes joined her, mixing drinks from the wet bar in her mother's room, sitting with her and making conversation about nothing. She could stand this until her mother began to slur her words, descending into self-pity and regret for a life lived outside of herself, revealing things too painful for her daughter to hear. That was when she would kiss the old lady on the cheek and say good night, leaving the door ajar in case her mother was to fall or drop a burning cigarette.

This, apparently, was a good morning. Her mother was up, sipping coffee, in a cheerful mood, and it was not even eight A.M. For the first time in a long time, she primped into a makeup mirror on the table beside her chaise lounge. Shug sat at her feet.

"I was just thinking," Kate said, "that the two of us should go on a little trip, go shopping in Atlanta like we used to do when you were a teenager."

"What's got you so fired up? Miss Sophie?" One barrier at a time, she thought. First Miss Sophie, then Rob, then Cecil.

"I do not want to talk about that woman right now."

"I know she called you. I know she wants to come over."

"Enough!"

The angry edge in her mother's voice played to the echoes of drunken rants in her memory. Shug spent so many years in fear of her mother's moods she almost retreated automatically, but today she forced herself on. "Oh, Mama, haven't you been stubborn enough about her?" Shug took a tube of lipstick from her mother's makeup bag, removed the top, and swiveled the angled bullet of color up and out, down and in.

"I will not talk about that woman right now. Do you hear me?"

Her mother spoke to her as if she were perpetually nine years old. And Shug always took it. Mustn't make Mama angry. My, how she will drink then. Mustn't make Mama cry. Mama will get extra drunk and fall down. At once it occurred to Shug that for all the pussy-footing around, all the times she held her tongue, none of it ever had any effect on when or how much her mother drank. It had all been a hoax, the messages she received, admonishments to be careful not to upset Miss

Kate lest she go on yet another binge. "Fine," Shug said. "Tell you what. I'll go on a trip to Atlanta if Miss Sophie can come along."

"It's a shame we won't be going, then," Kate snapped. "Hand me my lipstick."

Shug watched her mother press deep burgundy into the flesh framing her teeth. As a child Shug would sit at the master bath vanity next to her mother while Kate got dressed and made up for parties and teas, the daughter in awe of the artistic sweep of her mother's eyeliner, the way she sculpted her cheekbones and glazed the apples with blush. Now her mother's hand shook and her skin held the yellowish pallor of a long-time alcoholic.

"Mama?"

"Hmm?" Kate patted her face with a small powder pad, tilting her head to study the angles of her reflection in the mirror. "Goddamn, I am one beat-up old lady. But it's passable."

"You're beautiful," Shug said, venturing onto another patch of thin ice. "If you were happy you'd be even more beautiful."

Kate ignored the comment. "You know, you're right, in a way. Ever since that woman called the other day I've had an itch. To go. To do. What about New Orleans?"

"No."

"Well, why the hell not? We'll stay at the Monteleone, go all over the place, laugh at the crazy street people."

"I'll go if Miss Sophie can come along."

"Sugar Lee McCormick! Can you not leave that woman out of this conversation?"

For a moment Shug was, indeed, nine years old again, on the verge of scampering to her room until her mother calmed down or passed out. But the image of her mother, sitting there, tending to her aging face, afraid to be vulnerable enough to forgive her best friend, took the last slivers of fear out of her. "No, Mama. In fact, I am going to ask Miss Sophie to take a trip to New Orleans with me. I've about decided to invite Tammy, too. You can come along if you like."

Kate stared at her with stark shock in her eyes, motionless. Shug could almost see the truth sinking in as her mother leaned back in the chaise lounge. "Well," she exhaled. "Aren't we the little princess?"

Shug giggled. "Yes. We are."

"What will Almighty Rob think of a trip for girls only?"

Shug found another giggle. "Frankly, my dear, I don't give a damn what Rob thinks."

"I'll just be damned to dream on a porcupine pillow. You sound more like my baby all the time. What brought you to this new attitude?"

"I think you're right, that's all. I think Rob is not to be trusted, and I'll know for sure soon."

"How?"

"Not yet. I'll tell you later. Just remember you heard it here first." Two seeds had been sown, the Sophie seed and the Rob seed, but the third would take the sweetness out of the second one, Shug knew.

"You really are a princess this morning. Hand me my blush, your highness."

Shug rifled through the makeup bag, a rattle of plastic and mirrors. She handed a compact and a soft fat brush to her mother.

"Thank you, your highness. And now I require a Bloody Mary. Posthaste." She snapped her fingers.

Shug stood. "You'll have to get it yourself. I'm supposed to get together with Cecil this morning." She walked to the door, feeling the fresh wash of silence, knowing she had splintered a piece of her mother's barricade, even more of her own, and a surprising warmth of calm serenity rose up from her once nerve-knotted stomach.

"Cecil?" Kate half whispered.

"Yes. We have some important things to talk over."

Her mother's voice was defensive, riddled with apprehension. "But what could you have to talk over?"

Shug turned and met her mother's eyes, seeing more fear than she ever expected. "We're going to talk about...how to proceed. That's all." She pushed the door open, stepped out, then closed it, but not before she heard her mother give out a strangling little gasp as the barricade toppled. Shug leaned her ear to the door, hearing what she fully expected to hear. The clinking of ice into a glass, the rattle of liquor decanters, the snap of a plastic lid and the shake of a pill from a medicine bottle. Then the swish of feet against carpet, a metallic slide of heavy drapes being drawn shut, the click-click of a cigarette lighter, more tinkling ice in straight vodka, and, finally, the rustling of bedclothes as her mother slid back beneath the covers.

Shug stopped at another door, the door leading up to her old bedroom. Strange. For the first time it occurred to her how she was avoiding this door even more fiercely than her mother's. She had been back for seven months now and had not entered the room of her childhood, settling with Rob into one of the guest rooms without even paying the attic room a visit. Stranger, still, Rob never approached the door to the room or even asked about it. It seemed like one would be curious to see where one's spouse spent a childhood, would want to view a life on an intersecting path with his own, reminisce among the paraphernalia of puberty, teenaged treasures, and sacred mementos. But Rob never even acknowledged the room, or the fact that, yes, there once was a girl, once upon a time, a girl formed by years of living, constructing unalterable links of affection with others who might be even more significant than he was. She opened the door and took a seat on the third step.

She had not been able to go through with it last night, her plan to ingratiate herself to Rob, seduce information out of him, beat him at his own game. She was even losing some of her ancient bitterness toward Cash. Hours after her short visit with Cecil, the belief in devious assassination plots, let alone the need to retaliate against the conspirators, was so vague it was barely an echo, as if a waste of time was the only thing to be accomplished. As for her husband, she allowed herself to know, now, and on the deepest level, exactly what he was. Anything Cecil learned last night would be redundant.

When Rob stumbled in, sometime around midnight, smelling of Scotch, then crawled into bed uncommonly aroused, she feigned sleep. When he pressed hard into the back of her thighs, she wondered, but only for a second, what had gotten him all heated up. But it was not worth further wondering, she thought, amazed at how little she cared. When he mumbled curses and pouted off to the bathroom to spend some quality time with himself in the shower, she almost laughed out loud. Laughter. So unfamiliar and liberating. She decided right then she wanted to spend more time with Cecil and Tammy and laughter.

Shug stood and flipped the light switch, illuminating the room above. She looked up the stairs to where a wooden gateway bore a hand-painted sign. It had hung there as long as she could remember, reminding her to play her part in the family drama. The background was pale blue bordered by curlicues dipping at yellow pansies. In its center, in deep blue script letters, was a quote from *Proverbs*: "A merry heart maketh a cheerful countenance." She knew how to do the cheerful countenance; she was now ready to go after the merry heart.

She climbed the steps, each one taking her deeper into the realization she had been skirting ever since she came home, closer to freedom, further from the wasteland that was her mother's life. She lay on her old bed for a long time, gathering more strength from her past self; then, finally, rose to go take care of the present.

She went downstairs and out to the garage, where Rob's pristine white Mercedes was housed alongside her mother's car. The Rob-rubbed chrome and Windexed glass of the polished Mercedes winked reflections at her when she climbed into her mother's Cadillac. That goddamn Mercedes. He had never even put the top down. It was a goddamn convertible, but he was too uptight about it to even put the top down. She cranked her mother's car and backed out, closing the automatic door to keep field dust off her Great White husband's great white automobile. Then she headed for the café in town, thinking to carry breakfast to DoeRun, to rendezvous with Cecil, to share her heart with her brother.

Honey Drop Davis sat on the couch next to Ronnie Pierce, who brought her a glass of water and a wet rag. "Thanks, Sweet," she said, taking a long swallow, trying like crazy to maintain some kind of numbed composure. She put the rag to her face, battling the sweaty nausea that was still with her.

"He ought not to have done that," Ronnie said. "Sometimes I think he takes things over the line."

"No shit." She felt as if she were looking at everything from under water, far away, sounds muffled and wrapped in liquid. She was shaking when she emerged from the bedroom, where Claud left her after pushing into her with curses against her color, his ice-blue eyes squinting a perverse lust of hate down at her. She did not let her throat issue the faintest whimper, gave up not one surrendering sound throughout the attack. But the aftertaste of him made her stomach boil until she heaved and vomited off the porch of the trailer as he drove away.

"He's sure as hell mad at me," Ronnie said. "He ain't even got started good on kicking my narrow ass."

His voice seemed as far away as the rest of the world, way above the surface of the water, but she held on to her wits. She knew she had to get out of the orbit of the Pierces, somehow get the law out to where Cecil was, if he was still there, tangled up in the bedsheets with some whore. Where Claud was now headed, probably to bust in on Cecil making love to the woman who would replace Miss Honey Drop. She leaned back on the sofa. "I got to have my purse, Sweet."

"What for?"

"Because that's where my Tampons are," she said. "You ain't seen a mess till you seen a woman with a very heavy flow and no Tampons. I reckon your brother knocked it loose, 'cause here it comes."

"Shit. Where is it?"

"I think maybe it's in the back of your truck. Want me to get it?"

"Hell no. You're like to steal the truck and go to the laws. Then wouldn't my ass be grass." He got up and pushed back the screen door.

She stood, weak-kneed and wobbly. She walked over to the wall facing the couch and studied it through the liquid currents that wrapped around her emotions. It was covered with photographs thumb-tacked to the paneling, most of them featuring a large man who sometimes wore a policeman's uniform, sometimes civvies. The man with a shotgun. With a gutted deer. With a pistol aimed at the camera. With two little boys. Some of the photographs featured a man of the same stature, but hooded, dressed in white robes. Then there were larger groups of robed figures, crosses burning.

"Nice place you've got here, Claud," she muttered under her breath. "Real homey. Makes me feel kind of like one of the clan." She felt a sob trying to rise up in her, unable to break through the barrier she had placed between what she felt and what she allowed to enter her head.

She glanced into the kitchen area, where food on stacks of dirty dishes was in various stages of petrification. Ronnie's nine-millimeter lay on the kitchen table, its clip beside it. There might be a bullet in the chamber, might not.

"Here." Ronnie let the screen door slam, handed her pocketbook to her, and flopped back on the sofa.

"Thanks, Sweet. You been a real gentleman. I just want you to know that." She had to keep him engaged, on her side, in spite of what his brother had done.

"Like I said, Claud oughtn't to have done that. But you can't tell him nothing."

"Well, you got a lot on Claud, Sweet." She winked at him. Might as well stick with what works, at least with this one, she thought. She tucked her purse under her arm.

"I do love a blow job," he said, giving her a hopeful look.

"You'll be getting plenty. Don't worry. You just stick with your brother and you'll be getting all the mouth action you ever thought about."

"Huh?"

"Jail, Sweet. If your brother hurts Cecil you know he'll do jail time. And you'll be with him. An accessory. And it won't be no little county jail. And like I say, you'll get all the blow jobs you want if you play your cards right."

"Shit," Ronnie said. "Ain't no man going to gobble my goober. Anyway, Claud's too smart to get thrown in prison."

She resisted the urge to remind him of the penalty for rape. She fought down the rising need to scream and cry rising up in her again. She willed herself to be herself. Kim. One syllable the Pierces would remember. "Well I ain't worried about Claud," she said. "He ain't my type. You just take it easy while I go get myself all fresh. Then we'll talk business."

She turned on the faucet in the bathroom and opened her purse. This had gone way further than she ever thought it would and all she wanted was out—out of the Prices' trailer, out of Cole Couty, out of Alabama for good—and she planned to hit the road today. She felt filthy with the vile ejaculate of his race, and the slimy image of mating snakes, the snakes tattooed on Ronnie's arm, slithered behind her eyes. She had copulated with evil because she had to save herself and the stench of it clung to her thighs, her face. She wanted out and never to hear of Three Breezes, ever again. She was taking Ronnie Prices' truck, even if she had to shoot him to get it. She was driving to the station to get her car; then to some laws to give whatever statement they would need from her; to the Cole County Clinic, judging by the TV shows and movies she had seen; then to the bank to clean out her account; then by God north to Memphis. She would stop at her apartment in Columbus to take a bath, wash Claud Pierce off her skin, out of her insides, but she knew the branding of her practiced attitude, the brand burned into her confidence by his searing words, would stay with her; and the mutated reality that now resided in her, in the very heart of her, would never be purged. She only wanted out. She did not even plan to haul off many of her belongings. Hell, she wouldn't need any belongings. The promoter who was beckoning her to sign with him had way more money than Cecil, could get her a whole new wardrobe, an even more glamorous image.

She took the gun from her purse. She wasn't for one second worried about the contract. She would walk right out of this bathroom, point the gun at Ronnie Pierce, and make one phone call before she left this trailer for town. She would call that Wade Connors or Booty-Cop at the sheriff's office to tell him what happened and where to find Cecil. And she would send a message to Cecil via the sheriff: You're welcome for saving your ass from a crazy man. Now tear up that contract.

She lifted the weapon and held it out from her body, practicing her aim in the bathroom mirror. The revolver was loaded, stayed loaded, and she had six chances with it as opposed to maybe one or two without it. If it came down to it she would just have to keep pulling the trigger. It'll be hurt-your-ears loud, she told herself, and it'll spit fire, but remember to use both hands.

He had put on some music again. "Sweet Home, Alabama" sent its guitar rhythm throbbing through the trailer. She turned off the faucet, flushed the toilet, got her purse strap over her shoulder, and let the barrel of the revolver be the first thing he would see when she opened the door.

Tammy leaned forward in one of the heavy wooden chairs in Wade Connors' office, an open box of Krispy Kreme Doughnuts on the desk. Wade chewed on his cigar, marveling on the inside at Tammy's persistence, at Miss Sophie's strength, the old lady shade-dozing outside in the Wildwood Home minivan. "So y'all got some visiting to do this morning, huh?"

"Hell yeah," Tammy said. "First Earline. And then— well, don't you think Shug would be the logical person to visit after that? I mean, if we're going to finally hook up with Cecil? It's just that I've been pretty pissed at Shug, but Miss Sophie says I'm being petty."

"Oh, I think you've done enough," he said. "Besides, the way all this shit is flying around Cecil, I think it's better if you let me make both those visits. But get together with Shug at some point. She's going to need a friend here pretty soon."

"Oh, so you're finally going to do something? What changed your mind?"

"The universe," he said.

"What?"

"Like I was saying, it's kind of like the lining up of the planets for a cosmic event, all this shit around Cecil. It's order emerging out of a thin little slice of chaos."

"What in the hell do you mean?" she asked.

"Oh, nothing. It's just that you got big-ass rocks spinning all around the universe, pieces of matter flying all over the place and then, boom, here's a solar system. Perfect setup, right?"

"I guess. So what?"

"So shit falls into place when it's supposed to. You got atoms bouncing all around in the primordial soup, hooking and rehooking onto one another, making molecules that go to pulling in more molecules and the broth is just right, and one day it happens."

"What happens?"

"Life, fool." He chewed on the cigar, grinning.

"Wade, you are in a universe of your own. But at least it's not boring."

"What I'm getting at is, all this action revolving around Cecil, all these folks hitting each other like separate strings of dominoes, well, I got to believe the whole pattern is fixing to emerge. It's going to jump out at us like a double helix. And it's all about that murder."

"So you do believe Miss Sophie. I knew there was a brain in there somewhere."

"Well, let's just say all this craziness is going a long way toward backing her up, in my mind." He grinned again. "Not to mention you and your kissing self."

She slapped him, palm, backhand, palm. "At least I remember how."

"It's just a lot of craziness going on at once," he said.

"Crazy bad or crazy good? Us, I mean."

"I'll have to suspend judgment on that, collect up some more information. What if I come over this evening?"

"Only if you're going to kiss me back."

"I'll think on it."

She slapped him again when the phone rang. It would be weird, taking up with a man who was a long-time friend, but maybe that was how it was supposed to be. Maybe this was the way to go about it, as opposed to shooting a man into your vein, needing him like a fix, the way she had done Jerry Wayne Tolbert.

"Goddamn," Wade said, replacing the receiver. "That was Cecil's girlfriend on the phone. Hell, now I know the universe is just before making up a brand new solar system."

"What is it?"

He laughed. "I ain't telling you a damn thing. Hell, you'd just follow behind and insinuate yourself into the situation."

"Situation? What kind of a code word is that? What in the hell is going on?"

"I'll come by later." He was gathering up the keys to his patrol car.

"You can't do that. You can't leave me hanging. Are you taking your bullet? Is it a call for a bullet?"

He laughed. "Girl, you are crazy. I already told you it's a damn universe making up. Get on out of the way."

"But is it a call for a bullet?" she insisted, following him out the door as he left in a rush. "You better tell me that much or you're the biggest piece of pork in law enforcement."

He slammed the door to his car and backed out of the parking space.

"Answer me, goddamnit," Tammy yelled.

She heard him laugh again as he pulled away. "Yeah," he hollered from his open window. "I've got my bullet."

Earline sat at her kitchen table, sipping her third cup of coffee of the morning, pondering the visit she just had with Tammy Sims and Miss Sophie Price. The two women descended upon the quiet morning stillness of her home like a couple of complaining bluejays. Had she heard from Cecil? Did she have any idea where he might be? Did she think he was in some kind of trouble? After all, he had mysteriously gone off the air over eighteen hours ago. And wasn't she the least bit worried?

When Earline explained there were times her husband was gone for two or three days on the spur of the moment and she was not worried at all, they became agitated and fretful. And in fact she *was* worried, but about Miss Sophie. The old woman looked more bent and feeble than ever, and she was upset in a way Earline never seen before.

She hated she had promised Shug she would not let on to anyone where Cecil was. She wanted to reassure the old woman, but all the fuss over Cecil made her automatic tendency to protect him kick in. These events certainly were strange, folks all of a sudden concerned over Cecil, folks from years back, even. Shug's phone call, from out of nowhere, when the two women had only spoken a couple of times twenty years ago. And now these two, set on getting to Cecil. She was afraid to hope the visit signaled an end to her husband's silence, yet Miss Sophie's distraught tone tempted her to believe just that. And Tammy mentioned that she had been talking to the sheriff about Cecil. Could it be, Sweet Jesus, that this whole sorry business was finally going to be resolved?

As the women were leaving, Miss Sophie pulled her aside. "I am shedding my secrets, Earline," she said. "And there is one that Cecil will need to be told. It's about his mother and John McCormick. I think it's proper that he hear it from you."

"What now, Miss Sophie?" Tammy said, coming back into the house.

"Shoo!" the old woman said. "You go and sit in the van. Or better yet, go up to the Stop and Go and get us some more Krispy Kremes. I have to talk to Earline."

"If it's more deep dark stuff, then I want in," Tammy said. "I feel like I got the scoop on the whole county by now."

But Miss Sophie snapped, in an uncharacteristic way, "Shame on you, to treat this like gossip. This is something only Cecil can share with you if he chooses to."

"Yes, ma'am," Tammy said, her face flushing pink. "I'll get those doughnuts."

Miss Sophie took Earline's hands in hers as they stood there and told her about Renee's dealings with Big John McCormick and the rest of the white men, the men Earline wished, in spite of her earnest Christianity, would go straight to the bowels of hell, where she had known they belonged for a very long time.

Cecil had told her about Charity Collins soon after their engagement, and she sometimes wished he had not. Perhaps he needed someone to share his burden; perhaps he was hoping for absolution. It was clear he needed to come clean in order to cement the bond between himself and his fiance, and it worked.

She was always aware of some kind of eviscerating pain behind his eyes, ever since she met him at her daddy's church in Repass. He was twenty-one, two years her senior, tall, muscular, easy with words—when he was being his public self. He could talk smart-ass shit with his peers or spin out radio speeches with the polished finesse of a rich voice resonating with truth or outrageousness, as the situation demanded. Privately, however, he was quiet and innately gentle, and carried himself in a way so different from the self-conscious faux sophistication of the boys who usually courted her. He was an irresistible mix of kindly confidence, self-depreciation, and powerful words. He told her he thought of her as an arbitrary angel, one who would wield her power on a spiritual level, would guide him toward the warm center of her soul and nurture his own. Somehow, his saying it made it so. She came to feel a sense of duty spawned by honor, to help him stay tethered to a place where his torn spirit might someday heal.

They dated for a year, shared everything, climbed inside one another's skin and took a tour of secrets and fears, but she knew he held something back. He touched her with the care of one handling spun glass, tentative touches leaving her wanting more, yet he would not make love to her. It would not be right, he said, not until they reached the highest level of intimacy possible, transcending sex. She was not like the other girls he had been with, girls who clutched and drained his ability to give like emotional vampires. His regard for her was the most genuine he had ever known and he did not want to ruin it. It was beyond her understanding, though, and she felt cheapened by her desire, the low, behind-the-stomach flutterings making her wish he would tear her clothes off and breathe hard breaths into her flesh while he pushed against her, inside her.

Finally, when she agreed to marry him, it was as if she were presenting him with a vessel in which to place the full weight of his trust, and she promised to keep anything he told her in confidence tucked away in her heart forever. She promised, as he asked, not to ever give ultimatums or push him to do that which he knew to be wrong, and he promised to do the same for her. Finally, he said he had something to tell her, and if she could not live with him because of it, he would understand.

He drove her out to John McCormick's land, to a place near Round Swirl Creek, and walked her down to the bank, where they kicked off their shoes and waded out to a sandbar in the shallow water. "You like my woods?" he asked.

She nodded. And they were beautiful, the woods, unspoiled and powerful, spires of green spiking against a clouded blue dome.

"I come here a lot, all by myself," he said. "That's something I'll always do. When I'm out here I feel like I've crawled up inside the heart of God."

"That's how I always felt in my daddy's churches," she said, drawing circling loops in the sand with her index finger. "I don't guess I've ever been in a church that didn't make me feel that way. But then, I ain't never been in no white church so I reckon there's always a first time."

"Churches don't do it for me," he said. "But, you know, when I was ten years old, Miss Sophie took me to Temple Beth-El in Birmingham. I met the rabbi and they let me sit up in the balcony and watch a Bar Mitzvah. I guess that's the biggest building I'd ever been in. I thought it must be bigger than the White House or a castle or a cathedral. I felt real small in it. But significant. It was mysterious, and that white boy not much older than me was chanting in Hebrew, and it echoed all over. That's the only time I've ever felt close to God in a building."

"Did you ever get to go back there?"

"No. But I worried Miss Sophie to death about wanting to learn Hebrew and have me a Bar Mitzvah just like that white boy. And do you know she let me? I mean, she taught me herself, every afternoon out in the garage, and one day we just drove out here and had our own ceremony. Just me and her."

"That's a beautiful story, a beautiful thing to remember," Earline said.

"And that was when I really got to feeling like the deep woods was where God's heart was. And that's why I come here. To feel small and significant. It's sort of a private Beth-El. My own temple of trees, and it's really the only place I've ever belonged."

"I wish I could give you that," she said. "Belonging."

"Someday, maybe."

He apologized then and pulled off his shirt, but she was only overcome by a stifled urge to brush her fingertips across his chest, down to his jeans, to finally realize the fullness of her love for him. October sun dazzled over the currents and eddies surrounding them while he recounted everything vile and perverse he witnessed, the indignities inflicted on the woman who was as near a mother as he ever knew, the McCormick brand revealed like a coppery silk monogram on his shoulder, the lost piece of his spirit acknowledged, having curled up above the treetops along with Charity's. When she reached over to touch the scar with her fingertips, he drew back, flinching as if in physical pain, but she knew it was much more insidious than that.

Earline cried then, when he drew back, overwhelmed with Cecil's grief over Charity and her own grief over Cecil the child. But she also felt sick and furious, sobbing angry sounds, and when her revulsion subsided, she spoke. "It's been ten years, Cecil. You've got to tell the law. It's the right thing to do."

"I'm doing what I know to be right."

"You aren't going to let them get away with it."

"Did you hear what I said?" He invoked their promise. "I'm doing what I know to be right."

"How do you know?"

"There's people who would be hurt if I told. And I ain't meaning the ones that deserve it, either. I'm talking about ones close to me."

"You mean Miss Sophie? You really think somebody would hurt her?"

"Maybe. Maybe in ways nobody could see but her. Maybe not. Still, it's enough of a chance that I decided a long time ago to wait until she passes to even think about telling."

"That could be a long spell."

"I hope it is."

"To even think about it?"

"To even think about it."

"But why did you say there were others who could be hurt?"

"Because there's somebody else."

"Who?"

"Shug. Mr. Big John's daughter. I don't know what it would do to her to find out her daddy was in on a killing. I ain't going to do a damn thing to hurt Shug."

"But what's she to you?"

"Somebody I care about. Somebody I trust with my life. As much as I trust you."

"But she's white. She can't be those things to you."

"I know she can't. But she is. Look. I'm telling you these things because they spell the truth about me. My truth is hard and strange, and it don't change."

"I just don't understand how you can put that Charity girl's life down lower than some rich white girl who ain't even–Oh, God, Cecil. You been with her ain't you?"

"What?"

"You and that white girl. Y'all–"

He laughed. "Hell, no."

"Then why? Why else would you think some rich white girl is important enough to hide a killing? What are you to her if you ain't been with her?"

"Earline, she might be my half-sister."

"Jesus Lord."

"Even if she ain't, the deal stands. Look. I had me an unusual childhood. I'm steady living an unusual life. Bound to be strange to you. I ain't always known where I fit or how I fit or why my mama left me in the first place or nothing. If it ain't a regular enough life for you, I understand. I only thought it was fair to let you know, so you can decide you don't want no part of it. I won't think one bit less of you. I promise."

The water washed splashes and trills around them, soft breezes shuffling the leaves like thin playing cards. She knew it would be hard to keep her part of the bargain, resist interfering with his conscience, a conscience that was laid out before him to be drawn and quartered on a daily, sometimes hourly, basis. She could begin to trust Miss Sophie, she thought. She already liked her well enough, an acceptance etched with jealous suspicion of the dark-eyed, jewelry-flashing white lady who had raised Cecil Durgin. Earline and Cecil visited her at the big house in Three Breezes, shared some superficial conversations and stiffly elegant dinners. But now that she knew what Miss Sophie came through, something that would have broken so many others, Earline could feel respect burrowing into her heart.

But Shug was another matter. White folks as a rule were not to be trusted, and Shug was rich as the Pharoahs besides. Earline never laid eyes on her—had only seen photographs— but already hated her through and through. Maybe Cecil was secretly in love with her, making up this sister shit. Maybe he was one of those pathetic, turncoat Negroes who pined for the skin of privilege and held a secret disgust for their own women. But at once she knew that was not the case. It did not fit. Cecil was not a liar, not at all. And he was so adamant, so certain of Shug's worthiness. Suddenly Earline felt a snaking twinge of shame at her own lack of worthiness, and, in that moment, resolved to love him well and be the kind of wife he needed.

"Cecil?"

"Yeah."

"I'm with you. I want to be." She leaned in to kiss him, to finally touch the skin of his chest, avoiding the letters burned into his back.

"You won't be sorry," he said.

"You won't be faithful, will you?"

"I'm going to try like hell. It ain't going to be a promise, though. Not yet."

"I know." She kissed him again. "Cecil?"

"Yeah."

"Can we, now?"

"Yeah." And he stood to take off his jeans while she undid the buttons that went all the way down the front of her dress.

He made love to her as slowly as the sluggish current rolled bits of sand away from the little piece of earth where they lay, the most gentle pushes into sweet depths she had ever experienced. He moved his lips along her neck with heady, aching words of love, lush words, as slow as the cadence they set in the sand, a cadence that would stay with them throughout their marriage, through two children now grown and gone, through the women whose presence never failed to wound her, but never as much as Cecil had been wounded. And for all the longing she had, the yearning for the kind of lip-biting, nail-clawing, face-flushing sex that was fast moving and unfettered, it was apparently something he could only share with the peripheral women, those with whom he wounded her so uncharacteristically.

Earline took one more sip of coffee. Sometimes her love for her husband overwhelmed her with a hot rush of tearful empathy, a feeling her friends could never understand. They pointed out his infidelities, urged Earline to put her foot down, run him off if he didn't change his ways. But Earline knew. She was a keen observer of human nature and she knew there was always a compromise. She could easily have a man who would be faithful, but would he be as perfect a fit? Would he be as kind? Would he struggle as hard to understand her and himself? There would be a catch somewhere, she knew. There always was, but if Cecil could finally come clean, rise above his compulsion to save those sad replicas of Charity Collins, then there was a chance for their love to transcend it all.

Earline stood. Miss Sophie just shared the last bit of a puzzle that could at once complete Cecil and decimate him. It was the ugliest piece of a story beginning with a group of morally bankrupt white men making up a sick game for their idle amusement. But as disgusting and threatening as Miss Sophie's revelation was, Earline knew she would tell Cecil. She would tell him even though it might break him beyond the love they had built, because he needed to have every fragment, every sliver of the truth. She gathered up her car keys and set out for Camp DoeRun.

Tammy lay on the bed in Shug's old attic room, surrounded by yellow and blue and the feel of her youth, and pansies like the flowers she used to pull from the dark, behind her closed eyelids. Back then the petals she gathered in her head protected her, but lately they seemed to cover her like the floral blankets across caskets at Roper's Funeral Home, blooms and blossoms dragging at her heart.

She had left Miss Sophie downstairs at Miss Kate's door, Tammy adamant in refusing to join in on what was bound to be a very tense visit. Since she had always found Miss Kate to be intimidating, downright scary when she drank too much, Tammy admired Miss Sophie for even trying to make peace, reconnect with a deep and battered friendship. And now Tammy was falling into her own reminiscences, trying to keep to the good ones, like the nights spent in this room, so clean and big and all matched up, not at all like the little box of a room at Fat Forrest's house.

She remembered Shug's room being bright and frenzied and always cluttered with forty-fives skittered across the carpet, "Respect" or "Mony Mony" playing over and over on the stereo. There was a scatter of make up, Yardley cosmetics, and Dippity Do on the dresser and, on the bed, mounds of notes passed in schoolhouse hallways and across straight-rowed classrooms, notes to be read and reread, generating adolescent sagas, mini-soap operas of gossip and sordid dramas. It had been fun, those days before they grabbed on to adulthood, when they had the secure trust of fast, best friends to get them through the difficult moments, the brief heart-breaks, the wolves-in-sheep's-clothing friends. Tammy loved Shug like a sister forever, but instead chose Cecil to gift with her most shameful secret, the one that lived in the dark little coffin of a bedroom at Fat Forrest's house until she was ten, when it moved to live in tucked away patches of woods and creek banks until she was thirteen.

Cecil was kind to her when she told him about it, didn't think less of her at all, he said, but his look was one of a mourner at the wake of a child. It made her feel vulnerable, emotionally naked, a feeling that set terror tearing around in her bones, so she took refuge in half-truths and humor.

"Did you ever do this when you were a kid?" She scrunched the wrapper off a Dixie straw, then drizzled Coke on it, making it begin to expand.

"Yeah," he said. "I did."

She watched the writhing accordion of thin white paper twist and grow and seem to crawl with ringed muscles on the jockey's desk. "I used to want to kill myself," she said lightly. "But now I'm having too much fun. I'm going to hang around, I think." She was sitting across from where he sat in his low swivel chair.

"Tammy—"

She cut him off, feeling something in his tone threatening to burrow through the layers of flowers and get at her fear. "I know how to shoot Fat Forrest's pistol. He used to take me out to the creek to shoot bottles. But that was just an excuse to get me out of the house and

away from Mama. I could blow my brains out easy."
She said it tough and flip.

He studied her, seemed to know to join her in her
escape from what wanted to pull her under, even then.
Something in him understood. "You a good shot?" Cecil
asked.

"Damn good."

"Don't it make more sense then," he asked, "to
shoot Fat Forrest instead? Or at least shoot him first,
before you shoot yourself?"

They both laughed and she leaned her body into
the desk and put her hand, palm up, out to him. He took
it, held it a moment as though weighing something in
his mind while she watched him. Then he gave a half-
smile to himself and returned her hand to her side of the
table.

Tammy stood and walked over to one of the dormer
windows in Shug's room and raised it, looking out over
the land planted in lush, high-stalked corn and soybeans
in low green tangles. There were sirens echoing around
to the southwest, then going dimmer. She thought of the
homecoming dances and proms, dotted swiss and
daisies on a yellow gown she wore one year, daisies
pinned at her wrist and in her hair. She cocked her heart
toward the vision of innocence and wondered at the
turns she had taken, knowing she would take them
again, if they could lead to here, this moment, the possibilities she now came upon here in her best friend's
attic room.

She started for the stairs, to go join the two old

ladies, goad them into getting it together, promise them
she and Shug would do the same, when she heard the
sirens again, louder, as though they were circling out in
the distance. She went back to the open window and put
her head through, straining at the sound. The high,
squealing noise had come full around the property, was
growing even louder as it wove through the trees to her
north and west, out near the game preserve and Camp
DoeRun. For a second she thought she might ride over,
see what was going on, but in the next instant knew she
did not want to give him the satisfaction of being able to
predict her actions. She sat in the window seat, leaned
her chin on her arms on the window sill and let the
sound fire her imagination, knowing she would get the
details from him this evening, knowing she would want
to let him see who she really was. But that was a hell of
a long time to wait.

"Goddamn you, Wade Connors," she said to the
rich-soiled fields, the hidden creek banks littered with
broken glass and spent rounds, and the zinnias nodding
in manicured flower beds while a patch of black crows
rode the high August air.

Miss Sophie was not sure how far she would go, if
she would tell all she knew, when she turned the glass
doorknob to Kate's room, the room Shug once referred
to as "the mausoleum." It was an apt description. The
large room was dim, tomb-like, skinny little lines of sunlight sneaking through closed curtains. "This is ridicu-

lous," she said.

"Huh?" Kate rolled over, a wrapped chrysalis in a fat white comforter. "Go away. It's not even eleven yet," she mumbled.

"It's eleven-ten and you have company." She was struck by how liver-bloated and ill Kate looked, puffy-eyed, pale. She had let her hair go completely gray. Just two years ago she would not have been caught dead without her signature hair color, a deep toasted rust with honeyed-brown streaking highlights.

"Who?" Kate raised her head. "I haven't had enough sleep." She squinted. "Is that Sophie?"

"Where's your aspirin?" Sophie had walked over to the floor-to-ceiling windows and begun drawing back curtains, dousing splashes of sunlight across the room.

"Don't do that. God!" Kate covered her eyes with her palms.

"I'll get you an aspirin. Or three or four." It was sad. A person could age much better than that. A person could keep up her appearance, if she cared at all about herself.

"I don't need any aspirin. I'm not hung over. I just now got back to sleep."

"I'm bringing you some anyway," Sophie said.

"Well in that case make it a B.C. Powder. They're in the bathroom." Kate dragged herself into a sitting position and patted her hair. "What in the hell are you doing here?"

"I just thought it was about time," Sophie said from the bathroom. "We'll be catching the bus soon, so I decided not to squander what time is left."

"Speak for yourself. I'm not about to catch the bus." There was a hint of a slur to her speech, but also a vague touch of the feistiness of her younger years.

"By the looks of things I'd say you are, and you're way ahead of me." Sophie moved in an arthritic crouch across the bedroom.

"You're the one all humped over."

"I'd rather be humped over than hung over every day." Sophie rifled through an assortment of pill bottles in a brass basket next to the sink.

"Very funny. Glad to see you kept your sense of humor. But like I said, I'm not hung over. Not today."

Sophie caught her reflection in the bathroom mirror. They really were closing in on departure time, and she put her fingertips to her cheek, where the skin was loose and slickened with the talcum feel of aging flesh. She was coming upon her time, all right. Before long she would join the eternity of the stars and she damn sure wanted to leave the imprint of her existence on the lives bundled up with hers during this short journey.

"Why didn't you call first?" Kate said.

"Here." Sophie handed her the powder and a glass of water. An ashtray bearing a few butts sat on the bed-side table. There was a random pattern of cigarette burns on the carpet where Kate had missed her intoxicated aim. "It didn't occur to me. I never had to call first years ago."

"That was then. Things are very different now." She

let the white powder rest on the back of her tongue, then washed it on down with several gulps of water. She chased the water with the remnants of some watered-down vodka sitting in a puddle of ice cube sweat on the table.

"Yes, they certainly are. How are you doing since—well, the last time I saw you was at the funeral. And that's been such a long time ago." Her remarks felt hollow in the face of Kate's descent into the stagnation of the mausoleum, the crypt of her insular bedroom.

"Not long enough," Kate said. "Anyway, I'm doing great. Shug is home. Life is wonderful." Her eyes threw a belligerent gaze of reiteration at Sophie, who blundered on.

"I didn't get to talk with you very much at the wake. There were so many people. But I did want you to know how sorry—"

"Spare me. You have no idea how I felt. How I feel." Kate gulped down the remainder of the diluted vodka. Then she yanked open the drawer at her elbow, where a fresh bottle rolled against the wood.

"That isn't fair. I lost a husband, too, and I miss him every day."

"That is exactly what I mean. I do not miss John. And I doubt I ever had a husband. I need a smoke." She set the three-quarters empty Absolut bottle on the table and opened a satin cigarette case, withdrawing a Virginia Slim menthol.

Sophie lifted the ashtray and emptied it into a small trashcan by the bedside table, scattering butts like scurrying cockroaches over the bin of wadded Kleenex. It was too much. "You're looking bad, KiKi, real bad," she said. "Your eyes are all puffy. You're not taking care—"

"Don't call me that. And I'll have you know I already got up this morning. Even put on makeup, see?" She indicated her face. "And when did you become a doctor?" She lit her cigarette with a heavy gold table lighter and poured a splash of vodka in the empty glass.

"So why did you go back to bed?"

"Reality."

"What do you mean?"

"Just that. Reality spits in my soup on a regular basis. So I go to bed. What's it to you?"

"I'm just concerned."

"Now you are." Kate tossed back the shot of alcohol and let out a rush of a breath, an exhalation of appreciation.

"What does that mean?" But Sophie knew what it meant. It meant the damage was still splayed out between them, the wounds still fresh.

"Nothing. You know, I could use a Bloody Mary."

"Look at us, Kate. We're old. Truly old. Do you really hate me?"

"Yes. No. Why did you have to come here? Why can't we leave things alone?"

Sophie sat on the edge of the bed. "If you only knew how left alone things have been. Rotten. Things go rotten when they're left alone. And there are so many things I have to tell you, about back then, and about now. I came to prepare you for what's bound to come."

"What in the world do you mean? It sounds apocalyptic. Don't scare me like that." Kate sucked menthol deep into her lungs.

"I just mean that people's lives affect one another, especially when things are left alone and become more and more decayed. Dead animals bloat up and begin to stink after a while, you know. And someday it is bound to affect you and Shug."

"Shug? Now you really are scaring me, Sophie. I do not want my child hurt."

"I can thoroughly understand that." For a moment Sophie felt the camaraderie of earlier years, perched here on Kate's bed, unburdening herself, but she let a reflexive sprinkling of anger show. "My child has been hurt beyond anyone's suspicion and I have had enough of it."

"My God!" Kate flashed her most withering look of disgust at Sophie. "Isn't this a landmark day? I have certainly never heard you use that expression, 'my child.' He was always just 'Cecil' or 'the boy' or 'my tenant.' Since when did he become your 'child'?"

"Ever since the beginning, really." She took a deep breath. It had to be set out for the both of them. "Since John bought him. Paid for him."

"Paid? What in the hairy hell are you talking about?"

"He paid off Austin's debt so that we would be in a more comfortable position to care for Cecil."

"Jesus. Jesus God, I don't want to hear this." Kate held a palm to her ear. "Go away. Leave."

Sophie reached over and pulled her friend's hand

down, struck by how ancient their hands looked, skin transparent almost, veins prominent. Kate's nails were rough and unmanicured, something else which never would have happened if she were not so lost in regret. "If it had been only me, he needn't have bothered paying. I would have taken Cecil anyway. When you see a child so scared and so lonesome for his mother, well, how anyone could turn him away is beyond me."

Kate pulled her hand from Sophie's touch. "What are you saying? That I turned him away?"

"No, I don't mean that."

"Well, how could I turn him away when no one told me about him in the first place?" She blew a cloud of angry smoke. "And how could I have even considered it, anyway? A colored baby? Colored? Hell, look at Deb Mattox, adopting all those children from India and Africa and all—six kids in six different colors. That was only a few years back and she still gets talked about. And you think I could have taken in a colored baby forty years ago?"

"Maybe. I remember you not giving a damn about what people thought."

Kate stared off at nothing for a moment. "It's easy not to give a damn when you're Big John's wife and you've got all—this," she swept her arm in a large arch, "and everybody's scrapping around to be your friend." She put her fingertips to her forehead.

"I didn't scrap."

"No. You didn't scrap." Kate let her enjoy the compliment for only a second. "But that is neither here nor there. You are implying that I could have actually brought up a colored–"

"I did it, didn't I?"

"Get out! How dare you lord some kind of moral superiority over me when you stabbed me directly in the back and twisted the knife every day you let go by without telling me the truth. How dare you come here?"

Sophie was addled for a moment by the level of passion in Kate's outbursts, the volume and bulk of the anger she carried for so long. Then she was overcome with sadness for the years and years put by, the oblivious waste of it all. "No, Kate. I didn't mean to sound self-righteous. It's just that, well, you know better than anyone how desperate I was for a baby. How useless and anguished I felt all the time we tried. You know better than anyone else."

"So you took my husband's half breed of a bastard. That was very generous of you, Sophie." Kate pounded her cigarette on the edge of the crystal ashtray.

Sophie reached over and took her friend's hand. "You don't hate me. If you did, it wouldn't still hurt you so much. This whole business."

Kate snatched her hand away once again. "I cannot have this conversation."

"Yes, you can."

"Who do you think you are to come into my home and tell me how things are to be?"

"I'm someone who is trying to make what's coming easier for you and for Shug."

"There you go again, talking about Shug. And there

cannot be any more put between Shug and me. It would kill what little we have left."

"The truth will never kill anything. I promise. It will make things easier for us all."

"You'll never make anything easy. What are you going to do? What truth are you going to tell that you think I don't already know? Are you going to tell me about all of our mutual friends John screwed while I went without? The women he kissed and romanced and screwed while I sat up here alone, wondering why I'm thought to be so goddamn attractive when I can't even get my own husband into my bed? Well guess what? I saw through everything. And I did not go without."

"But I know about Chicago."

"Chicago just whetted my appetite."

This vein of conversation was unexpected and Sophie was tempted not to hear, did not want to know, but she at once recognized the hypocrisy of her reaction, attempted to comfort her friend. "Kate, it's all right. Anything that happened will be—"

"I did not go without and when you know what I contemplated you might not think it's so goddamn all right."

"Why would I—"

"About fifteen years ago I decided to get him where he lives, go after something that would hurt him more than anything. Just as coldly as you please. Premeditated seduction. Went after them with malice aforethought."

"Them?"

"His babies, of course. The boys he doted on, spent time with, pretended to have as sons. Cash and Lee. Big John's replacements for our own baby boy. Tantamount to incest, but worth it. So very worth it. And Sophie, I would have gone after Cecil, too. What a delicious little taboo that would have been, huh? I even thought about it. Can you imagine? I just never got the chance. So you see, I had a measure of revenge—a very private revenge that John never, ever knew about. So don't tell me what I ought to do now. You know nothing about me."

"Kate, my God. Cecil?"

"I was not ignorant about what John did. He gave me nothing and Cash was pretty much available on demand. Hell, he probably still is. And Lee tried, even though his heart wasn't in it. You see? I was not some simpering little fool who took it and took it. And there is nothing you can tell me that I don't already know."

"I never said you were a fool. Never."

"What money will do to us."

"Kate. You are not a fool."

"He waited until right before he died to say it, you know."

"To say what?"

"He let me coax and beg and carry on like some pathetic teenager. He let me lose every bit of dignity I ever had."

Sophie leaned toward Kate. "What did he wait to say?"

"That he stopped loving me when Shug was just a baby. God." Her voice caught and dissolved into a cluster of sobs before she snatched at a Kleenex, straightened her back, lifted the glass of vodka to her lips again.

"Kate, I'm so sorry."

"Just get out."

"You don't want me to get out. You need me back in. This is crazy. The things we have done. We need each other."

"Like hell."

Sophie sighed. "I can't believe—You wouldn't really have gone after Cecil, would you, Kate? It would be like Austin going after Shug. It's sickening."

"Are you leaving now?"

"Would you have? Cecil?" Sophie asked again, softly, catching a glance from Kate, a glance telling her yes, there might be a chance to mend. Just a faint chance, and she took it. "Eekh fahrshtay nit. I don't get it. Fahr vaws?"

The words evoked an odd sound from Kate, a guttural sob that turned into a forced sigh, and the words that followed were much softer. "I think so. And I'm not proud of it, but I think I would have sacrificed any feelings I had for you as a friend or an ex-friend or whatever the hell you are to me, in order to get even with John, even if it was only in my own head."

Sophie let it sink in, then, "Did you consider it as a way to get even with me, too?"

"Maybe," she said in a small voice. "I need you to leave now, please."

"Can I come back?"

"I don't know."

Sophie stood. "There are other things you need to know."

"Not now."

"Truly. It all has to be told."

"Not now."

"All right. Later." Sophie walked to the door, then turned. "Whatever happens, will you be kind to Cecil?"

"I don't know." Then, as Sophie touched the glass doorknob to leave, she heard Kate's whispered words. "Efshehr. Maybe."

Miss Sophie turned back to face her best friend, Kate, the lady with the large and outrageous personality, who never let anyone get the best of her, who now cried out with the most hopeless wail of grief Sophie could imagine. She walked back over to Kate's bed, once again sitting on the edge. She put out her hand, laying her palm upon her friend's shoulder as it shook violent sobs of loss into the space of years lost between them.

"I know," Sophie said. She leaned down and kissed Kate's head, the graying over of her years of false beauty. "I know," she said, hearing phantom footfalls in the sage brush at the radio station, seeing the dance of the trash barrel flames, feeling a slow tide of relief rising up, new and clean, up through the loneliness and the shame.

The long morning at Camp DoeRun was decep-
tively quiet so Cecil rested a long time, hoping for a little
bit of sleep, waiting for Shug and thinking on it all. He
finally got up around eleven and opened a can of pork
and beans for lunch, eating directly from the can with a
spoon, and wondered where the hell she was. He was
hung over and irritated with this waiting around shit,
but he reminded himself his sister was about to be
turned inside out by what he had to tell her. First were
the things he discovered about her fraud of a husband;
second, and much more threatening to her, Cecil had
come to the decision to tell her what her father and the
other men did, all those years ago. It was right. It was
simply right, and he would let her help him decide
whether to go to the law. If it would be too hard on Shug
for her dead daddy to be brought out into the daylight,
then Cecil would not push it, yet. Not until she was
ready. And even then, he had to take into account how
feeble and worn down Miss Sophie was, especially here
lately. He couldn't live with himself if his revelations
caused his mother to fade into forever, out of his life.

Cecil scooped another spoonful of pork and beans
from the can. He wished he could call Shug, tell her to
come on, now; enough spy, counterspy; he had things
to do today. But there had never been a phone at the

camp house. Big John always refused to put one in, insisting it would be an intrusion. For years, a hi-fi stereo and a radio were it, as far as electronic entertainment went, good enough for music or the news or whatever football games were being broadcast on any given autumn weekend. It was only after Bama won the national championship in 1961 when he agreed to have a television put in the place, twenty years later adding a Betamax, then a VHS VCR. But never a telephone. That made it too easy for wives and such to interfere.

Cecil wished he had not promised to stay until she came back. He paced, poked at the pork and beans with the spoon, mumbled at his poor judgment under his breath. He was already in a foul mood, having succeeded at getting only two or three hours of sleep on a long leather couch in the big living room. It was the first time he ever slept inside the camp house and there were just too damn many echoes of voices, mocking him, calling him a sorry excuse for a nigger, a spineless piece of shit who only knew how to save his own cowardly black ass.

He had walked miles last night, after the men left. First he collected up their empty glasses and stood washing them at the kitchen sink before he even realized he was performing one of his ingrained tasks, catching his reflection in the window, seeing himself outside, as a boy, peering in. He walked back into the great room then, and poured a drink of his own from the bar, then another. The sweet warmth of the whiskey accompanied him as he walked all over the house, up and down the porch, before joining her in the dark of the outdoors. He carried the bottle of Old Forester and a flashlight down to the skinning shed at three in the morning, to visit his own enigmatic secret, pay respects folded up in regrets at the grave of Charity Collins, as he had so many times before.

The barbecue pit, unblemished by fire or coals, sat like a parodied headstone on the rough concrete slab, and he seethed at Big John and Huck, who had crossed over to her side already, and without paying a price because of his own self-entrapment. He wished he believed in hell, especially when he thought of the men now dead. How blessed it must be, to have the cold comfort of a hot pit laid out for one's enemies, where they would slowly turn on Satan's spit, have the cooked flesh sliced inch by inch from their bodies, for all eternity. He ached for a hell for his enemies as he ran his palm over the cool brick and rough mortar of the barbecue pit headstone, knowing at the same moment if he really believed in the hole of fire it would only serve to lull him into further silence, just as his attempt to believe in a Savior had. It came to him, then, once and for all. He knew it was time to do the right thing, just the right goddamn thing, and not for redemption or the promise of heaven, but simply because it was the right thing to do and God would be pleased with him. And he knew it had to begin with Shug.

He sat in the dark, shaded from the full moon soaking overlying limbs in a warm bath of light. He sat against one of the beams supporting the tin roof of the skinning shed, sat facing the barbecue pit framed by a gutting beam, sipping brown whiskey and smoking and wishing for sprays of roses for her resting place. Breeze-whispered rustles of leaves called his eyes to search for her, sweeping the dense layers of leaves and under-growth, alerting him like a deer to find the place where she waited.

Back at the camp house, the old pit and grill, sooted and brick-chipped, marked the place where she was taunted and tortured by the one particular white man before his twelve-year-old eyes. Cecil could smell the smoldering oak logs in the fireplace while Elvis, Chuck, and Little Richard offered up surreal rock and roll sere-nades. He could feel the helplessness of being rooted to the damp dirt beneath the holly bush while the men took their turns with her inside the house, most of it out-side his vision, but not always his hearing. Big John apparently liked an audience, and she apparently liked whatever was being done to her. There were soft moans that grew into louder ones, into sharp exhalations; and quickening, frantic words encouraging, until she let loose a breathy shriek, followed shortly by a deep-voiced expletive from the white man. Then there was applause, whistles, shouts from the audience. Cecil stood, but they were still outside his view.

Shortly after her turn with Mr. Big John, Huck hollered, "Pin the tail on the piece of tail! Crawl, Baby!" and for ten minutes or so Cecil caught glimpses of her in and out of his line of vision, on all fours, the men chasing, slapping her behind, hard, taking turns aiming

Cash's souvenir mule's tail at the appropriate place near the back of her thighs. One minute she would be giggling, laughing, and the next there would be a cry of pain, a protest, and Cecil's bafflement tripled. Huck carried her over his shoulder, torso dangling down his back, across the room, hitting her on the pale flesh of her rear. He sat in a big chair across the room from Cecil's perspective, got her over his lap, both palms slapping at her while she struggled and laughed, then he leaned over and bit into her flesh, making a sound like a growling dog.

She screamed. "That hurts. You hurt me." She looked over her shoulder, put her fingers to the wound. "You broke the skin."

"Take it easy, Huck," Mr. Big John said, coming into the kitchen and opening the refrigerator. He wore boxers and an expression of exhaustion.

"Now you going to suck it, Baby," Huck commanded, standing her up, and she was swaying and giggling again, pain forgotten. "Over there 'cause I got lay down to have me a view of your ass."

"Is that right?" she said, leaning down so that her face was close to his. "You like that, huh?"

"Goddamn right." Huck stood and they moved out of Cecil's line of vision.

Mr. Big John gulped down some orange juice, straight out of the jug, put it back in the refrigerator, slammed the door, and scratched his butt. He sat in a straight chair at the table, arms resting on his thighs, head down.

Huck was hollering a steady stream of instructions to Charity. "Move it around, Baby. That's it. Yeah. Now go the other way. Damn."

Cash laughed. "Go on and chow down on it, man. You know that's what you want to do. Go on."

"Move it, Baby," Huck said. "Keep it moving."

"Go on," Cash said again.

There was a stinging sound of flesh being slapped, eleven, twelve, thirteen times while the other men whistled. Then it was quiet except for radio rock and roll, muffled moans, ice cubes clinking in the other men's glasses, until Huck had his big moment of release, more flesh slapping, and he yelled at the top of his lungs. Mr. Big John jumped, startled, having apparently been dozing. Then he stood.

The boy wanted to run as fast as he could, back to the skinning shed, erase everything he had seen, even the beautiful naked lady, but he was mesmerized inside a sickening feeling, fascinated by the raw, matter-of-fact way they were passing her from one to the next, to be used like a thing, like the sun-warmed watermelon Tony Mack Franklin had fucked one summer evening. Charity was no more to them than that. He could not imagine the men carrying on like this with their wives, or else why would they pay someone for it? Cecil knew he was looking into the men's guts, into the sexually malevolent parts of their brains. And he knew his observation, dangerous as it was, gave him a kind of upper hand, one they need never discover.

"How 'bout a visit to the old Circle J Ranch?" Lee

yelled. "Winner comes first. Hundred dollars. Come on, Big J!"

"I'm going to leave that with you, boys," Big John said, stumbling back out of the kitchen and toward one of the downstairs bedrooms.

"Ain't you good for more than one load?" Roscoe yelled.

"Y'all don't know how to save it up," Big John said. "I'm like old Hard Cat Cash. When I fuck 'em, they stay fucked." He closed the bedroom door.

Huck, too, was parting. "Goddamn, you got an ass," he panted, weaving over to the large leather chair and ottoman against the far wall, collapsing into the cushions

"Lay right here on the coffee table, Baby," he heard Lee say. "Do like that. No, put your legs like this here."

"Okay," Cash yelled. "Grease 'em up boys, and pass the Vaseline. Don't just lay there, girl, you got to put on a show."

Charity giggled. "Something like this?"

"Damn sure works for me," Cash said.

It was quiet for a while, the Chicago radio station filling in the silence. "It's twenty-seven degrees here in the Windy City. Baby, it's cold outside. Ten-twelve P.M. on a rocking Saturday night. Kinda gives me the 'Summertime Blues, 'so here's Eddie Cochran to warm you up." The disc jockey's mellow-cool voice led into another blast of music.

Cecil was glad he couldn't see their squenched-up, swollen-cheeked white faces while they masturbated.

He wondered what Charity thought of it all, if she wished she had not come to the party. But then, she seemed to enjoy most of it so far, especially whatever Big John had done to her.

"Hey!" Charity yelled in a while, then dissolved into laughter.

"Pay dirt!" Lee said. "Damn if Boscoe ain't got another nut."

"That's three, ain't it, Boscoe?" Cash said. "Get up, Baby, and go wash your face. I'm fixing to carry you off to my room for a real fucking. Damn if I want to kiss on none of Boscoe's jizm."

Roscoe came into his field of vision, stumbling into the kitchen, naked, hairy beer gut sheltering a shriveled up penis nestled in coarse curls. "Shit. I wanted to be last with her this time," Roscoe said, mopping at his genitals with a dishrag, "but I ain't going to make it. I got to go to damn bed."

"Hell, Roscoe, you know Lee's got a thing about being the last one of the night. Every time," Cash said, joining him in the kitchen, still working his fist to his penis, followed by a disoriented Charity, who stumbled over to the sink. She leaned over, turned on the faucet and splashed water to her face. "Ooh, yuck," she said. "It's all in my hair." She splashed more water to her head, then dried off with a dish towel. She raised the Venetian blinds and stared at the window above the sink, not three feet from where Cecil stood, watching her. She fixed her hair, swaying, looking into the window as if it were a mirror. She rubbed at smudged mascara beneath her eyes. "I look awful," she said. "I need to redo my makeup."

Cecil wanted to tap on the window, motion her to come out, take her down to the skinning shed and kiss her, stroke his fingers along her neck, tell her she didn't have to take money to have things she did not like done to her. Things that messed up her makeup.

"Fuck the makeup," Cash said. "I'm ready for some pussy. The Hard Cat man going to show you how it's done."

The corners of Charity's mouth turned up in a delicate little depraved grin, giving Cecil another charge of lust and confusion. She seemed to want Cash to show her how it was done. Probably she just liked Cash Cloy best. Hell, most women did. She turned, walked over to Cash, put her own fist around his penis, and led him away from the kitchen and out of view. Cecil heard a door shut.

Lee Davis sat naked in a kitchen chair with his Scotch and smoked a cigarette, serenaded by an occasional muffled squeal from Charity Collins. By the time he finished a second smoke, Charity was meandering her zigzagging way back into the kitchen, wrapped in a bed sheet, exposed flesh glazed with sweat.

"Cash said I ought to come back out here and take care of you. God, I'm wrung out!" she said.

"I'm just having a drink," he said. "Sit down."

She dropped into the chair. "He liked to wore me out." Her eyes were heavy-lidded. Her body swayed. "You seen the pecker on him, didn't you? Lord

Almighty."

Lee chuckled. He went to the bar, poured another drink, and brought it back to her.

"I'm past drunk already," she said, but she sipped it anyway. "What we going to do?"

"Sit right here and have a drink is all," Lee said.

"Don't you want none?"

"Tell you the truth, I lost the feeling. No offense."

"Oh, come on," she said, eyelids brushing down in a sleepy-drunk way. "I know you ain't too in-tox-i-ca-ted." She enunciated every syllable. "You been going slow on booze. I notice stuff."

"Ain't necessary."

"I notice a lot." Charity stood, unwrapped the sheet, then straddled his lap. "Please? I'm kind of curious about you. You ain't had a—you ain't blowed a nut all evening that I know of. Come on."

Cecil watched Lee, the familiar twitch of his jaw. He had the buck fever look Otis liked to laugh about. "That's real nice, but no, I'm going to pass this time."

Charity laughed. "This time? Just this time? Ain't this why you always go last?"

"What do you mean?"

"Come on," she said. "I notice things. You can tell me." She kissed his neck, but he pushed her back.

"I don't know what you're getting at."

"Yes, you do." She leaned in with the air of a confi-dante. "You know. Can't keep it up. So you just let everybody else go ahead. Right?" She ran pink finger-nails through his dark hair.

Lee squinted and cocked his head. "You think I can't keep it up?"

"Not for me."

"Shit. Wait here." He pushed her off his lap and went in the other room.

Here was his chance, Cecil told himself. Run to her, grab her by the hand, and take her off through the woods you know front, back, and sideways; go across the creek and into the game preserve. He could build a tree house like Tarzan did for Jane, like he saw at the picture show from the colored section up in the balcony. They could live off the land, off fish, wild blueberries and fresh game. He could save her from deadly animals who stalked her while she bathed her creamy breasts in Round Swirl creek, he could ride vines from tree to tree with her in his muscular Tarzan arms, and good would triumph every time over evil. But Lee Davis was coming back into the kitchen, carrying a blanket and a bottle of Scotch under one arm and a squat jar of Vaseline in the other hand.

"Swallow these," he said, opening his fist onto the table.

"Three of them?" she said. "But I'm already—"

"Do it. Now."

She picked up the pills, pushed them through her lips, and chased them with Scotch. "I better not get sick. I think you're fixing to show me something."

"Damn right. Bring the drinks and smokes and come on." He pushed the jar of Vaseline into the pile of material under his arm and took her by the elbow.

The screen door slammed and they stumbled down the steps, close enough for him to smell them, all funky with whiskey, sweat, and the damp musk of sex. Lee spread the blanket out on the grass next to the picnic table and the old barbecue pit, and Charity sat on the tabletop, her feet on the bench. Lee lifted the mesh from the barbecue pit and threw in some lighter knots and a couple of small logs he doused in charcoal fluid before throwing a match to it all.

"You ain't fooled me for one second. No sir-ee," she said, while he stirred at the flames and tossed in another log. With clumsy-drunk arms, she threw back the sheet wrapped around her and the light from the flames painted her skin in a yellow-white glow.

"What do you mean?" He walked over to stand in front of her, picking up his glass.

"I know what you want. I know who you want."

"Shit."

"You got the hots for Cash Cloy," she said.

"What? Good God Almighty. What kind of crazy bitch are you?"

"Hell I don't blame you. He's one good-looking guy. Ain't he?" she laughed.

"You're talking some sick shit. You need to shut the hell up."

"I seen how you watched him. I'm laying there on that coffee table, putting on a show, like Cash wanted. Hell, everybody's eyes was on me. All except you."

Lee set his drink hard on the table and grabbed her by the forearm. "Shut up! Shut the hell up!"

She giggled. "No, you had your eyes cut over to Cash the whole time. Over to that good-looking man's pecker. Did he put on a good show for you? I was watching you the whole—"

Lee came hard across her face with his palm, knocking her from the table to the bench, where she caught herself, wobbling, slipping. Her drink spilled and she let the glass fall from her hand and go rolling across the concrete with a slow, gritty, hollow sound. "You're a fucking liar," he said.

She pulled herself up to sit on the bench. She seemed oblivious to any kind of pain from having been struck. Cecil had seen drunk men fight and laugh while busted noses dripped blood, numbed as they were from the alcohol. "You know what I think?" She slapped her palm to the table. "I think you like having me after he's done been all over me, don't you," she challenged, aggressive and insistent. "You like to smell him on me, you want to get up inside of me and feel of his—"

Lee hit her again, this time with the back of his hand and harder, and she in turn skid-hit the concrete on her left side. She moaned. "That hurt," she breathed, crawling into a sitting position, running her hand down her stomach and hip. "You hurt me. I'm bleeding." Then she giggled, "You don't have to hurt me just because you got the hots for the Hard Cat." Her words were coming even more sluggish and Cecil strained to make them out.

Lee snatched her up by the arm, jerked her head back with a handful of hair. "You better not ever say that goddamn lie to anybody or I'll kill you."

She nodded. "Please. That hurts."

"Now sit down." He gave her a rough shove into the bench. Then he retrieved her glass and filled it with Scotch. "Drink up. I want you relaxed."

She took the glass and sipped. Lee pushed on it until liquor ran down her chin and she choked. "Stop," she said, coughing. "Look. Let's don't do nothing." She giggled again. "There ain't no point. You got the hots for Cash." She laughed louder at the joke she held over Lee with drunken insistence.

Lee yanked her up by both arms this time. "Shut your fucking filthy mouth!" He shook her hard as he spoke, her head nodding like a rag doll's, until he turned her around and pushed her to the table on her stomach.

"What?" she moaned, rising up, weight on her hands, then dropping back to the tabletop.

He went over to the blanket, picked up the jar of Vaseline, opened it, then set it back down on the bench. With his back to Cecil, he tugged on her legs, seemed to be sliding her toward him.

"Oh, ow," she yelled. "Splinters."

"Shut up. Get your knees under you."

"Oh, you," she said in a singsong, drunken voice. "You are so funny. You want to feel what Cash left behind."

"You're fixing to feel something, all right."

She giggled. "Well, show me then."

Lee leaned over and said something in a low voice. Cecil could not make it out, but Charity began to struggle. "No," she said. "Don't."

"Keep quiet," he said, holding her down. "I'm going to show you to shut your goddamn lying mouth."

"No, Lee, don't." Her voice was thick with alcohol. "Stop."

Lee dipped his fingers into the jar, then reached down in front of him, seemed to be grappling around between her legs, then he put the weight of his upper body on her back, elbow pumping as though her were punching her. Charity screamed, and Lee reached up around her head, Cecil presumed, to cover her mouth, because now her protests and moans were muffled. He counted as the white man's elbow drew back seven, eight, nine times to her smothered screams.

"You don't like that, huh," he said, standing. "Okay, we'll try something else."

Her voice was trembling. "No. Please." She tried to rise up on all fours, but he shoved her back against the rough wood. "You're hurting me. Leave me alone." Her words were thick, and she was crying.

"Don't you fucking move." He stuck his hand in the jar again, then put it to his crotch, arm working for a few seconds before he moved close to her, fumbling against her.

"Don't," she sobbed.

But Cecil saw Mr. Lee thrust his hips forward, hard, and she screamed again. The white man again lay over her, palm to her mouth, suffocating the sounds she tried to push from her throat. The boy did not want to hear her being hurt. He could slip into the house, he thought, get Mr. Big John. Mr. Big John would make Lee Davis stop. Or maybe Mr. Big John would not make him stop, would not care, would know what Cecil had seen.

Charity's stifled yells and sobs turned into a pathetic rhythm of whimpers that sounded like they had the breath knocked out of them with each thrust the man drove into her. Lee's hips pumped fast, had right off the bat, the man's steady "Uh, uh, uh," accompanying her breathless pain. With every motion came another crack in the idyllic forest fantasy Cecil had envisioned, until it shattered and tinkled through his brain in splintered shards, tears finally coming. Lee stood straight up, the muscles in his ass and thighs taut. He let go of her mouth so that her feeble sounds were clear now, heart-breaking, and Cecil was afraid his own crying would become audible. He had to get out of there. Another sound then, an explosion of air through clenched teeth, came to Cecil's ears and he was afraid he would be sick and reveal himself. He began to inch his way toward the corner of the house.

"Turn over," he heard Lee say. He looked back to see him roll Charity to the bench, pulling her up.

She moaned, "No. It hurts," and when he let go of her arms they dropped limp to her lap.

"Let's have a drink and smoke a cigarette. You know you got to smoke a cigarette after you fuck." A flame flared up. "And we ain't got started good, yet. Here Baby, have a cigarette." He pushed her down again, on the bench, her smothered moans and limp, half-flailing arms in a predetermined struggle against the dark

November woods. It was the last thing he saw or heard as he made his way around the side of the house and across the soft green lawn where the back trail would take him to the skinning shed.

Cecil thought he heard music, a car coming up the road, stopping at the red metal gate. He almost ducked out the back door, then thought he'd be goddamned if he was going to go hiding ever again, like a frightened child. Instead, he pitched the empty Van Camp's can into the trash and walked out on the front porch, its wide timber planks squaring around the south side of the house, heavy posts bearing a tin roof. It was bound to be Shug, he figured. And it was by god about time. She'd better have a good excuse for keeping him waiting so long.

But it was not Shug at all. There was an older model Monte Carlo parked there at the gate, and a man was climbing over, vaulting himself over, walking toward the house. He had a deliberate stride, a definite purpose about him. His presence grew larger and larger as he covered the expanse of lawn between the camp house and the gate, never betraying any hesitation, curiosity, or acknowledgment. There was no gesture of greeting thrown to Cecil, no words shouted ahead to clear the way for a friendly exchange, for a favor requested, for directions, gas, a phone. Aside from his carriage and demeanor, the man's dress was not what DoeRun was accustomed to seeing. He wore big-buckled boots, big-buckled jeans, and an open denim shirt with the sleeves cut away. A cluster of keys jangled against his thigh with each long step. Cecil watched him come closer and closer; the lines of ink etched on his forearm, longish blond hair pushed back from his face, his left eye cut at the lid and slightly swollen, coming into focus through a lens of blurry suspicion. It didn't feel right, and Cecil let his palm brush the long k-bar knife at his belt. "Can I help you?" he yelled as the approaching visitor came within thirty yards.

"I reckon you can," he said. "You're Cecil Durgin."

"Yeah." Cecil squinted his eyes at the man, still striding toward him, a man whose presence stirred up some kind of murky recollection he could not name. The open shirt revealed ink-laced skin at the left shoulder, some kind of hidden tattoo. "What does that make me to you?"

The man stood at the bottom step and leaned on the rail. "As far as I'm concerned, you're the piece of shit nigger that killed my daddy." He grinned and glared the malevolent blue of his eyes at Cecil.

It was an accusation that blindsided Cecil before he felt anger taking the shock away. He almost blurted curses back at the intruder, almost told him he wouldn't lay down for being called a nigger and a killer in one breath. But something about this man told him to keep to task. There had to be an explanation for the out of nowhere accusation. Maybe this was some kind of crazy man who had him mixed up with somebody else. "I think you come to the wrong place."

"Wrong place, hell. You killed him just as sure as if you'd put a gun at his head and fed his brains to the hogs and I'm looking at making it right."

"I think you better get off this land," Cecil said, risking a firm tone, not knowing to what degree a lost mind or a criminal history figured into the equation, still wondering why and how this hard-tail misfit had come to be here, at DoeRun.

"Oh, I'll get off this land, all right. But I got something to talk over with you first. I'm going to let you make it all up to my daddy by convincing you to let go of some of that influence you have when it gets to be election time."

Recognition rinsed out Cecil's initial suspicion and his presumption of insanity. So this was not some random aberration run amuck. No, this was an invited guest at a McCormick event. This was Lee Davis's guest. "You must be Claud," he said. "Claud Pierce, I think it is. Nice to meet you."

The man looked startled, but regained his threatening demeanor in a slice of a second. He sneered at Cecil, then offered a sound like something between a growl and a chuckle. "No, it ain't so nice to meet me. Not at all. I was told to let you know you need to keep them hands off the voters this time around."

"That right? What else did Lee Davis want you to tell me?"

Claud did not flinch this time. "Told me I could fuck you up a little bit if it made me happy. But if you do what I say, I might not have to fuck you up."

"If I agree to keep my hands out of the election, right?" Cecil could not quite get a bead on the degree to which he was being threatened. It seemed to be in a strange flux, one minute bordering on the absurd, the next immersed in ripening reality.

"You ain't as stupid as I thought." Claud approached the porch steps.

Cecil turned it over in his head. Odd that Claud would have come here to find him. Nothing near chance, not even in the universe of the coincidental. "So how much you making on this? About five hundred?"

"And a tip, if you do like you're supposed to," Claud said.

Cecil chuckled. "Sounds like Lee Davis runs you way more than he thinks he runs me."

"Don't nobody run me."

"You don't think so? And you with a pocket full of Lee Davis's money?" Cecil said, going with it, seeing the nerve he had hit, poking at it to find out if it would yield some hot-tempered information, anything to help Cecil size up what was unfolding here.

"I told you them pussies don't run me."

"*Them* pussies? More than one, you mean?" Cecil let a laugh punctuate his observation. "Oh, yeah. That would be Cash Cloy and Roscoe Bartley. Solid citizens, to a man. And they got you for a sanitation worker. Paying you a garbage collector's salary."

"Goddamnit, I don't work for nobody but me," Claud enunciated through clamp-jawed anger. "And I got my own quarrel with you, like I said."

Cecil was struck by the man's eyes, the blue ice of the irises, which seemed to go a different shade of frozen as the intensity of his glare deepened. "Well, Claud, that's interesting and all, but what you don't get is the fact that nobody runs me, either. Not since a long time ago does anybody run me."

"Ain't you the big fucking deal," Claud grinned. "You're the big boar nigger that runs the world when it's time for folks to vote."

"Maybe I am the big boar nigger," Cecil said, taking the words from Claud, stealing them, owning them. "But I ain't nobody else's nigger. So I think you better finish up and get on off the place."

A quick spray of words came from Claud like machine gun fire. "You're the big fucking killer, too, ain't you? You damn sure killed Old Man Pierce."

There it was again. Another reference to his daddy's death with a word made to hit him below the belt, connecting with Cecil's knowledge that he was, indeed, a killer by default. "You ain't got no business saying I killed anybody," Cecil said, "just like you ain't got no business here." All the while he was turning names and whispers from the past around in his head. Suddenly it occurred to him. Claud had tracked him here, had to have found him not through the white men, but through one of three women. His body jerked with a surge of rage. "What have you done to my wife?" he demanded.

"Wife? You got a wife? Oh, yeah, that's right, you do."

"You better hope you ain't had nothing to do with

her." Cecil felt himself on some kind of a precipice, a hidden verge of a feeling he did not know up close. It was a feeling destined to meet him as a stranger but, he sensed, would soon ooze recognition and finally couple with him in a union of ripe intimacy.

"Got a wife, by god, but you keep yourself in all kinds of pussy, don't you? Right good stuff, too," he laughed.

"Where's Kim?" He felt the upper hand slipping with Claud's read of the way his life was constructed. This son of a bitch was finding his weakness now, and vague instincts uncoiled and stretched up around his chest.

"Kim?" Claud gave a hoarse chuckle. "You must mean Miss Honey Hole. And it's a honey of a hole, too. Damn good snatch. You got good taste in nigger women, boy."

From the top step, and in one fluid motion, Cecil descended to the third to bottom step, raised his right knee and drove the bottom of his boot into Claud's chest, knocking him back, leaving his breath suspended in the air between them, arms thrown toward Cecil, then laid out in an attitude of crucifixion, legs unable to get beneath him. As he fell into the lawn, Cecil was on him, pounding his right fist into Claud's face, his cheek, his ear, before Claud could get his wind back and start struggling against him.

"You by god tell me what you done," Cecil demanded, raised up on his knees, fists gripping the denim shirt below him, the faded shirt matching the iced-over eyes that bore up at him.

Claud shook his head, some of the places where Cecil's fist had connected reddening. He grinned. "Goddamn, man," he said in the tone of a drinking buddy. "I was just fucking with you about that snatch. Why you want to be so goddamned serious?"

Another blind-sided moment took Cecil's clarity. He didn't feel any certainty about which version of Claud was fucking with him, this one or the previous one.

"Goddamn going to jump me for no goddamn reason. I ain't fucked with none of your folks. That ain't right, man."

"How'd you find me?" Cecil still held the denim shirt, feeling almost foolish, unaccustomed to letting fly what he kept caged at his core.

"Get the fuck off and I'll tell you. Goddamn, I ain't even took a swing at you. Don't you know nothing about no fair fighting?"

Cecil's heart still thudded fast, his body alerted by the same fight-flight feeling he had met on the one particular night long ago and with which he was only beginning to reacquaint himself. He stood and walked over to the porch to sit on the third step, forcing his mind to overrule his body, backtracking through the conversation, searching for what to believe and how to proceed. "Say your piece and get the hell gone," he said. "But first tell me how you found me here."

Claud pulled into a sitting position, then sat cross-legged, leaned back, reached into the front pocket of his jeans, and brought out a crumpled pack of cigarettes. "Shit. You done fucked up my smokes," he said, tossing a few broken ones in the grass until he gave up and found a filter with a short length of tobacco attached. He lit it with a red Bic lighter and squinted up at Cecil. "It's real simple." He sucked flat-lipped on the filter and blew a soft hiss of smoke. "I found out where all your scrapes and rubs are. It's just a basic process of elimination after that."

"Nobody would have looked here for me." He was getting all kinds of mixed messages, from Claud, from the white men the night before, from his own body's barely contained response. Nothing was straightforward. "Where's Kim?" he repeated.

"Why you want to keep asking me that?" With his cussing finger to his thumb, Claud thumped the piece of a cigarette, smoke streaking across the lawn, and stood. "It ain't like she's back at the trailer, taking it easy with my shit for brains brother."

The specific reference to his brother shot like quicksilver through Cecil's thoughts, at once blending names together, a string of names meeting him with the clear, cold image of two small boys, robed like their daddy was. The boys, the men, the fire in the trash barrel, and, finally, Miss Sophie, her eyes to the flames as they forced him to look at her, to put his lifeless fingers to the place between her thighs. "You're the son of a goddamn—"

"Be still, now," Claud said, on the other side of a gun, a gun that had appeared from thin air. "We'll have plenty of time to reminisce if you keep your head, don't get yourself killed." He walked over to where Cecil sat on the middle step. "You goddamn sure think you're the one in charge here, don't you? You been operating under false impressions for a long, long time, put my daddy in the grave, got used to being some kind of big nigger in town, ain't you?"

Cecil's thoughts were ripping right and left, making thin little incisions into the center of himself that held his rage, untapped even by the instinct that had already snaked out at Claud. One deep cut and he would give himself over to it, and gladly. This ofay motherfucker giggled while his daddy pushed Cecil's hand into the depth of flesh above his mother's thighs. This ofay motherfucker put a brand to his shoulder so that he would forever be reminded of her degradation and his. This meat-hunting motherfucker had done Big John McCormick's bidding all his life.

But you done Big John McCormick's bidding too, she whispered, just like I did. The sound of her breathless voice brought him up short, shushed at him through the mute leaves, as quiet as Charity's quiet frame was as she lay at Cecil's feet, Big John's ear to her stilled heart.

She came to him, finally, in the night, last night, just before he went inside. He was standing beside the holly bush outside the kitchen window, head hazy with whiskey, fingering the waxy, piercing leaves, when she stepped around the side of the house. She had been barefoot and wore a thin white cotton dress, loose at her shoulders, the pooling of it around her form letting the moonlight through. She watched him with an intense, wide-eyed stare, walking toward him with slow steps. Her mouth did not move, but somehow he knew she was saying, "It will be all right," over and over and over. When she stood before him he was twelve years old, confused, afraid, in love with her. Her eyes kept his as she leaned her lips to his cheek. He could feel them part against his skin, warm breaths brushing his skin between her parted lips, while she moved them along the side of his face in a slow, slow, arch. "It will be all right." Now he searched the woods for her, moved his head from side to side to find her form among the tree trunks, craned his neck to see around Claud Pierce.

"What the hell?" Claud was looking at him as if he had sprouted a growth in the middle of his forehead. "What the hell are you doing?" And he turned his own head for a small second to find what Cecil was looking at.

Cecil lunged upward, taking Claud's gun hand up and back with both of his hands, sending the ear-splitting sound of a double-fired pistol out across the lawn and through the thick walls of trees beyond. Claud staggered back, Cecil's weight pressing against him, like some kind of drunken dance partner.

Claud flailed at Cecil's flesh with his free hand, the two of them looping and pirouetting on the lawn, both of Cecil's hands cemented onto Claud's shooting wrist, elbows locked, legs pounding, aiming at tripping him up or finding Claud's sorry white cracker balls with his knee. They tangoed across the yard until Cecil's leg tangled up with Claud's and started a chain reaction, limb against limb against limb.

When Claud's back hit the ground, Cecil's weight full on top of him, the automatic blasted another round then went loose, hard steel clacketing against the soft earth. Cecil looked down into the blue eyes of Claud Pierce, the son of his mother's tormentor, and felt even more unfettered fury spilling into compartment after compartment, flooding his heart, the walls of his chest, pushing through every capillary outward.

She knew his rage, better than he did. Charity guarded it with the marred skin of her thigh, the rough lines scraping up her torso, the welted burns from the cigarette put to her shoulder and her breast while she screamed, while Cecil found his way away from her, in the dark, to the skinning shed. When he slipped her nightgown from her shoulders, letting the gown fall to a white cotton puddle in the shadow of the holly bush, the marks on her flesh took shape in his consciousness like a photograph materializing beneath a wash of chemicals. He drew her down to the dirt where he once sat with his knees against his chest, fighting back terror, tears, and coarse lust. He put his lips to her bare skin, to the place above her breast where Lee Davis had laid the fiery end of a cigarette. Cecil put his lips to her skin, finally, with a warming surge of tenderness, the kind of sweet gentleness the white men could not give her.

"Murdering nigger," Claud tooth-gritted at him, coming into the side of his head with the hard fist of one who had cultivated his punches over decades. They rolled across the rye grass, emerald green and still damp in shaded places, with the humid August air taking Charity into its hidden places, to the deep pockets of darkness nestled in the woods, where doe and fawn slept in the cover of limbs over cradling rooted earth. They rolled in a tangle until Cecil was able to kick into Claud's side with a heel, knocking him windless for a second. Cecil let his own knuckles bite into Claud's mouth, his nose, fueled by the unstoppable, blistering wrath that had by now swallowed him whole.

Her whisper swelled again through the trees, leaves like bits of paper tickling one another. "It will be all right." She had held her palm to his back, brushed it slowly up and down the back of his shirt, repeating the words as his lips found the wounds and the plains and hollows of flesh between and among the wounds. He let his mouth just touch, down the side of her chest, over the sharp push of her hipbone, never pressing into her with his lips. Their touches had been rough, those of the white men and the one man who made her cry out and struggle against the sheer force of his violation. Lee Davis's fist had pushed into her like he was beating some drunk in a bar fight, pummeling as if to make slick-knobbed, slimmering gristle of his face.

Then Claud was above him, dripping blood and snot into Cecil's face, spitting on him and calling him a murdering nigger, again and again. Cecil could taste warm blood in his own mouth, a taste sending his arms and fists flailing even harder. Then Claud was standing, far away and above him, and the buckle on his boot flashed a warning. It was enough of a warning for Cecil to half-cover his gut with his forearms before Claud drove his sole into Cecil's stomach, sending him doubled up and choking for air, but willing the breath back into his lungs.

Claud turned, took a step, then dropped to his knees, spitting and coughing into the grass, cursing as he dragged himself up to his feet again. As Claud staggered toward where the nine-millimeter was nestled in the rye grass, Cecil pushed himself up with his arms, drew in all he could from the reservoir of rage steady pouring its juices into his blood, and stood, swaying, slipping the k-bar from its leather scabbard.

Claud still snorted blood from his pulpy nostrils, his body moving from side to side, the gun at his feet. But just as he made to bend down, Cecil stumble-ran at his back, charged at him with the strength of his now unguarded truths, grabbing Claud around the chest, slinging him circle-ways, briefly pinning his arms and lifting him off the ground. Claud's legs kicked at the air and blood sprayed from his nose as he struggled to regain his arms. "You killed him," he grunted in a clenched-toothed voice, working his right arm loose. "Killed."

He knew she was watching, taking some satisfaction in the fact that he was finally doing what he should have done long before now. He had fallen upon the whole bunch of them, in the person of Claud Pierce, son of the man who raped his mother's pride. He could smell them, all Scotch and whiskey, perfumed sweat and rancid ejaculate, and he let the swell of unfiltered hate take him where he longed to be, to a place of honor, the place she promised him last night, as he touched her with his lips in the shadows.

Cecil drew back the knife, and Claud grasped at Cecil's arm, batted at the blade with his one free hand, blood spilling down his wrist. Cecil made several aborted jabs with Claud's hand riding his own before he brought the blade down into Claud's neck, into a point just back of, and a little below, his left ear lobe, plunged it in deeper, feeling the tip glance hard bone, and quick-dragged it forward around the throat with force fueled by once-hoarded emotions so that flesh, muscle, carti-lege all gave way just before Cecil pushed him into the ground. In that moment the severed jugular gushed its rhythmic jet of blood, a bright-red pulse becoming a rendering worthy of a big buck, a blood-let bog in the fine rye grass brushing like silky strands against her bare feet. Claud's eyes fixed up at him in some kind of dia-bolical disbelief, mouth moving as if to speak, the man-gled larynx yielding only raspy wet bubblings. Cecil, dispassionate, watched the pump of blood grow less furious by degree, the fangs of an ink-drawn reptile bathed in blood at Claud's shoulder, while Claud lay making struggling gestures, becoming more and more like the empty slough of a snake with each weakening throb of the vein.

Cecil leaned his head back, closed his eyes, opened them to blue sky and tree-topped clouds and to the thin, shrill, faraway drone of a siren; then he stepped away from the hand clutching faint and feeble grasps at his legs and walked back over to the porch. He collapsed on the steps, awash in some strange sense of relief set inside a raw amazement. The power of that which he had withheld from himself for so long, the pure force of it, had risen up like the thick pine trunks pointing needled green limbs at white clouds. Another siren sound joined the first, then another, a small swarm of a noise against the hills. He felt no need to wonder or react to the sound, waiting, watching the breeze lift and play strands of Claud's hair, his sleeveless denim shirt billowing up with the gentle wind.

She stood barefoot in the bloody puddle surrounding Claud Pierce, a marshy pool feathered with rye grass, head cocked, seeming at first disbelieving, then gave Cecil her full-on gaze. Her eyelashes dropped and opened once, twice, three times in the sunshine, and she brought her mouth up at the corners, into a suggestion of a smile. He felt the warm, wet, inside softness of her open mouth against his, even though she had not moved. She kissed him with the breeze, slid her lips across his, let her tongue push the taste of her into him. She brought one hand up and ran her fingers through her dark hair, her palm down the side of her face, holding it against her cheek with her head again cocked, looking into him. Finally she smiled one more time, turned, and stepped across the paisley-swirled lawn toward the old logging road leading down to the skinning shed. He watched the billowing purity of the white dress, the midnight curling into the dark waves of her hair, and the poetry of the emerald grass tickling her red-flecked ankles as she walked away.

Earline's eyes caught quick fragments of images through the trees as she approached DoeRun, and the pictures pounded into her heart with a rush of adrenaline. A sheriff's car, then two police cars, then the ambulance, all jump-cutting in her head like film projected from an antique reel to reel, blinking at her wherever the woods parted. Her breath went from her with a reflex assumption: the lineage of violence had, as it reached its end, eaten into her own world, consuming her husband in some awful way. He was gone.

As she drove through the open gate, past an older car parked there, she searched the yard with her eyes, needing to find him; but could only watch the ambulance pull away, the policemen milling and talking, cutting their eyes toward her, acknowledging her with an attitude of distant dread, as if hanging back with some message of loss, as if mentally drawing lots to see who would tell her Cecil was no longer with her. She braked the car and laid her forehead against the hard vinyl steering wheel, holding on, squeezing tight, talking to Jesus in her mind.

In a moment a door slammed, and she raised her head to see Wade coming down the porch steps, taking a woman she recognized as Shug McCormick by the elbow to help her down in a gesture of support, and Earline could only grasp the steering wheel more tightly, as if holding on, literally, would keep her from screaming and racing the car in a panic behind the ambulance. She watched them come toward where she sat, did not want to hear what they would tell her, and she moved her head slowly side to side, warning them away with her stare.

But they did not go away, stood instead beside her car. Shug's face, seeming old after her absence of two decades, was puffy and raccooned with smudged mascara, as though she had been crying in some fierce way, no delicate sniffling but full-out sobbing, and the welted red skin beneath her eyes was wet. Earline made to throw the car in reverse but Wade pulled back her door, which let out an anguished moan from its steel hinges. He leaned down. "It's all right, Earline," he said.

Shug knelt beside the open car door and took Earline's left hand off the steering wheel. "Cecil's all right," Shug said, and her voice broke into fresh tears. "He's in the house. He told me everything."

"Oh," was all Earline could manage, dropping her head back onto the steering wheel. "Oh." It came out in an exhalation of numbed relief, uncertain and couched in remnants of suspicion. "Oh."

"Hey, Danny," Wade yelled at one of the policemen. "How about driving Shug home. We'll get her car over to her later."

Shug shook Earline's arm until Cecil's wife looked over at the rich white girl, now a full grown woman, with whom she had once, very briefly, believed Cecil to be in love. Her cheeks warmed at the thought of how she had allowed her mind to follow along that false course of unfounded reasoning.

"He'll be all right," Shug said.

"But you said he *was* all right."

"He is. But Wade has to explain." Once again came a catch in her tone, and this time she gave an odd little whimper. "Earline, how can I make myself understand all this?"

For the first time in a lifetime, Earline felt Shug's kinship with Cecil. "Are you going to be all right?" Earline asked.

Shug closed her eyes, held them shut for several seconds, then opened them, tears spilling between swollen lids. "I don't really believe it yet. I mean, I believe Cecil, but not *it.* You know? If I believe it, then it's like losing my daddy the rest of the way." And she put her face in her open palm for a moment, letting bewildered sadness fall into it for a few minutes, Earline feeling helpless, wanting to go to Cecil. Shug looked up at her. "Do you see?"

"I think so." It glanced through her thoughts that she herself had more to tell her husband. And she could lose Cecil the rest of the way, too, in spite of his coming clean with his sister. "Yes, I do."

"God." Shug rubbed her hands up and down her face, wiping at wet cheeks. Then she held up both palms as if to say "enough" and pulled at a sad smile. "I'm mostly sick about Cecil. All these years. To have to feel that way for so long. God. We've all felt so bad for so long."

"Yes, Lord Jesus, Cecil's time has come to be at peace," Earline said.

"That's the damn truth," Wade, who until now had kept an uneasy silence, leaned down again. "Let's talk a minute, Earline."

"Yes," Shug said, standing. "I have to go see about Mama. See if she's sober enough to hear all this right now." She ran her hand through her hair, turned her face back toward the camp house, and her expression went at once from sad little girl to hard, angry woman as she added, "And Rob has some things to hear, too."

"Hey, Danny," Wade yelled again. "Check and see if Booty is getting everything he needs so we can proceed out here. Go on with him, Shug."

Shug leaned down again and hugged Earline, the first piece of affection ever set out between them and, with the denuding of the past, it was a bit of uneasy affection blanketed in potential. "Take care of Cecil," Shug whispered, then straightened up, giving Wade's arm what seemed to Earline a gentle squeeze of encouragement before the rich white girl, today a woman, today her sister-in-law, left.

"Where is he?"

"He's inside, like Shug said," Wade said.

"What about the ambulance? It wasn't in a hurry, didn't have any of the lights on." Earline's head was clearing, the initial numbness subsiding.

"Just let me explain what happened. Stay calm, you

hear?"

Earline had been so relieved Cecil was not being driven away in the soundless, slow-moving ambulance she overlooked the dark references being thrown at her. "Wade?" she said, a fresh tide of fear coming over her. "What kind of trouble is he in? What happened here? Take me to him."

"He ain't going anywhere," Wade said. "He's pretty bent out of shape. Let's just let him be for a few minutes while I explain things to you." He walked around to the passenger's side, got in, and reached over to turn the engine off. And in his slow, matter-of-fact drawl, Wade laid it all out for her, and for the first time she let herself notice the scarlet bog in the rye grass, Cecil's long knife sheathed now in blood. He laid it all out for her as she rocked back and forth, arms cross-laid over her stomach, brow wrinkled in an intense effort to grasp what it all meant for Cecil, what it would do to their lives. Wade seemed to read her mind. He began to launch into the legalities and lay out for her what he could. She shouldn't worry, he told her, but it was bad. He wasn't going to lie. Of course, he knew enough already to say in court right now, today, if he had to, that it was self-defense. And sure, it would be a sight easier all the way around if Cecil had not garroted Claud Pierce, had only stuck him once or twice in the neck and not tore him up so bad.

Earline felt her stomach rise up in her chest at the thought of how her husband was pushed up to that moment, that second on the cusp of a new hour in his life, when he could be capable of tearing a knife blade through life-filled human flesh. She moaned then, and Wade apologized for being so graphic, but goddamnit he wasn't going to dress it all up in a Sunday suit for her, he said. Still, she didn't need to go to pieces. She needed to stay together for Cecil, if nothing else. Cecil was pretty messed-up over all this.

She stopped rocking and looked over at Wade. "Will he go to prison?"

"I ain't saying he won't. But I ain't saying he will, either. He's got a lot on his side."

"He can't go to prison. He can't."

"You can't cry, Earline. Not now."

"You're going to arrest him, aren't you?"

"I don't have no choice."

"Sweet Baby Jesus."

"I look at it as a formality in this case. I don't even expect that high of a bail."

"Jesus."

"It will be all right."

"Will it?"

"I feel like it will. You just got to remember Cecil ain't a killer and he was defending himself. Hell, Claud Pierce wasn't nothing but a scavenger buzzard who's needed plucking from this world for a long spell. All them Pierces are kin to the wildebeest. And ain't none of them wrapped tight at all. Booty's done been out to the Pierce place, arrested Claud's brother. Says that property's full of tales and strange goings on. And that brother of Claud's is babbling like a myna bird on speed. Cecil done us all a favor, bottom line. Hell, it's a Boo Radley situation if I ever seen one, even if Cecil ain't simple-minded."

Earline gave a long, deep-breathed sigh. "Lord, when you get throwed a biscuit there ain't no butter, is there? But thank you, Wade. I know you'll stand by him."

"Damn straight. He's my hero," Wade said. "Always has been."

She smiled, warmed by Wade's words and loyalty to her husband. "And thank the Lord he finally told all he knows."

"Yeah," Wade said. "Told me to get a jackhammer out here, and an air compressor. Hell, a backhoe, too. Said he was almost positive we'd find what we needed under that barbecue pit out by the skinning shed."

"Praise Jesus," Earline breathed. "Praise Jesus."

"You go see about him," Wade said. "Be easy, now. He ain't real pretty, and Jim Frank on the ambulance gone yonder said he's going to need a few stitches in his mouth, maybe ought get his ribs looked at, so be easy."

Wade got out of the car, walked around, and took Earline's arm to help her stand. She kept her eyes away from the reddened patch of grass and focused on the big porch, tall windows above and below its green roof. She wouldn't cry. She would try to let him see, once and for all, what she was made of, what she wished he could accept and finally give back. She got the railing beneath her palm and pulled herself up the porch steps, slow and determined, feigning strength.

Tammy twisted the ends of a joint and ran it through her lips, wetting the thin paper, then she laid it on Shug's bed with the other two she had just rolled. "So when do I get to meet this Rob person? I kind of want to do him a favor and kick his ass."

"Do me a favor, you mean. Well, his note says he's gone to town in the pickup, to the Co-op, I think. But I can introduce you to his car."

"What?"

"Come with me." Shug stood. She reached for a Kleenex, blew her nose, and pitched the wadded-up paper handkerchief into a small purple wastebasket.

"Are you sure you're all right?" Tammy asked. When Shug had run up the stairs and through the gate to her old room all of Tammy's doubt and dread disintegrated inside a heartbeat. Time had not passed. Walls had not been built strong enough to keep out their history together. And seeing the devastation of what Shug's daddy had done was enough for Tammy. She let Shug cry in her arms, like so many nights, sitting on the third step, listening to her parents yelling at one another.

"No. I'm not all right," Shug said. "But I will be. And I think this is the first time in my life when I've known for sure that I will be all right. So come on. Bring your shit."

When they reached the second-floor landing at the top of the wide staircase, Tammy nudged her. "Want to go see what's going on with your mother and Miss Sophie?"

"Hell no," Shug laughed, taking some car keys from an oriental bowl on a small marble-topped table. "I haven't heard any yelling or furniture being thrown in there, so let's leave well enough alone. It'll be bad enough when I tell Mama about all that's happened." There was a shake to her voice. She sighed, glancing down at the floor.

"No, you don't," Tammy said. "You already had your big cry upstairs." Then she invoked the admonishment of their youth. "Let's don't feel sorry for ourselves, okay?" She took Shug by the arm and pulled her down the stairs.

They entered the garage through the kitchen door, Rob's Mercedes slick and unblemished, white on white, pure as a virgin bride.

"Tammy, Rob's car. Rob's car, Tammy," Shug said.

"Nice to meet you, I'm sure."

"He parks it in precisely the same spot every time. Three steps from the back. See?" Shug went over and leaned against the back wall of the garage, then took three steps forward, ending up with her legs touching the front bumper of the car. "And he refuses to put the top down. He buys a convertible, but he won't put the top down."

"Why?"

"Two reasons. First of all, he doesn't want the leather upholstery exposed to the road dust or any unforeseen elements of nature."

"And?"

Shug giggled. "He doesn't want his hair to get

mussed."

"What an anus," Tammy said. "Señor retento grande."

"God, how could I have stayed with him for so long?"

"You're allowed to be stupid, just like I was. But I have to ask. If he's such a jerk in everyday life, what's he like in bed?"

"As fastidious as you can imagine, but not about pleasing me, of course. Let's see, two minutes of kissing, on the lips, then kiss each boob for twenty seconds, insert finger until I'm almost ready—you know, mois-turewise—climb on, give it forty-seven thrusts, and you're done."

Tammy's eyes went large. "You count the thrusts?"

"Nothing better to do. Sometimes I count back from forty-seven to zero, kind of like a rocket launch in my head."

"Man," Tammy shook her head. "Only forty-seven?"

"Yep."

"Shit. That ain't near enough."

"Well, it seems like an eternity when you're wishing it to be over." Shug shuddered. "I might as well have been a corpse for all the attention he gave me in bed."

"And you never had anybody on the side? Damn, girl, you better get busy."

"Well I take the edge off every once in a while. I keep a vibrator in my boots along with the birth control pills."

"What a dweeb," Tammy said. "Not you. Rob." She

pulled a lighter from the pocket of her jeans and held the flame to the joint. "You know what we should do?"

"What?"

"Take a ride." She passed the joint to Shug.

"Of course we should." Shug at once became more animated. She sucked smoke into her lungs. "Hey, I'll even put the goddamn top down."

"And we'll hit every dirt road in the county by dark, just like we used to do."

"Hell, we might even go over to the PlayMore Club. Find some cowboy types to dance with. I'll leave a note for Wade back at home. Tell him to come and be the designated driver."

Shug handed the joint back to Tammy, got in Rob's car, and slid the key in the ignition. "Here we go," she said.

"Scared?"

"No more. I already know what I'm going to say to him. And it won't be much."

"What will you say?" Tammy asked, getting into the passenger's seat.

Shug unlatched the car's top and hit the button to lower it. "I'm going to say, to quote an ex-love of mine, 'This here is all played out, Ass Hole. You need to go.'"

"Does he even have an ass hole? Or is it so pinched up it's grown together? Have you ever actually seen an ass hole in that man's butt?"

Shug laughed. "I'm telling him. Tonight."

"And if he fights it?"

"Then I tell him the four things he doesn't know:

I've been eating birth control pills all these years, I only enjoy sex with a vibrating machine, my brother is black and we're going to spend a hell of a lot of time together, and I want him to get the hell out of my mother's house and take his hands off my mother's money. Then I call Wade to kick his ass out."

She cranked the car and used a small remote control to open the garage door.

Tammy turned on the radio, searching for the Oldies station out of Birmingham. Shug backed the car around and headed down the long paved driveway until the Mercedes' tires—clean, black, Armor-All-ed rubber surrounding the whitest of whitewalls and mirror-finished hubcaps—hit dirt road. Then she accelerated, speed building. "Want to do a Duke boys?" she yelled over the music, a Stones tune.

"You don't remember how."

"Want to bet?" And she sped up even more, smiled over at Tammy, then snatched the emergency brake, cut the wheels, and the car spun to face the opposite direction, dust boiling up around them while they shrieked hysterical laughter and coughed, waving their palms through the dirt cloud, trying to wave it away.

"Look what you've done to the nice white upholstery," Tammy said. "Tisk tisk."

"Goodness, what a mess. And to think it will just turn into mud after we go swimming at Tippin's Eddy tomorrow." Shug backed the car around and headed down the dirt road again, tires grinding into gravel. She let the car slide on the curves, and when she got to the dried-up remnants of an ancient cornfield near the highway she bounced the automobile across worn-down furrows, braked, and spun a doughnut in the dirt, sending another mushroom cloud of dust to swallow Rob's once obsessively-compulsively hours-spent polished conveyance. "Satisfaction" blared from the radio while Shug carved circle after circle into the abandoned field, fogging it with billows of red dust rising and fading. When she turned onto the blacktop, the car was drenched in dust, inside and out, the two of them, Shug and Tammy, gritty and peppered over with dirt and laughter.

DoeRun was a huge camp house, and when Earline opened the door the great beamed ceiling rose above her head with such overpowering presence she hesitated, feeling small and intimidated. There were dead animals everywhere, stuffed and mounted. A bobcat lounged in lazy petrification over a door frame, a fox had become statuetted in mid-trot, large-mouth bass curved their rigid tails against moth-balled air, and generations of regal deer, their racks cobwebbing the walls like woods lace, tines spiking above penetrating eyes of soulless glass, stared down at where Cecil sat on the leather sofa. A large red stain was bibbed down the front of his shirt; he had a wet dish towel against his mouth.

She went to him, held on to him, keeping back the panicked tears backing up in her throat. They didn't speak. She went to the kitchen, brought out clean wet rags and another towel wrapped around a Ziplock bag of frozen deer meat. She helped him out of his shirt and took it to the kitchen trash can, wondering for a second if it was some kind of evidence she was discarding. She sat beside him and he let her lean, but gently, against his shoulder, while he offered up answers to what he thought were her questions. Then, in an unanimated tone, he clarified, reiterated, explained it all again, while she reassured with the words Wade had given her: "It's a Boo Radley defense. Nothing to worry about." And she set about examining and fussing over his battered face, the scratched welts on his arm where Claud's fingernails had torn long lines in his skin, the tattered flesh at his knuckles quick-gnawed back by blows into Claud's teeth.

"I'm sorry, Baby," he said.

"Sorry for keeping yourself from being taken from me? And you need not think I could ever change what I've always seen in you. Not because of this."

"I'm trying to get clear in my thinking," he said. "Trying to understand."

"Don't you let yourself believe for a second it could've been any different. You did what you had to. That is the end of it."

He looked at her with the anguished eyes of one not certain whether he believed her words but needed to believe them lest he find the task of living with his deeds too overwhelming. Earline leaned forward, got her eyes level with his, and found a place on his hand to lay across with her own. "The truth is all anybody can ask for."

Then, knowing his emotional insides were laid open and ready to receive the last bits of the puzzling mosaic of his past, she repeated for him the account Miss Sophie gave her of his conception. She spoke of the visits Big John McCormick paid to Pitch Hill; the flirtatious shine he took to Renee Joyce, then a full-breasted teenager all giggles, with the charm of an inno-cent vamp; how he spent scattered evenings there in Otis's shotgun, rutting in the early hours beyond mid-night while Otis sat on the front porch with an old oil lamp glowing fire and a whittling stick peeled to nothing, listening to the moths slap their helpless wings against the thin globe while he worked his pocketknife.

When Renee turned up pregnant, Big John's infatu-ation with her soured fast. Still, even though he was done with her, there was a point to be made, to let her know where she fit relative to Big John's family and the rest of the world of Three Breezes, and it was choreo-graphed with the precision of all the other perverse points made by the white men over the years. Big John told Otis there was to be a poker weekend at the camp, just the regular group for the games they enjoyed. Otis was to come, as usual, to cook and clean up for them. And he was to bring along his niece, Renee. He was to bring his niece, Cecil's mother, so the men would have one woman for their entertainment. And even though she was a child-woman of only seventeen, Cecil just then a moment of a fetus membraned and suspended from the frothy wall of her womb, the men would not be denied

her. Even though she was courted and bedded by Big
John McCormick, she was now to be passed from man to
man on a forced tour of that which her child's mind could
not begin to dissect or comprehend or forget.

Otis tended to her during the months of Cecil's ges-
tation, she a solemn ghost frightened of herself, frightened of everyone. She refused to cross the threshold,
would only lie all day on the cast-off couch of some white
family or another inside her uncle's shotgun, counting
the particles of dust swimming in the slats of sunshine
that came through cracks in the walls. Otis brought her
shelled pecans and buttermilk, meals of fried fish and
collards, sometimes a vanilla coke from Wall's
Pharmacy, and by the time she delivered a son she had
begun to come part way back to a semblance of herself.
But within a few months Big John started coming around
once again, this time intrigued, not with Renee, but with
the male child he failed to produce elsewhere, a boy he
might want to keep close by, color be damned. And he
came around more and more frequently, hinting at his
intentions, until the unyielding transaction was put
before Otis, with Renee wailing like a wounded coyote.
Sheriff Huck took her to the train station in
Birmingham, bound for her cousin Loula and a steady
wage as a presser in a Chicago cleaning store owned by
one of Miss Kate's old beaus. Just below the Tennessee
line she tried to leap from the train, and the porters had
to lock her in the baggage car. They had her sedated at
the first stop where they could find a doctor willing to
go to the trouble for a hysterical colored girl.

The room at DoeRun was huge and hollow, Earline's voice circling up to the beamed ceiling while Cecil sat slumped into the couch, head back against the leather. It was only then, having already undergone the purging of his own hidden venom, the phantom tears came through a silent, surrendering stare as he listened to his wife. His eyes reflected the swooping revolutions of the ceiling fan above him while his mother's defiled portrait took on a density and dimension it had lacked forever. Earline let the whole of Otis's truth fill the room, knowing Cecil could now get inside his mother's skin and understand. Finally. He could know the desperation of a young girl straining at the deck of a passenger car to hurl her emptied body to the rails and clicketing wheels beneath her because she wanted her child. He could know what his mother suffered from the white men because he had seen it with his own child's eyes when he watched Charity Collins, when he witnessed Miss Sophie's humiliation. He could know his mother did not run from him; in fact, loved him. And Earline could feel something more in the space of her words in the daunting room of the camp house, something she knew as well as she knew her husband, more whole now than on the day prior. She felt Cecil accepting, receiving his mother's love like a viaticum, an absolution for the twelve-year-old boy who had allowed juvenile voyeurism to carry him from the secure isolation of his near-slumber by the skinning shed campfire and into perdition.

Earline lay her head against his chest, careful to

avoid his hurts, to be easy with him. She ran her hand up over his left shoulder, fingertips brushing the satin-skinned scar resting there. She traced its outline with her index finger, again and again, to the cadence of the swooshing ceiling fan, as if to gently erode it into insignificance.

Cash Cloy, Lee Davis, and Roscoe Bartley were framed in glass, like "Nighthawks at the Diner." The men sat at their usual booth, front and center, behind the plate-glass window, at the Southernaire Eatery in Three Breezes, having an early supper. Cash ordered chicken fried steak, Roscoe had liver and onions, and Lee chose the catfish filet with a generous side of cole slaw. Sandra Lawson, the waitress, came over with a pitcher of tea and freshened up their glasses. Cash looked up at her, smiling, then said something to make her throw her head back and laugh along with the three men. When she turned to walk away, the men leaned their heads in, mouths moving as in low conversation, then wide and open and laughing again, their eyes watching Sandra's hips, her backside shrouded in mint green and topped with the crisp white bow of an apron.

Customers paid, walked outside, into stifling August air. Buddy Jeter bused tables, stacking plates in a square gray-plastic tub. And while the men framed in the plate glass window, "Eatery" in script across its face, enjoyed their food together, a Three Breezes police car pulled into a parking space at the curb. The men cut bite-sized bits of meat, stabbed forks into salads and scooped at side dishes of black-eyed peas and mashed potatoes. Lee hit his palm on the bottom of a ketchup bottle and Roscoe brought another forkful of onion-smothered liver to his mouth. They sipped their sweet tea, leaned their heads in again, and laughed some more, Roscoe gesturing with his knife now, in between cuts, as a second cruiser pulled in to the curb, both Crown Victoria motors idling, air conditioners blowing. In a while Sandra brought over dessert, peach cobbler and warm apple pie topped with vanilla ice cream, and the men leaned back in the booth, laid their palms on their stomachs, and made faces exaggerating their fullness. And the pairs of officers in the two cars waited, watching, a couple of them smoking cigarettes, another reading the *Birmingham News Journal*, until a third police car, one called over from Tuscaloosa as backup, pulled up beside them. Then car doors opened, slammed shut. As the men inside swallowed down the last larded and sugared morsels of their desserts, the little bell on the café's door announced the presence of three officers bearing warrants and silver-slick handcuffs.

The great room at DoeRun was growing dim with the afternoon. Cecil eased himself up, wincing at the pull of muscle against his injured ribs, and stood. He and Earline walked out on the porch where Earline leaned against the railing, Cecil behind her. He set his left palm low on her waist, fingertips at her hipbone, and wrapped his right arm around her whole torso. She let her body lean back into his, careful to be gentle but with no hesitation, soothed by a new transcendence into the next level. With her back against his chest, his arm enfolding her, she sensed a new and electric field of warmth between them, felt a mysterious, fey power in his touch he had never before offered her.

A whole afternoon had gone by, and dusk was taking the trees. The two of them stared out into the dense clusters of browns and grays topped by green, pine needles like soldiers' plumes against the clouds, wild magnolia's oversized leaves glazed in a waxy green depth, blackjack oak, sweet gum, cedar, and finally, osage orange, the fabled tree of Noah–bois d'arc, indestructible preserver of life. Their trunks stood powerful and proud in verdant loveliness, all nestled in tangled privet, honeysuckle, and rambling wisteria. Cecil leaned his lips into the left side of Earline's neck. And even though he drew back in pain from the cuts in his mouth, it was the first kiss he ever gave her that was so full of promise.

Booty Cop was just pulling into the yard, and he lifted a finger, the standard Cole County greeting, as he drove by. He was followed by a flatbed carrying a backhoe. The jagged jaws of the big machine nodded as the truck rolled over ruts and washed out slashes in the dirt. Thick-linked chains anchoring it to the flatbed rattled slapped-steel echoes out into the August forest. The brakes squealed, truck cab knocking at low pine limbs. Cecil and his wife watched it lumber like a misplaced

river barge down the narrow road leading to the skinning shed, to the place where a single small vestibule, a
portal to the temple of the whole of his heart, would be
sanctified once again.

Acknowledgments

Thank you to Sonny Brewer for harassing me into a return to writing; to Louisiana Lanaux, sidekick extraordinaire; to Joe Taylor at Livingston University Press; and to William, Frank, Jim, Melinda, Sydney and Jennifer, Watson, Bev, *all* the writers who are always so encouraging; and to David, Pat, Scott, and the unbelievably nice folks at MacAdam/Cage. Also to the Hudson boys, Gene, John, Wilson, and Joe, for technical advice to add to Stephen's and Ben's. Thanks to Booda, for reading it without getting the vapors; and to Catherine, Kay, Kelsey (of the original Four Funny Chicks) and the rest of my posse. Norman and Tammy, you have been more than kind, definitely cool, to offer the cabin in the deep woods as a refuge for me, a hideout where I get so much work done.

And finally, this book is in memory of Jeff Martin, for being there in the beginning, forever ago, a spiritual imprint, truly a critical piece of fate, in John Craig Stewart's creative writing class. Here's to the Old Gentleman.